I0754865

Missing Sister

ALSO BY JOSHILYN JACKSON

With My Little Eye

Mother May I

Never Have I Ever

The Almost Sisters

The Opposite of Everyone

Someone Else's Love Story

A Grown-Up Kind of Pretty

Backseat Saints

The Girl Who Stopped Swimming

Between, Georgia

gods in Alabama

SHORT STORY

"My Own Miraculous"

Missing Sister

A Novel

Joshilyn Jackson

WM

WILLIAM MORROW
An Imprint of HarperCollins*Publishers*

 For information, address HarperCollins Publishers, 195 Broadway, New York, NY 10007. In Europe, HarperCollins Publishers, Macken House, 39/40 Mayor Street Upper, Dublin 1, D01 C9W8, Ireland.

HarperCollins books may be purchased for educational, business, or sales promotional use. For information, please email the Special Markets Department at SPsales@harpercollins.com.

hc.com

FIRST EDITION

Designed by Michele Cameron

Library of Congress Cataloging-in-Publication Data has been applied for.

ISBN 978-0-06-315871-9

Printed in the United States of America

25 26 27 28 29 LBC 5 4 3 2 1

For every single hand-seller who has ever put one of my books into the hands of a reader. I love my job, and I love you for helping me keep it.

Missing Sister

1

From the first night I laid eyes on Thalia Gray, I knew she was a stone-cold killer.

Granted, she was sitting on a back-alley stoop at two in the morning, soaked in gore from the waist down with a wet, red box cutter beside her. The blood was so fresh it was still tacky in places, plus I'd just walked off a murder scene; it would be fair to say, *Penny. This is not some big, intuitive leap.*

No one else was going to make that leap, though. I wasn't going to let anyone else make it, especially the cops. The real cops, I mean, because that was the night I learned I had no business being one.

Half an hour earlier, when the radio squawked and dispatch called a Signal 48 on Peony Lane, my field training officer had lifted up one shoulder in a shrug and turned the car around, completely matter-of-fact. This was the precinct code for a possible fatality, but here in quiet Kennesaw, it almost always meant a heart attack or some sad accident. I radioed that we were en route, almost as cool about it as Delilah, until dispatch added more codes. Fourteen-twelve. One-eleven.

Delilah's spine straightened as she punched the gas. "That's a major crime alert."

I sat up tall now, too, as if I were her shorter, less confident shadow. I'd never heard those codes outside a classroom. "Yeah, and one-one-one means notify the coroner," I said and was rewarded with a quick, approving nod. I liked it. Maybe a little too much. I'd always been a sucker for a sticker chart, and Delilah Williams had taken me on like a true mentor.

She was a pro, both kind and canny, and if I was really going to be a cop, well, she was goals.

She flashed lights to get around a dawdling Pontiac, then ran a hand over the short twists of her hair. "Full moon, Albright. People get nuts."

She didn't sound worried. She was energized, eager. I felt it, too, like I'd caught her vibe. So far, I'd mostly handled DUIs and traffic violations, fender benders and domestics. I'd been to the scene of an armed robbery, but the doer was gone long before we got there, and no one had been hurt. The worst call, for me anyway, was an OD down on Lester Street. He was a kid, seventeen years old, lying on a broken sidewalk, his lips already going blue. One of his "friends" used the dying boy's phone to call 911, and then they rolled him out of the car and left him. I'd been cool about it, taking lead, getting the Narcan up his nose before he stopped breathing, keeping him talking until the paramedics came.

I didn't fall apart until I pulled into my parents' driveway, where I sat sobbing in the car until my sweet, slope-shouldered dad came out to get the paper. "Penny-pen, your soft heart," he said. "Is this really the job for you?" Then I dried it up. Cop life hadn't been my childhood dream, but my end-of-shift assessments praised my observational skills, my facility for details, my creative thinking. My heart might be soft, but it wanted to protect and serve.

I squared my shoulders up and asked Delilah, "Fourteen-twelve plus one-eleven equals murder, right? A murder."

"I'm thinking, yeah."

Zooming toward a murder through the pleasant suburb where I'd grown up felt so unreal. Peony Lane was one of many flower-named roads that ran through an upscale shopping village called the Shoppes, where boutiques and galleries and cafés sat in pastel clusters. Murder seemed impossible that close to Clara's Closet, a bougie consignment shop where my twin sister, Nix, and I once bought our junior prom dresses.

Delilah turned into a small parking lot and pulled up beside three other cop cars, their strobing lights washing the storefronts red. The engine was barely off before she was getting out, giving me quick *You good to go?* eyebrows. I was, though my mouth had gone dry. Something awful and unfair had happened, and we had to try to make it right. This, right here, was exactly why I became a cop.

I moved more slowly than she did, but I still followed her into the lopsided star of service roads that ran behind this clump of stores, narrow and lined with back entrances and dumpsters. Ahead, where these service roads converged, bright floodlights illuminated the prone form of a man. He had on a nice gray suit, like a regular person, but he was splayed on his belly and centered in a large, shallow pool of liquid that shone dark against the faded asphalt.

I froze in place, feeling my heart pound. Once. Twice. He was still. So very, very still. I'd gone still, too, but inside I buzzed and thrummed with electricity. My skin shivered, my lungs gulped fresh, spring air. This man was done with all that.

I wanted Nix then, with such a big, bad want. So bad that it was like a sickness. Bad as it had been right after we lost her. I knew exactly how her hazel eyes would kindle as she rushed forward, how the floodlights would spark the red in her brown hair. When a road forked into "fear" or "curiosity," my twin had always chosen right. Thinking of her, I made my feet move me forward again. Slowly. Delilah was already at the scene.

It helped to take my focus off the body and put it on the cops surrounding it. The guy still fussing with the floodlights was Doolich, a milk-fed-looking person with pink-rimmed, blinky eyes. He was the only rookie in the department who was fresher than I was. His own field training officer stood to the side, arms crossed, serious, briefing Delilah. No one was trying CPR. No one was touching the downed man at all. I felt my stomach do a slow, unsettled flip.

Delilah turned, scanning for me. She jerked her head in a *hurry up* gesture, just as the shift sergeant, Gimbel, appeared beside me, jacked up and barking.

"Albright! We're going to get lookie-loos on this one. Staties, even the damn campus police. Start a log. If they have to sign in and explain what they think they're doing here, they'll clear out." He pushed a clipboard into my hands and shooed me back toward the alley mouth.

I took it on reflex, pleased to hear my voice was mostly steady as I asked, "What happened?"

"Stabbing. And the body's barely cold," Gimbel told me. "Security here is a joke, but we caught a break. Kids usually only smoke weed and get each other pregnant here on weekends, but God bless if some little potheads didn't decide to get baked on a Tuesday . . ."

I kept my eyes fixed on him, spine shuddering. A stabbing? Barely cold? So very recently, someone took a blade and opened up another human being. On purpose. My gaze flicked to the dark glossy pool surrounding the man. His blood, which had been contained inside his body doing its good work, was now congealing on the asphalt. Gimbel was sending me away from him, and I felt completely fine about that.

Or I did until Delilah joined us, her sharp scowl pointed at my clipboard. "You're giving Albright the mom job?"

He didn't like the question. "Little busy here, Williams. What's your problem?"

She jerked a thumb up toward the crime scene. "You got mint-in-package Doolich up there learning how to handle Baby's First Murder, while Albright, who is about to get her ass shoved out of the nest, gets mommed?"

Mixed metaphors aside, she had a point. Doolich had weeks of training ahead of him. I was almost finished with my stint on nights, and then I'd do four shifts with the training supervisor. After that, I'd be a real cop with my own car, my own beat, and no experienced partner buckled on like training wheels.

Gimbel chewed on it, not loving the taste, but finally he said, "Point taken." I fought the urge to hang on as he yanked the clipboard away from me, then lifted his radio to call for Doolich.

Delilah went into full teacher mode as we started back up the alley. "Some cops, older men especially, will save the paperwork for the FOSWAV." I'd heard her use this acronym before; it meant *First on scene with a vagina.* "Gimbel is a good cop, but he's older than most dinosaurs, and he has daughters. He will perma-mom you, if you let him." She paused to fix me with a skewering gaze. "Albright? Don't let him."

I nodded, hoping I wouldn't embarrass myself and let Delilah down. All that blood. I put one foot in front of the other, every step taking me deeper into disbelief. What was I doing in an alley full of murdered person? Five years ago, I was living happy and brown-mouse-quiet in the house where I grew up, slow-walking toward marriage with my high school sweetheart, Bodie, and working as a sous-chef at a French café.

It was Nix who was Velma for Halloween three years running, then Katniss, then slutty Katniss, then Lisbeth Salander. As kids, she invented Crime Girl, a game in which she was a vigilante superhero who wreaked dreadful vengeance on evildoers, and I was everybody else. Not that my twin would have ever been a cop. She'd been gunning for law school, and her endgame was politics. Ironic, to think of Nix studying rules, but as she herself once told me, *You have to know 'em really well if you are gonna break 'em, Pen-Pen. Government is the dirtiest game going. I promise, though, to use my powers for good.* The world was wrong, we both knew that, but she was the one who planned to dive into the filth and fix it.

Crazy. Well, she was crazy, a little. When she was up, she'd wax-wing straight into the sun, and when she fell, she'd plummet into trenches so deep and murky, only I could find her. I anchored her whether she was soaring or sinking, and she saved me from being Penny-in-the-Middle, fading cozy and quiet into a haze of endless gray.

Then in the spring semester of her senior year at the University of Georgia, Nix put her law school acceptance letters in the trash, threw some clothes into a bag, and moved to Savannah. She didn't say a word to me beforehand. She stopped answering her texts, doing her damned-est to avoid everyone who loved her. I thought it was another low, the lowest low of all, but she never came out of it. I couldn't pull her out of it. A couple years later, she took a dose of Molly that had been cut with fentanyl. She died in a filthy bathroom stall at an after-hours club, all by herself.

She'd left the broken world unfixed, and now I had to live in it without her. I was twenty-six years old, single, fresh off two years at Kennesaw State, where I'd stacked an improbable BS in Criminal Justice and then a police academy certificate on top of a Restaurant Management AA that had been mostly about menu design and pastry. Yet here I was, walking with a certified baddie toward a dead man.

You can't be Nicki for us. Not and still be Penny, too, Mom kept telling me. I wasn't trying to be Nix, though, even though she would have rocked the uniform. There was no world in which wild Nix became a cop, even though making the world fair had been her mission. Well, if the world had ever been fair, at all, at all, I would still have my twin sister. So I had to take the mission. I had to try, anyhow. This was me, trying.

I promised Delilah, "Next time, I'll advocate for myself."

Doolich was passing us now; he paused to have a tiny tantrum. "What the hell? I was right in the middle of something cool, Albright." He said my name with sneer in it. Last week, he'd asked me out, and I'd told him I didn't date men I worked with. Ever since then he'd been weird, negging me, making little snorts when I asked questions.

I said, "Take it up with Gimbel," and kept on walking. We'd left the sergeant looking like he was sucking a lime slice. Gimbel had respected Delilah's input, but he didn't love being in the wrong. Good luck, Doolich!

"Where's your head, Albright? Get present," Delilah said as we came to the edge of the lopsided intersection with a corpse in the center of it. "Pretend you're first on scene. What questions are you asking yourself?"

I steeled myself and looked right at the body, glad he was faced away from us. "It's a lot of blood. Is that normal?"

"The doer got him deep in the upper thigh," Delilah told me. "Slashed the femoral artery. Poor guy emptied out like a garden hose on max."

"How long would it take him to lose consciousness?" I asked, grateful to be pushed into learning mode, hoping to calm the thunder of my pulse.

"Less than a minute," Delilah answered. "No detectives here yet. Take a quick walk around the scene, then tell me what you'd need to do to secure it."

I didn't need Delilah's body language to tell me that I couldn't cry here. No matter what. Under my light vest and cop jacket, I was wearing an old T-shirt of Nix's that said "Good Trouble, Better South"; I wouldn't be both in her clothes and a coward, right now, in real time. It would make my absent twin feel even goner.

I pressed my lips together, hard, and then moved out, past two older cops who stood outside the light, talking quietly. They looked shiny to me, their skin gleaming sweat. I was glad to see I wasn't being frail; this was raw enough to trouble even veterans.

I canted left, careful not to disturb the scene or step in evidence. I knew that eventually I would come to the correct angle to see his face. I made myself go forward anyway. I was going to do my small part to help the great machine of the law find justice for a man who could no longer ask for it himself. Nix's voice in my head assured me, *You are where you're supposed to be. Doing what's right is often hard.* I nodded. Doing what was right was often hardest. I knew then that I wasn't going to break, not even a little, though I dreaded seeing if his eyes were open and what kind of an expression he'd made as he died. Two more steps, and I would know.

I took them, and I forced myself to look. It was worse than hardest. It was—

My understanding was slow to rise, like an actual dawning. This face, so individual, so specific, even with its cheek flattened against the pavement. This broad forehead. That Roman nose. These full lips, set sulky even when crumpled open. His tongue was out, so dry that it seemed nubbled, the tip mashed into his own dumped blood like he was lapping at it, trying to get it back inside. My body knew before my mind did; my heart contracted, and my breath stopped.

I thought I might spontaneously combust. Or scream. Or faint. Or drive my boot into his corpse, kicking it over and over, hard as I could. I didn't, though. My own face formed a rictus and my eyes seized. I could not look away.

"You done, Albright?" called Delilah.

I hadn't seen this man in person for years. His gray suit made his bloodless visage even paler, but I recognized him. Even streaked with gore and filth. Even glassy eyed and gawp mouthed.

I'd hoped to never, never see this smug face in real life, not ever again. Or if I had to, I had prayed that it would be under circumstances much like this—where he was dead and sprawled like roadkill. I squinched my eyes shut for almost a full second, and then I looked back to be sure I wasn't hallucinating or letting my mind turn some similar-looking man into someone that I wanted to see dead.

It was him, though. It was Danny Bowery. And if someone had only thought to let all his blood out of his body five years earlier, then I had no doubt that Nix, my twin, my other half, would still be alive.

2

Albright?" Delilah's voice. She sounded far away.

I stared down at Danny Bowery's dead face, and a stream of black joy swelled up inside my skin, filling me until I felt like I was floating, dizzy and unmoored.

I knew this bitter, galling gladness. I'd felt it before, once, a couple of months ago, when Danny's old running buddy, Xav Castillo, got himself murdered. Someone had picked up Xav's own souvenir Braves baseball bat, hand-signed by Chipper Jones, and bashed his brains out. A botched robbery, the news called it. No suspects. No arrests.

Now, every dark and starless piece of night sky had aligned and brought me here to see the fresh-dead face of Danny Bowery. A glad, hard voice inside of me said, *Two down.* Nix? I didn't finish her thought, though. Not right then. Instead, my training kept me questioning: *Two down in two months. Can that be a coincidence?* Then the guilt came, hitting like a low blow to the stomach, bending me inward. Had I somehow willed this violence into being?

Delilah materialized beside me. Her voice was low and fierce. "Do not puke on the crime scene, Albright." I got her message, loud and clear: *Don't be the girl who proves the unfitness of all girl-kind to be cops.*

I straightened and faced her. "I'm fine." The words sounded so steady, she believed me. I wasn't fooled. I was a thousand miles from fine.

"Albright!" Gimbel came hustling up, waving one arm in a big circle. "Doolich caught some dumbass tourist with a police scanner trying to slither in for a gander. I need you to close off this whole cluster of stores."

I blinked. The guy who'd used the knife on Bowery was in the wind, and Gimbel wanted me running crime scene tape out past Shoe Consortium and the Tea Spot. I wanted to ask, *By myself?*

I chewed up that question and swallowed it, quick as I could, but I must have thought it pretty loud. Delilah's ramrod-straight spine somehow went one degree straighter as she sent *Don't you dare* beams directly to my brain, and Gimbel's smile became benevolent. He wouldn't send me out alone if he hadn't cleared the scene well past the new perimeter, and I was two words away from one of his famous invitations. Every trainee received one at some point: *Officer, once you're off duty, let's you and me sit down. Let's reconsider.* He rarely issued them to me, but it happened almost daily to Doolich. I wasn't going to be that cop.

"On it," I said.

It was a relief to walk away, to let the sounds of the investigation fade. Once I was alone in the near dark, a noise got out of me. A laugh or some arid form of sobbing. As I made my way around the lopsided cluster of stores, crisscrossing iconic tape across the alley openings, I played a horrifying game of Clue inside my head. Xav Castillo in the living room with a bat. Danny Bowery in the alley with a blade. How personal. How very up close. *Two down,* Nix's voice sounded in my head again, and this time I let her finish: *one to go.* Of the three men that I hated most on earth, only Jordan Banks was still breathing. Unless someone had gone by his place to complete the set? Jordan Banks with a rope in the dining room. Jordan Banks with a wrench in the hall. I had no way to know, because I sure as hell wasn't going to use my work phone to check.

I breathed in deep and slow through my nose, trying to calm my rioting mess of red feelings, and I smelled a drift of mint and cumin. It pulled me out of my head, and that was a mercy. My head was a bad place to be. The scent was so faint I lost it almost instantly, but I'm one of those irritating people who can pick up toffee and tobacco notes hiding in red wine. I put my head up, huffing the air like one of my dad's dogs, and I caught it again, coming from another cluster of stores across a wide street.

There was a day spa over there, so it was likely expired products in their trash, but checking was an excuse to stay out here alone. I had to calm down. Red joy still flared in sparks and spasms, hot and avid, spiced with anxiety and guilt. I radioed Delilah to let her know what I was doing, then crossed the street. The spa's big dumpster was empty, and the scent was still beyond me, calling me onward. I followed it all the way through this second store cluster. Nothing, but there was a candle shop across the next big road.

I went, though I was too far from the scene now. I knew it. My teeth felt dry, and I realized I'd been grimacing or grinning with my lips peeled back. I had to get myself together and go back. As I paused, trying to make my face have some regular expression, a strong drift of scent rolled over me from a short, unlit cross-alley between a bakery and a noodle bar. I followed it.

The bakery had a recessed back entrance, and as I turned to check it, I saw a headless, ghostly form tucked back deep in the alcove. It was only a torso, really, glowing like old ivory. I almost screamed, and then the shape resolved into a woman wearing black pants and a pale, polka-dot blouse. The security light was off or broken, but the light of the full moon revealed her sitting quietly on the steps. She was vaping. That was the smell.

"You startled me," I said, thinking, *Witness*. Not, *Doer*. Danny Bowery had been a big guy, with at least sixty pounds on this slender blonde.

Her mouth leaked mint and herbs. She was around my age, with dark blond hair that had likely started in a bun. It was a mess now, with waves of loose hair all around her face. And what a face. A fat, downturned mouth on a sharp jaw, wide-set eyes, a long, elegant nose. Unusual enough to move her past pretty. Way past.

I felt a sharp twinge of recognition. I knew her, didn't I? We'd met before, at least, or—

"Aren't you a little short for a stormtrooper?" she asked. Her voice was low, almost raspy, too deep for her slim frame. She slow-blinked, and her right eye reopened faster than her left. She had some viscous darkness spattered on her face, making her eyelashes tacky.

My breath caught. The left hip and waistband of her pants were ivory. Her pants only looked black because they had been dyed with inky red liquid. The dots on her pale blouse and even the spray of freckles dusting her cheeks and nose were tiny blood drops. My gaze went skittering over her, skipping from blood to blood: the soaked linen pants, the streaked hand holding the vaping mod. I took an inadvertent step back, feeling so far away from the lights and swarming cops, and then I saw the gory, silver rectangle that sat beside her on the step. A box cutter.

I couldn't swallow. I heard Dad's mild voice in my head, saying, *Penny-Pen, is this really the job for you?*

Our eyes met, and that was when it all went so much weirder. Hers were a brown so pale that they were almost gold, like lion eyes. They were absolutely blank.

Predator, I thought. *Stone-cold killer, killed him, killed Danny Bowery like it was nothing,* and then my wild and rabid joy rose up again. Her gold gaze intensified, and I felt it like a slow, cool finger pressing through my skin, my skull, sinking deep into my brain. She knew me. Or at least, she knew my vehement gladness, shining clear and plain. It was as if I'd bent to gently unstick a bloody tendril of pale hair from her cheek and told her, *Hey, good job with that utility knife, girl. Good, good job.* Her blank eyes unglazed and lit, and what I saw in her face now was more, so much more, than an absence of remorse. She shared my ugly joy in his death, and her version was pure and unapologetic. I knew it. I felt it.

Twin thing, I thought.

That made no sense, but understanding surged between us anyway, the way it used to between Nix and me. It was physical, as if she'd somehow, without touching me, reset my heart to beat with hers. We were together in this. No one else understood. No one else mattered or existed. Just us. Only us. It was the least lonely that I had felt in years.

I stood locked in it with her for what might have been a breath or an hour, and when I finally spoke, my voice was a weird, wheezy whisper, "Do you need help?" As soon as I asked, I clocked the faint ligature marks on her neck. New ones. Reddish. They needed time to bloom. Tomorrow she would look like she was wearing a blue-and-purple scarf, though I had only seen this in pictures in a textbook. *Danny Bowery did that. This was self-defense,* I thought. It was the exact kind of rookie jumping-to-conclusions that Delilah warned against. "Are you hurt?"

She smiled. "You should see the other guy." She was still reading my mind; she must have been, because almost immediately, she added, "Oh. You have seen the other guy. You're looking for me." I hadn't been, not really, but I nodded, and her chin tipped down. "How's he feeling?"

"He's dead." She had no reaction. She already knew that. "You severed his femoral artery."

She smiled wider. "Lucky him. I was going for the dick."

Without missing a beat, almost feeling Nix talk through me, I said, "Lucky me. I don't want to bag *that* evidence." She barked out a raspy laugh that turned into a small cough. Oh, he'd hurt her, all right. I tried to regain some vague connection to professionalism. "Is your airway obstructed?"

"It's working good enough for this, Officer Albright," she said and took another hit off her rig. Her vape kit was silver and boxy, the metal engraved with fat, elaborate mums. It looked like art. Expensive art. Everything about her looked like art, actually. Her flat-heeled, elegant boots were probably worth more than my battered Honda. I couldn't help thinking, *Or they were before she made Danny Bowery bleed out all over them.* She clicked the unit off and held it up. "Don't tell me this is how you found me. This far?" When I nodded, she said, "Well, shit."

I touched my own nose, apologetically. "I'm a chef."

She chuckled and eyed my uniform, my gun. "Yeah. I see that."

That pulled my focus to her own weapon, sitting beside her on the step.

"What's your name?" I asked the box cutter. The bloody blade was both less frightening and less absorbing than her flat gaze. When she didn't answer, my hand went to my cuffs. The cool metal was a wake-up call. I was a cop. This was a killer. I couldn't stand here trading gallows humor with her. I needed to do a hundred things, all in the right order. It was only that it was very hard to think of what they were right now.

She said, "Thalia. Thalia Gray."

Okay, then. I'd asked for a name, she'd given me a name. That was procedure, and procedure was good. I knew what to do next. "I need you to move away from the weapon, Ms. Gray." I pushed my voice into its lower register, willing it not to shake. "Stand up, please, no sudden moves, and step down to your left."

She muttered another curse, but she rose to her feet slowly, as I'd instructed. Unfolded, she was taller than I'd thought, looming half a head over me even after she stepped down off the stairs. As she came out of the shadowed alcove, it struck me again that I'd seen her before. Also she'd said my name. I was wearing a brass tag, but the alley was dimly lit. Had she read it, or had she recognized me too?

"Do we know each other?" I asked.

"No," she said. Fast, definitive.

"You look familiar," I insisted.

"I've got one of those faces."

She didn't.

She took a sliding step left, easy. Next, I needed to make her face the wall. Then I should radio for backup, cuff her, and search her. That was right. That was the order. Instead, I fumbled out an evidence bag and put it inside-out over my hand. I leaned into the steps, sideways, watching her the whole time. I picked the box cutter up inside the bag like it was a dog turd, then straightened and sealed it. As I stuffed it in my pocket, my gaze caught on her bruised throat, and my heart lurched. I made myself focus on the perfect arch of the one eyebrow that didn't have blood in it.

"Do you need medical attention?"

Her gaze was level, her voice so calm. "Officer Albright, I can't afford any kind of attention."

"Ma'am, you are in for some, whether you can afford it or not. Face the wall, please." She didn't. I swallowed. "I have to take you in." I sounded like I was apologizing. More than that. I sounded damn reluctant.

She heard it, too, and her gaze sharpened even as her voice went soft. "No, you don't. You haven't said a word to anybody on that radio, and it's squawked at you twice." Had it? I hadn't noticed. "You could go back up this alley. Maybe you never saw me. Maybe you never came this way at all. Chef."

I said, "That is insane," which was not the same as saying no. I got louder. "I can't do that." At the same time, Nix was in my head, saying, *Sure, you can*. More words came out of me in a fast tumble, trying to be louder than her voice. "Look, it's obvious he hurt you. You have a great case for self-defense. Don't answer questions. Say you want a lawyer." She could afford a good one, if her boots were any indication.

I was out of line to say those things, but it wasn't enough for her. I could see it in her flat gold gaze as she told me, "I can't let you take me in."

Was she threatening me? She didn't move, exactly, but her energy changed, as if in some internal way, she'd coiled. My radio released white noise, then Doolich's voice, saying words that went past me in an electric squall. I'd shifted my own stance, too, I realized. Now my hand hovered over my gun.

She tilted her head like a raptor. "Don't. I'm so much faster than you." She said it like it was a fact. I heard more static, Doolich saying more words. My mother's voice was in my head, too, worried, telling me to use my radio, get help, pull my weapon if I had to. I wanted to turn my back and walk away, but that was not a thing that I would ever do. That would be impulsive, instinctive, insane. Nix owned all those words. I was good old Penny, and I owned words like *methodical, patient, thoughtful*. Or I used to, back before I quit my job, broke my engagement, and set off to put the world right via traffic stops and fruitless intervention at domestic violence calls. Come to think of it, I hadn't seen good old Penny in a while. No one had. Now I wavered in a back alley feeling alive for the first time in years, and was I smiling?

I was. Smiling like a mad thing at a woman who was soaked in the blood of Danny Bowery, a woman who smiled back while we decided on some primal level if we were going to fight each other, and I hadn't felt my twin so close in years. Nix was a presence, a gaze over my shoulder, the only voice I wanted to hear, and she said, *Pennest. Let her go.*

Thalia Gray leaned in, just an inch. "Walk away. This is not a story about a rookie who stumbles onto a killer and solves the case and becomes a big damn hero." Her voice was so much softer now. Almost gentle.

"Albright?" Doolich again. Not over the radio. I heard him calling. I had backup, now, and Thalia and I both knew it. My window to make Nix's choice was closing, and we both knew that, too.

She said, even softer, "This is not a story about cops at all." That coiling deepened in her body. Her smile became toothy, predatory. Warm as her voice was, this was a threat.

I flicked open the strap that held my gun, even as I said back, "This is a story?" She nodded. I wanted her to spin a tale that would convince me to take the lunatic's option, but there was no time. We could both hear Doolich's big feet slapping the asphalt. He was almost to the corner. It was too late.

I asked anyway. "What is it about, then?"

"Sisters," she said.

All the fight and all the fear went out of me. From the moment I'd seen Danny Bowery's dead face, the only story I could hear was Nix's. His death did belong to my sister. My twin.

How did Thalia know? My hand dropped away from my weapon. She'd given me only one word, but for me it was the right one, a bigger word than *rules* or *law* or *rightful*. It was a bigger word than any other that I owned. I stepped back and I straightened, and I gave her the single word she needed back:

"Run."

3

My life was made almost entirely out of stories about sisters. The parts that mattered, anyway. Nix's, too, when she was alive.

She had one story that was hers alone, but everybody in the world already heard that one. It was too common for anyone to do much more than shrug and sigh at the badness of the world. Or say, *Things are different now; we believe women. There's even a hashtag.*

Sure.

People still think all the awful things. More quietly these days, but still. *What was she doing there?* Or, *What was she wearing?* Or, *Why didn't she fight or run or—* They have a thousand ways to end that one, and all of them push the blame toward the girl who got herself hurt. People cannot bear to believe certain things about their husband or their son, their pastor or coach, or even about some fine, upstanding citizen. They tell themselves, *She caused it.* They tell themselves, *Girls lie.*

Here are the facts in my sister's story, or at least those parts that no one would dispute.

Nix, hot off her first major breakup, went of her own free will to Party Town, a huge, crumbling rental house off campus. She wore a short skirt and joyfully drank several ladles of deadly trash can punch. She flirted lightly with a sophomore named Jordan Banks, one of the self-replacing beer pong guys who lived there. Banks told her Danny Bowery and Xav Castillo had snuck off to the attic rec room to smoke a blunt on the quiet, and he suggested they go have a puff. Danny and Xav were both seniors, like her. She'd danced with one a time or two. Played Truth or Dare with the other. Everyone knew those dude-bros because they always had weed and knew where to get Molly.

Jordan was in tight with them, their lapdog-slash-delivery boy. Nix went upstairs with him, undrugged, undragged, a little drunk, and a lot cheerful.

Danny said, "Nixie! I heard you got single, you poor baby. Want a consolation toke?"

"Hell, yeah. Pass the pity pot," she said, unfussed. She was the one who broke it off, surprising everyone but me. Mom and Dad had practically adopted Michael by then. He'd spent the last two Christmases with us, done family camping trips. They'd hoped Nix had grown past wild boys and wastrels, but I knew my twin wasn't going to marry a button-shirt guy who liked baseball and accountancy. Michael was my type, not hers. Even Nix said that after she dumped him. *I thought it was love, but turns out I was trying on your plain brown boots, Pen. You want 'em? They're an upgrade.* She thought Bodie was basic. Point was, that night at Party Town, she was feeling free, not hurting.

The four of them passed the blunt around and then played foosball, two-v-two. Nix was a deadeye, and no matter how they switched it up, her team won. My twin was a born crower. She boasted she could take on any two of them alone and still come out on top. Was it dirty talk? Sure. She was joking around, taunting them, flirting. Nix herself told me all that. Eventually.

They took the challenge, and for three straight games, she handed them their asses. They got hot about it. While she trounced Banks and Castillo for the second time, Danny Bowery came up behind her and grabbed her hips, grinding to make her miss her shot. Nix mocked him for cheating when it was already two on one, and she was still winning. She laughed at them for losing. Losing to a girl.

They didn't like that. It got contentious. Or so she said. There were no witnesses with handy phone cams on this floor of the rundown rental house. Her own phone was in her purse, which she'd hurled into a corner. When Danny flipped her skirt up and made her miss a block, she lost her temper and smacked his roaming hands, then shoved him. He shoved back. Then there were three boys in a pack around her, pushing and jostling. Allegedly. They left my twin sister crying in the beanbags by the foosball table. Allegedly.

She walked back to her own off-campus apartment, over two miles away, where she showered until there was no hot water left in the whole building. The next day, she canceled her weekend home. Flu, she said. The next weekend, she told me not to come to Athens. Still flu. Another week, and again, she didn't come home. Her texts were weird and short, and she wouldn't answer my calls.

She did answer the call from her adviser, who was concerned about three weeks of missed classes. Nix went to the office, where she promptly fell apart and told that woman everything. Her adviser had prepared a makeup schedule for missed tests and late papers. She was unprepared for this. She made some horrified and sympathetic noises, but she also said, basically, that Nix had gotten herself raped all wrong if she wanted to press charges.

I took a class called Social Science and the American Problem when I went back to school for my criminal justice degree, and that awful woman was dead right. With no rape kit or even pictures of Nix's injuries, it was her lone word against all three of theirs. Jordan was in the Honors College on a merit scholarship. Danny and Xav volunteered at Habitat for Humanity and had families who could afford attorneys. They would have "torn her up." That was the threat the adviser leveled at her. My straight-A twin, who dropped out and moved to Savannah and ghosted her family and abandoned her ambitions and stayed drunk and high until she took that Molly laced with fentanyl and died—she would have been "torn up," if she'd demanded justice.

I didn't let her go easy. None of us did. Me, Mom and Dad, our older brother, Gand, and his daughter, Shadow—all of us drove over to Savannah so many times, alone and in pairs and in groups. We begged her to come home, to go to AA meetings, to at least answer her damn phone.

I need to reinvent myself, she told me, by which she apparently meant, *As a person who does so much drugs.* It was a year before she told me what had happened. Later still, she told Gand, and she made us both swear silence.

We weren't even allowed to tell our parents. I honored that, and he did, too, though maybe we shouldn't have. I went over it a million times after she died. What if I had told Mom and Dad? Would things have come out different? What if I'd said this, or done that, been here instead of there?

Most of all, I wondered, *What if I had answered my phone on the night she died?* She called me from the long, thin unisex bathroom of an after-hours club. I didn't pick up, and a few hours later, the manager found her body curled on the tiles in the last stall. She left me a message. I still have it saved on my phone, her voice threading in and out of the low bass thumping through from the dance floor, running water, flushing toilets, a drunk woman hollering invective at her boyfriend, someone laughing, shoes clacking on tile, all the noises of a world of people unaware my twin was dying on the other side of a flimsy metal door.

. . . cold and bad, Pen . . . I'm scared of my . . . Please, can you . . . feel like a ghost already.

It took me hundreds of listens to decipher that much. It took me thousands to accept that I'd never be able to make out enough words to know what had felt "cold and bad." The bathroom floor or her own body or simply the world? I'd never know what had frightened her, or what she wanted me to please do, or if she called herself a ghost because she knew that she was dying. I'd never get to lie and say I wasn't mad, or tell the truth that no matter how mad I was, I loved her so damn much it didn't matter. The connection cut off, and then she died, shivering, and scared, and wanting me, while I slept with my phone on silent like a girl whose twin was not in crisis.

"Like a girl whose twin was in crisis for more than two years," Gand had said, when I played him the message. I appreciated his attempt at absolution, but it didn't help.

Meanwhile, none of those three men failed out of school or fell into addictions. I doubt they even blew a midterm. Danny and Xav strutted along to "Pomp and Circumstance" to pick up their degrees soon after Nix dropped out, Jordan two years later, and they went their separate ways: Xav to a law school, which felt like a direct kick to my stomach, Danny to nepo-baby it up at his dad's company, Jordan to play Friendly Local Banker in the burbs. I saw their lives unfolding through the rosy filters of social media. I couldn't look away, though their joy was gall and bile to me.

At least until two months ago, when someone smashed in Xav Castillo's head. As memorial posts poured onto the internet, I'd tried not to be some vicious version of happy. Tried, and failed. He was killed a couple of days before the second anniversary of Nix's death. That felt fitting. It felt fair.

In the wake of Xav's death, I remourned hers. I couldn't stop replaying her final phone call or remembering all the times I drove to Savannah with Gand or our parents or alone to stage failed interventions. The last time Gand was with me, we invaded the bar where she worked. We sat on rickety stools drinking soda and pretending we hadn't shown up before, asked before, begged before. That night, it finally went down different. At last call, she gave me the ghost of her old Nix smile.

"It's late, and raining, and what with all the lecturing, you two must be exhausted. If you promise not to prune-mouth at me, you can stay over."

She'd never invited us inside her place before. It was a moldy basement room in a "historic" home that was falling into chunks. The water in the shared bathroom ran yellow, and the floors squeaked and sagged, but I said nothing. I made no faces, even. She'd let me a little ways back in. I was so scared to jinx it.

Gand slept on the floor, and Nix and I shared a futon in a cheap black metal frame that smelled like cat pee and old books. My twin was restless, so we drifted in and out of sleep, whispering on and off. It was like being back in the womb, the two of us fitting and refitting, me the small spoon and then her, or curling toward each other with our legs tangling, breathing in each other's breath. Two bodies making room for each other in a too small space. Nicolette and Penelope. Penny and Nicki. Nix and Pen. Pen-Nix.

Gand's snoring woke us up early. We were facing each other in little curls, like a closed set of parentheses. The basement room had one long, narrow window up by the ceiling, and the predawn light touched her so gently, I could see the echo of my face in hers. We weren't identical, but we had looked a lot alike, before salt air and hard living turned her skin so dry and papery. Before she'd hacked her long hair off and fried it butter-blond. Before she'd gotten skeletally thin.

She whispered, "Do you want to sneak out and get coffee? We can watch the sun come up over the river. I love to hear the water swirling past me, on and on. It would break my heart to leave that sound."

I held my breath for a beat, scared to break some spell where Nix was conjuring a future, but I had to ask. "Why would you leave it?"

She closed her eyes against whatever desperate hope my face was making. "Don't go full Penny on me. Smother the optimism. There's no way to wind a clock backwards. I can't be that stupid girl who secretly believed she was invincible. Okay? But. I emailed my old head of department from UGA last week to see if I can maybe finish up online. She remembers me."

"Of course she does." I tried to keep my voice steady and calm. This was new, and it felt delicate. I didn't press, but I did think, stupidly, *It's going to be okay. She is going to be okay.*

A month later, we buried her in a wild, green cemetery with no headstones, no curated lawns, only woods and meadows. I have almost no memories of the weeks after she died. I didn't quit my job so much as I simply stopped going. I must have packed up her scant things while I was in Savannah, or someone did it for me, because I had her clothes, and her glass horse, and half a dozen books that I read over and over to see her slanted notes cramped in the margins.

I couldn't stop going back over all the ways I could have done things differently. The hinge moments. Couldn't stop thinking, *If only this, if only that*. But I couldn't change the past. That rock-hard truth made me ask myself, *What can I change?*

There was a time when my twin, the same girl who accused me of optimism, would have answered with, *The whole world, Pen. We can change the whole damn world*. That was before her college adviser told her no one would believe her. I wondered, *What if she had called the cops, and gotten someone—well, someone like me?* I slept through her final call, but what if I could answer someone else's?

So I applied to Kennesaw. I got flack from my friends for it. They were city people in food service, plenty jaded about cops. They rolled their eyes when I said I planned to be a good one. I meant it, though. If I could make the world safer, fairer, I could . . . I wasn't sure. Honor Nix? Keep her close? My twin had once believed the world could be made fair. I'll say this; studying the criminal justice system hadn't helped me share that faith. Not at all. I still thought it was work worth doing, though.

My fiancé told me I'd gone nuts. Bodie kept asking who I was, and I didn't know, so I broke up with him, this sweet boy who had been mine since homecoming sophomore year. Mom and Dad and Shadow were too shell-shocked by Nix's death to stop me burning down my life, but Gand said a lot of the same things Bodie said. I told him it was trickier to break up with a brother, but I could likely find a way. He promised to let it go if I promised to talk to someone. I agreed.

He meant a therapist, but the only person I wanted to discuss it with was Nix. I got in my Honda and made the four-hour drive out to the coast. The green cemetery was way outside the city, near the river. I had a map to find the willow tree we'd put her under. I sat on the damp ground by the roots and told her that if she said I was nuts, too, well, I'd go another way.

My woo-woo brother might have heard an answer in the sudden storm that rolled in off the water, but fuck that. I wanted Nix to speak. She didn't. She said exactly nothing, again, when I visited her only two months ago to tell her someone had bashed in Xav Castillo's brains. I asked her if that felt like justice. I got silence, then a lone bird calling. It sounded mournful; I had to feel my curdled joy alone.

Now, Danny Bowery was dead, and this stranger, Thalia Gray, shared my sense of awful triumph. We felt the same dark feelings, except that hers were unapologetic.

Sisters, she said. I'd followed my good nose into a sister story. When I said, *Run*, she'd responded instantly, melting to the mouth of the alley and slipping around the corner. I hurried the other way, and there was Doolich stamping fast toward me in a fuss. He stopped short, and I all but ran to him. I didn't want him coming even one more step this way.

"What's happening?" Doolich's big eyes bulged like eggs as he peered around, riled and uncertain. "Were you talking to someone?"

"No." I looked where he was looking. The mouth of the alley was empty, and all at once, I was bereft. I'd let her go, and the idea that I might never see her again stung at my skin.

Doolich flared his nostrils, torqued. "Why didn't you answer your radio, Albright? When I turned the corner, I heard—"

I interrupted him, "I was talking to myself, maybe? I do that sometimes. When I'm anxious. This is pretty intense." Why did I feel like crying? Her familiar face—where had I seen Thalia Gray before? If this was a sister story, the connection was Nix. How did she know Nix?

He scoffed, playing hard cop. "If you say so. Gimbel wants you back, ASAP."

"Okay." I walked past him toward the crime scene, willing him to turn away, to fall in step beside me, and to shut up.

I got two of the three. First he asked, "Why did you come out so far? Did you hear women talking?" I shook my head. Then he said, "I definitely heard voices. Maybe someone else is here? Should we go look?"

I kept going. "You said he wants me ASAP."

He humphed and then got busy with his radio, updating his training officer. With the wrong codes. I didn't correct him. I was too busy trying to get my story straight. *Sister* story. That was real, but what could I say to Delilah? I couldn't lie. She'd smell it, sure as I'd smelled Thalia vaping. I had to tell the truth: that I'd followed a scent, just like I'd said when I'd radioed her, and that I'd checked out the spa and a candle shop. The end. No lies detected, only some truths left out. I could do that. It would be easier, though, if I could stop feeling that my heart was trying to fight its way out of my chest.

Doolich finished with the radio and told me, "That hot chick with the braids from the coroner's office—"

"Leslie," I said automatically.

"—is here now, and detectives from CID. We've had a bunch of calls come in. You and Williams are going to bust up some off-campus college party that got loud, and I'm staying here. Because we were here first, and I'm running the log, after all, which could have been you, but . . ." Was he being smug? Yes, he was getting back at me, or thought he was. "Did you finish with the tape?"

I hadn't. I wasn't even sure where I'd left the rolls. I was happy to be ordered off the scene, though, so floored by what I'd done. I couldn't tell if I was sorry. Thalia was so gone she felt pretend, as if I was in a movie where I'd summoned a revenant to enact a cold revenge. If Doolich hadn't heard our voices, I might believe I'd made the whole thing up.

Did Thalia own a piece of *my* sister's story? One that I never heard? I'd let her go with no idea of how to find her again, and that thought made me stumble. I nearly went down, but I caught myself, my hand going instinctively to my pocket to keep the hidden box cutter from falling out. I felt the rectangular outline. Solid. Real.

"You okay?" Doolich said.

"I should turn on my Maglite, huh." I sounded both too hollow and too hearty.

We clopped in tandem down the street. I kept my gaze down as if watching my footing, but I was fighting to keep a wild, strained smile from stretching itself across my face. I had the weapon. It was proof. Not only of her presence. Of her crime. My heart swelled with a fear-tinged exultation. I didn't have to find her. She would come to me, to claim it. And when she did? I would get so much more from her than that one word.

4

I fumbled with my seat belt; my fingers felt thick, buzzing with pent-up blood as if I'd sat on them for half an hour. Then I had to shove down a bray of wild laughter at the effort I put in to virtuously buckle up over a pocket full of stolen evidence.

As Delilah drove us off into the night, some small, scared, very Penny part of me was saying that I'd yanked the good guy hat off the victim, and that was fair, but then I'd handed it with crazy faith to Thalia Gray. I wanted to blurt out everything and hand Delilah the bagged, bloody weapon. Now. Immediately. With every passing minute, my felonies compounded. *Tell now, and you might get probation instead of prison,* the girl I used to be was saying. I'd be fired, at the very least, but that was good. Not because I was too soft for the job, as Dad kept saying, but because I was too broken to be a trustworthy cop. The world already had enough shady ones.

My spine vibrated like a plucked violin string, but I didn't hurl my head into Delilah's lap and burst into tearful confession. The girl I was now didn't tell Delilah damn-all. Instead, I flipped the AC on. Georgia weather in March was a fickle thing; tonight was on the cooler side, but I was blazing hot. I touched the lump the utility knife made in my pocket, trying to breathe normally. I tried to simply *be,* as my older brother was always saying I should. It wasn't working for me, though.

It never had. Gand used hashtags like #centerandbestill under pictures of him doing beautiful yoga. He lived in an old mini–school bus that he'd rehabbed into a house with a working kitchenette and a composting toilet. He made his living peddling surfboards and vegan protein shakes to his thousands of Instagram followers. Gand worried about literally nothing. He shed even the things that ought to worry him—not seeing his daughter for weeks at a time, for example—and let them waft away like autumn leaves dropped in a river. I regularly spent time asking Gand to please worry more.

Delilah's voice cut through my swirling panic. "For the record, you handled yourself well at the worst call I've ever gotten." I thanked her, but I felt outside myself, as if I was a panicked cat hanging from the car roof by my claws, watching Penny smile at her mentor. Meanwhile, the tires rolled, moving me farther and farther away from the scene of my crime. She went on, "It was also the most interesting, but I tell you what, I'd rather be back on college party patrol than be the detective that has to tell that dead guy's family. He looked like a citizen to me. Nice suit, nice shoes. He had a wedding ring, did you clock that?"

I nodded, though I hadn't looked at his hands. I'd seen Danny Bowery's wedding pics all over Insta. His wife's socials were full-on house porn; Danny was a VP at his father's bougie import company. I'd curled my lip at shots of Danny and Fiona twining arms to drink champagne at their new macassar ebony dining table from Argentina and kissing in front of their custom Brazilian-tile backsplash. Their newlywed status made it even stranger that he'd been in a suburban shopping plaza in the middle of the night, getting stabbed by a blonde who wasn't sorry.

I knew that once the family was notified, their feeds would fill with shocked dismay, then memorial posts, then funeral plans. Danny's flaws would be washed away, same as Xav Castillo's had been. With Xav, people talked about his love of craft beers and the Braves and his big dumb bulldog, Betsy. I'd felt so damn sorry for the dog, because dogs are too pure to know when they love assholes. No one said a single bad word about him, not even that he was living way beyond his means and deep in debt. I had to learn that from the news. It surprised me, considering how much money corporate lawyers made, even ones fresh out of law school. No one intimated he was culpable, though there were no signs of a break-in, so he must have let his killer in the house. *Well, if his killer was a hot blonde in pricey boots—*

"Penny for 'em, Albright," Delilah said.

She was going for the eye roll with a joke I'd heard a million times, but I didn't have one for her. "Still processing. Hell of a night." My thoughts were worth more, anyway, because I was thinking, *And it* was *a blonde in pricey boots, because what are the chances these killings aren't related? Two men who committed a violent felony together get murdered in the same city, in the same year, the first right before the anniversary of that shared crime? It was her. It had to be her. Right?*

No cop was going to connect Danny Bowery's death to Xav Castillo's unsolved homicide, though, because no other cop knew what they had done to Nix. My silence meant those cases would stay open and unconnected, probably forever. *Fine,* I thought. *Good. Anyway, I promised Nix that I would never tell.*

"You okay to take this call?" Delilah asked. We were almost to the address dispatch gave us, and I realized I was rocking myself, faintly.

"I'm good," I said. I wasn't.

I was remembering the last time I saw Nix alive. I went back to Savannah, alone, a week after we'd watched the sun come up together. I felt so much hope, so much patience. I spent the night again, and she tucked in close to whisper, the way we used to on stormy nights when we were small. I could smell her toothpaste breath over the skunky pot smoke that had sunk deep into the futon.

"I should be more interesting and powerful now. Since I got raped." I'd started to protest, and she had laughed, bitter, but real. "That's what I see in the movies. Rape turns soft young silly girls like us into wild and fascinating superheroes. Stronger and smarter. Without it we're, what? Dull? Weak? I should send thank-you notes, because now I'm a girl who might one day get up off this bed and burn the whole world down."

I had put my forehead against hers and whispered back. "You were always that girl, dummy. You still are. You still can." I believed it, too, right up until the day she died.

Thalia struck me as the same, a natural-born dark knight. Not a victim, even with those bruises on her throat. The opposite, in fact. Her face was so familiar. Had I seen her in Savannah? She must have known Nix. She must have loved Nix, because two men were dead.

Two—so far, I thought, and then Delilah parked and we headed into a swirl of garage band bass and pot smoke. We'd come to shut the party down, but I wished I could plunge into it, instead, and disappear into the black lights and moving bodies. I was so off my game that Delilah let me clock out without our usual postmortem.

"Get some sleep," she said, and I fled for home. I didn't even change out of my uniform.

I parked my car on the stretch of patchy grass beside my parents' driveway. All around me, nice neighbors slept in nice houses while golden light touched the gray horizon. This felt thematically wrong. The sun should be snuffing itself out. The box cutter whispered and thrummed like a live thing in my pocket, and a cold hand grabbed my heart and squeezed until I felt the edges of it squishing out between the spectral fingers.

Common sense said I should chuck the knife into the Chattahoochee River. A toss, a splash, gone. *What box cutter? What murder?* Then I could be normal. When Thalia contacted me, I could say, *I got rid of it. You're fine.* I would ask no questions. I wouldn't wonder, for example, if she'd killed Xav. Or if the third man, Jordan Banks was up next on some cosmic list. Or some real, actual paper list in her pocket. I would step back from what felt like a cliff's edge and onto a nice, safe road where I worked a beat. I'd deescalate domestics, take drunk drivers off the roads, and administer Narcan to dying kids on Lester Street. What was I doing?

Having a panic attack, my mother's voice said calmly in my head.

Well, that seemed reasonable. I needed Nix—when didn't I?—but now I was scared enough to say her name out loud, as if I hoped my sister might respond. I said it again, and then again, like an invocation. "Nix, Nix, Nix," desperate for an answer.

For the first time since her death, I got one. Not words. It was more a feeling that I was not sitting in my car alone. The hand around my heart loosened its awful grip. Air came into me easier. I felt tears rising in my eyes and I could smell her: sweet rose undercut by sandalwood and oud.

"Okay, then," I said out loud. "Okay."

Mom used to sing a song to us when we were little, because we were so twin about things:

Penny and Nicki, Nix and Pen,
Where does one stop and the other begin?

I wanted to tell her now, *Here, Mom. I've been standing frozen still ever since she stopped. I've been waiting to start. This is me starting.*

I'd gone to Nix's grave so many times to summon her and felt nothing but sunshine or wind or rain, heard only birdsong. But now? Here she was, present in the hot sweep of my carbonated blood. Here she was in the electric spark of a pocket full of felony, in the surge of bright current between me and a murderer. The act of letting Thalia go, perhaps even giving her permission to continue—that was what it took for me to feel I wasn't utterly alone.

I wanted to see Thalia Gray again. I needed her to tell me how she knew Nix. To make my own choices make sense. I got my personal phone out of my glove compartment and typed the name she'd given to me into Google. There were a few "Thalia Gray"s and "Grey"s on various socials, but none were her. Too old, too young, the wrong race, the wrong face. I'd have to wait until she came to me. I needed it to happen. Soon. Sooner than soon.

I got out of the car and paused in front of the basic builder 1980s split-level where Nix and I grew up. I wanted the knife close. I wanted to call *her* close. I wished I could tuck it under my pillow as if it were a baby tooth and wait for Thalia Gray to fairy in my window and retrieve it, but what if Shadow found it?

Technically speaking, I didn't live with her and my parents. Back when Bodie asked me to marry him, I told him I couldn't leave my niece, and he told me he loved my mom and dad, but not as roomies. As a compromise, we'd walled off the six hundred square feet of unfinished storage over the garage, hiring pros to do the wiring and add a skylight. Dad did the plumbing, giving us a working kitchen corner and a bathroom. My neighborhood was zoned to allow mother-in-law suites, no matter what our prune-mouthed neighbor Mrs. Blanchard might say; we'd added outdoor stairs that ran up the side wall to a private entrance, but Shadow thought of my place as part of home, same as the downstairs. I couldn't risk her stumbling across the box cutter.

Instead, I went toward the backyard, where I heard eight big paws thumping across the grass. Brandy and Timbo surged up to the tall, chain link fence, pushing their big snouts into the holes. They were brother and sister, boxer-mastiff mutts, vigilant and smart. They weren't barking their fool heads off because they knew the sound of my engine.

"Good babies," I told them softly. They must have needed to pee in predawn hours and bothered Dad to let them out. The Boston terrier, Bosch, was likely still tucked in my mother's armpit, snoring.

I let myself in, pushing the dogs back. As the gate swung shut behind me, the weighty sound of the lock reengaging, more thunk than click, gave me the illusion of security. It was still too dark to walk around except in such a familiar landscape. My feet knew the slopes and trip points so well that my biggest risk was dog bombs as I made my way past our ancient, gently rotting swing set. I felt safer here in the dingy predawn, with curious Brandy and helpful Timbo flanking me like an honor guard. I thought about burying the knife, but Timbo was a digger. I flinched, imagining him bringing this bloody relic right to Dad like a prize. I spun in a circle, pressing one hand to my forehead, trying to think inside a storm of conflicting impulses.

The coming sun backlit the uneven line of live oaks and pine trees into a jagged silhouette, and then I knew the perfect spot. Our old tree house. It had once been a platform, roofless and simple. It was now a few bug-ridden, rotty planks, disdained by Shadow and her techie friends. I hadn't been up there in years. No one had. It was a ghost place, a Nix place. Perfect.

In the wooded part of the huge yard, all the big oak trees looked much the same. Gand had nailed slats into the trunk to be our ladder, but I had to run my hands down the rough bark of three oaks before I found them. Brandy pushed in close, her snuffle-y nose questing along with my hands.

A couple of the rungs had fallen off. I wasn't positive I could get up there, but I was in the best shape of my life, thanks to prepping for the police force fitness test. I scrambled up, testing the remaining rungs as I went, until I was belly down on the sagging planks, panting from the effort. I pushed myself gingerly up onto my knees, then felt around the trunk, seeking our secret knothole. In my memory, this hole was higher up; we'd been shorter when we found it. Nix and I used to leave notes and prizes there, being Scout and Boo Radley for each other. We stopped after I gifted her a half a pack of Hubba Bubba and it turned into a ball of ants.

I turned on my phone's flashlight and pointed it down into the shaft. My light bounced off a round shape, bright and violet, and for one dizzy second I thought Nix had sneaked back from being dead to hide a present for me here. I reached in and pulled out an ancient plastic monster figurine, a Happy Meal prize from some long-ago kiddie movie. Moss had grown in the crevices of his dopey grin.

I dashed away a couple of unwelcome tears, then leaned back to dig the evidence bag out of my pocket. Even in my hands, it felt unreal. I turned my flashlight app on, needing to see it. It was a plain, flat rectangle made of matte silver metal, simple and generic. My dad had one exactly like it. Almost. His wasn't stained and clotted with dried blood. I turned it over, and the light caught on a thumbprint. Thalia

Gray's whorls and loops were perfectly preserved in Danny Bowery's dark blood. It was as if she'd signed her murder.

She was real, then. This was real. My body flooded with guilt and gratitude, grief and vindication. I didn't want to feel these things, or any things. I wanted to be quiet now, and sleep. I scrabbled in the hole for a fistful of ancient, rotted leaves and twigs, then tucked the box cutter way down deep and packed the purple plastic guardian and the detritus back in on top of it. Buried. Invisible. Gone.

Gone enough. I dusted off my hands, clambered carefully down, and hurried back toward the gate with the dogs flanking me again. Every step I took away was both sorrow and relief. Every step away, I felt more like myself, and yet I still felt a presence. It perhaps was only the remains of the vibrating connection that I'd forged with Thalia, but even if that were so, my twin existed in the echo. She was with me. Nix. It was so true and palpable that as I reached for the gate, I heard my sister call my name. Not in my head. I really heard her.

"Penny." That so familiar voice. I knew it better than I knew my own. "Pen. What are you doing?"

5

I stayed outwardly calm. Calm enough that we were spared the drama of two big dogs activating their barkholes and thundering in mad circles. At the same time, my heart was blooming in fast motion, opening in something like a burst. I turned toward the voice, dizzy with stupid hope, even as I recognized that this was Shadow. My niece was recently fifteen, and she'd grown three inches in the last year. Her voice had changed, too. She sounded so like Nix now. I wasn't used to it. I wasn't sure I ever would be. Now that voice had called me softly from the unlit screened porch under the deck.

"Nothin'. What are you doing?" I replied, trying not to sound as pure shook as I felt. My heart thumped and pounded, slow to get the memo that I was fine. Maybe I wasn't. The yard was brightening from black to a gold-edged gray. Had Shadow seen what I was doing?

I went closer, waiting for her to ask, *Pen, what terrible crime were you hiding way up in that rotty tree house?* But all she said was, "I dunno. Sulking. Being sad. I couldn't sleep."

God bless teenagers, who wander about in a cloud of drama and emotion, blind to the idea that something of interest might be happening with adults. Even the ones they loved most. There was the flare of a plastic lighter, and she touched the flame to the wicks of the citronella candles on the low table. Now I saw she was curled on the glider sofa, swaddled in blankets. No phone, no iPad, no laptop. Off as I was, this still struck me as weird. Shadow loved a screen.

"Want coffee?" She lifted up a fat, ceramic mug.

"No, thanks." I didn't want coffee, much less the brown sugar and hot milk with a splash of Folgers she perpetrated. I also didn't want company, but she was sunk in the old, deflated cushions looking like a pile of laundry. Shadow was kinetic, with none of my yoga-brother's tolerance for stillness. Even when she was deepest in her screens, Shadow jittered a leg, spun in her chair, tapped, hummed. Well, her father hadn't bothered to come home for almost three months now, a wide stretch even by Gandian standards. We all knew, the longer his absence, the bigger she'd act out. Now, tonight of all nights, I sensed a doozy was upon us. I opened the screen door, and the dogs pushed past me and began milling all around the table, picking up on her distress. "What happened?"

She patted at them and said to me, aggrieved, "I got suspended. For the rest of the week, and then probably two more weeks after that."

I shoved my hair back behind my ears. Shadow was a good student, a good kid. She'd never even had detention. I was still in uniform, though I'd stored my gun and my heavy kit at work, and I was churning with anxiety and exhaustion, feeling filthy from my tree climb and my choices. I was so desperate to shower and sleep, I didn't even want to dig in my old texts for any hint of Nix knowing a "Thalia." But in the way of teenagers and cats, this least convenient moment was when she needed me.

Where was Gand? A rhetorical question if ever I heard one. This was a job for a full-on parent, but Shadow didn't have any of those. When Gand was a sophomore, he knocked up Victoria Delevet. She was a junior with a perfect GPA, a head for STEM, and crazy-ambitious parents. Scared of disappointing them, she hid the pregnancy for months. When it finally came out, the Delevets wanted an adoption so closed it was practically the condom packet in my brother's wallet. Gand signed away all rights to seek financial support, and in return, my parents got full custody. Victoria gave birth halfway through the summer, and mere weeks later the entire clan moved up to Boston. She never even held the baby.

My brother did. A nurse put her in his arms when she was seven minutes old. Then my parents took turns holding her, and then me and Nix together, our four skinny girl arms making a cradle as we clasped her between us. From that day on, she'd had five partial parents.

Shadow was seven when Nix and I graduated from high school, and there was no way we could both leave her for college. I was happy to stay home with her—Kennesaw had Bodie and culinary school—but Nix needed a prestige degree to set her up for law school. Even after she moved to Athens to go to UGA, she came home to Shadow every other weekend. More than Gand did.

Poor kid was down to four partial parents now, so I had to stay here and step up. So much for bed. "Do Mom and Dad know?"

She snorted. "Yes. They called Mom at work. Dad came home early, and they super grounded me." She lifted the blanket and then pushed Brandy back with a foot, clearly wanting me to tuck in with her. I sat down and let her wrap me up, and Brandy and Timbo settled, too, flopping at our feet. Shadow had her mother's mouth and Gand's cherry-cola hair, but all I saw in the gold glow of the candles were Nix's wide-set eyes, true hazel, red and swollen now from crying. "No phone, no friends, no computer, no streaming. All I can do is sit on this porch and age."

My own, lighter hazel eyes went wide. Mom and Dad were so much more indulgent with her than they had ever been with us. She had no bedtime. No chore chart. She didn't have to choke down all her broccoli and she never ironed anything. When she was thirteen, she was wild to get parental permission for a stupid anime cat tattoo, and they had actually considered it.

It had been Gand—Gand of all people—who stopped her, saying, "Tats should hold deep meaning. I want us to go together when you are ready to commit to your first tattoo."

My brother, who was unable to commit to a girlfriend or a street address or even his own kid, really said those pretty, stupid words with his pretty, stupid mouth. When Shadow insisted that she did want to "commit," he bribed her with piercings. Her ears were full of titanium and teeny amethysts, and her nose had a delicate ring in the center and a bead on the side. She buzzed her hair down to an inch, and she wore rumpled layers of oversize everything and slouched around like she'd had a spinectomy, and my parents never blinked.

I said, "Oh, dear! What happened?"

She laughed a little then. "I like it when you talk like Pooh Bear, Pen-Pen. *Oh, dear! Oh, bother!*" She even had a lopsided smile like Nix, with just one dimple, while Gand had two and I had none. "So there's this girl at school, Portia, who has terminal hamster nose, always damp and on the whiffle. She's cringy, like she's expecting to get tortured every second. So people torture her. You know?"

"I do know." Some kids picked on weaker kids to feel powerful. Some people never stopped.

Not without the timely intervention of a blonde with a box cutter, Nix said sharply in my mind, while Shadow's matching voice swirled soft around me.

"There's this *Gossip Girl* wannabe site for our school with its own Discord. No one knows who runs it. They put up a purity test, and literally everyone was taking it. I did. They posted the results so you could compare, but with no names."

"Mm-hmm," I said, encouraging. She had yet to get to the part that mattered, and my anxious mind was again trying to place Thalia Gray. That face gave me such déjà vu. If she'd known Nix, it was in Savannah, or I would have known her, too. Our childhood had been truly ours, and even during college, I spent every other weekend in Athens, being young and kid-free with her. I tried to picture Thalia in Nix's moldy rented room or Momo's, the blue-collar sports bar where she had served up shots and PBRs. Thalia Gray? Head-bopping as the crackly, ancient speakers blared out "Eye of the Tiger" and sports-ball broadcasts filled the screens? Not in those boots.

Shadow was oblivious to the slosh and surge inside me. "They posted Portia's results with her name and picture as the 'purest,' like it was an award. Pen-Pen, that girl has never done anything. She got a perfect zero. Can you even? People left comments, really graphic and so mean, describing how gross it would be to do this or that sex thing from the test with her. She got crap at school about it, too, endlessly. Portia was literally dying." I felt more than saw her shoulders reset themselves under the blankets. "I couldn't stand for it."

Those words hit me hard and low. Nix had been this way, always. She hated to see people punch down, and she punched back. Shadow punched back, too, even though she was too weird and too uninterested in being pretty to be part of the in-crowd. Her three best friends were spotty computer boys, pale and bug-eyed from never coming into the sunshine. Gawky Piotre, whispery Darcy, and the improbably named Jeff had zero social currency, but Shadow had Nix's born don't-give-a-fuckness.

"What did you do?" I asked.

"Me and Jeff hacked the site. Turns out, Bryce Thomlinson set it up. Him and his girlfriend, Mandy, and their snotty friends were the meanest commenters, too."

She was absolutely forbidden from hacking, but—well. I still made cassoulet from scratch in my tiny kitchen. When you are very, very good at a thing, it's hard not to do it. At the same time, no one gets suspended for hacking kiddie-mean-book sites. "Then what?"

Shadow looked away. "Then I posted all *their* purity tests. With names. On the front page of our school website."

Now, at last, she had my full attention. "Shadow, tell me you didn't hack the school's computer system."

"Well, I did, though. Just me. Not Jeff." I did not believe that for one red second, but she was still talking. "All their parents lost their minds, and Mandy realized Bryce was cheating because his test said he'd done stuff that he didn't do with her, and Emma F. and Tulsa aren't speaking because—I mean, who cares. Basically, the Übermensch are wrecked and they deserved it."

Nix's voice, her eyes, her volunteer-as-tribute choices. God, this child was killing me, but I was deep down shook. Shadow and I had near simultaneously qualified for a bed and three meals at Lee Arrendale State Prison. In a rising bubble of hysteria, I thought, *Hey, we can be roomies.*

Out loud—so out loud the dogs both put their heads up—I said, "Shadow, did you change anything else? In the school computer system? A grade or—" She shook her head. "I'm serious! Because that's a felony, several felonies, and they could charge you as an adult." It had happened in Georgia before.

"I didn't. Anyway, I only got caught at all because Principal Straughn ran a mini-inquisition, and some butthead said Piotre did it. They grilled him, so hard, and they were going to call his parents and the cops." She set her mouth. "So I confessed."

"Shadow! Why didn't you call me?"

"Well, I was mad. Piotre was crying, and, also, like, Piotre? Please. I love him, Pen, but I can code circles around him. No one suspected me because I have tits, and everyone knows tits make you stupid."

I yanked her back to the part that mattered. "Did they call the police?"

"No. Because I came forward. But, Pen, two weeks' suspension pushes me out of the race." Shadow began crying in earnest, snotting so hard that the dogs activated and stood up, pushing their noses around our blankets, concerned. For valedictorian, she meant. The mother Shadow didn't know had been salutatorian before going to Yale. Shadow wanted to outdo her, as if this might get Victoria's attention. Oh, kid. Good luck. "I'm not sorry," she insisted, her voice hitching. The dogs milled, restless and worried. God, the drowning eyes, the winged brows, the narrow nose, and the courage of her convictions. Nix, Nix, Nix. Shadow was only Victoria from the mouth down.

"I'll talk to Mom and Dad and get you ungrounded sooner if you promise—"

She was already rising on her knees to throw her arms around me, swearing there would be no more hacking. None at all. Not ever.

Sure, kid. Sure.

"Pen, can I maybe use your computer on the sly? If I'm super, super desperate? Just for Discord, or—"

"We'll see." That meant *probably,* and she knew it. She squeezed me so tight. Was I undermining, or did she need a soft place now? When Gand was home, I could be more sister or cool aunt, and Mom and Dad could act like grands instead of parents, all of us flexing in and out of the overlapping roles of what we'd lost and who we really were to one another. But when he—

Shadow interrupted my thoughts, going stiff and yelling, "Oh my god!" She tore herself away from me, scattering throws and pillows. I was left suddenly cold in the spring air, and she went running for the screen door.

There, framed in it, was my erstwhile brother himself. He opened his arms, and she leaped up and into them, crying happy tears now. Both dogs followed, turned from anxious to joyous in a blip. Gand caught her and lifted her, hugging her while she kicked her feet. He looked at me over her head, grinning. "Jinkies. It's the cops."

Shadow craned around, her face incandescent. "He came home!" as if I couldn't see him right there wearing those stupid raw-silk drop crotch pants and looking a little high. As if the dogs weren't zooming around in a flurry, tails windmilling joy. She turned back to him. "Gand, Gand!" She called my brother by his stupid ancient nickname, like everyone.

"Hi, Gand. Welcome home." I made sure my tone was mild, even though I half wanted to kill him. Gand was a daisy sniffer who played the mandolin and, FFS, the pan flute. He melted away from conflict, retreating to Canada or the Keys if shit got real. To be fair, travel was his job-like thing. He sold a lot of supplements with posts of his hair and pecs gleaming as he did shirtless crow pose in this or that national park, or sharing sunset zoodles with a series of yoga chicks sporting 4Ocean bracelets and wearing lululemon bralettes as tops. He genuinely cared about his carbon footprint, but it irked me to see him tag things

#caretaker and #BeTheFuture when every day, I saw the actual future sitting at Mom's kitchen table eating Lucky Charms and wishing for a father. "Did Mom text you?"

"Texted? She emailed me a novel," he said, setting Shadow down.

So he had come for her. Good. I needed him to handle this. I had my own felonies to worry about.

He tousled at her buzz cut. "I drove all night to get here." Shadow squeezed him again, eyes shining, but I thought, *Hey, thanks, superhero.* He grinned back down at her. "I don't suppose you can make me a coffee, eh, Shadsy? I'm dying."

"Of course!" She was more eager to please him than even the dogs were, and Timbo was about to wag himself in half. Off they went in a Shadow-led pack to do his bidding in the kitchen.

As soon as she was gone, he lifted up surrender hands. "Don't shoot, Officer. I know, okay? But I talk to her every day."

He meant over social media. Shadow followed him, commenting on all his posts and reels, which wasn't great. At fifteen, do you need to know what your dad did at Burning Man? (Peyote, and a girl named Waterfall.) Do you need to know that your father has discovered the (imaginary, or at least quite dubious) health benefits of sunning his b-hole, or track his pilgrimage to lift this nether eye up to catch vitamin D at the edge of the Grand Canyon? This was Gand all over, irresponsible, carefree, barely twice her age, not great at boundaries.

His real name was Garrett, and as a kid he'd been a living blur, the boy who had to swim out farthest, bike-jump highest, play guitar the loudest. He'd go up to bed and pop directly out his window, shimmy down a tree, and hare off into the night. Girls adored him, so much so that the grosser guys at school dubbed him the Pussy Wizard. In public, this became codified as Gandalf, and soon everyone, even teachers, even his own mother, called him Gand, though most were mercifully clueless about his nickname's etymology.

Outside, the yard had filled with a pale gold morning. I'd have loved nothing more than to ream out my brother for his long absence, but I was so weary that I was seeing double. I got up to go, and then I realized that I had to tell him about Danny Bowery. If he heard it from the news, he would rabbit, instantly becoming a smudge on the horizon. He'd give me no chance to guilt him into staying, and then Shadow would pull a bank heist or kick-start a revolution, and I'd be left with all of it.

I went right to him, and I gave it to him blunt. "You're going to hear that Danny Bowery got killed. I have to know, right now, if I can for just this one time count on you to stay around."

His face flashed surprise and then a thousand other things, too fast to read. "Killed? Killed how?" he asked. "You mean like an accident." He said this with no uptilt on the end. It wasn't a question, he was willing it to be true.

"I don't," I said. "I'm sorry. He was knifed."

Gand sucked in his breath. We could hear Shadow banging around in the kitchen through the window behind us. He glanced that way, and then he put his face in his big hands. "I can't," he told his palms. "It makes it all come back. I can't hear this."

Quick as a cat, I dashed around him, getting between him and the screen door. I kept my voice low, but I spoke so fiercely that it felt like screaming. "Well, how do you think I feel? Gand, I was on duty when it happened, and every cop car in Kennesaw went to that call. I had to learn by looking at his damned dead hateful face. All by myself."

He shook his head, *No*, into his hands. I tugged fruitlessly at his thick arms until he relented and dropped them. He had tears in his eyes. Rage flushed through me. Surely he wasn't crying over Danny Bowery? His reaction held no tinge of the dark joy that I had shared with Thalia Gray. My brother couldn't bear to feel such unclean things, and I could feel every muscle in his body bending him away from this—from me, from here, from Shadow.

I said, "If you dare run. If you run, if you leave me with this, again, and leave me with Shadow, when I am . . . when she is so . . . I swear, Gand. If you leave—"

We both heard Shadow clattering back, and Gand near instantly smoothed his face into a blank yoga expression. Vapid smile, distant eyes. Above pain. Beyond impurity. I smiled, too, though mine felt more like bared teeth.

She came out with one of Mom's lidded glass cups from Starbucks, caroling, "I put in oat milk!" She skipped lightly to her father, sloshing out drops of coffee from the drinking slot. "Do you want to go running? Before it gets ungodly hot?"

Shadow only ran when he was home. Only sang her sentences like songs when he was home. Only skipped like she was nine when—

"Sure, baby. Let me change. I'd love to run," he said.

I had to work hard not to snort and say, *I bet you'd love to run, you coward*. We faced off, me in my blue uniform, and him in a sustainable bamboo T-shirt that said "Earth First." Shadow was between us, and in that space, I knew we couldn't rely on him. He could stay, or he could be gone tomorrow. Or in an hour.

Shiny, happy Shadow knew it, too. She'd even put his coffee in a travel cup.

6

In my apartment, the word *bedroom* was literal; there was room for nothing else in the narrow space under the eaves. We'd put a skylight in the sloping ceiling to appease the fire code, and back when I was engaged, I'd loved falling asleep with Bodie, cozy and safe under the stars. Since I'd started night shifts that skylight had been the bane of my REM cycle. I'd used half a roll of duct tape and a thick towel to black out the room. I clicked the light off and lay down, thinking of dead men and my choices, wondering if my brother was already halfway to Mexico. My body shut itself down anyway, I think in self-defense.

I came to with a jerk, sure that I was not alone in my apartment. A weird feeling these days. Common sense said it was Shadow, doing a little B&E to get her grubby, grounded paws on my computer, but I bolted upright in the bed anyway. What if it was Thalia, come already to retrieve her blade? It wasn't hard to picture her with lockpicks or a crowbar. She didn't seem the type to knock. I wanted this, so badly. I needed to feel again our shared toxic joy, or at least my sense of déjà vu. I'd let her leave her own crime scene. I'd lied for her, to Delilah. On the power of one word? I had to hear Thalia's sister story.

All my clothes were in the other room, but I was decent enough in my huge sleeping T-shirt. I slithered out of the bed barefoot and pushed through the flowered curtain that separated this "room" from the rest of the apartment.

It wasn't Thalia, though, or even Shadow. It was Gand, eyes closed, palms up, sitting crisscross vegan applesauce in the exact middle of my floor. I stopped abruptly, biting back a snarky comment about how he was literally centering himself. To be fair, it was the only open space. Every corner in my main room had a function: kitchen, living room, office, and then the hanging rack and dresser that I had instead of closet space.

At least he hadn't bolted. Yet. I went over to my "closet," and I spoke with plasticine good humor. "Don't you dare om at me this early." Technically it was late afternoon, but Gand knew what I meant. I rummaged in my dresser for a pair of sweatpants.

He opened his eyes and unfolded, standing in a single, smooth motion. His mild tone felt as forced as mine. "Dammit, Pen. I've been looking for that T-shirt for a decade."

Oh, right, this was his. It was worn thin and soft from a thousand washings, but the yawping white monster mouth and the red block that read "Eminem x Rihanna" had held up.

"Nix stole it. She slept in it for years." We both knew that meant it was mine now. He held up double peace fingers, but I still felt so contentious toward him. "I thought we traded spare keys for emergencies."

"The last twenty-four hours feel like a rolling tide of emergencies." That was true enough to be fair. And to justify a fistful of homemade macarons for breakfast. As soon as I had pants on, I got them out of the fridge and hit the button on my electric kettle. My brother eyed my breakfast doubtfully. "I have fig and nut butter energy balls out in the Shred Shed." I rolled my eyes at both his idea of cookies and his dumbass hashtaggy name for his converted school bus, but he persisted. "Want me to run get you some? High protein and fiber, and they're just as tasty as those French Oreos."

I knew from experience this was a dirty, dirty lie. "I put a dozen raspberries in the filling, so it's healthy, as long as I eat a lot of them to get the fruit," I told him with my mouth full. "I hope you didn't come to say goodbye. Shadow really needs you home."

Instead of reassuring me, he said, "She really gunned it through some fences, huh?" He sounded almost admiring.

I kept my focus on measuring out coffee, but I said, quite sharply, "The suspension was a gift. They could have expelled her. Hell, they could have had her arrested."

"I'll talk to her today," he said, crowding in to get mugs out for us and giving me his most charming smile. "I'll tell her real hackers don't confess."

I was not in the mood for humor on this topic. "You're lucky she's not facing felony charges, Gand."

That paused him. "I know. Sorry. I'm only being flip because . . . because . . . the other thing. It's fraught."

Fraught was exactly right. Everything felt fraught, and it would, for me, until Thalia came for her weapon. Or at least until I remembered where I'd seen that singular face before. "If you mean Danny Bowery—" He blanched at the very name, then turned away, suddenly very busy searching my fridge for a nondairy milk option. "We can't run away from it." By *we*, I meant him. I wasn't going any-damn-where. I never had.

Gand offered me a weak nod. Bowery, Castillo, and Banks had hurt our family about as badly as we could be hurt, but Gand could not stomach violence. His goodness made me feel as if I had a monster in myself. Still, he was here, which was worlds better than what I got when I called to tell him Xav Castillo was dead.

He had been on the road for weeks when I called him, camping to and from the Crazy Horse Memorial. His last post on social media was from Mouse Landing State Park in Tennessee, so I knew he was close. That was good, with the anniversary of Nix's death looming. I called him from my bed, already weeping before he picked up, talking over his hello. He was the only person on earth who could understand why this death felt so personal.

"Gand, listen. Somebody killed Xav Castillo." I waited for questions, but he had none. Not at first. I talked into his stunned silence, telling him everything I'd pieced together using Google and local news and posts from Castillo's grieving friends and family. He breathed ragged breaths, no words at all, until I said, "Is it bad if part of me is happy? Is it bad if part of me even wishes—Gand, I wish I'd done it." I wasn't blowing off steam. In that moment, I meant it. "I wish I'd been the one to grab up that Braves baseball bat and smash his head until he was sprawled out on his bougie hardwood floors. Maybe if I had done it years ago, right when Nix told me what happened, if I had wiped him off the earth, Nix might still be—"

I heard the phone drop, a thump of feet, and then distant retching. I'd shocked myself, saying it, but his disgust still burned. I'd imagined a hundred thousand karmic horrors destroying those men a hundred thousand times, but I'd never fantasized that I would be the karmic horror. Not until I'd said it aloud to a man who wouldn't even smack mosquitoes. I held the line, waiting, twisting up with shame and rage and guilt.

He came back faster than I thought he would. He said my name, so soft and loving. "Penny? You don't mean that. You're not bad."

His kindness and the fact that he was so damn wrong made me cry harder. "I'm sorry. I'm sorry," I said. I was sorry he was sickened, but I didn't take it back.

My brother tried to take it back for me. "It's okay to say that and to feel that. It's not true, though, Pen. You wouldn't have done it. You're just reacting. People can't help how they react to things, you know? People can't help what they say or wish right in a moment, sometimes. I love you and I validate your feelings, but you are so good, and you would never do that."

I cried harder at his kindness and how wrong he was, and he stayed with me, silent but keeping the line open. I listened to him breathing, regulated and steady, until I had no tears left and I fell asleep.

I hoped he would start home right away, be there when I woke up in the morning. He wasn't, but I began working on a batch of low-sugar vegan sweet rolls anyway, expecting his skoolie to roll up any minute. I wanted to lean on his broad shoulder, have him look me in the eye, and promise me again that I was good, because I didn't feel good. I still meant every word I'd said.

When he hadn't shown by ten, I checked his Insta and saw fresh-posted pictures of Gand in fallen angel pose, barefoot and serene beside some famous hot spring out in Arkansas. Geography told me he hadn't gone to sleep when I had. He'd driven all night, away from us. Away from me and my rage. He hadn't been home since.

I'd felt his long absence like a judgment. I still did, and Shadow felt it like abandonment. I couldn't push him away again now, not when his kid was in a mess and I was shipwrecked by my own wild choices. At the same time, with my empathetic brother in the room, I was forced to remember that both Xav Castillo and Danny Bowery had mothers and lovers, friends and pets, all of whom had never done one damn thing to harm our family. Danny's loved ones would be hurting in a way that I knew intimately. Their pain was not a thing that I could revel in or even want. Gand's empathetic gaze insisted that I realize exactly what I'd given my blessing to when I told Thalia Gray to run.

He said, "Okay, then. If you need to talk. We can."

My brother was more comfortable with silence than I was. Hell, he probably would prefer an endless silence to this conversation. He waited me out, while I got shelf-stable almond milk from the cabinet and fixed our coffees and took them over to my sagging orange love seat. He sat in stillness, eyes closed, waiting until I could find the words. I told him about answering the radio call, and the scene, and then the world-tilting moment I'd recognized Danny Bowery's face. I was hesitant and careful, but he had an arm around me before I was five sentences in, and that made it easier. I stopped there, though. I didn't mention Thalia Gray at all, or the bleak joy we shared, much less that I had nicked the murder weapon.

I did say, "Two of the men who hurt Nix, dead. I'd hate to be Jordan Banks, hearing about it this morning. I bet he's freaking out."

His eyes were so sad and serious they hardly seemed like his. "That's not our concern. If—" He stopped short and sat up very straight. "You haven't been still lurking around their socials?"

Of course I was. I ignored his stupid question and asked, "You got your phone with you?"

He didn't, of course. Unless Gand was actually creating content, he lived as unplugged as a Luddite. Mine was charging on the floor beside my bed. I went to grab it while Gand mother-henned at me from the love seat, "Forget about Banks. Whatever happened to Danny Bowery, it isn't connected to Xav Castillo."

I came back through the curtain to boggle at him, phone in hand. "Of course it is!" He had to know that. There was no way not to know it, barring willful blindness.

"I don't see it," Gand said, willful as all hell.

I wanted to hurl my phone right at his serene head. He wasn't a wise person, my brother, for all he'd read *The Tao of Pooh* nine times, but he was smart. What he meant was, he didn't want these deaths to be related. Not to Nix, not to us.

I dropped belligerently back onto the love seat and punched at my phone with stiff, angry fingers, navigating straight to Banks's fiancée's feed. Bare hours before Danny Bowery got his femoral artery cut, she'd posted a selfie taken in a local pizza place. She was gazing up at Jordan Banks while he gave the camera a shit-eating grin. Still life with asshole, filtered to be perfect.

"Who's that?" Gand asked, disconcerted to see that while he was busy centering-in-place, Jordan's life had marched cheerfully forward.

"Kaitlin. His fiancée." I sounded sour. I'd watched this romance unfold in real time on Insta in a story too normcore-cute for even a Hallmark movie to stomach; Jordan and Kaitlin met at a charity dog wash for a no-kill shelter that was sponsored by his bank. Now he was living the kind of sweet, small life that I'd wanted with Bodie. Meanwhile, I was single. Meanwhile, I'd learned to shoot a gun, snap on handcuffs, work a Taser, and the world remained unfair. Meanwhile, Nix was still dead.

That was the worst part. My twin, who had changed lipsticks and boyfriends and weekend plans with mad abandon, was going to keep on being dead, forever, on and on, dead without end, amen.

I needed Nix here to give Marcia Brady's *Sure, Jan* face and tell me that poor Kaitlin faked every orgasm and Jordan watched bug-squish porn after she cried herself to sleep. All I had was Gand, though, and my organs felt like they were curdling in bile as I watched his reaction turn into relief.

He said, "We checked. He's fine."

I snapped, "Fine for now. Fine this morning. But there were two months between Castillo and Bowery, so he may not be so fine come April." Gand drew a sharp breath, and I added, "I don't care. It's not my job to care if this man, out of every asshole breathing on the earth, is fine." A guilty little voice inside my head had an answer: *Well, kinda. Because you are a cop. Protect and serve.* Not to mention, I'd personally let his friend's killer go strolling off the crime scene.

Gand agreed with me, however. "Of course not. Your job right now is, stop looking." I didn't understand him until he reached over and swiped away Kaitlin with her earnest spray of freckles, her snubby nose, her adoring smile aimed squarely at Banks. "It's spiritually bad for you to watch him."

"What is that, some kind of Zen koan? Not looking doesn't change the facts. Jordan Banks isn't a tree in a forest. If he gets killed next, and I don't hear about it, believe me, it still made a sound."

He stood up abruptly, which was the Gandian equivalent of hurling a chair across a room. He even raised his melodious voice. A little. "Penny, he won't be killed. Watching them like this has given you tunnel vision. What happened last night has nothing to do with Xav Castillo. Or Nix. Or us." He stomped as far away from me as my apartment allowed.

I stood up, too, sparking. "But if it's not connected, why—" I stopped abruptly. If I told him about Thalia Gray, I risked making him culpable. My accomplice after the fact.

I hadn't finished the question, but he answered anyway. "Because those guys are—were—broad-spectrum assholes. I'm sure they've each done things to give awful people good reasons to go after them, individually." I opened my mouth for a retort and didn't have one. "Penny, back in college, they were drug dealers."

I scoffed. "They were not. I mean, they knew where to get pot, so they would get it for other people, too. And sometimes Molly. For money." I stopped talking, pressing my hands to my head. He was right. "Oh, shit. They were drug dealers."

Gand nodded. "They also sold Valium. Dilaudid. Adderall. They hooked me up with a full-on sheet of acid for Burning Man one year. Nix called Bowery, and he told us to PayPal Castillo, and then Jordan Banks delivered it. That's organized. That's a business."

I'd been too close to it to see a thing that my cop self would have clocked from space. To me, they were guys I'd met a time or two at UGA. *Party dudes. Connected. Got the hookup.* That's what everybody said about them. Nix called Bowery a *pot-trepreneur,* like it was cute, but Gand—Gand, of all people—had reframed them for me. They had been drug dealers. And drug dealers got killed.

I shook my head no anyway. "Why, though? They didn't need the money. Why take the risk?"

Gand had an answer ready. "It's who they were. It's probably who Banks still is. They did bad shit they didn't need to do all the time. Bowery and Castillo had parents paying for their school and fat allowances. They sold drugs anyway. They had dates and hookups with all kinds of girls. They hurt Nix anyway."

I churned back and forth, wishing I had room to pace. "That was five years ago. They wouldn't still be selling drugs any more than they would go to frat house keggers. Xav got drafted by a high-end firm right out of law school. Danny's a VP at his daddy's company. Jordan is Mr. Citizen, managing a hometown bank out in—" Listening to myself, my fresh cop training started to kick in. My voice cut out and I stopped dead. I stared, big-eyed, at my brother.

"What?" he said.

I was still putting it together, but I took him with me, saying it all out loud. "Danny's dad owns an import-export company that specializes in goods from South America, and a lot of that stuff is shipped to the US through Mexico. The amount of drug traffic, including opioids, that comes into the US from our neighbors to the south is—it's a lot. Xav's firm does international trade law. He probably had all kinds of connections with customs. Jordan is a banker. He must know how to hide or clean up money. Jesus, you could be right."

Gand shrugged, wry. "Guys who do bad stuff and never once get called on it do not one day spontaneously embrace the thought that rules do apply to them."

My body felt so stiff and anxious. What if the three of them had stayed in the drug business? If Thalia Gray, with her dead-eyed smile and her expensive everything, was some kind of cartel hired gun, then I hated her. The opioid "industry" had ended Nix's life as sure as those three men had. This idea felt like ice water dumped over my head, and I'd been blind to it because Nix was so big in my vision. *Sisters,* Thalia said, and that was all it took to turn me. Delilah had warned me: A cop gut takes years to grow, and jumping to conclusions and then bending facts to support my set ideas was about the dumbest thing I could do.

"Their deaths could still be related. If they were still working together—" I began, and my brother threw his hands up in the air, frustrated.

"You're the one stalking them. Were they all up in each other's business?"

"No." There was close to zero crossover on their social media. Just occasional alumni stuff they all might see. The coppest bit of me thought this strengthened the theory. I said, "If they *were* still in business, they'd downplay their connections. Even back in college, they didn't room together. Plus, Castillo may have opened the door for his killer, which makes sense if—"

"Stop!" Gand interrupted, blanching. He didn't like to think about the details. "Drug dealers get killed. It's not our business."

It all made sense, and they might have been working together, but I didn't believe that this was why they died. Thalia Gray was not some impersonal killer working for a drug lord. She had told me it wasn't a story about cops, and it was not this story Gand was telling, either. *Sisters.*

Even before she said that word, I'd seen her joy. Bowery's death was personal to her. I knew it. No one alive could understand that because no one alive knew that I was desperate with loneliness every second. Hell, I was lonely now with my brother in the room. But I hadn't been lonely when Thalia Gray's eyes met mine. I hadn't been lonely in the car this morning, touching that bloody knife and feeling Nix's presence.

I thought, *She's going to come to me, and not only to get her weapon. She'll come because she is as empty inside as I am. I saw it, and she saw me, clear and true.*

Gand wasn't one to keep on pressing into conflict. When I stayed silent, his brow smoothed. "Can we move forward? In all things. Simply go forward, staying open to possibilities."

"Sure," I said, but I had to work hard to not add, *You walking fortune cookie.* "As long as you can move forward while staying here. We need you."

I was looking for a commitment. Not his specialty.

He said, "I'm taking Shadow to Krog Street Market to bum around, get some dinner." This was his way of saying he wasn't going to run. Not today, anyway. We looked at each other uneasily, and then he added, "Why don't you come? Get out of your head. Window-shop with us. Eat a vegetable."

What else was I going to do? Sit here and stew in my terrors and my speculations? I nodded, and he ducked at me and hugged me. I yanked his big head down and hugged him back even though every bit of ground between us felt unstable.

After Gand left, I showered and dressed, wishing for someone I could talk to about Thalia Gray, or at least about my choices. I wanted Delilah, with her sharp brain and instincts, but that road was closed. I gave Bodie our mutual friends in the breakup. My newer friends were cops or from the criminal justice program at KSU, and they all had firm ideas about the rule of law.

As I blew my hair out, my phone began vibrating. The screen

showed me a number I didn't know. It was probably a scammer or a robot telemarketer, but my thumping heart said it was Thalia, calling from a burner to avoid leaving a trail.

I picked up and said, "Hello?" sounding more urgent than I had intended.

"Penny?" Not her. A man. His voice sounded familiar.

I said, "Yes," very neutral, feeling like an idiot. No answer. "Hello?"

A ragged breath, and then: "I don't know how to say this. Not to you. But—Danny Bowery got killed. I didn't know who else to call. Xav Castillo was killed, too. Murdered. Now another one? I can't stop thinking about Nix—" he said, and his voice broke when he said her name.

I knew him by then. Michael Sullivan. Nix's final ex, the steady, quiet man she'd dated for more than two years. Trying on my plain brown boots, she'd said, and that was fair. If I'd met him first, I might have called dibs, or at least insisted on a round of rock-paper-scissors. I hadn't seen him since her funeral. The real one, at the green space outside Savannah, not the big memorial here. Michael took off work and drove four hours on a Wednesday morning to sit silent in the near-empty room with us, looking like his collar was too tight for him to truly breathe. After, Mom had hugged him, crying, while Dad thumped at his back. Michael had spent two Christmases at our house, two Thanksgivings, two Easters. A lot of birthdays, but he and Nix had been broken up for quite some time by then. I hadn't seen him since. Now he was calling me, telling me facts I knew already, and there was only one explanation: "You *know*."

He misunderstood me. "Yeah. I'm on this UGA alum page, and someone posted that Danny Bowery was ki—"

I cut him off. "Michael. I don't need you to explain the internet." The family was notified hours ago, so of course the word was spreading. "I mean, you *know*. How?" I thought Gand and I were the only people on the earth who would connect Bowery's and Castillo's deaths to Nix. Not even our own mother knew what those men did to my sister.

A recalibrating pause, and then he said, "Nix told me."

"When?" I asked, my voice gone harsh, my hand so tight on the phone now it was cramping.

"When she was living in Savannah. I visited her a few times." I blinked. She'd never mentioned this to me. Well, not specifically, though she'd bitched about people she knew from school showing up uninvited and, as she put it, *Making blah-blah noises about therapy.* "She was getting better, Pen. She was thinking about . . . coming back to . . ." These were hard sentences, and he was having a hard time finishing them. "Anyway, she told me. Not long before she— Before."

This resonated. I'd truly felt a shift, like she was readying to rise up bright and burning from her own ashes.

I was choked up past speaking, and into my silence, this good man who had loved my twin said, "Now two of them are dead. Fucking murdered. It has to be connected. Right?" I could hear repressed emotion in his steady voice. Michael felt it, too, what I felt. He was acknowledging the truths that Gand refused, and he didn't even know about Thalia Gray.

"Right. Exactly right. I was—" I cut myself off, abruptly. "I can't really get into it now." I didn't trust myself to not say too much.

"Mm. Can we meet later? Or tomorrow?"

I hesitated. I had the next two days off, but it was such a bad idea, with me this scared and reeling. Still, I heard real regret in my voice when I said, "It's not a great week. We have a family situation." This was sort of true. Shadow, unbusy with school and grounded from machines, was trouble. "Then I work all through the weekend."

"Next weekend then. Sunday?" Maybe he heard the coming no in my silence, because he added, quietly, "We don't have to talk about all that. No questions, no pressure. The news dredged up a lot for me, Penny. I'd like to see your face. Can we do that?"

He didn't say, *Because it's similar to her face.* Not out loud. I heard it, all the same.

"Sure we can, Michael," I said, very gently. "Sure, we can."

7

The next day, Thursday, I woke up to see a human shape crouched on the foot of my bed, trying to stare me awake. I bolted upright, and I almost said, *Thalia*. It was Shadow, though. Of course it was. The clock said it was past noon.

I grumped, "No, you cannot use my laptop, evil child-ghoul. Get off my bed."

She held my own phone under her face, lighting herself Halloween style. "Buuuut I neeeeeed iiiiiiit."

"No, you do not, and give me that." The screen was locked, thank god. At least she hadn't resorted to hovering it over my sleeping face. Probably because Gand left his phone lying around, and she knew his code. He didn't have a laptop, not even a tablet or an e-reader, so here she was.

She said, "I didn't come up here to beg for 'puter time. Not all the way. I'm worried about you, Pen-Pen."

"Me? Why on earth?" Though truthfully, I was worried about me, too. The longer I heard nothing from Thalia Gray, the more I doubted my decisions. She knew my name. She sure as hell knew where I worked. Why hadn't she made contact? I scrubbed at my eyes and swung my legs off the bed.

"You were weird, yesterday. At Krog. Really weird."

Okay, fair. I told her the least incriminating truth I had. "Me and your dad are disagreeing on some things."

She swung her legs around, too, and scooched in close beside me. "Things about me?"

If only that were all! I avoided lying with a tidy, "We're working through it."

I started to get up, but she pulled me back, relentless. "Gand said you got called to kind of an upsetting crime scene."

Thanks, Gand, I thought. *Thanks for this.*

She read my mind and added hastily, "He figured I'd hear about it anyway. People from school go to where they found the body. To make out and stuff. So yeah, it's blowing up my group chats."

I put my arm around her. "Not gonna lie, last shift was hard." My tone was so light, so neutral. I was proud, but the flip words still made me flash back to the scene. Danny Bowery. Thalia, drenched in his blood. Our awful joy. "It's not like on TV, or even like Nana's funeral where she was all tidy and nice in her blue dress."

Shadow felt the flinch in my body and turned sideways to clip onto me like a koala bear, tucking her face into my shoulder. "Nana did not look nice. She looked like a waxy Muppet, completely fake and terrible."

"You thought that? You were so little." Mom and Dad hadn't wanted her to come to the viewing at all, but Gand said death was part of the natural cycle, not something to be hidden or demonized.

She gave a theatrical shudder. "I still have dreams about it."

I did, too, honestly. Everyone said how peaceful she looked, but to Nix and me, it was as if the real Nana had scampered off to Monte Carlo in a feather boa and gold shoes and left a haunted doll behind to trick us. Danny Bowery had been worse, though. Messy. Deflated. Personal. Still, I had a policy of being honest with this kid, so I gave her as much truth as I could.

"The person I saw didn't look fake. He looked really real." I stopped there. I couldn't say, *Plus I wanted him dead, and he's not the only one, and I feel so damn conflicted about that,* even though this was a conversation I was desperate to have. Not with a kid, though, or my pious brother, or my gentle dad or wounded mother, and sure as hell not with a cop. It would be dangerous to even talk to Michael. The person I wanted most was permanently unavailable, and Thalia hadn't come. Yet.

"That makes sense, I guess," Shadow said. I had no idea what she was referring to. I'd lost track of the conversation. Oh, right, why I was being weird. She went on. "Did you have to touch anything or, like, was there blood you had to—"

"Shadow." I tried to get up. She clipped on hard, holding me. "I'm not going to answer stuff like that."

She blew a short, soft raspberry. "I'm not a toddler, Pen. You can talk to me. If you're upset or scared or whatever. I know you wish I'd talked to you before I hacked the school." I was wildly touched by this, and it must have shown on my face because she let me go and scooted back. "Don't go all damp at me, ugh. It's patronizing, and I'm being serious. You have such a weird vibe, and—and—" She was stuck, her eyebrows pushing together.

I cut her off. "Shadow, I've been vibe free since 2003. I'm fine. Really. Scoot, okay? I need to get dressed. But hey, later on, when the day cools down, why don't we harness up the dogs and hit the Silver Comet Trail?"

Her mouth turned farther down and she considered it, but she shook her head. "Nah. Thanks, but Mom and Dad decided I could hang with friends, just no electronics. I'm walking over to Jeff's as soon as he gets home."

"That's great!" Kids who didn't have enough to do got very bad ideas, especially very bright, very angry kids.

She got up to go, but then paused, framed by the curtain I had instead of a door. "For the record, I don't think you're okay, and I do think you should talk to me, and if you leave for hiking before I go, do you think I could use your laptop a bare tiny little? I'll only do virtuous school things about learning, I swear. My young mind is atrophying, Pen."

I hurled my pillow at her head, laughing. "Out, devil," I said, and out she went.

Both my days off were like that. There were moments that seemed perfectly normal, baking with Shadow, helping my mother repaint a plant stand. Then it would hit me all over again. I'd been irked with

Gand for telling Shadow about the crime scene, but it turned out to be a stroke of genius. He'd talked to Mom and Dad, too, and they were so sweet and careful with me. My faith that Thalia Gray would contact me ebbed. I really expected her to show up to our little house on Walnut Street? Tap on the window while I comfort-watched *Parks and Rec* for the fifty millionth time, and say, *Oh, hi, so, like I was saying at the crime scene . . .*

Maybe she'd assumed that I was smart enough to get rid of the utility knife. Maybe she was a cartel killer, after all, and I was a stupid rookie who got suckered. Maybe I'd made up our connection in my head, and she hadn't even said *Sisters*. I could have heard what I wanted to hear, and really she said, *Pistols* or *Blisters* or *Lasers* or nothing because there never was a blood-soaked blonde in the alley because when I saw dead Danny Bowery I slipped into a fugue state and dreamed her up.

Late afternoon on Friday, with my parents both at work and Gand and Shadow out running with the dogs, I couldn't manage my doubts any longer. I had an almost physical need to check on the bagged knife. It was proof that everything had happened as I remembered it. I wanted to touch it through the bag and study the whorls and loops of Thalia's thumbprint. No one was home. I could slip across our wooded backyard and slither up the tree.

I went outside and started down the stairs, and then I froze, stopping dead on an instinct as unerring as a wild deer's. I was being watched. Delilah said cop gut took years, but this was more a female thing. Every hair on the back of my neck went up as an unseen gaze crawled across my body. I told myself, *It's probably Mrs. Blanchard, tallying up our weeds.* I looked across the road. There was no nosy neighbor craning her neck to ogle me from her porch, and her old Buick wasn't in her carport.

My whole skin flushed and prickled. I thought, *Thalia*. She was here. Somewhere. I spun on the landing, seeking her, and now every window in every neighbor's house looked like an eye. There were only a few cars parked on the street, and I recognized all of them as belonging to neighbors except for two. A green Ford Explorer sat catty-corner from my house, across the street, and some kind of Subaru was close to the corner. Both had deeply tinted windows. There were also plenty of tall trees around, the thick spring foliage making them into perfect perches. If Thalia was here, I couldn't lead her right to the knife; she could come and yank it when I slept.

Instead, I stayed out on my landing for a solid five minutes. I wanted to yell, *I know you're here. Come talk to me,* but I didn't want to call any neighborly attention. I hoped my long pause read as an invitation. I went inside and opened all my curtains, showing her that I was alone.

Then I paced and frothed and waited. She didn't ring the bell or slither in a window. When darkness fell, I turned every light I had on. I made dinner and ate, every move feeling like a performance. The night hours came and crawled along, and still, she didn't come. I went back outside sometime after midnight, all my skin set to quiver, but my sense of being watched was gone. So was the Explorer.

The next day, shaky from bad sleep and roiling doubts, I had to go back to work. Walking into the building, my very presence felt like a violation. My face had forgotten how to make normal expressions. What was a person's mouth shaped like when they hadn't stolen evidence and let a killer go? How low or high did people set their gaze when they weren't walking through a sea of cops while hiding information that could radically change the course of two murder investigations? I could feel secrets clogging my veins, making my blood feel thick and hot.

I changed in the women's locker room, got a cup of coffee, then joined the stream of shift cops gathering for roll call in the briefing room. Absolutely no one talked about the murder. Carter was showing Wainwright pictures of her weekend trip, and Blane was bitching to Demarco about some chick he met on Hinge. I fought the urge to interrupt and ask, *Hey, any movement on that murder?* I got red and sweaty considering even that casual inquiry, but I was also scared that it would look weird if I didn't ask.

Delilah breezed in right before the meeting started, looking like a shady spot in hell. I went right to her with my face flushed, flop sweat challenging the chemicals in my deodorant. She flashed a normal smile and asked how my days off went.

I said, "Oh, I was great. Good days," and her eyebrows went up.

"You okay, Albright?"

I wasn't, but I babbled something out about Shadow and her suspension. Delilah's expression shifted to sympathetic; she herself had a much younger brother, Marcus, that she'd helped parent. He still didn't have his ish together in his thirties. Not the same, but her feelings about Marcus could mirror my feelings about Gand or Shadow, depending on Marcus's most recent bad choices. As I told her about the hacking, I started feeling eyes on me. Again. *Nerves,* I told myself, because no way Thalia would be bold and dumb enough to surveil me here. Then my uneasy gaze found Doolich. He was staring at me from the doorway, baleful, biting off the edges of a Danish with methodical resentment. He wasn't even blinking.

I interrupted my babble to ask Delilah, "What's his problem?"

She glanced his way, then snorted. "Is he still sulking about getting stuck with clipboard duty? What a toddler." She gave him a stare-down, and he turned away.

We found seats as the lieutenant hustled through to the podium to update us on leftover day-shift business and go over important APBs and BOLOs. I thought for sure I'd get some information then, but he didn't mention the murder at all. When he said "Any questions?" at the end, no one asked for an update. That seemed bizarre, but I didn't want to be the one to do it. I tried to tell myself that no news was good news. If there was movement in the Bowery case, he'd have briefed us. As a budding criminal sitting right beside the kind of high-standards cop I'd hoped to be, the relief I felt shamed me.

The meeting broke. I stood up, and there was Doolich, leaning beside the doorway, staring me down. He tapped his temple with an index finger, then pointed that same finger right at me. He had his chin tipped back so far that if I had been closer I'd have seen straight up his nose to where he kept his brains. Allegedly.

I started toward him, determined to put my face up near his face and ask him what the hell that meant. Every other cop in the room was getting up, too, though, clogging my path. Doolich slipped out first. By the time I got out of the room, he was long gone.

8

Saturdays were crazy in a college town. Delilah and I got a call right off, and it did not let up for hours. We didn't even have time to grab a coffee, and I was glad for it. Busy was good. It was almost three o'clock Sunday morning when the radio finally stopped squawking. We grabbed a sack of burgers at the all-night Krystal and sat down at one of the round tables outside. Delilah habitually spent our meal breaks in teacher mode, going over our last few shifts, so I thought that surely now the murder would come up.

Instead, she told me, "You've got me this week, and then your final four shifts, and then you're on your own, baby bird. Let's go back over all the ways a cop can get a feel for the rhythms of their beat. You need to know your streets, your hot spots, the locals. If something is off, you should feel it in the very air."

This time of night, even the deepest night crawlers had wound down, and the earliest birds were still dreaming. We got to finish our review and our burgers with no interruptions, and then she wanted to put the lesson into practice by patrolling a subdivision where there'd been a string of predawn car break-ins.

"This is how cops get those 'lucky' busts. They know their problem areas, they put in methodical hard work."

We made our quiet, crafty way up and down the blocks, and I got antsier and antsier. Busy had been better. I finally hit a tipping point where bringing up the murder felt less weird than all the silence.

"Has there been any movement on that big case? From last shift?"

Delilah pushed her lips out and blew air, a disappointed noise.

"Nothing of substance. The vic's name was Daniel Bowery. A citizen, like I thought. He lived in the city, though. Northside."

I knew all that. I wanted her to tell me things I didn't know. "So what was he doing way out here in the middle of the night at a closed shopping mall?"

Delilah gave me an approving head tilt. "That is a good cop question, Albright."

Great, but why didn't she answer it? I reminded myself that this was a normal thing to be interested in, and I pushed her. "Well, what's a good cop answer?"

She paused at a stop sign and met my gaze, as if measuring my interest. I looked back as blandly as I could.

It felt like mercy when she started moving again. It was an even bigger mercy when she started talking. "So. Earlier that night, Bowery was at the Sea Salt Grill." I knew the place, an upscale steak house just down the road from the front entrance to The Shoppes. "Bowery's a VP at his family's import/export company, and if there's one thing we have in Kennesaw, it's retail. He's got a lot of clients out here, and he does schmoozy dinners for them pretty regular. It was a big table, a big check with lots of drinks, so the staff remembers him. The bartender said that early on, while he was waiting for his guests to show, Bowery hit on a blonde at the bar." I tried hard not to react, which was difficult as Delilah stopped talking abruptly. She stopped the car as well, peering past me down a long driveway. "Is that— Nah, it's a dog."

I didn't care about some dog. Or car break-ins, for that matter. Not tonight. "So they are looking for a blonde?" The question came out overloud.

Delilah started forward again. "Why would you think that?"

I shrugged, wordless, and after another minute that lasted about nine years, she went on. "She paid cash, so we can't find her to confirm, but the staff agrees she left long before he did. You think there's something there?"

I did. I really did, but I tried to make a noncommittal noise. "That would be leaping ahead to a conclusion before I knew all the facts. Or any of the facts. Which would set me up for 'confirmation bias out the wazoo.'"

She grinned, because I was quoting her. "Good girl. Yeah. Bowery left last as he had to close the tab. We found his car still at the restaurant. Apparently, after dinner he decided to schlep across muddy, wet grass in his expensive Italian leather shoes to visit an outdoor mall with zero open stores. As you do."

"As you do," I agreed, facetious.

"So he's strolling along real normal-like, into a normal web of dark, deserted alleys, and then he gets into a tussle and someone slices his artery in half with a short, sharp blade." We had completed the circuit of the neighborhood, but instead of leaving, she went past the entrance to the subdivision and began to mow our slow way through the whole thing again.

"You got this from Gimbel?" The sergeant was her beer buddy.

"Some from him. Some from the chief." She said that last with no small pride. Delilah started copping back in 1999. She'd gotten a lot of pushback, a lot of hazing. Now she was inner circle, trusted and respected; she valued it because it had come to her so hard. "I got a theory, though. You want to hear it?"

Of course I did. I tried to be cool as I nodded.

"I think it was a woman."

I knew it was a woman, and I couldn't help getting big-eyed. "Why?"

She slowed even further. "You tell me."

"How would I know?" Too loud. Again.

She gave me a quizzical eyebrow. "You can't know. I want you to think it through."

I was thinking, in a frantic mental buzz. I believed Thalia was the blonde in the bar. If she had lured Bowery to the alley specifically to kill him, then I'd aided and abetted premeditated murder on the strength of a feeling and a single word. First-degree murder was a death penalty crime in Georgia. I swallowed audibly.

"Albright?" Delilah said.

"I'm working on it." The car rolled on, slow and smooth in the darkness. "Okay. You suspect it was a woman because that's a thing a man would mess up shoes for. A sex thing."

"Bingo."

"But he's married," I blurted, and she tilted her head, curious.

"How do you know that?"

Alarm bells went off all over my body, even as I said, "I don't." I had to be more careful. I was wrung out and knew way too much; it was too easy to slip. "He had on a wedding ring. You pointed it out on scene, remember?"

"Oh, yeah. That's right." She chuckled then, raising a cynical eyebrow. "He was married. Amazing how those little golden bands make people keep their pants on."

I flushed, but I wasn't being naive. I knew what Danny Bowery was capable of doing better than anyone. "Okay, but you described a successful guy with a business, a wife, and a reputation to think about. Going to a spot teens use on the weekends feels off-brand. Why not a hotel? He could afford it. Meeting a stranger for sex in an alley and then attacking her feels sloppy and impulsive for a guy like that."

She said, "Attacking? So you think he was the aggressor."

"I mean— I don't know." I did, though. That was the problem. I'd seen the bruises on Thalia's throat, and I had damn good reasons to want it to be self-defense. I'd said too much, again. Easy to do with Delilah.

She pulled over and turned the headlights out. "This is a good learning opportunity. I want you to talk your theory out. We can watch the street at the same time."

The cooling engine ticked. My eyes had to adjust, but I felt her gaze on me. That was her job, though, to evaluate me. I tried to stay cool and think it through as if I was any cop and the stakes here were all professional.

Thalia Gray could have used the promise of sex to lure him to the deserted Shoppes. It would be easy to ice him there and stroll away, but I didn't buy it. It felt impersonal, and the woman I'd met had felt all kinds of personal about his death. What if Bowery had suspected her of killing Xav? Maybe *he* lured *her*. He could have gone in with the kind of bad intentions I knew he was prone to having. I realized then, with some relief, that I did believe, one hundred percent, that however it started, Danny Bowery had tried to rape and kill Thalia. He'd hurt her badly enough that she'd needed to sit down once she was clean away. It was pure dumb luck that the body got discovered that fast. It felt more like fate that me and my chef's nose got sent to secure the scene.

I didn't realize how completely quiet I'd gone until Delilah said, "Albright, stop chewing and spit. You think he was the aggressor, and I want to know why."

I felt the silence like a void. My secrets clogged my throat, wanting out. The urge to confess, to put it all into Delilah's lap and get her help, came roaring back, so strong.

The radio saved me. It crackled loud enough to make me jump, and dispatch asked for officers to respond to a domestic violence call a mile or so to our east.

Delilah's full lips pressed together. "Let's keep on this car break-in thing."

I reached for the radio anyway. Someone else would take it if I gave it thirty seconds, and I needed to be moving. "That address is so close."

"Mm. I know this couple. Cue and Beth Wyland. We're at that house twice a month, minimum. He'll show belly like a dog, and she won't press charges. But, hey, your call."

It was. I ran the shift, and then she evaluated my choices. I usually took her guidance, but I was too scared of what I'd spill. I told dispatch we were on the way,

She started up the car again. "You got a card?"

On my first shift with Delilah, she'd shown me a stack of business cards she gave to DV victims. They had nothing but her very female name and her cell number under a logo shaped like a bottle of nail polish, in case the husband or the boyfriend found one. I'd ordered my own from an online printing service, but they hadn't come yet. In the meantime, I'd tucked some of Delilah's into my Narcan kit. I checked the zippered case now and nodded.

She set out for the address. "Tell me the theory you were chewing while we're on the way."

I had more than a theory. I had actual knowledge, and I'd learned how easy it was to say too much. "Maybe it was a sex thing, but that doesn't mean he went to meet a woman." That was the opposite of jumping to conclusions, and it also pushed Delilah back an inch from the truth.

"That is facts," she said. "The down-low crowd is more prone to hookups in outdoor, deserted venues. Women don't feel safe there, generally speaking. Anything else stand out to you?"

"Not right off. Let me think?" I didn't want to think. I wanted out of this dangerous conversation.

Delilah nodded, then turned into a neighborhood full of starter homes, tidy and cute. A couple of blocks in, a man stood waiting for us near the curb, outlined in the porch lights behind him. His saggy ranch house, with its peeling paint and cracked driveway, didn't fit here. Delilah pulled over at the top of his balding yard. As we got out, he grinned and bobbed and held up placating hands high so we could see that they were empty. This guy knew the drill.

"It's okay, Officers, it's okay, all a misunderstanding," Cue Wyland yodeled. He was short and as skinny as a skink. His wiry, pale arms were covered in tattoos that were mostly tits and demons.

Delilah said, "Another misunderstanding? Tell you what, Cue, it's nigh on morning. Go to your brother's place, right now, and sleep this off, and I won't arrest you." She was waving me toward the porch, where a single dead gardenia bush lifted skeletal arms to heaven.

"Arrest me? I ain't do nothing!" Cue protested.

Delilah formed her mouth into a firm line. "Public intoxication, how about?"

He ducked his head and grinned like a dog who'd found the litter box. "I ain't been drinkin'."

The smell of tequila was coming out of his pores, so strong I almost got a proximity buzz as I passed by him. The front door opened as I went up the three cracked steps, and his wife came out to meet me. Beth Wyland was a tiny, bug-eyed blonde who shook like a Chihuahua as she apologized for calling and for being a bother, and for "riling him." I bet she'd have apologized for breathing if he said it bugged him. She insisted he hadn't hurt her, but she was wearing a shapeless flowered dress with no sleeves, and I could see her upper arms were red. "It was just I got him yelling, is all. I shoont've got him mad. I shoont've called you."

"Did he do that to your arms?" I asked.

"Naw. I get hives, is all," she lied. There was a hand-shaped pattern to the "hives," as if someone had grabbed her hard and shaken her. "I get real emotional, is all, and then I hive up. I don't want to press no charges."

I asked if she had a friend she could go stay with, but I couldn't get anything but papery apologies out of her. By then, Delilah was walking over, saying that a Lyft was on the way for Cue. Beth busted out in tears.

"Please don't send him off," she begged while Cue insisted loudly from the curb that he had his forty-five-day chip, and Beth backed him. "He don't drink no more, or anything. For real."

Delilah was implacable, but she let them ramble out lies and excuses in stereo while we waited for the car. Finally a Civic with a Lyft sticker arrived, and Cue loaded himself drunkenly into it. Beth stared wistfully at the receding taillights, and Delilah walked down to the road to make sure the Civic kept on going-going-gone with Cue inside it.

Beth shot a poisonous look at her back and said to me, "She shoont've sent Cue off that way. This here's his own house. His mama left it to him, free and clear."

I got one of Delilah's cards from my Narcan kit and held it out to her. "This won't get better, Beth. If you want out, or if you're scared, you can call us. Day or night. For now, it's better that he cools off at his brother's."

"You ever met a man?" Beth said, blinking her watery blue eyes at the card. "Probably not. You look like you was raised inside that Christmas movie with all the songs and nuns. I bet at home, you got a closet full of dresses made of drapes." With him gone, she had some sass in her, and I realized she was my age, maybe younger. Her posture had been so hunched, her face so stressed, that it had aged her. "He ain't going to his brother's, you baby. He's going to my ex-friend Deb's, and he's gonna cheat on me again, because y'all sent him off."

Something tipped in me, then. Why were there always women ready to love awful men? Beth Wyland hugged herself, rubbing her own bruised arms and blaming cops for Cue's behavior. Jordan Banks and the batted and box-cut members of his trio had loving mothers, sisters, girlfriends. A woman had flat married Danny Bowery. He'd looked good on paper, I guess, but Flannery O'Connor had it right when she said a good man is hard to find. I'd been on the apps. It was true. I knew what I was supposed to tell Beth: *Help is available. You deserve better. One day, he could kill you.* All these things were true, and professional, and if they were repeated often enough, the message might land. But I'd had a long two days, and what came out didn't sound pro. It didn't even sound like something I would say.

"Not my job to make sure any lady-punching that goes on is strictly monogamous." She blinked, shocked, and then she clapped a hand hard over her mouth. I could see a laugh was happening in her eyes and in her shaking shoulders. I took the opportunity to lean in close and add, "Fuck that. Pack your things and get out while he's busy beating Deb."

She laughed out loud then, instantly looking guilty for it. I looked back, also guilty, working hard to not clap a hand over my mouth, too. God, but it felt good to say a raw, bad truth.

"Are you really a cop?" she asked.

I nodded, but then I added, "I guess," and my whole face felt red hot. I started to turn away, but Beth darted at me and snatched Delilah's card. She jammed it in her bra, her jaw set to belligerent. I gave her a single bob of my head, and then I left.

Once we were on the road, heading toward a fender bender near the college, Delilah said, "I saw she took the card. Good work." I flushed, hoping she hadn't heard me. I also hoped it was good work. I wanted to believe that one day Beth would call that number. I tried to imagine her fleeing to a safe house, or pressing charges, even picking a better man next time. As if she was reading my mind or my mood, Delilah added, "You never know what's going to be a tipping point for someone, Albright."

Nix spoke in my head again: *The fastest way out for Beth would be if Thalia Gray came to see Cue—and brought a box cutter.*

I made a noncommittal noise that must have sounded cynical, because she added, "Cops get jaded. Even cops in a nice town like this. We meet so many assholes. Everyone lies. Even regular good citizens panic and lie to us. Cops even lie to each other. Some of us are bitter shitheads. But not you. Not yet, anyway. You want to help people, Albright. I see it in you. It's a job of work to keep that, but it's worth the effort. The best cops keep that."

I muttered a thank-you, and it came out cracked because my eyes were watering. Delilah Williams, a great cop by any measure, was saying I could be one as well.

She was so wrong.

She eased onto the highway. I watched all the brake lights flashing as drivers clocked the cop car joining them and slowed. I thought she would say more, keep teaching me, but instead she got so quiet, letting her praise linger in the car.

At last I said, "I wish you could have met my twin."

Her eyebrows went up. "You have a twin?"

"Had," I said, and it was enough.

"I'm sorry," she told me. "Identical?"

"No, but we looked a lot alike," I said. More truthfully, I looked like a photocopy of Nix. A little softer, with blurrier edges. Telling her about Nix's death was akin to an apology because I wasn't ever going to become the cop Delilah saw in me. I wasn't sure I could stay a cop at all. I couldn't take another night like this.

"Was it drugs?" Delilah asked me. My surprise must have shown, because she added, "You've never forgotten your Narcan kit, not once. When we went to that OD down on Lester, you knew exactly what to do for that kid."

"Fentanyl." In that one word, any cop would hear a whole big story. Not too far off from the truth. "Nix was living in a place worse than that house we just left. She was drinking all the time, doing drugs. She fell right off the world." I didn't say, *I let her,* but maybe Delilah heard it. She had a way of hearing more than people said. It made her valuable. For me, tonight, it also made her dangerous.

"Do you have anyone to talk to? Someone who carries it with you?"

Nix was the one I could always talk to. I was more myself with her than anyone on earth, including Bodie, even when we were engaged. "Not really. I'm close with my family, but there's things I can't say, even to them."

"Oh, I get that," Delilah said, rueful. "Cops only talk to each other, and that right there is a sad song called 'How Delilah Got Divorced.'" She quirked a half smile at me, her eyes on the road. "I hope you know that you have me, Albright. I'm an ear, no matter what's eating you. I am on your side. I'm true-blue, through and through."

God, it was tempting. I trusted her so much. I could feel a thousand words rising as silence stretched out in the car between us. The desire to fill it, to unburden, was a pressure in my chest. What if I was wrong? What if I'd loosed some cold-blooded cartel killer who never knew my sister?

"I don't think I'm a good cop. I'm not true-blue," I said these words to my lap, not her face. I didn't want to see her reaction or be reassured. She'd poured so much work into me, not knowing I was cracked in half.

"I think you are. I think you are solid, kid. When you see a person like Beth Wyland, you remember your twin, yeah? You have a big heart, and you're open. You're just feeling sideways tonight. What's eating at you?" Delilah asked, so soft.

The car rolled along, blanketed in a solid, quiet blackness. The world felt empty of everyone but us. I felt so safe with her. I breathed in, readying to breathe out the truth. I turned toward her, the taste of confession sweet in my mouth already, and then I felt Nix again. A warning hand, cold on my shoulder.

No. The silence stretched and stretched between us, Delilah waiting, patient, for me to fill it, and in my head, Nix's voice told me, *This is not a conversation, dummy. This is an interrogation.*

The breath I'd taken pushed out in a gasp. Oh, hell, it was. A good one. Masterful. All shift long, Delilah had used every damn technique I'd studied in cop school, things she had gone over with me, practiced with me. She'd waited for my anxiety to crest, so that I broached the topic. Then she'd offered open-ended questions. Carefully worded solicitations. Camaraderie. Silences she'd created and maintained. These were all gambits.

Fear trilled up my spine, but I made my voice go flat. "I'm fine, Williams."

The mood she'd crafted between us shattered. She was busted, and she knew it. I saw her white teeth flash in the darkness. Was she proud of me? For seeing through her?

She said, "Let's head for home. There's some detectives there that want to have a word with you."

I faced forward and sat on my hands to keep them from clenching into visible, stressed fists. I was sorting through everything she'd asked, trying to figure out how much they knew. They at least suspected that the person who stabbed Bowery was female; Delilah had used that fact to bait a trap. It was possible they were looking for Thalia, specifically. Maybe they already had her. Maybe she'd given me up to catch a break. If I wanted to get ahead of this—

That was panic talking. Delilah's silence helped it grow. She knew how difficult it was to keep from filling it. I pressed my lips together hard enough to make them tingle.

As we got close to the station, Delilah said, "I looked back at my evaluations, and what I saw there, what I still see here in the car with me, is the makings of a stellar cop."

The way she used the present tense filled me up with instant hope, and then an almost instant anger. God, she was good. I said nothing.

We were very close now. At the final intersection, she took a long pause at the stop sign. She picked her phone up and typed into it, but she didn't send a text, Instead, she turned the screen toward me so I could read what she had written:

You should talk to me. Really. But inside, the only word you say is, Lawyer.

Then she erased it, letter by letter, until it was completely gone.

9

They were waiting for me right inside the door. Two detectives, both in their forties, one a round-faced dad type with his salt-and-pepper hair buzzed short and the other a sharp, thin woman with wet eyes. Delilah walked me in, but she dropped back as soon as we were inside, under the harsh fluorescent lighting of the station house. The woman, Brinks, went with me to the women's locker room, where I stored my gun and changed into jeans and a T-shirt. I pretended to be calm, but I could feel my hands shaking, and every building doubt I'd felt coalesced, and I was thinking, *What do I know, really, about Thalia Gray?*

We'd shared a look, a feeling, a felony. And they knew. Somehow, they knew. I was deep in it with Thalia, scary deep, drowning deep, over a connection that all came down to one word. One word! At the same time, I remembered the huskiness of her voice, the intensity of her eyes. *Sisters.* I wasn't on the side of the angels, I knew that, but maybe I had enough spine to stand firm with a Fury.

If not? I better find some, I thought, as I went with Brinks to Interview Room Two and sat down at the heavy table with the handcuff ring in the center. My hands were free, and I fought the urge to sit on them again. Jameson, the other detective, offered me coffee, and when I said okay, they left me.

I'd only ever been inside here when I got my rookie's tour of the station house. It was a plain, gray-green room with a table, three chairs, one door, and a large, dark one-way window. I knew there were people behind it, evaluating me. My posture. My expression. Was Delilah there? I knew I was being recorded. I wondered if the door was locked. It was a physical challenge not to get up and cross the room and check.

I reminded myself it was okay to look anxious. Innocent people were anxious here. Delilah told me once, "I know a guy is guilty and also hard as hell if he falls asleep in the interview room." I was guilty, but I was also in no danger of sleeping. Time stretched, untrackable and endless. There was no clock in the room. My work cell phone was in my locker. My personal cell was locked in the glove compartment of my car. I felt as if I had been sitting here for hours, which could not possibly be true.

I'd read about the pressure suspects feel in a room like this, but I hadn't fully understood it. Now that pressure sat itself down on my chest, heavy and unwieldy. I couldn't get my breath to go down into the bottom of my lungs. I felt like I was only getting oxygen in tiny snatches.

After an endless span, the detectives came back. Brinks stayed by the door, hard-eyeing me, while Jameson set two Styrofoam cups down on the table and said, "Milk. Milk and sugar." I took the second option, because I knew how bad the station coffee was. He sat down in one of the battered chairs across from me, his expression friendly and casual. "So, Officer Albright—Penny. May I call you Penny? Don't be scared. You're still in training, and it's okay if you made a mistake. We're not out to get you. We're here so you can help us clear up a few things."

Sure. We were simply a trio of colleagues having coffee together in a room that had been crafted for confession.

"Okay," I said. One word, but it wasn't *Lawyer.* I felt, as so many people who had sat down in this room before me, that not talking at all would be suspicious. Most of those other people were now in prison.

"Can you take me through what happened on your last shift? Not the whole thing. Start when you and Williams arrived at The Shoppes." Here was Good Cop. Brinks leaned against the wall, and I felt her gaze like a fleet of needles, poking lightly all over my skin. "So Williams parks . . ." Jameson prompted.

"Right. There were some black-and-whites there already. I think three . . ." I took him through it, how I walked the scene with Delilah, then went to run tape for Gimbel. I told the truth, but not the whole truth. The lack of air in the room kept me succinct as I described catching a whiff of something herbal, distant but out of place. "I radioed Delilah, then went to check it out."

"Were you scared?" Jameson asked, so fatherly. He had light brown eyes, a shade lighter than his complexion, and they seemed so warm and kind.

Brinks snorted. "Don't baby her."

"I'm not," he snapped back, and then more softly to me, "It would be normal to feel anxious. Did you?" I shook my head in a mute no. "Why not?"

"I know The Shoppes pretty well. I assumed I was smelling something from the day spa. Checking felt like due diligence." That was true. I had to remind myself that it was true. Everything I said felt suspect when subjected to Brinks's flat gaze.

"But it wasn't the spa," Jameson said, prompting me forward again.

"It wasn't," I agreed. "So I kept going. That was a mistake, but then Doolich came, and I went back with him."

Brinks punctuated my last sentence with a skeptical snort. Textbook Bad Cop. The whole setup had seemed obvious, known, even a little silly when I'd studied interview techniques in books. I'd seen it used on a hundred detective shows. Everyone had. And yet, I hated her. I felt myself wanting to please him. It was bizarre to be inside of it and know exactly what they were doing and feel it working on me, anyway.

"Then what?" Jameson asked.

"Delilah and I were sent back on patrol," I told him with finality. "Can I go home?"

Brinks made a scoffing noise. "That's your question? We pull you in here like some dirtbag, grill you like a perp, and you don't ask us what's going on. Pretty weird, Albright. Most cops would be mad. Most cops would at least want to know why."

By then I had figured out why I was here. I rose to this bait, feeling like her chump even as I did it. "Because I know why. Doolich. He thought he heard voices. He asked me if I heard people talking. I said I hadn't, and apparently he went to his training officer and had some kind of meltdown over it. Now you're wondering if I did hear someone."

"That's pretty much it." Jameson smiled, bland and genial.

He was lying. If that was "pretty much it," these detectives could have asked me, casually, when I came to work. Doolich having better ears wouldn't incite them to shove me in this room and, yes, treat me like a dirtbag.

Then I remembered Thalia sitting on the steps in her blood-soaked pants. When Doolich told his training officer, they must have gone back to the alley where he'd found me. There, in the dark nook behind Cupcake Heaven, they would have found forensic evidence that someone had been in that alley with me. Someone covered in blood. I did my level best to keep understanding from dawning on my face under the falcon-sharp eyes of Brinks.

Jameson settled into his chair like a man who planned to be here for a while. "I do wonder why you wandered so far from the cleared scene. Weren't you afraid?"

I told the truth. "Yes. I was. But the scene upset me, and I was getting myself together. I know it was a poor decision." I started to say more, then shut my mouth. His job was to get me talking.

"Hey, I get it. That was a rough call. So you thought it was the day spa, but you were way past the spa when Doolich found you. I'm a little confused. Maybe take me through it one more time?"

I knew this tactic, too. He wanted me to repeat myself, because if I gave them a tiny inconsistency, they could pull at it, like one little loop of picked wool in a sweater, and then they would unravel me. Or if I told it exactly the same way, they'd know I'd been rehearsing it, and rehearsed stories were usually lies. I had Delilah Williams in my head, chanting, *Lawyer, Lawyer, Lawyer,* but I told it to him again, anyway. Good, obedient Penny, brought up to be polite, born to keep the rules. Everything I'd said was the truth, so I knew it was consistent, but I told it shorter. Scene. Tape. Smell. Doolich. My sins were all sins of omission.

Brinks activated then, coming over to the table to loom and pepper me with questions. What exactly had I smelled? Herbal? Like shampoo or cooking? Had I seen anything? Heard anything? Exactly how far down that final alley had I gone? To the end? To the middle? Had I seen the entrance to the shopping center?

She was trying to lull me into giving short answers quickly, so that when she threw in a zinger, I'd answer without thinking. I tried to resist her machine-gun urgency, and I leaned hard on, *I don't know,* and *I'm not sure,* but I could feel myself falling into her rhythm. I didn't say *Lawyer,* though, because in the nonexistent space between her questions, I was learning, too. I was now certain that they had found Bowery's blood on the stoop, but with the lights out over the bakery's back door, and without my confirmation of exactly how far down the alley I had gone, they could not be sure—or could not prove—I'd seen it.

Brinks threw her curveball then. "Did you see the taillights leaving the back entrance?"

I almost said, *No.* Easy enough. I hadn't. But hidden in that negation was a tacit admission that I'd seen that entrance—and that would place me at the alley's end. It was a good trick. Dumb criminals fell right into traps like this. The smart ones thought they were safe because they saw it coming, and then they fell right into the next one. It didn't matter that I knew all the tricks; the tricks still worked. If Delilah was watching through that one-way window, she was likely annoyed to see me being so damn stupid.

I stopped talking. I put my face into my hands. Brinks repeated the question about nonexistent taillights. It was time to take Delilah's good advice and stop talking. Delilah would not sit here having manners. Neither would my twin, for that matter. Nix would not eat a single bite of the pap Jameson was spooning into my bowl. Nix, taller, bolder, darker, sharper, would stand up. I stood up.

Nix wouldn't give answers to a woman so obviously out to get her. Nix would go on the offensive. I went. "I'm done. I'm tired, and you're freaking me out. I'm going home." I came around the table, staring at Brinks, and only Brinks, sharpening myself against her hardness.

Brinks moved to stand in front of the door, blocking my only way out as Jameson said, "We need your help, Penny."

I ignored him. "Are you going to arrest me?"

I got a half smile and cold eyes. "Do you think we should?"

I shrugged while Jameson blustered kindly, "This doesn't have to be contentious, we need to—"

I talked over him, to her. "No. I also see no reason for you to question me like I'm a dirtbag." I stepped in to her, closer than was comfortable. "I'm going home. If you want to arrest me for smelling things and being bad at police tape, then do it."

Jameson stood up and came after me, his tone propitiating. "Penny, we're on the same team. Help me clear up these discrepancies—"

"Get me a lawyer," Nix said with my mouth. "Or get out of my way."

No clock in the room, but I could hear each passing second as an endless tick. One. Two. Three, and then Brinks moved aside, shrugging like she couldn't believe how stupid I was being. I was so scared the door would be locked, that this was another tricky little trap to break me down.

The knob turned under my fingers, though. The door swung open. Beyond was the regular white hall with its fluorescent lighting, and once I stepped outside, the air seemed like it had oxygen that had been lacking in that tight green-gray space.

I headed for the front exit as steadily as I could, forcing myself not to hurry. Jameson came up beside me, matching my pace.

"If you leave, you're going on suspension. It won't look good on your record." He sounded so regretful. "Delilah Williams says you're the real deal, kid. Let us protect you. We have to clear this up."

Brinks stomped along heavy-footed behind us. I kept on going, feeling side-eye from every cop I passed on the way out. I didn't see

Delilah, or Sergeant Gimbel, or even Doolich. I shoved the glass doors open and stepped out into the parking lot. The sky was beginning to turn gold with the early morning sun. Jameson dropped back. He and Brinks went left to get into an older model Ford Explorer. Green. With deeply tinted windows. I'd seen that car before, on Friday, parked on my street. I'd come out of my house and felt so watched. I'd thought it was Thalia, but no. It had been Brinks and Jameson. I got into my own car quickly, my knees gone watery. I might have led them right to the knife! I could be in jail right now.

As I navigated out of the parking lot, they did, too. I turned right, and they turned right. They didn't even bother to let a car or two get in between us, not that there were many at this hour. *Intimidation,* I thought. I kept expecting them to peel off, but they stuck, turn after turn. I drove like any civilian with a cop car behind her, three miles below the speed limit, full stops at every sign, acting as if signaling my turns was part of my religion. My heart felt swollen and too high, seated way up in my chest.

I thought, *When I get home, I'll go inside. They can't sit in front of the house all day, staring at my closed curtains. The department can't afford to waste them that way. They'll leave. Once I am home, everything will be immediately better.*

I was wrong, though. It was worse.

10

Our most awful neighbor, Mrs. Blanchard, was standing by the road in bare feet, that's how bad it was. She was a pencil-thin older lady with a rigid spine and no discernible sense of humor. She'd been crusading to form a neighborhood association to "unify the color palette and limit tacky lawn decor" for almost twenty years now. Her dearest dream was to measure our grass with a ruler and then tape official reprimands to our mailbox. She'd never gotten the traction, so she solaced herself by talking thinly veiled shit about my mother on Next Door. Shoeless for Mrs. Blanchard was like starkers for normal people.

She saw my car coming and revolved in place to orient on me. Her bathrobe belt was cinched tight enough to shape her thin body into a wasp shape. She turned with me as I passed, her face a rictus of delighted horror.

Catty-corner across the road at my house, three patrol cars were pulled up to the curb. I didn't see any uniforms, but that was almost worse. Where were they? My parents, Gand, and Shadow huddled in a knot at the end of the driveway. Mom wore one of Dad's T-shirts and sweatpants, and her hair stuck up all over her head like the tail of a wild chicken. My father, tidy in his usual TV Dad striped PJs, waved me down, as if he was afraid I'd drive past and keep on driving. If only I could! I wanted to floor the gas and zoom away, even as I parked on the street a few feet beyond them. Then I wished I could lock the doors and never get out and never explain anything. That felt like a reasonable compromise. I couldn't make my legs work anyway.

Not until I looked at Shadow squatting on the drive, swabbing savagely at the concrete with red sidewalk chalk. Gand hovered over her, wearing nothing but a voluminous pair of brightly patterned raw-silk pants. He looked like an escaped genie with his thick arms crossed over his bare chest. His presence had to help, but I still had to get out of the car, if only to offer the kid some empty reassurance.

As soon as I opened the door, Dad called, "Penny. They woke us up, and they had this—"

He waved a paper form at me, frantic. I recognized a search warrant when I saw one. Now I knew where the officers were. Crammed into my small apartment, rummaging. I hoped so, anyway. Anywhere but the backyard. Anywhere but our old tree house. My hand came up to cover my mouth too fast for me to stop it. I made that bad, confessional hand reach for the paperwork instead, and I could see it shaking. Brinks could, too. I had no doubt.

She'd driven past my car to park in front of it. Jameson stayed in the passenger seat, but she'd gotten out when I did. Now she leaned on her car door, blatantly watching and listening.

Mom asked, "What's going on, Pen?" Her voice was steady. She was the activities director at a nursing home with a dementia wing; she could keep calm in any crisis.

I joined them, standing close to Shadow. She stayed folded into a small wad on her haunches, her hands chalk-stained. She'd written *ACAB* in jagged letters and was now circling the acronym with coils of red barbed wire.

Again, I felt a wash of gratitude that my brother had told my family about the murder scene. They had no idea that the victim meant anything to me—to us—but it let me shorthand an explanation. "The other night, at The Shoppes, I was sent to run tape around the perimeter. That other trainee, Doolich, told the chief that he heard me talking with someone out there." Which was true. "Which is ridiculous." Lying to them was easier than lying to cops in that cold, hard room, but it felt worse. A hundred thousand times worse.

"That *is* ridiculous!" my father said, overloud.

"Don't react," I told him. "Nothing you say can make it better." My mother's face had become thunderous. She turned a dagger-filled, calm gaze toward Brinks. I put my hand on her arm. "It might make it worse. Let it go."

Not my mother's specialty. She'd given birth to both Gand and Nix, after all. She said, "Did you tell them that this Doolish person asked you out on a date, and that you shot him down? Some men can't manage rejection." She spoke in level tones, but loud enough to make damn sure Brinks heard her.

"Mom!" I said, and she subsided. I felt sorry for Doolich, sloppy and anxious, always getting lectured. Now, he was one hundred percent in the right. I wasn't willing to go to prison so he could finally get a gold star on an end-of-shift report, but I also couldn't let my mother make this justified search of my house into Doolich being a creep.

Shadow glanced up at me, and I ran my hand over the feather-soft burr of her hair. "It's going to be fine."

"I know," she said instantly. Shadow's misplaced faith in me burned, and it also made me love her so, so hard. She dropped back onto her butt and leaned against my legs, scoffing, "These idiots aren't going to find shit."

"Language," Mom said mildly.

I saw my kitchen curtains move. They were in there, all right. What were they searching for? Surely not the murder weapon. Which I had. Hidden in a tree house not fifty yards away. A tree house! How childish, to tuck what amounted to a bloody confession in a place a kid might hide a pink diary with a flimsy heart-shaped lock.

The warrant would tell me. It would set parameters. Cops couldn't dig around any old place that pleased them for "evidence" on a vague suspicion of shenanigans. They had to have cause and a compelling theory. If they were looking for the weapon, however, the warrant might well let them search the yard. I scanned it, skipping the legal boilerplate and finding the typed-in specifics.

Dad said, "Penny, if this young man thinks you—"

My eyes flashed him a warning, but it was Gand who interrupted him. "Dad. Later." It was the first time my brother had spoken. He'd rallied behind me as solidly as the rest of them, but he wasn't fooled. He knew too much. His gaze was asking me who the hell I had been talking to at Danny Bowery's murder scene. "Later," he repeated, just for me.

"Fine," Mom agreed, emitting a field of such controlled protective rage I could almost see the air heat-warp around her sleep-wild hair. The Penny my parents and Shadow knew would never do anything to legitimately attract this level of law enforcement. "Right now all I need to know is if everyone you work with has lost their ever-loving minds, or if they're evil?" She had not lowered her volume.

"Mm. Maybe neither? I'll put a fiver on flat stupid," my brother said, serene.

"I'll take evil," Dad said. They shook on it.

I was heartened by their theatrical rally around me, even though I was terrified that any second someone in the backyard would start yelling about bloody knives and I would be handcuffed and arrested right here in front of God and Mrs. Blanchard.

I made myself focus on the warrant. It limited their search to any and all parts of my police kit and uniforms, including shoes, and any dry cleaning tickets or laundromat receipts. That meant the yard was not included. No one kept clothes or their paperwork inside an oak tree. I breathed a little easier, at least until the front door to the main house opened and a cop came out.

I wheeled to face Brinks. "That's my parents' house. Not mine."

Her expression didn't change. "So, you have a washer-dryer in your apartment?" I shut my mouth. I did use Mom and Dad's washer and dryer, so the scope of the warrant let them access the laundry room at least. They'd push the limits as hard as they could. In my apartment, the warrant would let them search every drawer and cabinet, looking for a dry cleaning ticket. They'd no doubt already been through my locker at work, my car, and my purse while I was out on patrol. The thought of Delilah keeping me out of the way and prying at me while they set this up made my eyes sting. She'd done what she thought was right—what the law for sure said was right—but it still hurt. At the same time, I couldn't reconcile her unsent text offering me good advice with her stealthy interrogation.

I looked up when I heard a door slam. Doolich had come out of my apartment with a large evidence bag full of my uniforms. He thunked down the stairs with his training officer, Graves, right behind him. Graves's half-apologetic glance swamped me with more guilt. I'd had ten shifts with him before I went on nights; his assessments had been very positive. The same could not be said for his assessments of Doolich. Doolich tilted his chin up at me, all smug defiance. He was in the right, which was an awful feeling, and he'd been pawing through my dresser and my bookshelves, touching my pillows and my family pictures, which was worse. I had a sudden visceral flash of memory; I'd left yesterday's underwear, socks, and sleep shirt on the floor by the shower. The thought of Doolich sifting through these items turned my stomach.

Their next step would be to check my uniforms and shoes for Danny Bowery's blood. Any trace, any speck, would prove I'd seen the blood and kept it quiet. That would ratify Doolich's claim that he had heard me talking to someone. They'd have me on obstructing an active investigation, maybe tampering with evidence, which was fair, because that's exactly what I'd done. I tried to remember how close I'd stepped to the stairs in the bakery alcove. What had I touched? All I knew for certain was that I had not touched Thalia. I would have remembered that.

Doolich passed by, lofting the large bag at me as if to say, *Gotcha*. I stared back, pressing my lips together hard enough to hurt.

Dad said, "This is harassment. You should sue. Or at least tell them all where to go and quit."

I told him, "I'm suspended anyway."

Shadow let out a small laugh like a bark. "Really? We can form a club." She unfolded and stood beside me, less freaked out than my parents. She took my hand in her chalky one.

"With pay, I hope?" Mom asked. When I nodded, she said, "Good. Sit home and take their money. They owe you. How can they even think it of you? Have none of them actually met you?" Her bright-dark eyes snapped fire. The Penny she knew would not keep bad secrets, much less hide murder weapons in the yard. The Penny she knew wasn't here.

I said to Brinks, "I would have turned over my uniforms if you'd asked me."

"How cooperative," she said with flat disbelief. "So, tell us where else we should be looking. Left a jacket at a friend's place, maybe?"

I kept my eyes trained on her face. If I looked to Gand or his skoolie, she could try to use that as an admission or an excuse to go right in. I wouldn't put it past my brother to have magic mushrooms sitting in the fruit bowl with his organic plums. Then they'd arrest him and use those charges to pressure me—I was projecting far down a chain of known tactics and my own fears. I made myself stop doom spiraling and concentrated on matching my breathing to my brother's. He was probably doing some kind of yoga thing to make his brain release calm hormones.

It might have worked, if a uniformed officer hadn't emerged from my backyard just then. I saw the top of a plastic evidence bag in his hands. I tried to imitate the yoga face that Gand was wearing. Faint smile. Peaceful gaze. Thinking of exactly zero. If I'd known this day was coming, I would have spent more time holding an agonizing plank while wearing the expression of a girl who'd been lobotomized past pain.

"I don't keep any laundry in the yard, I can promise that," I snapped at Brinks.

Mom was now busy eye-stabbing Mrs. Blanchard, who had crept closer, down to the corner of her yard, but Dad said, "Penny. You said not to talk to them. Should you talk to them?"

Brinks spread her hands, her face all amused innocence. "They're checking the trash. For dry cleaning receipts."

Surely that was what was in the bag. A receipt from Sunshine Cleaners for Dad's sports jacket and Mom's Sunday skirts. I couldn't see for sure, and the cop walked away from me, over to his partner.

They convened on our wide porch, all of them, even Brinks, talking too quietly for us to hear.

I was sandwiched between Mom and Shadow, and I think they both felt me shivering. Their grips on me tightened. Dad and Gand stepped closer, too, in tandem. Even so, I was completely unprotected, and I knew it.

If it was the weapon, I still might not be officially arrested. They'd wait for forensics. They'd want to match blood type, at least. They'd have cause to bring me in, though. My chest felt squeezed as the huddle on the porch broke, and Brinks came toward me. Every step she took, my spine got tighter. She stopped right in front of me and gave me a cool appraisal. If that cop had Thalia Gray's knife in the bag, I was going right back to Interrogation Two, or straight to holding.

"Don't leave town," she told me, like they say in movies. She wasn't joking. Then she wheeled away and got back in her car.

One by one, the black-and-whites started up and trundled off under the gimlet eye of Mrs. Blanchard, and a few more neighbors who had come out on their porches. It was bad, but I could breathe again. They hadn't found the knife. I was safe. For now.

Even as relief surged through me, I found myself spinning a slow circle. I searched the street, the trees, the houses, wondering if Thalia was watching. If she saw this much heat coming at me, I'd never hear from her. I could go to prison for what I'd done, but in that moment, that felt dwarfed by the threat of never knowing. I couldn't stand it. If Thalia didn't come to me, then what?

Nix was only a voice in my head, but it was a voice that knew the answer: *Then you have to find her.*

11

They had tossed my place so hard.

Every cabinet was empty, the doors hanging open. Every drawer had been emptied out and then pulled from its socket to lie on the floor. My clothes lay in drifts and scatters, all the pockets inside out. I had to clear a path through sweaters and dishes, as well as trampled books and trash and silverware to cross the room. My bed was utterly dismantled, the mattress leaning on my breakfast bar. The vent covers were off, which was bullshit. Who kept dry cleaning receipts in the vents? One of the vintage Bourgeat copper pans that I had scrimped to buy was dented, and that made me cry. In the bathroom, even my most personal toiletries were heaped in the sink and on the shower floor. Worst of all, my sleeping T-shirt and dirty socks sat by the overturned bath mat alone. The underpants that I had remembered with such mortification were flat gone.

It took me the better part of two days to put my tiny place back together, and those underpants didn't turn up in any other space.

Doolich had them. I knew it. He'd taken my stupid lemon yellow panties with the daisy on the butt. No way they were in evidence. As if. He'd taken them to make me feel small, humiliated. Mission accomplished. My skin burned and my throat felt tight to think of him walking past me with my old underpants stuffed in his pocket. It burned worse remembering that I'd felt sorry for him and a little guilty for turning down a date. Doolich, who had long envied my good end-of-shift reports, had gotten the chance to legitimately be the better cop. He'd used it to take the lowest road possible.

I cleaned up all by myself, feeling too invaded to want help and too raw to manage conversation, even with my family. Mom and Dad and Shadow were blindly on my side, but Gand's third eye was open. He had as many questions as Brinks did about who I'd been talking to on the scene where one of the three men I hated most on earth had died.

Once my place was put back together, there was nothing I could do but wait. How surreal it felt to spend the next week grocery shopping, hiking with the dogs, cooking, keeping Shadow busy, avoiding alone time with my brother, knowing that back at my job, cops I knew were building a file with my name in it. Doing normal things felt anything but normal. I had a dizzy moment in the soup aisle at Kroger, unable to remember the brand of vegetable stock I'd used for literal years. I felt itchy and watched all the time. I didn't know if it was my imagination, or the cops, or Thalia Gray, looking for a safe approach.

If anyone was watching, they were doing a bang-up job. I didn't see faces or cars I recognized. The department's budget had no room for round-the-clock surveillance, but there had been one murder in Kennesaw last year, exactly none the year before; this case had high priority. Every day I fought off wild urges to climb the tree and get the knife they hadn't found. I wanted to take it out to Lake Lanier and throw it as far as I could, letting it sink and be lost in the dead town rotting under those haunted waters. I didn't. What if I led Brinks right to my secret? I remembered Delilah taking me to mow the streets where the car break-ins had happened, saying this was how cops got lucky breaks. They might not be on me twenty-four seven, but I'd be stupid to assume no one was checking up.

Shadow, bored and restless, haunted my apartment whenever Gand was busy making reels or prowling the city. We baked and played endless games of Scrabble and trained Bosch to add Spin to his trick repertoire. All the while she weaseled at me, wanting to get on my computer. No doubt she was sneaking screen time at her friends' houses, but these school days spent at home were long. She begged and tugged, telling me it was vital, she would die, but she also said these exact same things when she "needed" takeout from Hippie

Hibachi. Mom and Dad were holding firm on the tech grounding because Shadow had done an actual felony. I tried very hard not to think about the fact that if felonies were the bar, Mom and Dad needed to block me from their Netflix and take away my iPhone, too.

I lived for my meetup with Michael Sullivan. Thalia hadn't come, but Michael's feelings also matched mine. Gand's accusing gaze tracked me every time we were in the same room, but Michael had promised not to pressure me or ask me questions. On Sunday morning, he texted me suggesting Tasca, a trendy Midtown tapas place that the old chef me would have been wild to try. I sparked to it. I missed being that girl. Getting ready felt like dressing for a respite from my life.

On my way out, I ran into my mother in the driveway, fresh home from work. She was wearing her bright red jeans and wide-stripe blouse instead of one of her dark, pilled cardis, so I knew it had been game day in the Memory Care wing. The bright, familiar outfit helped the residents recognize her, but her stormy expression did not match the vibe.

"What's wrong?" I asked her, instantly on point.

"Mrs. Blanchard's fomenting a revolt against the Shred Shed parking here. Her post on Next Door about it is titled *It's a crime*."

"Mrs. Blanchard is a crime," I said, rolling my eyes like a normal person who was tired of Mrs. Blanchard. In some real corner of my heart, I was very, very tired of Mrs. Blanchard, but mostly I was happy to hear about a normal problem that had zero to do with murder or me.

She lightened up as she took in my flowered dress and ankle boots. I'd put on a little makeup, too. "Wow! Where are you off to, pretty girl?"

Under her warm gaze, I realized how much hell I'd looked like recently. I couldn't remember the last time I had gotten out of sweatpants, or taken an everything shower, or bothered to conceal the violet circles that had grown under my eyes.

I couldn't stand to tell my mother one more lie, but it still felt weird to say, "I'm going into town to have dinner with Michael."

"Michael . . ." Her smile froze in place as she trailed off, making room for me to supply a last name.

"We only know one Michael, Mom. He wanted to—" Now her mouth turned down. "Mom. Make your face look a different way." She didn't. "This is not a date, if that's what you're worried about." Men don't call up and ask for dates with an opening line like, *Hey, did you hear a man that we both hate got murdered?*

"All right, sweetheart. I'm not worried," my mother lied with bland love, smoothing her frown lines away. "You could ask him to dinner here, instead. We'd all like to see him. And if it's not a date, why not?" When I narrowed my eyes at her, she capitulated, her point made. "Another time, maybe. On your way out, can you go by Mrs. Blanchard's house and bop her a good one on the head?"

I sighed with mock regret. "Alas, I'm Ubering."

She sighed louder. "Well, rats. I'll have a hard time sneaking up on her." She touched her garish top. "My 'fun' blouse sets the wrong tone for a smackdown. Clothes do send a message." Even though she straightened my collar as she spoke, she was at the front door before the line landed. She had me dead to rights; this was a date night outfit.

"No one ever sees you coming, Mom," I called after her.

She often was unnoticed when she left, too, but in between those unheralded events, the woman who had contributed half of Nix's genes got her way an awful lot of the time. She gave me a salute and went inside.

I got into my Uber feeling unsettled. Why had I put this dress on for Michael Sullivan? And straightened my hair. And bought new lip stain. I felt weirded out, worried he'd take one look at me and assume it was a date. Or worse, think that I was expecting a date. It was more than half an hour from my place to Midtown, but I was so tangled up in my anxiety that it didn't occur to me until I was getting out at the restaurant that I'd left my laptop sitting on my breakfast bar. If I was serious about keeping Shadow off it, I should have brought it with me. Or at least locked it in my car's trunk. With a tiger sleeping on top of it.

Too late now. Also way too late to change clothes and scrub off my concealer and try to look a little more like hell. In I went.

The air inside of Tasca smelled of saffron and toasted cinnamon, and the lights were low and soft. Some exposed brick and pipe gave it an industrial edge that kept it more hip than cozy, but the deep red walls, wine racks, and Spanish tile floor said, *Rustic tavern, far from home, a place for spilling secrets.*

I saw Michael before he saw me, installed in a two-seater booth against a wall. He looked so chill, pointing at something on the menu. As the waiter left, Michael checked the door and saw me. His body froze in a physical stutter. It passed faster than a blink, and he smiled a greeting. It made me feel better to know he wasn't quite as cool and easy as he looked.

I threaded my way toward him, slowly because every table was full. Of course I'd peeped at him online. All he had was a stiff LinkedIn profile, but his mother's Facebook was a gold mine. I'd wondered how the pasty, long-faced accountant in her pictures, stiff and dour, had ever captured Nix's eye. Now, walking toward the real thing, I remembered that Michael washed out and blurred in photos, as if his innate stillness was actually vibration. This effect was amplified when he was with his family, posed in their picture-ready, icy home.

In person, he was elegant and handsome: lanky body, blue eyes fringed in thick black lashes, dark hair brushed forward in a short, sharp Roman cut. He'd paired a soft Henley T-shirt with well-cut pants and scuffed brown boots. The right amount of scuffed. Nix had been able to spot guys who understood their boots should look like this from space.

Michael stood up and shook his head as I came close. Not a no, but like a man trying to wake up or stop himself from staring. "Penny. It's been a while."

"Too long," I said, and then we fell into that embarrassing thing where one person (me) tries to shake hands while the other leans in for the hug. He jerked to a halt just as I dropped my hand and lurched at him, and then we both stopped, dead awkward.

I said, "This is dumb. Come here," and pulled him close.

He smelled the same, damn my chef's nose, like spicy leather with notes of orange oil and coffee, as if he'd stepped into my arms straight out of my past. Nothing triggered memory like scent, and the two years Nix was with Michael were our last good years. He graduated soon after they started dating, but he'd stayed in Athens to do his MBA. Clouded in this scent, my head became a slideshow of a thousand joyful moments. Me and Bodie, Michael and Nix, camping and clubbing, apple picking, going to pop-ups. One New Year's Eve, Nix had us at a piano bar singing show tunes with a hundred gay men in their seventies, and on the first bong of the clock, Nix kissed my forehead like a blessing before snogging Michael half to death. Remembering, it was hard to let him go. I wanted only to be back in that piece of the past. With Nix gone, none of the three of us ever saw one another anymore. *We never were a square,* I thought now. *We were three planets that revolved around my twin.*

Bodie eye-rolled at Nix's extra, and in private called her my "manic pixie dream twin," but Michael never eye-rolled once. He'd watched Nix like she was his favorite show. His own family was chilly and status conscious, and he had basked in the warm chaos of our house. He fit. I hadn't felt a gap when she broke up with him, though; Nix disappeared into Savannah so soon after, and the gap she left eclipsed all others.

I held him too hard and for sure too long, but I felt like it could not be long enough. I'd scrolled back on his own mom's highly curated Facebook page a long way without seeing an "other" significant enough to make it to her pictures. I liked that, even though it was unkind. I didn't want his chances for love to permanently end because Nix's life had, especially since she'd dumped him. Still, an unreasonable part of me would have a hard time liking any man who'd gotten over Nix. In this moment, I knew how deeply he still grieved her, and it made me feel as if we'd called her into the charged air around us. If I let go, she'd be gone.

She was gone, though. She was already gone. I knew this. When I finally released him, my eyes were wet.

I said, "It's weird, right? This is weird?"

He said, "A little," passing a hand over his face. "I wasn't ready for how much you look like her. More like her than I remembered."

He wasn't wrong. I'd put in auburn lowlights to soften the required, severe cop updo, plus training for the PT test meant I was thin, for me. Nix had been naturally less curvy, plus when she was happy, she forgot to eat, which, what? I'd never once forgotten to eat in my whole life. Back when we loved Harry Potter, Nix said my Patronus was the perfect grilled cheese sandwich.

We sat down, the high-backed booth making me feel instantly alone with him, and safe. Michael was good at creating a mood. Water was already on the table, along with a bowl of fragrant herbed olives. Penny-of-Yore would have strapped that bowl on her face like a feedbag, excited to eat at a place with a James Beard–nominated chef. I wasn't sure that I could even swallow, though.

"So," I said. So what? "This is nice."

"We can skip the small talk. I'm bad at it, anyway," he said. "Is that rude?"

"Not at all." I didn't want it, either, but I wasn't sure how to begin. I couldn't blurt out, *Hey, awesome pair of murders,* like a psycho. "You said we didn't have to talk about it. But now—" I stopped. Now what? I'd been interrogated, twice, once by my own mentor. I'd been suspended and my house had been searched. My brother was eye-stalking me, disappointed with my choices, and a pink-eyed blinky rabbit that I used to work with had stolen my panties. "Now I want to. If you do."

Michael put both elbows on the table and steepled his fingers together. "Thank god. It's been eating at me. I don't believe in coincidences, Penny. When Castillo was killed—I don't know what I thought. Something like, *So, Karma is real after all.* But now Bowery? It has to be connected."

His words were balm. Gand had started out dismissive and moved on to suspicious. "Not small talk, but I changed careers. I was working as a cop out in Kennesaw when it happened." Michael made a surprised face, but it lasted too long. I'd learned from Delilah, whose bullshit radar was legendary, that long surprise was manufactured. Real surprise flashes, then transitions in a blink to sorrow or joy or denial or laughter or anger. "You knew that. You googled me," I said, amused.

This time his surprise was genuine, moving near instantly to sheepish. "What gave me away?"

I chuckled. "You kept your eyebrows up too long. Human brains adjust fast; it's how our dumbass species has survived. My favorite training officer once told me, 'Fire surprises no one more than the arsonist.'"

He flushed, faintly, just as a very beautiful, androgynous young waiter loomed over us with a wine bottle. The tall booth and his all-black clothes had hidden his approach.

"The Rioja!" He flashed the label, then began theatrically opening it. He was paler than Michael, his dead-black hair swept back from a widow's peak, and his full lips were oddly red.

Michael mouthed, *Vampire?* at me silently.

I dipped my chin in the barest hint of a nod, working not to laugh, and right then, I remembered another reason Nix had liked him. Michael was fun.

Out loud, Michael asked, "Would you rather have a cocktail? Or a coke?"

"This is great."

"I ordered some small plates, too. They'll come out as—" He stopped himself and smiled, rueful. "Sorry. I'm not going to mansplain tapas to a chef. Want to add some things?" He pushed a menu toward me.

I said, "Former aspiring chef." Count Waitula finished decorking with a flourish and then gave me an inquisitive head tilt. "Whatever he ordered is fine, thank you."

Waitula leaned down conspiratorially and made sexy, evil-dead eyebrow shapes at me. "Fine? Try exquisite. Your date has perfect taste."

I stopped myself from explaining that this was not a date, but I couldn't stop my blush. If Michael was embarrassed, it didn't show as the waiter poured a splash for the standard tasting ritual.

"She's the one who knows wine," Michael began, but I demurred.

Michael sloshed it about, then wafted the smell toward him with a hoity-toity hand before he drank. "Mm. Notes of Uncle Purvis's cigar smoke with sea monkeys at the finish. Vindictive, yet saucy. It should amuse you." He was so dryly la-di-da about it that I had to laugh. The waiter chuckled, too, and spilled generous portions into our fat-bellied glasses before he walked away. Michael lifted his in a silent what-the-hell toast, then drank deep.

I followed suit. The wine was rich and dry, old enough for the tannins to fully develop. I knew right then the bill was going to hurt, especially since I might soon be unemployed. But so what. I let the good wine flood my mouth. This was a hard conversation. Why not let some of the night be sweet? Michael must have felt the same, because he pushed the olive bowl toward me. I took one, and it was smoky and perfect. I tasted lemon, coriander, thyme.

As soon as the waiter was out of earshot, Michael fessed up. "Guilty, Officer Albright. I googled you."

I grinned. "Same. You're pretty stealth, but your mom's Facebook is an endless Christmas letter. Hey, are you some kind of big-time financial adviser who has worked for multiple Fortune 500s? I wasn't sure. She only mentioned it in every other post."

He lifted his glass in a salute. "Who needs small talk when your mother thinks she's your publicist." A joke, his tone perfectly light, but I knew there was pain behind it. His chilly mother talked about him much more than she talked to him.

"To be honest, I came away not understanding what your job is, only that you're good enough at it to buy a Lexus," I said. "What exactly do you do?"

"I'm a consultant," he said. "So almost nothing." We both laughed. "No. I work for corporations that have grounded themselves, fiscally. I help them retrench, and then I disappear, leaving order and profitability in my wake. Ideally. Of course, my father tells me that if I was actually good enough, I'd have a BMW." Another joke, but I felt the sting behind it. Back in college, his disdainful father only saw the minus in his sea of *A*'s. Michael turned the conversation back to me. "I was sure you and Bodie would be married, and you'd be running a kitchen somewhere. I was glad to be wrong." My eyebrows went up, and he clarified. "About your job. The news was short on details about Bowery's death. As a cop, I bet you know more than a chef."

I looked around and drank some wine before I answered. This was one of the best tables in the place, very private, not too near the bathroom with a sight line to the open kitchen. Michael always did have unerring instincts for what was good. Case in point: He'd loved Nix. She'd loved him back in part because of his taste; Michael wore Chelsea boots and Madhappy hoodies when most UGA guys jammed their manky troll feet into rubber flip-flops and sported shredders off Shein. He'd smelled like Tom Ford instead of armpit or Old Spice from Kroger. But he was too vanilla for her, long term. My twin didn't like or even get the subtler flavors. She'd have killed it on *Hot Ones*.

I'd paused too long, thinking, and Michael said, "Are you not allowed to tell me? Can you say if—was it *like* Castillo? Same MO?"

It was eating at him, same as me. "Not at all." He still looked uncertain. "Believe me. This isn't something I heard." I swallowed. Met his eyes. "Michael. I know exactly what it was like when Danny Bowery died. I know because I was there."

His face flashed shock. "That's not possible."

Even his microexpressions were more micro than those of most people, but Delilah said I was good at reading people, and I understood him. He thought I meant that I was there when Bowery was *murdered*. That I was confessing to a killing, maybe two, over a bowl of woodfired olives. Did he look relieved now? Yes. Maybe even glad. I felt it. My heart jumped in an echo of that moment when my gaze had met Thalia's and we'd both been glad, together. He looked away, perhaps ashamed, but I loved his reaction. It was so pure and true and animal. So different from my brother. When Castillo died, Gand had puked because I *wished* it had been me who smashed his head in.

I let out a laugh that sounded giddy and shook, both. "You don't think I have it in me."

"No, I don't. Are you reading my mind? I don't remember you being—" He waved a hand, but he had himself under tight control now.

His upbringing had been a boot camp for not feeling things or showing them, and this time I had no idea what he meant. This had been one of Nix's big problems with him. After she broke it off, she told me, "I thought Michael-never-Mike must have a dark side. Not like, torturing puppies in a secret basement, but some wild kink. A red room. An unspoken yearning for specific outfits. If he does, it's buried too deep for even him to know. All I found under the WASPy reserve is even more WASPy reserve."

That was Nix all over. "You dumped him for being a good egg?"

She laughed and said, "Pen-Pen, I don't want to fuck an egg. Good or bad."

Had I disconcerted Michael by seeing through him earlier? He wasn't used to it. He leaned back, eyes shuttered, mouth still, like a man who wasn't sure he wanted to be vulnerable and open with the twin of his dead ex. Fair. Maybe he needed me to go first. I took a big breath and a bigger sip of wine.

"I didn't kill Danny Bowery. I worked the crime scene. Hell, every cop in Kennesaw came to that call," I clarified.

He digested that, then said, "I didn't kill him, either." It was so dispassionate it would have read as a lie if I didn't know how buttoned-up he could be. And if I hadn't met the killer on the scene.

"I know you didn't." I sounded so sure of this that his eyebrows went up.

"You have a suspect." It wasn't a question.

I held my hands up, palms out. "I have no idea who did it." This was a lie, and it was the wrong lie, too. He'd meant the police, and I'd answered it as if he'd meant me, personally. A small silence fell. Somehow our wineglasses had gotten themselves empty. Michael rectified the situation, waiting me out until I added, more truthfully, "The police have no leads, and they haven't drawn the faintest line between Bowery's and Castillo's murders. They can't. Because no one knows what you and I know. Well. Except Gand. Who has yet to file a report." That made him chuckle. We both knew Gand wouldn't voluntarily speak to a cop who was not his blood relation. "I'm not going to tell them, Michael. I promised Nix I'd never tell anyone."

"Mm," he said. A nonjudgmental noise. He leaned across the table and dropped his voice. "I made her the same promise. I plan to keep it. To be honest, I don't care if whoever killed them is never brought to justice." His face was still carefully blank, but his next words felt so vulnerable. "Does that make me a bad person?"

Gand would say yes. Me? I felt tears close again, moved that Michael still cared about the vow he made my twin. "No. As an officer I ought to feel an obligation, but, hey, I'm on suspension." That was plenty, but I kept right on, talking so quietly he had to lean across the table. "I went off down an alley by myself. Way too far. Another officer, Doolich, came to get me, and he heard me talking to someone. Someone I found. Someone with a knife who was soaked in Bowery's blood. Maybe he heard me tell that person to run. Allegedly."

I ate another olive, shocked at my own recklessness. But Thalia hadn't come, and Michael felt the way I felt, knew the secrets I knew. I was so tired of being so alone. I picked my wineglass up and closed my eyes and drank off what was left.

When I looked back to him, all color had left his face. Even his lips were white, but his eyes blazed blue, and his voice was measured. "Penny Albright. My god. Aren't you a surprise."

12

Michael poured out the rest of the bottle between our glasses. We drank, measuring each other's mettle like gunslingers while all around us people laughed and talked and flirted and ate. He didn't ask me anything. I appreciated that. The waiter zoomed over to drop off shrimp in classic garlic sauce and a cast-iron pan with albóndigas sizzling in a salsa española.

"Now these? These are special," the pale waiter said, waggling his perfectly groomed eyebrows as he set down the meatballs.

"We'd better have another bottle," Michael told him calmly.

So not like Gand. I'd given Michael every sin my brother wanted me to confess, but Michael wasn't asking for repentance. If anything, my recklessness sparked his approval, and that made me remember in my whole body how much this man had loved Nix, my Nix, my bold, wild twin.

All of a sudden, I was starving. It was as if I'd had a pound of gravel in my stomach, and now it magically disappeared. I shoveled food onto our plates, and we both tucked in. The wine and his acceptance mixed and went right to my head. I leaned in, too, feeling an impetuous energy gather between us like a giddy whirlwind swirling with anxiety.

"Gand says the murders aren't connected to what they did to Nix. So if I did hypothetically let the killer leave, then I pretty much assisted some drug cartel asshole."

Michael's mouth curled with distaste at that thought. Not because he was uptight. He was a one-or-two-beers person, like me, but he hadn't fussed when Nix tried shrooms in college. I remembered him laughing when she lit a blunt and told him solemnly, *This is my duty as a future senator. The first step in changing dumb laws is to break 'em.* He didn't like the thought that I'd been some drug moll's dupe. Drugs had helped kill Nix.

He said, "Are you saying you didn't know this person? You let a stranger leave? Hypothetically."

"I know how it sounds, but she—" My voice cut out abruptly, and I clapped my hand over my mouth, my eyes gone wide. Too late. The feminine pronoun had already escaped it.

He waved a hand, like, *Don't worry about it.* "The only side I'm on in all of this is Nix's." We both knew that was the exact same thing as saying he was on my side.

I drank more wine and then started again. "Okay. It was a she. She looked familiar, but I couldn't place her. Gand says it's possible Bowery, Castillo, and Banks were still selling drugs together after college, but he also says bad people don't suddenly stop being bad, so they'd each have their own enemies by now. Gand also wonders if this is about Nix, then why is the third guy still living his best life?"

Michael dismissed that, just as I had. "Maybe she hasn't gotten to Banks yet. Maybe he's up next. If I was him, I'd sure as shit be worried now."

I nodded. "If Banks is on her list, well, I let her go. If she uses that freedom to complete the set, then I—"

He cut me off, scoffing. "Fuck that, Pen. Did she say, 'Let me go, so I can do more murders?' No. Don't put that on yourself."

I was glad enough to leave that thorny thought and get back on topic. "Do you think they were still selling drugs together? After college, I mean."

Michael thought it through before he answered. "I knew those guys, back at UGA. Everybody did." His tone was calm, analytical, but the words themselves stank of rage. "I can't see Castillo, Bowery, and Banks leading the kind of double life required to have jobs like theirs and also work for a cartel. I also can't see them being clever and careful enough to found a side hustle crime empire. They were not still waters, Penny. They did not run deep."

His opinion did a lot to balance out Gand's, but I couldn't quite keep faith that I had done the right thing. Not when Thalia never came to get her knife. I smiled, but it didn't quite get to my eyes.

"Penny. What am I missing?"

I took a deep swallow of wine, then another. I could feel my heartbeat in my face. *Calm your tits,* my twin would say, if she was here. *Let your tits be calm as little swans upon the blessed waters.* I'd told Michael a lot, and I didn't want to lie to him, but the bloody knife still felt like mine alone. Or, no. Not alone. Mine and Thalia's. Our only connection. Doubt-filled and disheartened as I was, I couldn't quite let go of my dumb hope that this really was a sister story, as she'd said.

The vampire waiter saved me, appearing with a second bottle and a narrow oval plate holding three fat bombas sitting in a row. I helped myself to one and slid another on Michael's plate while the waiter took out the cork. We tried them as the waiter refilled our glasses and left.

Michael blinked and reached for his water. "Damn, that's so hot."

It wasn't. Crispy outside, with potato and spiced lamb inside, drizzled with smoked tomato aioli.

"No, it's perfect, very balanced. Remember how Nix used to call you Toddler Mouth?"

"Pah," he said, smiling. "Because I didn't like hot chicken set to blister. Nix would call this bland and douse it in Romesco. She'd eat the fire right off that candle. Do you remember—" His voice cut out, and he looked to me so gently, as if asking for permission to invoke her. I nodded, and he continued. "Do you remember when we went tubing down the Hooch?"

I laughed out loud. Of course I remembered. Nix and I wore stained, torn polyester prom gowns from 1982 that we dug out of the dollar bin at the Salvation Army, all ruffles. The boys were less formal in swim trunks and tuxedo T-shirts. "Why did I let her pack the picnic?

It was ninety percent hot sauce and alcohol." We'd gotten dangerously blasted, gulping grocery-store prosecco out of plastic coupes to sooth our burning mouths.

By some silent accord, all talk of felonies, mine and other people's, was tabled as more plates came. We tried perfect bites of this and that, eating way too much and reminiscing. What a luxury it was to slip away into the past, to tell each other stories we already knew because we'd both been there. We were laughing, mostly. So deeply that my sides hurt from it. At some point, he poured out the last drops from the second bottle, and then he set it down with a deliberate thunk.

"My whole life before Nix was limits. My family is all walls, you know?" I did. Nix had told me that when Michael was a kid, his punishment for misbehavior or mistakes was the silent treatment. He'd walk around his house like a ghost, eating off the stove or out of the refrigerator because they wouldn't set a place for him at the table. They refused to even see a child who might embarrass them. "That's no way to live. Walled in. Nix was boundless. She would reach for it, whatever it was. She unleashed me. Made me into myself."

I'd never seen him so open. It made me open, too. "Sometimes, I think I was her limits. I was the wall around her."

"No." He was vehement. "I might have said you were, before tonight. I'm seldom surprised, Pen. But you've surprised me. And as we've been sifting through the past, what I see over and over is you cheering her on toward her best impulses. You never held her back."

I said, "Yeah. Not back. But maybe I held her safe? Maybe it's not great to be completely boundless. If I'd been a better wall, maybe she wouldn't have fallen off the world." It was suddenly serious again. I was thinking about that missed call. . . . *cold and bad, Pen . . . I'm scared of my . . . Please, can you . . . feel like a ghost already.* Her voice, drowned out by relentless bass and running water. My twin, surrounded by people, but dying all alone.

"I refute that, too," Michael told me, and again, his words spread over me like balm. Or I was drunk. Or both. "She did what she wanted.

Remember when we went to that Battle of the Bands thing, out in that muddy field?"

"Oh my god, I told her not to wear those shoes!"

"Right. You told her. But you didn't yank them off her feet and burn them." He spread his hands like a lawyer making some great closing argument out of a pair of ruined, high-heeled sandals. It was a small absolution, but it landed with me.

He called the waiter over and ordered us flan and tres leches cake with a Muscat de Beaumes-de-Venise. The drinks came fast, in tiny tulip-shaped glasses, while Michael and I wandered through more of our shared past, the good times only. The highlights reel. I don't know what was sweeter, to eat these perfect bites with the floral digestif or to remember and remember and remember. People outside my immediate family shied away from even saying her name to me. As if bringing her up would remind me she was dead. As if I had forgotten. I never forgot, not ever, not for a single breath. Now, we laughed so hard, remembering her absoluteness, her impulsive surety, her good, bright heart. I was so glad I'd come, so grateful.

After the coffee came, I said, "Not to mood-kill, but do you mind if I ask you something serious?"

"Naw," he said, his old South accent escaping and stretching at the vowel. He'd had his fair share of the wine. "You can ask me anything."

I swallowed. "If Gand is right, if this woman I let go was a random cartel killer—" I stopped. I had her thumbprint, locked onto the knife in Bowery's blood. If she was some tawdry, awful drug person, I wanted to tell Michael about the knife, and then take it to Delilah, and go to prison, so the cops could use it to find Thalia. She could go to prison, too, and then to hell. I felt my mouth crunch up, suddenly near tears. If she'd known Nix, or loved Nix, if this really was a story about sisters, then why hadn't she ever come? She would have wanted to talk to me, Nix's twin, as much as I wanted to talk to her. It would have rung in her, way down deep, like bells, the way it rang in me. Days and days of nothing had gone by, and if it wasn't for Michael, I'd be all alone in this.

I finished, "—then I have to tell the cops. She has to be found. And punished. Right?"

Michael reached across the table and put his hand over mine, cool and firm. "No. Who cares." Now he had surprised me. "Penny, those guys deserved what they got. Look. I get it. You want to know. Okay, well, I want to know, too. You need to find her. For your peace of mind. There has to be a way. We can put our heads together. Sometimes a little detail that you don't notice that you're noticing can—"

He was still talking, but I no longer heard the words. His voice became a drone of soothing nonsense. At that very moment, just as I despaired, I had my answer. I sat up very straight, all my doubts shut down, half my questions answered. It wasn't drugs. It wasn't separate from Nix. It was personal. Gand was stupid. I'd been right, all along, and the bells were back, ringing through my veins like crazy, vindicated joy, because Thalia Gray was here. She was staring right at me, like she'd been here for hours now, waiting for me to notice.

As soon as I saw her, I dropped my gaze to the white tablecloth. I could still see her in my peripheral vision, leaning casually beside the ornate front door. She was monochrome again, wearing silvery-gray fitted pants and an exquisitely cut jacket that made her glow like a slim beam of moonlight against the deep red of the wall. I took my hand out from under Michael's and I put it to my forehead. Behind this cover, I risked another glance. She was still looking at me, only me, and when our eyes met, it happened again. That click. Awful, wrongful joy rose in me, and I felt incandescent, as if there was a switch in me, and she had flipped it.

"Penny?" Michael had seen the charge enter my body, but he didn't understand the source. "What did you remember?" he asked, as if the light was some internal flare. It wasn't. It was an open channel, bright energy surging from her to me and back.

I opened my mouth. Shut it again. I fixed my gaze on him, waiting for my body to remember how to breathe and make words. In my peripheral vision, Thalia lifted one lazy hand, open, palm to the ceiling, and then folded her fingers toward herself twice in that sharp, beckoning gesture that means *Come here*. Or *Bring it*. Sometimes both. Then she rolled on her shoulder and disappeared out the front door.

I found I was already standing. "I need to go."

"Penny? Are you—"

I talked over him. "I'll Venmo you for this."

"No, this is on me, I— Penny? Penny!"

I was already slipping sideways through the crowded tables, calling back, "I'll Venmo you."

I dodged a woman heading for the restroom, a waiter whose slow pace made me consider brief, decisive violence, a man shoving his chair back from the table. I felt like I was dream-running, trying to get to some strange meeting place through thick, congealing air. I slithered through a group of women coming in as I was going out, and I dove into the darkness after Thalia Gray.

13

Déjà vu swamped me again as I plunged out and down the stairs. I felt like I was diving deep, reaching for something lost. Something I'd tried to catch before. I stumbled on the last step, and I almost ended up face-planting. Instead, I careened into the valet. He mostly caught me, and I grabbed his jacket and jerked myself upright, staring all around.

Thalia Gray wasn't there. Not right there, not waiting for me. I felt weirdly bereft, blinking, clutching the valet, and I realized I had slipped past buzzed half a bottle back. I was drunk.

"You okay?" the young man asked. His worried face was a pale oval hovering over me.

I pushed off and lurched past him toward the intersection where this one-way Midtown street hit a major thoroughfare. This way, Tasca's covered bar patio faced a broad sidewalk and the lights of other city nightspots. If she'd gone toward the patio, she was already out of sight around the corner.

"Do, uh, you want me to get your car?" the valet asked behind me.

"Do I seem like I'm in any shape to drive?" I asked back. I spun to face the other way, peering down the narrow side road where the sidewalk dwindled into darkness. "She went this way, didn't she? The blonde."

"Yeah," he said. I started walking, hearing him call after me, "Do you need a cab?"

I waved a vague negating hand at him and left the cheery lights of the valet stand. I weaved my way into a dark too thick for easy breathing. As the night closed around me, I felt as if the ground itself was sloshing and surging, pulling me inexorably onward. My body moved as if moon-pulled, and I understood I wasn't having déjà vu; the night reminded me of something real.

All at once, I was thirteen years old again, snorkeling with Nix on a family beach trip. All day we'd darted in and out of bright blue water, the sugar-white sand a dazzle in our eyes, but now the sun was an orange ball on the horizon and the water had darkened down to navy.

We kept swimming anyway, diving and letting our snorkels fill, pushing hard with our fins to reach the bottom and grab shells. We let our own held breath carry us up, then blasted our exhales to clear the tubes, spouting like whales. Every shell we'd found so far had little crabs inside, and so we'd put them back.

Mom and Dad were on the beach with baby Shadow. Any minute they would call us in. Nix began kicking away from the shore, trying to get out of earshot, grabbing my hand to pull me along. The sea got deep so fast, and as we dove, we could feel it going cold in layers. The sun became a sliver, and the first faint star shone, visible. Now it took five or six strong kicks down before we could see the white sand glimmering. When we surfaced, treading water, I told her it was time to head back.

She told me, "We can't. It hasn't happened yet." She couldn't say what *it* was, only that she felt it coming.

Our father bellowed for us then. "Girls! Girls!"

"I didn't hear that," Nix said, grinning. She sucked in a huge breath, put her mouthpiece back in, and down she went. I went with her. I always went with her, and the water was so dark, my only sense of up came from the tug of the air inside me. Then the white sand shimmered into view, and Nix pointed, excited. She'd spotted a curved, golden rectangle, darker than the sand around it, pale enough to gleam in the dark water. An olive shell, the biggest one I'd ever seen.

The water was at least fifteen feet deep, perhaps closer to twenty. My ears popped, and every foot that we descended made me colder. The light was all behind us now. We kicked hard, down and down toward her prize.

Nix was a little bit ahead of me, already reaching. Her hand was inches from closing on the "shell" when I understood that it was looking at us with a single inset eye, big as a plum. I grabbed her shoulder, yanking her back just as a seven-foot circle of sand clouded into the water directly beneath us. We both went still, our limbs spread out, floating like a pair of starfish. Our held breath pulled us upward as the huge stingray unearthed herself, rippling more sand away, her sleek skin shining. Nix had been reaching for one side of the dome that housed her eyes, as if it was a thing that we could own and pocket and take home.

I rose faster, so that I saw my twin's pale limbs and baby-pink swimsuit framed like a reverse silhouette against the vast, golden-brown disc. The ray undulated, rippling forward; we felt her muscular movement as a push. She glided off as we rose, her deadly tail with its serrated spines trailing behind her. I came up shaking, but Nix was screaming with joy to have come so close to something so big and deadly and buried and not ours. Something beautiful and wild.

Now, I plunged into a darkness that also seemed to get colder in layers as I hurried after Thalia Gray. No one was with me to pull my hand back, urge me up. At the other end of the block, I could see another place with a rowdy patio bar. Color and sounds and life. The music was very faint, very far. Between here and there, the dark was broken in dim splotches by security bulbs over the doors of these closed businesses. The road itself was too old to have streetlamps.

The dark intensified as I came to a dead building with a failed coffee shop on the ground floor. No lights. Boards over the big windows. The next building was a tall, historic-looking home on a narrow lot, clearly now some kind of office. A narrow drive went snaking in between these places. I peered down it, and I caught a whiff of something herbal and intense.

My nose never fails me, I thought, and then I knew I wasn't simply drunk. No, I was destroyed, and stupid with it.

I turned toward her scent. Never mind that the last person who followed Thalia Gray out of a restaurant and down a dark alley was

Danny Bowery. Never mind how that worked out for him. The gravel rolled under my unsteady feet. I kept going, my hands reaching out in front of me to catch me if I fell. Ahead, near the end of the buildings, the silver line of her slim, straight form coalesced out of the darkness. Behind her, the drive opened onto a gravel parking lot. There was a tall streetlamp back there, but it was broken. Had she smashed the bulb herself, or simply made use of the dark it offered? Two more steps, and I saw a harder line of silver gleaming in her hand.

I thought, *It's the box cutter. The one I stole. That's why the cops didn't find it. She came to my house and sniffed for blood, then slithered up the tree and fished it out.* That was nuts, though. I hurried forward, my body shaking, my smile too wide, thinking, *Anyway, her blades are not for me.*

As I got close, I saw the silver she held was only her vape kit with its profusion of engraved fat mums. Something in her body language made me slow and drop my hands. I dove directly into conversation. "That cop who interrupted us? He heard us talking. So they know they're looking for a woman." I stopped between her and the brick wall of the taller building. "They suspended me. They searched my house. They put me in the box and talked at me, but I didn't talk back."

Her head ticked sideways in a movement that read as strange, inhuman. Like she was some inquisitive bird of prey, or an ancient reptile on the hunt. *Clever girl,* I thought, but she had no pack, and she wasn't the distraction. She was it.

"Good. You'd have sent yourself to prison." Her voice was mezzo more than alto now. Her bruised throat had healed.

"I've been waiting for you to come and get your knife."

One eyebrow went up. "You didn't get rid of it? It—"

"—incriminates me, yeah, I get that. I kept it because I hoped that you would come for it. That night, I felt like you really saw me, and I saw you. We connected." I hated the whole English language then. I didn't want to borrow vocab from *The Bachelor,* but I didn't know how else to say it.

A considering pause, and then she said, "Did we." It was too flat to sound like a question. She stepped in fast, and all at once she was way too close. "Is that what that was?" She leaned closer. We weren't touching, but I could feel her body like a heat. I smelled juniper, faint bitters, even fainter rose. Her breath brushed my cheek. "Is this why you said *Run?*"

My body flattened to the wall, palms on the rough brick. Did she think I was slinging some kind of weird sex vibe at her?

"Stop it," I said, flushing with hot impatience. I reached one hand up to push her back, but she melted away before I could, all that forceful energy dissipating. We were still too close, but I could breathe, at least, in the small space between us.

"I prefer not to be touched." She looked at my hand, so I dropped it. "I don't like it when people touch my stuff, either. And yet you're practically teething on it."

I shook my head, and the dark world sloshed around me. "It's my stuff, too. Anyway, you're the one who's following me, and you're the one who—whatever the hell that was, so who is touching who? Or whom. Or whom's stuff." I was wound up in the words. "You have to talk to me."

"Oh, do I, Officer Albright," she sounded almost amused, and she came down hard on the word *officer.*

"I don't have to be a cop," I blurted out. Up went the eyebrow again. "I'm already suspended. I could quit. I should quit, anyway, because I've been so bad at it. I let you go. After we . . . after we . . ." I pointed from her eyes to mine with two fingers, waving them back and forth between us. "I'm just Penny, here with you. Just Penny. It's safe. You're safe."

"Am I." Everything she said ended too flat to sound like a question.

I answered anyway. "Yes, with me, you're safe. I told you to run. I hid your bloody knife. I didn't tell the cops that Bowery's death was connected to Xav Castillo's case."

I saw the name land with her, narrowing her eyes. She took a long sip off the vape, then said, "You *are* in this, aren't you. Deep. Forgive me. I'm recalibrating," I had no idea what that meant. "Are you armed?"

I said, "Of course not. I'm suspended, remember? They took my gun. Listen, those men have been doing bad things together since they met in college, all three of them. They were selling drugs, back then. One was the face, one did the money, one delivered—"

Thalia held up a hand to stop my voice. "I know all that. Stop talking. Are you recording this?" I shook my head, a vehement no. "Forgive me," she said, again. "I have to be sure."

She turned off her rig and tucked it into her breast pocket, then leaned toward me. The gravel drive was already narrow, barely worth the name *alley*, and I was suddenly so scared I flattened to the wall again, so fast I banged my head. I had kicked my way down, down, down, into a drowning space, and now her pale gold killer's eyes came in so close.

"I'm not recording this. I'm not armed," I said, as sincerely as I could.

"I'm not a trusting person," she said, mimicking my inflections. She put her hands on my shoulders, spinning me, leaning me back up against the wall, pushing my arms high. This is what I should have done to her, last time we were in an alley. I pressed my palms to the cold bricks.

"I'm not going to stop you," I said, and in response, she kicked my feet apart like a pro. I meant the search, didn't I? I was giving her permission to search me, not to go ahead and make it a trifecta by killing Jordan Banks.

"Good," she said, her hands moving over my dress, checking seams and pockets. "Because you can't."

She found my phone. I felt its small weight lifting as she took it. After a pause, she put it back. I couldn't blame her for the caution. The cops had staked me out and searched my house and questioned me. They were likely watching me on and off. Her hands on me, her fingers running along my underwire, told me this was personal as hell for her. I held still and let it happen. Let her happen. She crouched to run her hands along my bare legs, both sides, then checked my boots, meticulous. She straightened up and ruffled through my hair. Her search techniques were textbook. She did everything but make me squat and cough, and then I felt air rush in between us like a chill. I had enough room to turn around then, so I did.

"No weapon. Why? You went to cop school," she said, getting her vape back out.

"Why would I need a weapon?"

"Look around." She blew out a dismissive puff of air. "You're small and female, so you can't afford to lose. You need a fast, definitive victory; you should bring a knife to a fistfight."

"We aren't fighting." I wasn't fighting, anyway, but I was unable to stop myself from asking, "What do I bring to a gunfight?"

One side of her mouth quirked up. "Avoid them. Too random. Too easy to kill the wrong people. A knife, you have to be close. You have to mean it."

She was cagey, but she'd decided to let me in, a little. Or I'd said enough to make her acknowledge that I was already in. Whatever. I pushed it further. "Same with a baseball bat."

Her gaze sharpened. "If you find such a thing to hand." A measuring pause. "Okay, suspended Officer Albright. What do you want from me?"

"You said *Sisters* to me. You knew this was a story about sisters. You have to tell me."

That made her head tilt back the other way. "Tell you what, Danger Mouse? I'm going to need you to be a little more specific." She leaked steam as she spoke.

I cut right to it. "Did you know Nix? My twin. Those three men hurt her. They hurt her, and she died. You know that, right? You knew her. Maybe you even loved her." It was odd to say this after she'd weaponized a bunch of sex at me, but shared grief could pull people in strange ways. So she'd kind of hit on me, this woman who didn't like to be touched. So what. Hard to judge her when I was fresh out of an intimate dinner with the last man Nix had ever loved. "I don't get why

Nix wouldn't have told me if she was gay or bi or what-the-who-cares-ever, but those were bad years. She shut me out of a lot. I'm glad if you loved her. I'm so glad if she wasn't all alone."

Thalia Gray's eyes flashed a thing that might have been a feeling then. "I didn't know your twin. This isn't about her." She said it soft, and I believed her. It hurt to believe her, and I hated to believe her, but I did. It also changed the way we were connected. Not by love, as I had hoped. The thing that chained us to each other was altogether darker.

"Then why? Why did you say the story was about sisters?" It hurt to ask, as if the words themselves were sharp. I'd wanted it so bad. "It's why I let you go!"

Her mouth thinned, but her eyes welled with a dark pain that matched my own. When she spoke, she had none of my anger. "This story is about my sister. Mine."

I was too drunk, and I'd come out with too much certainty to process this. Then I remembered Gand saying, *They had dates and hookups with all kinds of girls. They hurt Nix anyway.* No, it was more than that. We'd been talking about the three of them back in the day, and he had told me, *Guys who do bad stuff and never once get called on it do not one day spontaneously embrace the thought that rules do apply to them.*

"Your sister," I said finally. I fought the urge to step in and take her in my arms. *I prefer not to be touched,* she'd said. I tried to reach toward her with my words. "We're the same, then. You and me. Your sister and mine, both. That's what connected us. You felt it. You know it happened."

She said, "Okay. Yes. We had a moment. You had a sister. You're on some kind of mission, and I respect that. You think it's intersecting with mine, and maybe it is. But I don't need help. You're touching my stuff now."

I shivered in the balmy air. Her stuff was murder. She was saying she didn't need my help to murder, as if I had come out here to offer. Maybe I had, because sober Penny was one hundred percent horrified. Was this plotting? Was I asking to be an accomplice in a killing? This was the exact opposite of every choice my brother had made so far. Drunk Penny, all id, did not give one single solitary shit.

Her gaze was so intense I looked down; I had to, focusing on the lapel of her jacket. I saw she wasn't immaculate after all. She had a little piece of lint there, so pale the silvery fabric camouflaged it. I reached out to pick it off, and I saw her hating it. She hadn't minded touching me, but my fingers coming toward her, oh, she hated it. She stayed dead-animal still, though, and I understood that for her to allow this was a softness toward me. I picked it away delicately, carefully, making no real contact, and knew she understood my carefulness was a softness toward her. I pinched my fingers together, so hard I felt the blood leaving them.

I said, "I hate—I hated—all three of them so much, but I didn't do anything. I couldn't. Maybe I don't have the spine for it, or my brother's right and it's wrong, no matter what. But they're so bad, and . . . and . . ." I'd lost the thread. I was rambling. I hauled myself back on track. "I can't pretend that this is not my stuff. Nix was my twin. I lost my other half. They broke her, and she died. Most days I feel like I lost half of me. Can you understand that?"

She stopped moving as I spoke. Entirely. It was as if she'd died. Her body ignored gravity, refused to collapse, but she'd gone way too still to be a living creature. "I can. I'm sorry." Her eyes were like my own eyes, and it hurt to meet them. She felt it, too, because this time she was the one to look away. She said, mostly to herself, "I need to get the hell out of this city." Then back to me: "You don't understand the scope of what I'm doing, and you're going to fuck it up. Get rid of the goddamn box cutter and stay out of my way for three days, so I can finish."

My eyes went wide. Was she going to move faster now because of me, or was her plan already in motion? *Finish.* What a word. Did that mean *Banks* would be finished? Dead. Removed. *Just because the other two died doesn't mean that's her plan for him,* I thought belligerently, but I didn't want to ask her because I didn't want to know for sure. If I knew, if I knew for sure, could I let it happen? Even asking the question made me wonder if I was more like my brother than I thought.

Perhaps she sensed me wavering, because she leaned in. "Three days. Then, I'll get out of *your* way. What you do after that—it's nothing to me."

It was the first note that rang false for me, and I was drunk enough to say so. "It's not nothing to you. I have seen you somewhere before. I do know your face."

Her eyes narrowed. "You don't."

Mine narrowed right back. "My best training officer, a woman named Delilah Williams, once told me it takes years for a girl to get a cop gut, so maybe I'm wrong. But I think I have the tiny seedlike start of one, and it's pretty damn sure that right this second, you are lying."

Right then we both heard Michael calling. "Penny?" I felt an instant flash of irrational, drunk rage. Why could no one leave me be when I was plotting in dark alleys?

Thalia's body went liquid, readying to fight or maybe ooze away into the dark. Damn that helpful valet guy! She barely acknowledged I had a stake in this, so she wasn't going to stand around to be peacefully introduced to my twin's former ex-boyfriend. All I'd really gotten from her was felt up and a bit of lint, still pinched between my fingers like an eyelash that I planned to wish on later. I'd given her my sister story. She owed me hers. I dropped my voice to a whisper. "We're not finished. You want that knife destroyed? Come get it."

Her eyes widened, incredulous, and we heard Michael call again, closer. She leaned to put her mouth right by my ear and said, so soft it felt like my imagination, "You're touching my stuff. You don't want me touching yours. Believe it."

She stepped back from me and pointed to her own eyes, then to mine, like I had done, but her way felt like a threat. A threat from a person who had killed. Up close and personal. A baseball bat to a man's temple. A blade, a thigh, a quick, decisive gash, then all that blood. I refused to drop my gaze, though my knees felt like they might give way. I was glad to have the wall behind me.

This story was *ours*, though, whether she admitted it or not. I didn't back down, and she stepped past me and went around the corner, out of sight.

I stumbled the other way, toward Michael's voice. Before I reached the alley mouth, I paused. My pinching fingers were still pressed together so damn hard they tingled. I opened them, but my hands were sweating. The curved sliver had flattened and stuck.

It wasn't lint at all. It was the teeniest, tiniest small feather. I stared at it, entranced, as if it was hers, truly. As if under her jacket she had wings folded away, wings with big feathers, sleek and layered, and tiny blue-white feathers like this one under. This was the finest down, soft and powdery, insubstantial as spun sugar in my hand. I tucked it safe into my pocket. I had plucked another piece of her, and I was going to keep it.

14

Michael had already passed by the narrow alley mouth, but when he heard me crunching out through the gravel, he came back to meet me.

"You okay?"

When I nodded, he offered me a small tin of mints. I stared for one stupid second, then realized he thought I'd run out here to puke. I blinked, nonplussed. Why would I dash past a perfectly good ladies' room? I took a whole damn handful anyway, like a confirmation. They were Altoids, so strong my sinuses began to burn. I chewed them into slivers, trying to make them melt faster.

I was listing slightly to the left, and Michael put a steadying arm around me, smiling. I looked up at him as big-eyed and grateful as a rescued princess. *Delilah Williams would not approve,* I thought, and then I had to clap my hand over my mouth to stop myself from spewing candy in a bray of shaky, inappropriate laughter. I heard my mom say, very clearly, in my mind, *You, my girl, are overwrought.*

He said, "That second bottle might have been an error."

Michael and my imaginary mother were both right. Second bottle, bad. Overwrought, for sure.

"I need an Uber," I said around about a thousand shards of Altoid. Drunk as I was, I thought it was very clever, very stealthy, to smell of so much righteous mint. It covered the fact that I had not been sick and the faint cling of herbs from her vape kit. Thalia was my secret, personal and private, and I was going to keep her. She would come back to me, though she'd said it like a threat more than a promise. I felt the tiny feather in my dress pocket as if it had weight.

I got my phone out, but the screen was dark. Thalia must have turned the power off while she'd had it. *Trust issues*, I thought. I pressed the power buttons. Michael fished his own phone out, one-handed, and began thumbing in my home address to call a car while my phone rebooted.

As we walked back toward the restaurant together, I was thinking, *Over in three days*. Over was good, for all that her version of over was so violent and specific. The three men I hated most had fucked around with the wrong person, and they were finding out. Not on my behalf, though, or Nix's. Thalia had a sister, too. Did that absolve me? Gand wouldn't think so. It was not my circus, but they arguably were my monkeys. And anyway, I knew her. I knew her face.

I swallowed the remains of the Altoids, then I tilted my head back onto Michael's arm and peered owlishly up at him. "Michael. I'm keeping Nix's secret. We both think it's right to do. I'll never tell the cops that the cases are connected, or about the woman in the alley. I'm sure now. I'm positive."

He looked down at me, a little amused, his face looming close. "Two bottles' worth of positive."

"Okay, fair. I mean it, though. It's only—" My own arm went around his back, because with my face turned up this way, the broken city sidewalk felt alive, shifting under my feet.

"Only what?"

I shrugged, and that made the world spin more, so I held on to him tighter, and I told him, "I wish I knew why she killed them."

"Mm. You could find her. Ask her."

I tilted my head back farther and we stopped walking while I mulled this over. We were approaching the light spill from Tasca now.

"How could a person find her?" I hoped I didn't have to, because Thalia was already mine. She didn't want to be mine, but she was. Would she come for her knife, now? "She gave me a name, but I got nothing from it. So how?"

He smiled. "That sounds like a question for some sober people. Let's figure it out in the morning."

"You're sweet. A sweet man," I said. He was offering to help me. I wanted Thalia to myself, but if she hadn't come in two days, maybe I would take him up on it. I told him, "I feel like things are moving fast."

I could see how serious he was in the ambient light. "Do you need them to move slowly?"

I turned toward him, or perhaps he turned me. If he did, I let him. "No," I said. "I can't be slow."

Because I had three days before she got the hell out of the city; that was what I meant. We weren't talking about the same things. Or maybe we were, because as he bent to me, I tilted my face up and rose onto my tiptoes. Thalia Gray might not like to be touched, but I did. It was only that I'd forgotten in the last bleak years.

Michael smelled of spicy leather and the prettiest parts of our shared past, a warm scent remembered from across a gulf of loss and grief. My eyes stayed open, even though I knew that he was going to kiss me. I thought it would be barely anything. A brush of lips. The kind of kiss that seals a promise; he promised me I wasn't bad, and that he would help me if I asked. He promised he remembered her, like I did. That was how it started, as a tiny friction, his lips sliding past mine. Then he pulled me in close. I felt myself go boneless, bending to him, shaped by his arms. His mouth opened mine and I learned he tasted of the past, too, all dark coffee and orange oil.

I felt history come alive, electric between us. Maybe he did, too, because there was a pause, a pulling back. I sighed then, or maybe it was the start of a laugh. A push of breath moved between us, my breath, and it was all bright mint. Fresh and bold, reminding us of nothing. A new taste, wholly new, and then he was kissing me again. My hands found their way into his hair; his found my hips. The world spun, and I was lost in him, in the scent of something starting, so crisp and clean. A now. Maybe a future.

At least until a small, amused voice at the far back of my brain said, *Pen, your plain brown boots sure as hell know how to kiss.* Nix's voice. That's what made me pull back.

I stared at him with my eyes gone wide, and what I said was, "My mother told me not to wear this dress."

Michael grinned and passed a hand over his eyes. The other stayed firmly on my waist. "It's a good dress. Don't blame it."

He turned us back toward the restaurant and we kept walking. That valet watched us with unabashed interest. He'd seen two women dashing off into the night, and now the man who had followed was man-walking me back with me leaning on his man-arm like a fragile flower, after pausing for a sidewalk make-out sesh. The valet wouldn't think, *So, they were clearly all discussing crime.* It probably looked to him like a regulation love triangle. He would cast me as Wronged Wifey and Thalia as the Femme Fatale.

Oh, valet, how right you are about that fatale *part,* I thought. I stopped and turned my back on the valet to ask, quietly, "Michael, was that bad? Am I bad?"

Two different questions. I think he heard it as one. "No, Penny. We're just lonely."

"Well, are we stupid?"

I was. I'd gone haring off after a shark to watch it vape and threaten. I was mildly surprised to find that I had not been eaten, but it was also more my shark now. A shark on my team. A shark that didn't want to be on any team at all. It had flashed teeth and reminded me: Sharks aren't team players. I was drunk and tossing metaphors like salad. Michael thought that I had tossed my cookies, and he'd fed me fifty mints and kissed me anyway. I was giddy with wine and guilt and the feeling of not being killed, which was a good, good feeling, and the feeling of kissing a man for the first time in literally years, and that was good, too. Thalia had threatened me. I still had her knife. I'd threatened her. A man was probably going to die in three days, and I knew it. He was a bad man, though, and I hated him. I would not tell Gand or Delilah.

The world felt cut in half. I was walking out of one side, where Thalia held her secrets about sisters in dark alleys, and into the other. Here, I was giving my twin's most important ex lies and kisses in the kind of dress girls wore when they went out on dates, and damn, but my mother was so smart.

"We are not stupid," Michael said, certain.

"Is there a way to find her?" Other than the knife, I meant.

"Yes. Maybe. There's no reason not to try."

Yes, there is. She told me not to, and that's a reason, I thought. It felt good to have a person who wanted to be on my team, though, so I said, "Thank you. I needed tonight. All the parts." I clutched his arm harder. "I'm sorry I got drunk. I'm sorry I ran out of the restaurant." He waved that off, but I wasn't done apologizing. We were in the lot now, waiting. The valet was pretending to look at his phone, but he was trying to listen. Drama, drama. An older couple came out and handed him a ticket, so he had to peel himself away before he knew the end. *Can this marriage be saved?* God, I needed to be home. "I'm sorry that I stuck you with the bill. Hit me up on Venmo. Same name as my Instagram."

His voice was gentle and amused. "Penny. I always planned to pay. Before the second bottle. Before we kissed." I started to protest, and he said, "Hit me back, then. Take me to your favorite food truck. Buy me tacos."

He remembered my abiding love of food trucks, where rookie chefs could be innovative and cut their teeth with low overhead. I'd dragged Nix and Bodie and Michael to so many. "Deal."

This time of night in Midtown every other car had an Uber sticker. We watched three or four slide past before the black Saab that was to cart me home pulled into the turnaround. Michael opened the door and folded my drunk ass in. I struggled with the buckle until I heard the click, then leaned back and let it drive me off into the night.

I think I dozed, because the city lights blended into the stars, and it seemed bare minutes passed before we pulled up to my house. I thanked the driver and got out, my legs unsteady. I needed to sleep, but the idea of climbing alone into my wide cold bed was vile. My body felt awake, and I didn't want to lie down in that wasteland. My hand went to my mouth, remembering. Touch. Not sex, though tonight I had remembered what it felt like to want sex. Now what I felt was a more primal drive than even that. What I wanted was my mother. What I needed was Nix. I wanted to be held by a person that I belonged to. Someone, anyone, who loved me. Or liked me or was nice or at least alive. Any heartbeat, any warm and living body. Anything at all that meant that I was not alone.

I bypassed the stairs up to my place and went to Mom and Dad's front door instead, even though all the lights were off inside. The porch light was off, too. Maybe I could borrow some dogs, or climb in bed with Shadow.

It took me a sec to get the key in the lock, it was so dark, and I was so far from sober. Finally it caught. As the door swung open, I stumbled in, toe catching on the stoop, and slammed straight into another human body.

What had she said? *You're touching my stuff.*

Her bloody knife was hidden not two hundred feet away. Even closer, everyone I loved best in all the world was sleeping. The people in this house were the only things that mattered to me.

You don't want me touching yours. Believe it.

Now someone was slipping out the front door just as I was slipping in.

15

I almost screamed my head off before I realized it was Gand. "Oh my god, you weirdo, what are you doing lurking about in the dark?" By then I was laughing, though I could hear it had a sharp edge of hysteria.

He wasn't laughing. Not at all. "Meditating. Waiting for you. I heard the car, so I was heading up to your place."

I pushed past him, weaving into the den. He followed, looming over me as I told him, "I need to steal a bunch of dogs."

He cocked his head. "Penny, are you drunk?"

"A little," I said, defensive. "Like you don't wine." Hell, he made his own vegan pot gummies. He ate mushrooms and peyote. He'd sworn off Molly and LSD when he gave up meat, but any plant was fair game.

"I'm not giving you shit about drinking," he said as I made my way around the dimly lit family room, checking the sofa and then the dog bed by the fireplace for Bosch. Gand stayed close, his voice low, but his tone urgent. "Pen. Stop a sec. Mom said you went out with Michael. Nix's Michael. On a date?"

I blew my air out like a horse. "I don't know. Call him up and ask him. That will be so comfortable for everyone."

Gand was not amused. "I hope it was a date, honestly, because the alternative—" He leaned down and got very in my face. "What were you doing with Michael, really?"

I stopped looking for Bosch and got belligerent back. "Eating tapas."

He said a soft, explosive, "Bullshit." I held my ground. "I checked that Instagram. Jordan Banks's fiancée? She hasn't posted since the pizza thing we looked at, and that was more than a week ago."

I goaded him back by reflex. "Oh, I thought we weren't looking at those socials. Because it's bad."

Then his words pushed through all the wine, and I scrabbled in my bag for my phone. I went to Jordan Banks's own feed as Gand watched, chewing at his lip. Banks hadn't posted for two weeks. He tended to puke up mansplainy discourse in fits and starts, so that wasn't too unusual. Kaitlin, however, sold ceramic cats on Etsy and never met a brunch she wouldn't photograph. She posted at least twice a week. Their silence, plus Thalia telling me she'd be done in three days, made my heartbeat ramp up, pushing blood fast through me. Damn Gand for guilting me off their socials. I should have been watching.

I said, "I'm sure it's nothing," but my voice came out too high, too loud. I tried to push past him again, this time to get back out.

He grabbed my upper arm in his big hand. "Pen. Who did the other trainee cop hear you talking to at the crime scene?" And there it was, finally asked out loud, in the open. Doolich's claims had been credible enough to get me suspended and deploy a team of cops to search my house, and Gand knew the victim was a man I hated. He was so scared that Doolich was telling the truth.

I wrenched my arm away. "Back off me, Gand!"

He put his hands on either side of his head like he was manually working to keep it from exploding, his volume rising. "I've been backed off. I gave you space. And you went to Michael?"

"Michael didn't judge me. Also? Michael won't flee to Kansas or Cancun if shit gets hard."

"That's not fair," he said, but it was so, so fair. "What are you mixed up in?"

"Hey! Hey, guys," Shadow said. We were so deep into it, we hadn't heard her coming. She was standing in the middle of the stairs, baby-cradling Bosch. They both were perked, eyes wide with anxiety. "You're being super loud."

Gand dropped his volume, but none of his intensity. His eyes stayed trained on me. "Shadow, go back to bed."

She clutched the dog to her chest and came down to the bottom landing. "No. What's going on?"

"Nothing," I said, trying to glare him out of my way. He needed to stop touching *my* stuff. I groped in my wine-soaked brain for Thalia's threatening words. I found some, and I said them with as much of her cold menace as I could bring to bear. "You don't understand the scope of what I'm scoped to, so back off me before—"

"Stop it!" Shadow cut me off. She always did this. Gand left her every other minute, and yet she always came in on his side. She'd even defend his right to abandon her.

I did not let her distract me from channeling Thalia at my brother. "—before you fuck it up. I need some time. I'm going to figure it all out and finish it. Myself. Tomorrow."

"Like hell! Tomorrow?" Gand snapped back.

"What's wrong with you?" Shadow yelled. She moved between us, and Bosch snorked. She was holding him too tight. I drew my spine up tall, tears close, but determined to defend myself, when she added, "Lay off Penny!" She was talking to her father. I think my jaw unhinged. I know his did.

"Uh, yeah," I said, too shocked to be remotely articulate.

Shadow articulated for me, so fierce. "Sometimes you have to do a thing because you know it's right, Gand. No matter what anyone else tells you, or what the rules say." Bosch squirmed so hard she put him down, and he ran in a frantic loop around us, barking. Shadow yelled over him, "And sometimes other people need to fuck off and let you, even if they don't understand it."

"Exactly," I chimed in, and at the same time my mom said, "Language!" She was hurrying down the stairs, barefoot, her hair sticking up in tufts. "Why is everyone screaming?"

Gand answered her, cold and tight and loud. "Penelope here just told my kid that she was right to hack into the school computer."

Had I? My head was swimming, and poor Bosch had lost his mind. Shadow was berating the father that she coddled because any hint of conflict made him leave. I was making a big, loud conflict about murder in the den.

Mom clicked the lights on, making us all blink and flinch. "Everyone stop yelling. We'll have Mrs. Blanchard ringing the bell in another minute. Bosch, shut up, buddy." He didn't.

Dad was thumping down the stairs now, too, fumbling with his glasses and growling to clear his sleep-clogged throat. His pajamas with their ironed creases were the only orderly thing in the whole room. "Who's fighting?" The big dogs slithered anxiously down past him and joined the general canine milling and upset, but at least they didn't bark about it.

My eyes met Gand's, and here we could agree. Gand was thirty, I was twenty-six, and there were still things we hid from the 'rents as if we were children. Or as if they were. I balled my fists into the skirt of my dress, and in a flash of drunken inspiration, I killed about a thousand birds with one loud stone:

"Michael Sullivan kissed me. On my face. I let him. I might kiss him more. Bosch, please."

"Oh, snap, as the olds say." Shadow's eyes had gone so wide.

My mother flared her nostrils and gave my dress a telling stare as Dad said, "Honey! Honey. Okay, well. We can talk about that calmly, I would think. Come sit down."

Gand said, "Like hell. She needs to talk to me. My place. Now." He reached for me again.

I jumped back. "Gand. Stop. You hurt me."

He looked and saw his own grip printed in red onto my arm. It was faint, too faint to leave a bruise, but he was horrified to see that he'd forgotten his own strength. "I can't—I can't—"

Mom went to him, instantly worried he was setting up to flee. She put a soothing arm around him and said to me, "Honey. Please. Your brother—"

Shadow scooped up Bosch and hollered, "Everybody lay off Penny!" She tucked the freaked-out dog into an armpit, his stiff legs all poked down, and he was surprised enough to shut up. She looked a dagger at her dad. "Penny said what she said." She gave my parents more eye daggers. "She did what she did." Then that miracle of a girl-child got between me and all of them and said, "She will not be taking questions at this time." With that, she grabbed me with her other arm and steered me out the door.

Every single one of us was shocked enough to simply let her pull me out of the house. She shut the door on all of them, and there we were, out in the sudden peace and darkness, under stars, together.

"Wow," I said. "I mean, wow. Shads. What was that?"

"Let's go before they follow us." Bosch wriggled and craned his neck up to lick at her face until she set him down so he could have a pee, and then we all three went up the outdoor stairs and into my place. Once the door closed behind us, she asked me in a small, unsteady voice, "Will he be here in the morning?"

"He'd better be." I threw my dress one way and kicked off my ankle boots another while Shadow got me a sleep shirt from my closet corner. By the time I'd struggled into it, she was handing me a mason jar she'd filled with water. I drank until I felt like I was sloshing as Shadow steered me to my spinning bed. Bosch leaped in after me, stamping around while I jerked at the duct-taped towel over the skylight until it fell on me. Shadow clicked the light off and then got in, too. In the sudden dark, I saw the stars revolving in the skylight's frame.

Shadow snapped, "Settle!," and I turned obediently on my side before I realized she was talking to Bosch. We faced each other in little curls, patting and lying to the dog between us, telling him that all was well within his pack. He believed us. He coiled into a tidy ball.

"I didn't mean you should have hacked the school website," I whispered. She scooched closer, pressing her knees to mine. I could smell her sweet, young sleep-breath and her gardenia shampoo.

"I know you didn't," she whispered back.

"We'll slash Gand's tires to keep him, if we have to, and you are ungrounded. Starting now. I'll tell Mom and Dad. On my head be it. Right or wrong."

I didn't know if I was taking responsibility for ending her grounding or for letting Thalia go, but Shadow couldn't leave it unanswered. Or maybe it was Nix who couldn't. I wasn't sure who was talking, this girl I loved as if she were my own, or my twin, who was so my own that the only place she ever spoke was in my head. Either way, the words came to me so clearly: *It's hard to know what's right, sometimes.*

My stomach sloshed and the bed spun; it seemed to me that I could hear the river. The stars went dark, and I could smell the rain-fat water, coming here all the way from Savannah. It rose until it reached the roof, and then it waterfalled down on us. It gathered and swirled, pushing through my apartment. It picked up the whole bed, washing us out of the house, carrying us toward the coast. The bed turned black beneath me, and I smelled ancient skunky pot smoke and mildew. This was not my bed after all. This was Nix's last bed. Under the ground.

The futon frame creaked as I turned toward her, asking, "Am I bad?" My twin, I knew, would tell me no. She was on my side, always.

Instead, she curled in closer and repeated, "It's hard to know what's right sometimes. You can't puss out and do nothing, though."

I looked into her dark-bright eyes, true hazel, flecked with green and gold. "I'm braver than I look, Nix." Delilah had told me so with words and reports and her hard-won respect. Then she got me in the car and grilled me like a prawn.

Where were we? I didn't know this dark river, floating us down and down. Nix took a bright coin out of her mouth so she could say, *Thalia isn't her real name. You know that, right?*

I was too dizzy to nod agreement, but I didn't have to. Not with Nix. I asked, *I've seen her before, haven't I?*

Nix told me plain, *You know we did.*

She has her own sister, though. She didn't love you.

It wasn't a question, but that wasn't why Nix didn't answer. She didn't answer because she was so cold. Her lips were tinged blue, like the lips of the boy I'd saved on Lester Street. I said her name. *Nix*. Nothing. *Nix*. Nothing.

She was no longer in the bed. She was so far from me, and she was calling . . . *cold and bad, Pen . . . I'm scared of my . . . Please, can you . . . feel like a ghost already . . .* Heavy bass thumped like a heartbeat in the background. Nix's own heartbeat was hidden by it, fading. I called her name again, so loud I woke my damn self up.

In the space between dreams and the waking world, I felt her with me, sleeping as we often had, turned toward each other like a closed set of parentheses. Then I shifted past dreams entirely, and I knew again it was Shadow. Sunshine streamed over us from the skylight, and her eyes were open, looking at me over the coiled form of the dog. Shadow was awake, but barely, her body so settled in that she looked melted.

"Did you call me Nix?" Her voice was creaky with morning.

"I was dreaming." I felt okay, I realized, except I needed to pee. "Thank you. For last night."

"I got your back." She did, too, though I could see she was anxious. Well, she'd stood up to her father. Was she mad at him, or simply growing up? Either way, this was an important first, and I hoped he wasn't a big enough shit to run now. She'd feel punished for it.

I told her, "You're a good kid, Shads."

She made a wheedling face, all big eyes. "So did you mean it when you said I was ungrounded?" At my solemn nod, she scrambled to her feet so quick it shook the bed. Bosch didn't stir, even when Shadow dashed off to my kitchen corner to peer out the window. "The Shred Shed is still here," she announced, and her bright grin upped its wattage to a million. "And now, because I am amazing, and you are probably hungover, I will make you coffee before I go play Xbox until my eyes fall out."

"Goddess level reached," I told her.

I saw my phone on the floor. I leaned off the bed to get it, irking the dog, but not enough to shift him. He'd stay until the bed was empty or he exploded from holding his own pee. I might die the exact same way if I didn't get up soon. I saw Michael had texted late last night, checking that I'd gotten home okay. Then I remembered announcing to my family that I had kissed him, Nix's most important ex, and that I might again. I groaned. Perfect. Now I'd have to figure out if I had meant it with every worried Albright nose poked in and sniffing at me. And this was the easy problem, compared to the dangerous murderer I'd baited last night. *You want that knife destroyed? Come get it.*

I texted Michael back:

SORRY! Just saw this. The Uber lady didn't abduct me.

It barely landed before he was calling. I had my ringer off, but I saw it incoming, and I swiped the connection open. In the kitchen Shadow was clattering around and singing some pop anthem about bad ideas and boys. I rolled to face the wall and kept my voice low. "Hi."

He chuckled. I was sure he could hear her belting. "How's your head?"

"Good." He meant the wine, probably, but I added, "I have it on straight." I wasn't sure exactly what we were discussing: my compounding felonies, or the fact that we had kissed. I'd pulled Michael into the larger mess with me, but he was ankle-deep and I was pretty much on scuba. "Michael. We agreed to keep Nix's secret. Did you think it through? If we say nothing, the killer could go after the third guy."

"I thought about that. Sure." He sounded so casual about it.

I pressed. "You don't care if Jordan Banks gets murdered?"

With zero pause, he said, "I don't see how that's our business."

His matter-of-fact words lifted some weight off me. Why could Gand not give me this? I changed the subject. "I may have indicated to my family that last night was a date."

Again he chuckled. "Wasn't it?"

"How would I know? I haven't dated much, post-Bodie."

Understatement. Last year, pressured by Gand's endless string of you-need-to-truly-live speeches, I'd gotten on a couple of the "swipe right for bullshit" dating apps where my brother found his recovering

VSCO girls and pansexual yoginis. I'd met two D-bags, three players, and a Himbo before giving up.

The first D-bag, Carl, had been a pity swipe. He looked like a fixer-upper, what with the pornstache and the shiny bowling shirt. He'd been crafty enough to pose with an adoring dog to look nice, which ought to be a crime: falsifying evidence. I was internet-dating-dumb enough to let him pick me up at my place. Despite my careful directions, Carl knocked on the house door downstairs. Nix would have said, right then, *Hell, no, Pen, this boy does not listen*. Mom invited him in for hot tea, for god's sake, and Dad drilled him with a slew of personal questions while he sent me frantic texts asking for rescue.

That right there could have been a meet-cute. In the car, he told me, "When your mom answered the door, I was, like, 'Wow, this girl really needs to update her pictures.'" We were both laughing until he added, "They say all women turn into their moms. I hope you've started up the diet early."

I stopped. Even my smile faded. "I think my mom is beautiful."

"Sure. I mean, to you. But you gotta admit, she's given up."

I loved my mother's dear, rounded body swathed in old, pilled sweaters. I thought, *I need Nix to text me that the cat we don't have has been rushed into emergency surgery for brain worms or dyspepsia, so I can bail,* and it rendered me suddenly bereft. Luckily, Carl talked enough for both of us. I paid for my own drink and Ubered home as soon as I politely could. I got some aggrieved texts, mad I hadn't remitted unto him one sex for all his troubles. I blocked him, and after that I met my Swipe Rights out at coffee shops. Five vanilla lattes and no desire for any second dates later, I deleted the apps.

I told Michael, "I'm not sure I'd recognize a date if one came up and bit me."

He said, "Last night quacked like one. We can leave it there, for now."

"I like that." I could admit that we might be walking toward a thing, but nothing more. My hesitation didn't come from Nix. Nix and I had never once in our whole lives gotten in a fuss about a boy. We would not start here, wholly in my own head, over the one she'd called my plain brown boots. Nix had preferred her guys a little cocky, a little broken, the kind who kept her guessing, while Michael had been blatantly devoted to her. When she broke up with him, she'd jokingly wondered how long common decency required her to wait before she tried to set us up. Maybe, in another life—well, who knows. Instead, she went to the wrong party, and here we were. "I owe you tacos, anyway."

The silence that fell then was comfortable and brief. I could feel us both being pleased inside it.

From the kitchen Shadow called, "Coffee is readyyyyyy."

I dropped my voice even lower, though Shadow was the last Albright who would give me any crap. She'd proved that last night. "I need to go."

"Okay. But let's do food trucks soon. I've been thinking about ways to find her."

We both knew who *her* was; his confidence alarmed me. I didn't want her found by anyone but me. I said, "Yeah. Real soon." I needed to know what his ideas were, so I could protect her or use them myself, though I'd woken up with an idea of my own.

Shadow yodeled from the kitchen, "Get your booty up, Pennest. No one is bringing you coffee in bed!"

We said quick goodbyes, and then I went to grab Shads and squeeze her and rock her while using the dopiest voice I owned to say, "My perfect, precious coffee angel! My beautiful caffeinating baby!" until she was laughing and pushing me away. She went to dig Bosch out of my covers and then took him down to pee and eat. The first thing I did was go to the bathroom, too, but second, even before I poured myself a cup, I dug in the pocket of my abandoned dress to find the feather I had plucked off Thalia Gray. It was tiny, but real, curved like the half-moon of my pinkie nail, proof last night had happened. The morning sun revealed the color was more blue than white.

On the high shelf of my wardrobe in the closet corner, I still had my copy of everyone's childhood jewelry box with the spinning ballerina. Nix had owned a matching one, but she threw it out as baby stuff years back. The spring on mine had broken, so the plastic dancer listed and flopped, but it could still grind out a plink-plunk version of "Swan Lake." I added the feather to the flat drawer under the main compartment where I kept Nana's pearls.

Michael had texted again, wanting to make concrete plans, but I left him on read. I wanted to try finding Thalia my way, first. She and I had different sister stories, but as she'd pointed out, there was plenty of overlap. I had a strong guess as to where she'd turn her attention next, and even when, since she had said she only needed three days to *finish*. I wasn't sure exactly what that word meant for Jordan Banks, but it felt plenty ominous.

I was a cop. On paper, anyway. I'd been trained on how to run a stakeout. I couldn't handle a twenty-four-hour watch all on my own for three straight days, but Thalia seemed to be nocturnal. I'd only ever seen her in the deeps of night, anyway, and the sun had been long down when both Bowery and Castillo had crossed paths with her. I'd nap this afternoon, and tonight, I'd go to Jordan Banks's house and see why he and Kaitlin had gone silent. A scared, very Penny voice said, *You mean to see if he's still breathing.* I ignored it.

Thalia Gray had given me a single word. *Sisters.* In return, I'd given her a felony. I'd given her both my story and my silence. She owed me more. She owed me the truth, and I was going to get it.

16

No way the cops had probable cause for a warrant to put a tracker on my car, but I didn't trust Detective Brinks not to color outside the lines. Cop school had taught me where and how to look; I made sure my Honda was clean before I left home to begin my stakeout. I knew where Jordan Banks's neighborhood was. Theoretically. I'd never driven out there to glare at his house in person, though.

Because that would be insane, I thought, and a bray of laughter that sounded absolutely nuts got out of me. I sure as hell was going now, well after sundown, dressed all in black like a cat burglar and with my phone preset to silent. At the police academy, I'd taken a Saturday seminar on tactical lockpicking, so I'd also packed an expired credit card, a screwdriver, my dad's old handheld drill, and some stiff wire into a grocery bag.

It sat on the passenger seat, a physical reminder of the reason I might need to get inside: if Banks was dead already. Every time I glanced at the bag, awful, imaginary pictures of his body rotting undiscovered in his living room flashed through my brain. Poor Kaitlin might be dead beside him, because what did I know about Thalia, really? The idea that I'd helped a woman too cold-blooded to care about collateral damage was one in a long list of doubts and terrors plaguing me. Like what if Brinks was better at placing trackers than I was at finding them, or what if Gand bugged out while I was gone, and what if Shadow blamed herself because she'd finally stood up to him, and how could I help her through that if I went to prison, and by the way, what the hell did I think I was doing with Michael?

So it went, my mind churning as I drove southwest through the deepening night. The entrance to Banks's subdivision was on a country road lined with heaps of kudzu and tall pine trees. The sign was so overgrown by brambles that I overshot it. I slammed on the brakes—*Oh, very subtle, Penny*—and then U-turned into it. His '70s neighborhood had a lot of big trees and no streetlights. No sidewalks either. None of the houses had garages, and the driveways and curbs were filled by well-kept older sedans and trucks. My Honda looked like it belonged here. This far out of the city, the chance of cameras catching me cruising the neighborhood was slim. All these things felt like cover, and my nerves dialed back enough to let anger creep along my edges.

The cute split-levels in various shades of pastel siding reminded me of my own neighborhood. Banks's house was on Appletree Lane, a street name so wholesome it was practically Americana. My lips thinned. He shouldn't get to live in this sweet place, camouflaged as some nice man, some good neighbor, readying to buy a Big Green Egg and build a Home Depot play fort. *For when he has kids,* I thought. Nix never would now, would she.

I turned down his street and found only five houses on each side before it ended in a cul-de-sac. His place was fourth on the left, a pale lemon with a near-identical powder blue on one side and a soft peach on the other. As I approached, I recognized his cherry-red Mazda 3 parked in the drive. He'd posted a string of brag-tweets when he bought it, and I'd hoped it was true that people with red cars got more speeding tickets, because I was that petty.

Even though his car was there, the house was completely dark, the only one on the whole block without at least a porch light. Did that mean she'd already come and gone? Thalia could have cut the power. I oozed past, peering down each side yard as I went. I saw no light in his side windows, not even a blue TV glow or the faint spark of a bathroom night-light. I circled the cul-de-sac, then clicked my lights off and waited, letting my eyes adjust and seeing if I'd caught anyone's attention, or if another car had followed me. With Brinks still in my mind,

I gave it a good twenty minutes before I crept my car to Banks's place and parked in front of an old pickup truck. My car's nose now pointed toward a fast escape, and I had plenty of peel-out space left between me and a white VW Jetta.

Maybe he was already asleep. Or sprawled in a congealing puddle of dark fluid, his eyes gone glassy, staring at nothing. Or out of town. Or sunk deep among the ghosts of Lake Lanier. Or tied to a chair alongside Kaitlin in the dark house with Thalia standing over them. This shuddered me, but I had no way to know. I settled in, Delilah in my head reminding me, *Ninety-nine percent of cop work is patience and paperwork, kid.* At least I would be spared the forms.

I already needed to pee, but that was psychology. I sucked on hard candies, and I waited. The moon rose higher. One of his neighbors walked right by me with a big dog, and I sank deep in my seat, grateful for the darkness. A minivan came and parked in the blue house's driveway. I watched in my rearview as a young couple wrestled some tired little kids out of the back and took them inside. As ten o'clock went past, and then eleven, lights began to go out in the other houses. The chirring of night bugs and frogs got louder, a peaceful sound in a peaceful place, but the idea that Banks was in there, dead, felt realer and realer. Thalia Gray, with a box cutter, in the dining room. Thalia Gray, with a baseball bat, in the hall. What could I possibly learn by loitering outside, if she'd already come and gone?

Well, when I put it that way. I hadn't brought that bag of tools for nothing. I got out of the car and jammed my phone into a back pocket. His yard was the darkest on the street, but I still hurried across it, feeling exposed. The grass was damp and long enough to bother his neighborhood's Mrs. Blanchard. Water soaked through my tennis shoes and into my socks.

Banks's wide front porch had a low, wrought iron railing and four steps. On either side, monkey grass–lined beds held tall, fat azaleas that offered me some merciful cover. Even better, I didn't spot any security cameras, and he had a regular button doorbell instead of a Ring.

Up I went, and I was relieved and horrified in equal measure to see his door had an old-fashioned warded lock that my bag of tools could pop right open. Was I really going to add breaking and entering to my growing list of crimes on the strength of Kaitlin's internet silence and a burned-out porch light? I should at least try to look before I leaped. The large, low windows on either side of the front door had blinds, not curtains. They were closed, but I had seen his big tuxedo tomcat on his social media. God bless Oreo, both sets of blinds had end slats that were bent or skewed or missing. Dark outside, dark in. I went to the left window and cupped my hands near the glass. Peering in, I could make out a farmhouse table with a bench on one side, chairs on the other, and a large china cabinet against one wall. No still form was sprawled with limbs akimbo on the floor or slumped in a chair.

I'd taken only a single step toward the other window when I felt more than saw headlights turning onto the street. I swore under my breath and crouched, hoping the car would stop at one of the first few houses. No such luck. It kept on coming.

I clambered over the low porch rail and dropped down between the wall of the house and a bud-laden azalea bush. The bed had been recently mulched, and the new pine straw was slippery. I rolled my ankle and spilled backward, flat onto my butt, the shopping bag landing with a clatter of tools beside me. The top of my head was practically level with the low porch. I got my legs under me and crouched, my every move rustling and crackling the fresh straw, then froze instinctively as light spilled over me in little speckles through the thick waxy leaves. My heart rate ratcheted up another notch. The car had turned into his drive and stopped. My lips shaped a word, and it was, *Thalia*.

I leaned forward far enough to see a dark-colored muscle car, black or maybe navy, with fancy orange rims on the tires. Its big, loud engine was still going, rivaling the frogs. I ducked back as the passenger door opened and Jordan Banks got out. Hale and hearty, for all his pale shirt and skin were washed out by the moonlight. Even his light brown hair seemed colorless, as if he was some leached specter. As he crossed in front of the car, the headlights bloomed him into colors, but they also lit him from beneath, making his pug-nosed, boyish face look ghoulish. He had his hands in the pockets of his khakis, his wide shoulders hunched up. He stamped his feet down hard as he walked toward his front porch. Toward me.

There was zero chance he wouldn't see me. The porch wasn't tall enough. The space between the wall and the bush was too open, too obvious. I was on the side close to the driveway, already speckled in light from the wide, bright headlamps. I couldn't sneak quietly around the corner of the house, either, not in this new straw. I had no options, no way to escape. He was eight feet from the first step. What would he do? Then six. Then four.

I braced my body to make a scampering, mad run for my car when a female voice, throaty and smoky, hollered, "Hey!"

While I'd frozen, watching him come at me, the driver's-side window had scrolled down.

He wheeled back to the car. "Hush it, Liza. It's late."

She hooked her elbow on the door and leaned her head out the window. I peered through the bush, silently holding aside a few leafy branches for a better view. I saw long, copper-colored hair and big teeth bared in a wide smile.

"C'mere'n make me." She sounded like she had been drinking.

He took two stiff-legged steps toward her. "Go home. This was a mistake."

Her smile dimmed not at all. "You said it was a mistake last time, too, but here we are."

He kept on talking over her. "Well, I'm done making it."

The woman's grin stretched wider. "You said that the time before last."

Nothing low that this man did could possibly surprise me, but I was set back by the sheer audacity. The mask he wore for Kaitlin, his parents, his customers was usually screwed on so tight that even he might believe it was his face, but he was showing who he really was right now. I scrabbled in my back pocket for my phone.

She said, "At least come kiss me bye. Since we are really done." She drawled out the word *really* with such skepticism.

"In front of my own house?" Banks wasn't as loud as she was, but I could hear him.

I dimmed my phone light as low as it could go, then opened my camera to video and pressed record. I extended my arm, trying to find a quiet path through the leaves to get a visual.

She said, "Nobody's looking. We aren't HBO, you stupid man."

"I'm not going to be a cheating husband."

Too late, I mouthed, silent, just as the redhead in the car said the same damn words. It was like I was lip-syncing her.

Affronted, he got a little louder. "I've been under stress. You have no idea." This sounded raw and truthful. I hoped it was because he'd heard about Castillo, and now Bowery. I hoped he dreamed of Nix, and that he was afraid. "This won't happen after I'm married."

She laughed, and I wanted to. "Sure, babe. You'll rent a tux and smash cake in her face, and everything'll change."

"Liza. Go on." Oh, he was so mad. I felt a splash of fear on her behalf, and for me as well, trapped with his angry body between me and my car.

"You're not married tonight, so kiss me bye like a gentleman. Least you can do, considering everything this mouth did for you earlier." She pointed emphatically at her own irrepressible smile. She sounded downright amused, dulled by alcohol or confidence, not seeing that this man was born to punch down. I'd bet a thousand bucks his customers loved him, while hatred for him bloomed in the breast of every teller.

He hustled over, fury writ into his posture. "Get the fuck out of here."

Palpable bad energy rolled off him. Surely he wouldn't hurt her in view of so many windows? They were dark, though, and drunk people could be so stupid. My leaf-addled, imperfect view got shakier, and I realized I was trembling as I held my phone toward them between the branches.

She blew a raspberry, saucy, but she pulled her elbow in. As the window rolled up, she called to him, "Next time li'l Kaitlin's out of town, you can eff yourself for a change, you di—" The window closed, cutting her last word off. The rumble of the car's big engine changed as she shifted into reverse. Once her headlights were gone, my phone, dim as it was, would be a spotlight. I stopped the video and shoved the phone back in my pocket. The big engine growled louder as she backed away, and I tried to use the sound to cover me as I crept backward toward the corner of the house. The pine straw crackled, and Banks spun to face me. I froze, listening as she drove away. I was alone with him now, unable to read his expression. His body swayed like a thick snake as he tried to peer through leaves and darkness.

"Who's that?"

He started toward me, moving with fast purpose, not like a man idly wondering if there might be a possum in his flower beds. Like a man who had been under "some stress," as he had told that woman. Like a man who was expecting to be stalked. I wished then I was still filming. Live streaming, even. In seconds he would be standing over me as I crouched like a felon in his bushes, and he would—what? Grab me, hit me, drag me out? I should get out of the bushes, onto the open stretch of lawn. If he laid one hand on me, I could scream the world down, wake his neighbors, terrify the frogs.

That might make him back away. Or release the violence I'd seen building in him. I had no time to make a better plan. I clenched my fist around the neck of the bag, grateful for the weight of the drill. I could swing it at him, if it came down to it. I had Thalia in my head, telling me to bring a knife to a fistfight. Telling me that I was small, and female, and I had to win fights fast, definitively, or— I tensed my legs and began to rise.

A car horn blasted behind him then, so loud, so long and blaring, that it seemed to me it broke the night itself in half. He let out a startled yelp and wheeled to face the road. For one tip-tilted moment, I thought someone must be in my car. The blast stopped, and the white VW Jetta roared to life and light.

Dear god, I thought, *Thalia's been there the whole time.*

She'd watched me park behind her. She'd watched me creepy-crawl to his porch, peer in his windows, hide in his bushes. Now she was saving me? Whatever she had come to do, I'd ruined it. I pressed my palm over my mouth. I had a good guess about what she had come to do. I'd stopped it, this thing I didn't want to want. Relief and rage and gratitude went to war in me. I scrambled to my feet, peering over the azalea as the white car peeled out so fast that I smelled burned rubber. The engine sounded like a furious growl. She'd said, *You're touching my stuff. You don't want me touching yours. Believe it.*

Banks sprinted after her, hollering, "Hey now! Hey! Who's there!"

In the Jetta's taillights, I saw a tattletale barcode sticker that meant it was a rental. Of course it was. A Jetta didn't go with the boots, the bespoke vaping rig, and anyway, who brings their own car to do crimes? Well, me, apparently. Then again, I hadn't come to kill him.

As the car zoomed off with Banks sprinting and yelling in pursuit, an upstairs window of the house across the street turned gold with sudden light. More lights came on farther down the road. She was saving me, and I was standing here in a bush, gobsmacked and wasting it. I leapt up and tore out of the bushes, dashing for my car.

My hands were shaking so hard I almost dropped my key fob like every stupid girl I'd ever yelled at in a movie. My fingers felt so thick and slow. My whole body did, even as the Jetta and Banks and the stars themselves seemed speeded up. I climbed in and drove after them in what felt like slow motion, but I understood that I was roaring down the street. Within seconds I saw Banks in my headlights, standing in the middle of the road. He whirled toward me, waving his arms, his mouth agape. I laid on the horn and didn't slow. He dove to the side of the road, then scrambled up and tore after me, screaming curse words. Porch and window lights lit in our wake.

I sped for the exit, going way too fast, leaning forward. My eyes burned with strain, trying to not run down someone's cat and searching for the Jetta's taillights. She'd talk to me now. She had to.

I made it all the way to the exit sign without seeing Thalia. Was there another way out? I paused at the intersection, wild-eyed, and peered left. Nothing. Looked right—and there she was. The Jetta idled on the shoulder like a pale miracle. As soon as I turned her way, she started moving again. I followed, and my car was shaking like I was blasting club music. Then I realized it wasn't the car. It was me. I was shaking. *You're touching my stuff.*

She kept going, winding us farther and farther away. Smart. Somebody had probably called the cops. The drive let me pull some breath into my body. Let me get some thoughts together. She'd see now that I would not give up.

We came to an intersection with a closed gas station across from an abandoned Aldi with the windows boarded up. She put a blinker on and turned into the grocery store's empty lot.

Mistake, I thought. Two cars meeting up in the lot of an abandoned building? Any cop alive would think, *Hey, look, a drug deal.* I followed anyway, and when the Jetta stopped, I stopped, too. I stayed behind her, engine idling, in case she meant to wait for me to get out and then roar away. The Jetta's lights went out, though, and the engine went off. Then the driver's-side door opened . . . It wasn't Thalia. My brother, Gand, got out and stood there in my blazing headlights, furious and beautiful and exactly the last person on the earth I expected to see.

17

Are you kidding me?" I stormed toward my brother like an absolute Fury across old asphalt and some shattered safety glass, and then I saw that he was crying. Really crying, tears falling unheeded in a torrent. All at once, my rage was whirled up into fifty thousand other feelings, and none of them had any place to go.

"Penny. Come on. Tell me. I know you didn't kill Danny Bowery. You were on duty when he died. You were patrolling with another cop. So I know, I know, you didn't kill him." He said it like a man who knew no such damn thing, his breathing ragged. "So you didn't kill him. Right?"

I froze, stunned out of movement. "Oh god, no!" Michael had wondered this for half a second, but it had never occurred to me that Gand would think it. "Of course not."

"But you *were* talking to somebody right near where Danny Bowery died. Was it Michael?"

"Oh, Gand, no," I said.

He came at me then, so fast that it was like a swoop, and put his big hands on my shoulders. He stared down at me, his dark eyes pleading. "So why the hell are you with Michael, Nix's Michael? Why are you stalking Banks? You told Michael what they did to her, didn't you? Did the two of you plan to kill Bowery? Or did you only find out after, and then cover for him?"

"Gand, none of that is right. I didn't. I swear." He was so swollen with fear, overstuffed even, I was afraid to touch him, as if he might burst. "*Nix* told Michael. Two years ago, in Savannah. He was visiting her there, like we did, the whole time. When Bowery died so soon after

Castillo, Michael called me, freaking out, because he thought it had to be connected, exactly like I did."

The more I talked, the more Gand visibly deflated into fraught relief. I stepped in and hugged him tight. I could feel individual muscles in his arms ticking and spasming, and his heartbeat was a thunder that reverberated through us both. He sobbed so violently, his words were hard to understand. "I've been so scared for you. That you'd go to prison, or that the guilt of it would wreck you."

Understanding dawned. He'd staked out Jordan Banks's house to see if I would come. Maybe to stop me from doing murder. My balanced brother, trying to save me from myself. I said, "Hush, now," patting his back as if he were an enormous, frantic baby.

His storming was too violent to sustain. As it ebbed, he told me, "I should have known. You aren't cold-blooded, Pen. But you wouldn't talk to me." He stepped back, hands still on my shoulders, his gaze searching my face. "What were you doing at Banks's place?"

I still wouldn't give up Thalia. It was a thousand percent possible that Gand and I hadn't been alone at Jordan Banks's house. If Thalia was there, she'd simply surveilled better. I was still determined to find her, but my brother could not go down any deeper into it with me.

I laughed, a little shaky. "Same as you. Watching. I still think it's all connected. I wanted to see if anything would happen." This was all true. I don't know if he believed me, but he nodded. "Thanks for luring him off me. I was so scared."

Around us, the night bugs chirred. He'd calmed enough to let me go and wiped at his eyes. "So when you said you were going to 'figure it all out' and 'finish it, tomorrow,' you meant you planned to watch Banks, because you thought whoever killed Bowery would come for him next." I nodded. "But then—" His brow furrowed. "Who were you talking to, Pen? At the crime scene. That other trainee heard you, and people don't risk their whole career filing false charges over a turned-down coffee date, no matter what Mom says."

This was killing Gand, and he wanted me to take it off him. His dark eyes pleaded with me for a lie he could believe. At the police academy, I'd studied ways to spot a liar. Liars avoid direct eye contact, or make it too intensely. They talk too loud or fast or quiet or slow. Their expressions may not match their words; they smile when saying sad things, or nod their heads while their mouths say no. I tried not to do any of those things as I lied right to my soft brother's face. "It was just me. He heard me talking to Nix."

Relief washed all the way through him, sagging his shoulders and closing his eyes in a grateful blink. He believed me because he wanted to, and maybe there was enough truth there for him to hear it. I had been talking to Nix that night. I was always talking to Nix.

"Gods, I'm tired," he said.

I wasn't. I didn't think I was ever going to be tired again. "Come get in my car. You have no business driving in this state. I can Uber out tomorrow and return the rental for you. I don't mind."

Gand was already shaking his head no, backing away from me. "I can't, Pen. I need to . . . I need to—"

I felt a little spark and sputter from the embers of my anger. "You need to come home, is what you need."

"I have to have some distance." He turned all the way around, heading for the Jetta.

Part of me wanted to let him. I wanted him out of my way, and safe. The idea that Thalia might have seen not one but fully two Albrights digging their hands so deep into "her stuff" was frightening. At the same time, Shadow had finally expressed her own opinion instead of catering to him. If he left now, what message would that send? I had to think about what she needed first, because her father wasn't going to. Not right this second, anyway.

I followed, pulling at his sleeve. "You cannot leave your kid right now. You hear me?"

He didn't answer. I couldn't physically stop him, or even slow him down. He got into the rental car and closed the door on my demands. I watched him drive away.

I didn't want to stand in some abandoned grocery store parking lot in the pitch-black hours of deepest night, all by myself, so I got into my own car before I absolutely lost my shit. I cried my guts out, ugly cried, leaning on the steering wheel. My big stakeout had yielded nothing but this schism. My cover was blown. I couldn't go sit on Banks's house again tomorrow; he would be on high alert. I'd put Thalia in danger, or at least messed up her plans. I was shoulder-deep in her "stuff," and she'd warned me off in a way that sounded like a threat. This was my one best shot at finding her, and I had blown it.

I had her thumbprint on the knife I'd stolen, but that did me no good. Suspended cops couldn't access the federal database. I sat up, hitching and scrubbing at my face with my hands. Delilah Williams could run it, but I could hardly go to my old mentor, the one who had interrogated me so ruthlessly, and say, *So, I happened to find this bloody knife that is completely unrelated to literally the only murder that's happened in this town for more than a year. I was wondering if you could illegally run the print for me under the number of some unsolved B-and-E case?*

The worst part was, Gand was on the run, again, and it felt like my fault. Again. Even after I stopped crying, I didn't calm down. I dreaded going home, scared I'd see the Shred Shed gone already, the Jetta abandoned curbside for Hertz to collect. I couldn't stay here, though. I dug out my phone, anyway, to get directions home and saw I had a string of texts from Michael.

Hey. Then, Did you already go to bed? Then, Okay. Call me tomorrow.

The last one had dropped less than an hour ago. I texted back, I had my phone on silent. Are you asleep?

He answered instantly. Nope. Night owl. Call me?

Three texts and now this? It felt a little urgent. As soon as I was on the road home, I told my phone to dial him. He picked up on the first ring. "Hello?"

"Is everything okay?" It came out short and sharp.

His voice went cautious. "Yeah. Why wouldn't it be?"

"Well, you texted me three times." I was trying to sound normal, but it came out aggrieved, with a big sniff at the end. My nose was still running from my massive weep.

"Sorry. I didn't mean to overtext," he said. Tight. Shut down.

I immediately felt a little terrible. *This is how nice men are when they like you, Penny,* I reminded myself. It had been a while, and with everything that I had happening, three texts felt like an emergency instead of a compliment. Siri filled the awkward pause with instructions, telling me to take the next left.

He said, "Are you in the car?"

"Yeah. My body still thinks I'm on night shift," I told him.

"You sound compressed. Like you're calling from underneath a piano someone dropped on you."

Siri talked again through the speakers. She'd found a route right to the big four-lane highway that would lead me most of the way to Kennesaw. I said, "Hold on a sec," and shut the directions off. Considering what I'd spilled drunkenly at dinner, there was no reason to hide tonight's debacle. "I staked out Jordan Banks's house. I thought the person—I thought she might show."

A long, low whistle, and the awkwardness in his tone was replaced by admiration. "Ballsy. Damn. I take it nothing happened?"

I snorted. "Oh. I wouldn't say that." I spilled most of it, telling him how Gand had saved me. "My brother thought you and I were in cahoots. Like, we'd been secretly dating for a while and when spring came, our young hearts' fancy turned to murder. He was worried."

"Are you worried?" Michael asked.

"About what? I know we didn't kill anyone!" There was an awkward pause that coincided with an intersection. Before the light went green, I realized he wasn't talking about crime. Just dating.

Finally he said, "I know you didn't love Bodie. Nix knew it, too."

I narrowed my eyes, instantly pissed. I didn't like people telling me what Nix knew or didn't know. "Bullshit. She'd have told me."

He backed off, but his mild tone didn't change. "I only meant that Nix was your person, and she knew it. If Nix and Bodie had both been drowning . . . " He trailed off in a way that made the hypothetical into a question.

I kept my eyes on the road, my hands tightening around the wheel, and I said not a damn word. He knew the answer, and so did I. Nix. Every time. Hell, if Nix and I had both been drowning, I'd still have picked her.

Michael interrupted that maudlin train of thought. "It went both ways. She was always more yours than mine." He didn't seem mad about it, though. "There was a time when I thought I'd marry Nix and become part of your family. You all are what I wished I'd had, when I was a kid. The breakup was worse because I didn't just lose her, you know? After, I gave her space, but I always thought we'd reconnect. Not romantically. I don't mean that. I mean—I was her friend."

If I'd had a damn tear left, that would have called it out of me. Even when she was so broken, and everyone but our family had given up, Michael kept going to Savannah, trying to call her back to us. "I'm glad she had you."

He chuckled, but it was a sad sound, somehow. "Yeah. I'd sit at Momo's and she'd bring me chicken wings and say, 'Go the fuck home, Michael. The only thing you can get here is salmonella.'"

That was so like her. The wide road was mostly empty now. The strip malls I was passing were all closed, the stores dark. I followed the bright path my headlights cut, feeling as if there was no one else on the planet right now. "We all did time at Momo's." All the family, I meant. The one he wasn't officially a part of, for all he'd acted like family toward her, simply out of love. "She *was* getting better. Thinking about her future, talking about finishing school. If you and I had had more time, I believe we could have pulled her out of it."

He echoed me. "I believe we could have. But here we are."

In his words, I felt a sense of rising, being pushed up and away from something buried. My voice rose, too. "So what do we do now? We wander the earth, you and I, with our guts pulled out, and nothing ever gets a single second better—"

He laughed then, dry but real, and the sound stopped me short. "Of course not. You'll have a good life, Penny." He said it like he believed it. Like it was true. "You'll marry someone, have kids, be happy. I will, too. It's only that you'll never love anyone the way that you loved her." He breathed in, then pushed the air back out. "Neither will I. Stupid. But there it is. Sometimes it happens that way."

I stared at the black asphalt, lighting up before me, calling me toward home. "God, that's bleak."

"Is it?" he asked. "I think of it as a thing we have in common." He sounded profoundly serious. "We'll never share that with anybody else. We'll never share her with anybody else."

I was stunned into such silence. Mom would say it was impossibly unhealthy for him to believe this. Dad would tell me it was more than unhealthy; it was brutal. A brutal way to see life and love. It was also honest. It was also true. The last thing that had lit me up at all was Karma. A body in an alley. Thalia Gray and her box cutter and her throaty way of speaking. This was less bleak than that.

He said, "All right. Enough. I want to see you. We need to put our heads together and find her."

It sounded more like a strategy sesh than a date, which really took the pressure off. I said, "I don't see how we can possibly track her down."

He said, "I told you, I bet you remember more than you think you do. If we talk it through, who knows what might come out. For example, did she have a Southern accent?"

"Yeah," I said, immediately, although I hadn't thought about it before. "A little. Like Atlanta people do." The urban accent was a background burr, softening a syllable here and there and pulling at a few of the vowels. I also realized that her *J*'s and her soft G's hit my ear a little strangely. "Holy crap, and something else. A little Frenchyness, is the best way I can explain it."

His voice quickened, too. "Southern. French. What does that say to you?"

"Louisiana," I said. "New Orleans, especially. Oh my god!" It might be nothing. Maybe she had a lisp or affected the slurring *J* to sound more cosmopolitan, or hell, maybe she was an Atlanta girl who had spent a lot of time in Canada or Paris. But it was something, and he'd pulled it out of me. I was close to home now and too tired to make good choices. I said, "Listen, I need to go. I'll text you in the morning."

There was a brief silence, and then he said, "Okay." I was glad he didn't press me, because I was smashed so flat already.

We hung up as I turned into my neighborhood. I dreaded the final stretch down my street. The Jetta wasn't at the house. Neither was Gand. I knew he hadn't gone far because his skoolie was parked beside the drive, killing the grass and irking Mrs. Blanchard. I went to bed praying I'd still see it when I woke up.

18

I slept well into the afternoon, as if I'd permanently gone nocturnal, too, in sync with Thalia Gray. Thalia planned to "finish" in three days, and I was already halfway through day two. If I couldn't find her, I'd have to live with my choices, never knowing how right or wrong I'd been to cut her loose.

I got up and went to put water on for coffee still in my underpants and a giant T-shirt, then sat down at the breakfast bar with my phone. I had a text from Shadow asking, Where is Gand? with an emoji storm of question marks and worried yellow faces. A glance out the kitchen window confirmed he hadn't crept home to snag his skoolie and flee to a far horizon, but I didn't see the Jetta either.

I texted him: TOUCH BASE WITH YOUR KID, ASSHAT!

I had a text from Michael, too: Thinking about you. Our talk at dinner. The walk after. How to find her. All of it. Let's get together. Soon.

Walking memory lane with Michael at Tasca had felt good, but it also seemed quite sad, in light of all he'd said last night. What could be a redder flag than both of us still loving Nix, first and best and forever? At the same time, kissing him had held the sharp, clean taste of a fresh start. I was too mired in history and crime to navigate these contrasts. Right now, I didn't need a date. I needed a coconspirator; Gand was too easily bruised, and Delilah Williams was much much much too cop. Michael was my best bet, but inviting him into my search for Thalia felt so intimate.

I decided to keep him as an *Oh, Shit* card I'd play tomorrow if I hadn't found her. I texted back:

Soon. For sure. I owe you tacos.

I used the word, not the picture. Sometimes a taco emoji was just a taco emoji, but I had zero brain space to unpack what I was ready for with Michael.

I left my texts to look at my brother's socials. Sure enough, he'd posted at midnight from Jenji, a twenty-four hour Korean spa near Buford Highway that was famous for their unisex bathhouse and their vegan food. Was this his way of telling me that he hadn't left town?

I hit the share button and sent the post to Shadow, then texted: Don't fret. He's out roaming.

I texted Gand again, this time with less name-calling and caps lock: Touch base with me, too. Please?

I killed a couple minutes grinding dark roasted coffee beans, loading my French press, and pouring in boiling water before I looked again. No answer. If Gand would consent to Life360 and keep his phone both charged and on him, how easy things would be, but even that level of commitment gave him hives. Instead, he'd gone to get exfoliated and cruise for girls with lotus blossom tramp-stamps, living wholly in the now. How nice for him, that he could do this; for me, the past hurt so damn bad, the future felt so murky. I wanted him to be strong enough to look back and push forward with me, instead of snoozing in some urban yurt while a chick named Wind or Lyric manifested avocado toast.

Shadow hadn't texted back, either. I should check on her right quick while my coffee steeped. I pulled on jeans and padded barefoot out my front door, only to jerk to a halt on the landing.

There was a woman sitting on my bottom step, all slim shoulders and straight spine. Her head and hair were hidden by a lightweight pink hoodie. I thought, *Thalia*, and I made some kind of squeak. She heard it, or she'd heard my door bang open, because she unfolded in a leisurely stretch and turned toward me.

It wasn't Thalia. The woman on my stairs was Delilah Williams. She held two huge Styrofoam to-go cups, one in each hand, unsmiling, her big dark eyes unreadable.

"Albright," she said in lieu of a hello.

"Oh, hi," I said, fighting the urge to leap backward into my apartment and slam the door. I asked her, very tart, "Are you here to arrest me?"

"You think I'd come arrest you in a hoodie?" Now she was smiling, already marching up my stairs. "I was going to knock as soon as I'd thought of a good opening line," she said. I tucked my bed hair behind my ears, feeling crusty-eyed and morning-breathed in front of this woman who was effortlessly making a baby-pink hoodie look cool-chick tough. It was the way she led from the hips more than the plain black letters spelling out "On Wednesdays We Smash the Patriarchy." As she reached the landing, she held one coffee toward me. I took it on instinct. "Can we talk?"

"Talk? Or is this another stealth vivisection?" It came out strident and hurt, when I'd been trying so damn hard to match her cool. Flustered, I accidentally sipped the coffee. It was lukewarm and bitter, no doubt from a gas station. Delilah liked caffeine, and she wasn't fussy about how she got it in her bloodstream.

She held up surrender hands. "Talk. You can trust me, Penny."

"Oh, I can, huh," I said. I wanted to invite her in, then use the very techniques she'd helped teach me to find out how much suspicion was still pointed my way. I wasn't good enough to turn the tables on her, though. Delilah was the deep end of the pool. Not to mention, I was actually guilty. I could almost hear the stolen murder weapon thumping around inside the tree behind us, alive, like the tell-tale knife.

"Yeah. You can," she said, meeting my gaze directly.

My gut said to believe her, though she was the one who had taught me I should trust facts over my instincts. Every fact I owned said I should tell her to go to hell. Well, almost every fact. She had told me to shut my mouth and get a lawyer, and I couldn't reconcile that with the smooth interrogator who'd been out to get me.

I heard myself say, "Okay. Come in. I can at least give you a coffee that won't melt your intestines."

She shook her cup and it sloshed, almost empty. "You know I'll never turn that down."

Once inside, I busied myself dumping out both to-go cups and getting down ceramic mugs, while she plopped onto a high stool at my breakfast bar, saying, "So last week I got a call from Beth Wyland. Remember her?"

Of course I did. The young woman with skinny, bruised arms and a bad husband. I'd given her Delilah's card. "You came to talk about Beth Wyland?"

"In part. Yeah. She called me." I was interested in spite of myself. I poured for us both and passed her a mug, black, the way she liked it. Delilah went on. "She was disappointed it was me that answered. She wanted you. You know how many times I tried with her? A lot of times. But you got right in there." Delilah sounded so admiring. Maybe she was working me over, but the compliment landed anyway. I felt it like a whole-body flush. "What did you say to her, Albright?" I flushed harder and shrugged, turning away to add a little milk and get a spoon. I'd said nothing kind or hopeful. I'd made a rather black-hearted joke. "Well, it worked. I picked her up and drove her to the shelter down on Forsyth. Who knows if it will take, but getting out of an abusive marriage is like quitting smoking. Most people have to try a lot of times before it sticks. She's taking her first shot at it, and that's on you. That was some A-plus copping."

"Thanks." I kept my stinging eyes down, fake busy stirring my coffee.

She said, "You're welcome, but I didn't come here to pat your ass."

I kept stirring, my throat too tight to swallow, unable to meet her gaze. "Why, then?"

She said, "To tell you forensics came back on your uniforms. No blood. Not even a fleck from a shaving nick."

A wave of unearned relief washed through me. I turned fully away to look out of my kitchen window, not sure if I was checking for the Jetta or hiding my expressions. Probably both. Gand was still not home, but someone was texting me. I could feel my phone buzzing in my back pocket. Meanwhile, the silence in my kitchen stretched itself down into a whole new level of awkward.

Delilah broke it. "I told them they wouldn't find anything, Albright. I want you to know that."

I said, "Bullshit." I believed her, though. Or at least, my dumb heart wanted to believe her.

"I'm serious. I went to bat for you. I wasn't the only one, either. Gimbel. Graves. Every officer who worked your training shifts, in fact."

That only made me feel worse. I quit futzing with the curtain and turned back to face her. "You know what, Delilah? Forget coffee." I set my mug down and opened the tall cabinet by the sink. "Let's see what liquor I've got on hand."

Her eyebrows went up. "It's barely two. I haven't had lunch."

"Yeah, but you work nights, so time is meaningless. Plus, if I make crepes, we can call it brunch. Everyone has a tipple at a brunch."

She grinned and threw her hands up in surrender, drinking her coffee as she watched me gather ingredients and make a shaker full of a deadly cocktail I'd invented called the Meadowyn. Two parts floral gin, one part strained lime juice, and one part Cloosterbitter, shaken and served up with a bar spoon of cherry juice and a champagne or soda floater to make it pink and fizzy. I needed all my wits about me, but if Delilah lost some inhibitions? Great. I turned my back, using my body to block her view as I poured an overly generous slug and then a very stingy one into a pair of champagne coupes. I topped them off with carbonated water until they looked even.

I handed her the strong one, which felt fair considering all the interrogation tactics she had used on me. I did say, "This can sneak up on you. Go careful." She lifted her glass in a toast and took a decidedly uncareful swallow. I lifted my glass back and took a very, very small one. "What happens now?"

Her smile was open, her gaze unguarded. "What do you want to happen?"

"I want to stop feeling watched," I said, with quite a bit of heat behind it. I opened the fridge, digging around for anything I could use for an impromptu crepe filling. As I dumped vegetables and cheese out on my square bit of countertop, I told her, "I want to be able to think nothing of it if there's a car I don't know parked near my house."

"Done," she said. "I'm not saying Brinks wasn't doing drive-bys, but there will be no more surveillance. That word came from on high. In fact, the chief himself is going to call you tomorrow to tell you to come back to work."

I digested that as I started on the crepe batter, using real chicken eggs, because fuck my absent, silent brother. I beat the crap out of it with the whisk, too, because fuck the chief.

"Are you killing the batter or just thinking furiously?" Delilah asked. When I made a who-the-hell-knows face, she answered for me. "I had a sneaking suspicion you might tell the chief where to stick it." That made me smile in spite of myself. "I wanted to get in before you set your bridges on fire. You should give the job another chance."

That almost made me set my whisk down and beef up my cocktail, in spite of my intentions to keep my head clear while she got loose and chatty. She hadn't picked her drink back up, I noticed. Maybe she had the same plan.

I said, "On our last shift, you worked me over like I was some perp in a back room."

She copped to it. "Yeah. But I wasn't recording. I wanted you to talk to me. Delilah. My official job was keeping you busy while they got a warrant and searched your locker. Believe me, no detective said, 'Hey, uniform, we sure need your help with our investigation.'"

I got my flat crepe pan out and started heating it. "So you grilled me for my own good," I said, heavy on the skepticism. Again, I wanted to believe her.

"Absolutely. Albright, you think I came at you hard? You should have seen me going after Doolich. Which, by the way, no one asked me to do. No one thanked me for it, either."

I didn't feel bad about that even though I was the liar, and Doolich had told the truth. That guy had zero business being a cop. "He took my underpants," I told Delilah.

Her eyebrows popped up. "He what now?"

I dipped the heated pan in the thin batter. It started cooking instantly, going brown and lacey. "You heard me. When they searched my house, he stole a pair of my underpants."

Delilah didn't ask me how I knew it was him, or if I was sure I hadn't misplaced them in the laundry. She simply accepted this truth. "What a little shit."

"Right?" I said, as if I'd expected no less. I was floored, though. Her immediate belief felt like a gift, when it ought to have felt normal. If Nix had had a cop like this— I turned away to chop up asparagus with a savage hand.

"Here's the thing," Delilah said. "Doolich doesn't have the imagination to make up hearing voices, much less the spine to stick to a lie. So yeah. I interrogated you." She laid her disbelief out next to her faith in me, and then she let both stay together in the quiet room.

I made myself focus on making a roux for the filling, ignoring the building pressure to talk. I was so tired of feeling bloated with secrets, but I could not be safely honest with Delilah. I let the silence stretch between us. She could sit there like a stone until the Second Coming, but I wouldn't be the one to break this time. I moved on to sautéing vegetables, checking the window every few minutes. I saw no Jetta, no Uber, no Gand stepping out of some chick's car.

Delilah waited, more comfortable than I was, quiet in her body. She didn't break the silence until I set a plate of perfect crepes filled with asparagus, mushrooms, goat cheese, and cream in front of her. "So you have a secret. You think that makes you unique?" I thought I'd won because she spoke first, but these words hit me sideways. She paused to fork up a bite, and then she paused harder, eyes widening. "Damn, Albright," she said after she swallowed. "You said you were a cook before, but—damn."

She wanted to talk food? Fine. That, I could do. "Really, the batter should have been made yesterday. It's better if it sits."

She ate another two big bites, then said, "Come back to work."

I boggled at her. "You say I'm keeping secrets. You believe Doolich. Why would you want me back?"

She shrugged and took a bigger bite. When she spoke again, it felt like she was opening a negotiation. "I don't know what Doolich heard, Albright. I'll never know, because I took my best shot in the car, and you rode it out. That means you have the spine for about damn anything the job can throw at you. Plus you're smart and principled, and excuse me for stating facts, you've had some excellent trainers who have put a lot of time and effort into you."

I had to look away. If I was so principled, would I have let Thalia run? I believed in the law, or so I'd vowed when I accepted a gun and a uniform. So why did I have an official evidence bag full of official bloody evidence hidden in a tree house?

I said, "I can't come back, Delilah."

She made a piffle noise as she laid into her second crepe. "Sure, you can. Maybe police work wasn't your first calling, and these are some compelling French breakfast burritos, but I've been at this long enough to have a gut, and mine says you're a born cop." She meant it, too. Her words had such conviction. "You want to do good in the world. I see that in you. So I decided whatever happened that night is not my business. I suspect you made a mistake. Okay. Rookies do. You won't make it again, because you're a person who learns from mistakes. I've seen it on our shifts. More importantly, I'm the one who let you make it. That was a difficult crime scene, and I was both thrown off and really interested. I took my focus off you. Whatever you did is on me, and I learn from my mistakes, too. I'll do better by my trainees going forward. Hey, guess what? In order to do better going forward, Albright, you have to actually go forward. Come back to work."

I wanted to believe her. I wished it was all true. But I wasn't a good cop. I wasn't even a particularly good person, sometimes. I said, "I can't."

She wasn't here to be told no. She settled her ass deeper into the cushion top of the tall stool. "Do you know, in places with diverse cops, more women particularly, domestic violence goes down? I don't mean it gets reported more. There are more arrests, and then the actual incidents go down. Better to let the wife be mouthy if popping her one means jail time or probation and a record."

I turned away, going back to the window to push my curtains aside yet again. This time, I saw a low-slung silver car had pulled into the driveway, a two-seater with a long, long nose. There was a sleek, leaping cat figure on the front; this was an old Jaguar, maybe from the sixties, so perfectly restored it gleamed like new. The soft black convertible top was up, but I could make out two figures inside through the smoked windows.

"Albright, what's your obsession with the window?" Delilah said, a little testy. "Are you bird-watching in the middle of my heartfelt plea?"

I glanced over my shoulder. "Sorry. My slutty brother never made it home last night. Not unusual, but he's not answering texts, and his kid is worried. I think this is him getting dropped off now."

Delilah had her own difficult brother; she sat back and made the sign of the cross at me. "Okay, absolved." She settled and waited while I looked again. The passenger door opened and sure enough, my brother rose up from the low seat, looking more relaxed than I'd seen him in days.

"Yep. It's him. All systems normal."

I was about to release the fabric when the driver's-side door opened, and a long slim shape unfolded, cool and blond and damningly familiar. I recognized her even though she was wearing what amounted to a costume: a gauzy copper-and-green skirt that ended in fringe, topped by a sheer gold half top that had long strings of little jewels and bells hanging down over the skirt. Both other times I'd seen Thalia, she'd been monochrome, androgynous, sleek. This was high-end hippie-chick fem-wear, for all she'd butched it up with mirrored aviator glasses. Her head tilted up then, toward my window, like the face of a flower shifting to point right at the sun, as if my own gaze was a hot, bright, telling beacon.

Gand was saying something to her, pointing at my stairs.

I let go of the curtain and stepped back, even though she'd see the movement. Now she knew for certain I was here.

"Albright?" Delilah said.

I swallowed, sick to the pit of me from the strange geometry. I felt myself teetering, soon to fall, at the tip of an intangible triangle: My very own murderer at the base of the stairs. Her stolen weapon, hidden in the yard. Now Delilah, this woman I so admired, was up here with me at the apex. Her suspect was in my driveway, the person I had failed to arrest or even search or cuff. I felt all the lives that I was living moving toward a horrible collision.

What the hell was Thalia Gray doing at my house, this moment of all moments? More importantly, what the hell had she done to my brother?

19

I could feel my smile stretching too wide, my eyes rounding too open, as I turned back to Delilah.

"Can you give me a sec?" I spoke with a lot of intensity, one hundred percent panicking. I was already moving past her, heading fast for the door.

"Everything okay?" She uncrossed her ankles, both feet on the ground now, as if she was a person who might get up on her feet and go to the window and see Thalia existing on my lawn.

"It's fine," I said, and it sounded like the blaring lie it was. I was talking like a drowning person, going under, airless and weighted down by swarms of awful secrets. I also felt an equal and opposing lift. I'd been frantic to find her, so frantic I'd been parsing vowel sounds with Michael. Now here she was, at last. "I need to have a tiny come-to-Jesus with my brother." *Enough truth there to sound true,* I thought. "He's about to go crash in his tiny house without bothering to tell his kid he's home safe."

She subsided, leaning back. "Got it. Go fix his little red wagon." She rolled her eyes and added, "Family. What can you do?"

"For real. Thanks," I said with overblown gratitude. "I'll be three minutes, tops. Okay? Okay."

I cracked my door open, slithered out, and shut it tight behind me. Gand and Thalia were already at the foot of my stairs. I was so relieved to see her, and excited, and horrified to think of my brother in her unsafe company—or custody—all night. They waited as I came galloping down, stopping two steps from the bottom. I wanted to stay between Thalia and Delilah, as if I was a forest or a wall, as if they would not be able to see each other through me.

"Morning, Penny." Gand was smiling, pleased and easy in his body. She was, too. "This is Polly."

"Polly" smiled and took the glasses off, showing me white teeth and dead eyes. "Hiya," she said, heavy on the vocal fry. *Jesus.*

"We were gonna beg your buckwheat pancakes," Gand said to me, then turned to my personal assassin. "Penny uses flax meal for the egg. They come out crazy fluffy."

I could barely rip my eyes away from Thalia long enough to say to Gand, real testy-like, "Go inside right now and let Shadow know you're home. She's been texting me, worrying."

"Aw, man, really? Why didn't you tell her—" He stopped there. Tell her what? That after he'd accused me of murder in an abandoned Aldi parking lot, he'd needed to destress by getting pumice stoned and laid? He turned to Polly. "Gimme a sec. I need to check in with my kid."

"Sure." Thalia smiled up at him, so very fetching. He was fetched. He slid an arm around her waist to pull her hips in toward him, and she bent, willowy and willing. He leaned down and planted one on her while I stood a few steps over them both, fuming, sick, afraid. The kiss was mouth to mouth, nothing gross, no tongue, but there was a moment of linger, and she used it to slide her eyes sideways and look at me. Her gaze was as blank as a basilisk's.

Gand broke it off. "Back in a sec. Are we go for pancakes, Pen? I can invite Shadow, too—"

"Like hell!" If this creature in her beads and bangles actually had been some hippie hookup, which she emphatically was not, he still shouldn't bring her to eat breakfast with his teenage daughter. Thalia being Thalia, I didn't want Shadow within miles of her. It came out harsh, amusing her and taking him aback. I made myself say, softer, "I have company upstairs."

Gand had the audacity to laugh. "Penn-ee! Good for you." He turned away and headed for the house.

"Not that kind of company," I snapped after him. I came down to stand on the lowest stair, right above her. I dropped my volume, but it took some effort. I was shaking. "You fucked my brother?"

She said, sotto voce, "I told you not to touch my stuff. Next time, I might not give him back."

God! She must have been at Banks's. Watching the *Gand and Penny Blow a Stakeout* show. I leaned to put my face close to her face, furious and scared sick. I had so many frantic things pushing to be first to get out of my mouth. I wanted to tell her she better keep her bloody Lady Macbeth hands off my brother. I wanted to say, *You still owe me your sister story*. I needed to say, *Get the hell out of here*, because the canniest cop I knew was thirteen stairsteps and one thin door away. If Delilah stepped out on the landing, this fraught interaction was not going to pass her vibe check.

What won the race was, "You said you don't like to be touched."

"Needs must," she said, and put her glasses back on, showing me my own reflection twice instead of her equally blank eyes. In the mirrored lenses, I looked exactly as freaked out as I was feeling. Below the glasses, her smile was crafted to be taunting, but that felt like more theater, no more sincere than the beads and the vocal fry. "He's nice. Obedient." Before I could gag on that, her voice dropped ten degrees, so cold I got a chill. "Such a healthy guy. All his blood still kept so tidy in his skin."

As if I needed that reminder. As if I wasn't shaking to know this murderer was watching me closer than the cops ever had. Either she was good enough to follow us from Banks's—Gand had waited at the neighborhood's entrance, after all—or she'd checked Gand's socials, seen his Jenji post, and gone straight there to scoop him up. This was a demo of how easy it would be for her to blow my world wide open. All night, she'd had my brother at her nonexistent mercy. Next time, it could be one of my parents. Shadow. I choked on my own fury. Some of it was aimed at her, and some at Gand, but mostly it was pointed right straight back at myself.

I leaned closer. "My company upstairs? It's my training officer. Best cop I know. Do you want your face in her head? She won't forget it, ever. She's great with faces."

Delilah told me that true surprise flashes fast, but Thalia Gray flashed absolutely nothing. Nothing I could see behind the glasses, anyway. She recalculated like computers do, in a click, then nodded. She reached into her skirt pocket and pulled out a business card. "Tonight. Six o'clock. Bring it."

Bring what? Did she mean that we were going to fight? She herself had told me that if a small female person got into a fight, she had to win. Every time. Then I realized she was being literal. "You want the box cutter back."

She gave me a quick sideways head tilt and some eyebrow, like, *Obviously*. "You should've gotten rid of it. Now, I want it in my hands."

If this was a fight, I'd just been asked to bring a knife to it. So why was I suddenly smiling in spite of all the adrenaline still zooming through my bloodstream? I knew why, though. She was giving me what I wanted at last. Her time. A place where I could find her. I took the card.

"I'll bring it. And you'll tell me the story. The sister story."

No answer. No reaction at all. She wheeled away and went fast to her car, her body moving entirely differently than it had when she was being Polly. No more hip swaying, no more willowy bending. This scything stride did not go with the skirt. She was safe behind smoked glass in seconds.

Her card was plain, off white, such heavy stock it was both as soft as fabric and sturdy as cardboard. It didn't say *Thalia Gray* on it, much less *Polly*. There was no name at all, no email address, no number. Only a Midtown street address written small in vehement dark letters that smeared a little under my finger. Pencil. Her handwriting was as neat as a French schoolgirl's in some 1800s novel, so uniform that I'd mistaken it for printing. The Jaguar's engine purred to life and she backed out of my drive. I stayed another thirty seconds to make sure her car kept moving away from me, my former mentor, my house, my brother. Every inch that widened between us both felt like a loss and let me breathe.

Gand came back out the front door in time to see the Jag disappear around the corner. He walked over to me, and I resisted the urge to grab him and squeeze him tight and tell him not to go off into the night with strangers, not again, not ever. I'd been told this all my life, but no one says this to men. Especially men who are 170 pounds of mostly muscle. Bowery had been a big guy, too, though, and how much good had that done him?

My brother was oblivious, looking down at me with mild exasperation. "Shadow's playing Xbox, so she can't have been that worried." I closed my eyes, and now, instead of hugging him, I wanted to shake him senseless. "Man, I wish Polly had waited. She was cool. So anyway, who you got upstairs?" He waggled his eyebrows.

"Idiot," I said, so fond, so furious. "It's my old partner, Delilah. I, for one, didn't drag home some rando."

"YOLO," he said, unapologetic. "Anyway. I came home."

I hopped down and went to hug him, unable to stop myself. My brother, warm and alive and safe and not running. I said into his shoulder, "Good. You do only live once, though. Not for very long if you don't get smarter fast." God, I could smell her on his skin. She was all over him. I let him go and stepped away. I didn't think her name was Polly any more than I believed that it was Thalia, but I'd take any crumb of knowledge I could get. "Do you at least know 'Polly's' last name?"

"Nah. Oh, wait. Yeah. I think she said that it was 'Amorous.'" He grinned and then made a rim-shot noise. "Get it? Polly Amorous?" I knuckle punched his arm, three times, fast and hard while he laughed and tried to dodge, hollering, "I'll be here all week. Try the veal!"

I laughed in spite of myself, mostly because I was so relieved that he was okay. Or to keep from bursting into tears. He'd spent the night with the person who had cut Bowery's femoral artery with a box cutter and smashed in Xav Castillo's brains, easy as I might throw a stick for Bosch.

"I'm glad you're home."

I heard the door then, and there was Delilah on the landing. "I better get going. Is this your brother? Hey. Delilah Williams."

As she came down, I told her, "This is Gand. He's fine. Except he probably got chlamydia."

Gand was smiling, about to greet her, but he interrupted himself to say, "Hey, now!" Delilah chuckled. Then he continued, "Listen, I told my kid I'd take her out for Thai food. Since no one is going to make us pancakes. Apparently?" My baleful glare was answer enough. "If you'll excuse me, then."

Delilah watched him get all the way into the main house before she spoke again. "Okay, I said my piece. I'm done badgering, but I hope I'm not done working with you."

"You okay to drive?" I asked even though I knew she'd barely touched her drink. I was making a point.

"I'm good. Are you good?" She was making a point, too. We'd both hoped the other would loosen up, maybe say more than we meant to about this or that. I knew it, she knew it, and yet neither of us was mad about it.

I said, "Yeah. Thanks for coming. You're on a crusade, and I respect that. It's a good one." I did not say, *I can't be part of it. I am on one of my own.*

I think she heard it anyway, because she gave me a sharp, two-finger salute and said, "I'm not done trying with you, Albright."

Delilah and I didn't have a lot in common past the cop thing, and that felt over. Also, a cop friend was the last thing I needed right now, considering Thalia's reappearance and Jordan Banks walking around still having a pulse. Even so, I found myself so grateful she had come. She felt like a safe place in a bad storm. I stepped in, and I hugged her. She froze, surprised, for half a second, and then she hugged me back.

I said, "Tin Man. I think I'm going to miss you, most of all."

"Well, shit. That feels like a firm no. Okay, Albright. Penny. You have to make your own decisions. Listen. I still have your back, okay? Maybe because I think in a year or so, you might change your mind. Maybe because my spidey senses say you're in some trouble. If I am right on either count? Click your heels, I'll come running." Her dark eyes were serious.

I nodded and said an awkward, "Thanks."

I watched her saunter to her car with my spine taut. I made myself wait until she'd driven fully out of sight. Then I made myself wait more. I sat on the steps and, checking my phone, saw the text I'd felt land had been from Michael, asking if tonight was good for me.

It wasn't. I had a date with Thalia to trade a knife for a sister story. I left Michael on read, sitting tight until Gand and Shadow came out and caught their Uber. Mom and Dad were at work, and the dogs were inside. I had the place to myself, but I felt spied on anyway. Delilah had said that all cop surveillance had been pulled, but I still gave the street a serious once-over, checking for unfamiliar cars or vans. Everything looked regular, and Mrs. Blanchard's carport was empty as an added blessing.

I got up and let myself into the backyard, trying to look like a normal person who needed to water the flowers, calm and casual. I closed the gate behind me, buzzing, even though I'd barely touched my drink. I hurried toward the stand of oak trees at the back, and I scrambled up the remains of Gand's ladder. Once I was sitting on the rotting planks, I jammed my hand down in the knothole, deep, not bothering to check for spiders, scrabbling in the mulch.

All I found was twigs and leaf detritus, damp and crumbling. No evidence bag. No bloody box cutter. No guardian purple toy, even. I kept digging until my fingernails were scraping bark and wood pulp at the bottom of the hole. I stirred my hand around. Nothing. Some sly Boo Radley had come and taken it. My stomach lurched.

I slid down the tree, scraping my shin, and when my feet touched the ground, I backed away. I was so dizzy. My stomach turned and soured. I found myself sagging against another oak while my mind ran in crazy circles. In the city, Thalia Gray was waiting for me. I wanted this meeting so bad that I had gotten in her way. More than once. I'd thwarted a violent woman with no limits, who had stalked me, who had absconded with my brother. Now she wanted her weaponry returned.

I didn't have it.

20

I was cop enough, still, that before I'd paced a hole into my carpet, I knew where Thalia's bloody box cutter had gone. I would have known immediately, if not for the way love worked. It made such blind spots. I also had a good idea of how to get it back.

You have to wait, I told myself. *Don't have a bunch of feelings.*

I killed time getting myself ready to go see Thalia Gray in her own territory. First, I brushed my teeth like I was trying to scrub off all my enamel and took a boiling shower before pulling on my favorite pair of black jeans and a lightweight lavender sweater that I always felt good wearing. I thought I was fine, putting on a little makeup, when I realized my reflection was too tall. My spine was so straight. It had elongated of its own anxious volition because Thalia had put her killer's hands all over my brother. Sure, he hadn't minded at the time, but it wasn't about him. She knew the thought of my only remaining sibling dozing beside her, unspooled and oblivious, would make my blood thicken and chill. I shook my shoulders out, relaxed my posture, but the mirror mercilessly reflected the anxiety in my eyes. Oh, well. I was going. No way I wasn't going.

Then there was nothing I could do but watch Life360 and pace. Time was my enemy. I wasn't sure what I would do if I couldn't get the knife back in my hands before our meeting. Every hour that passed took a solid year right off my life. I got two phone calls, first Michael, then the precinct. That was probably the chief, telling me I could return to work. I let both go right to voicemail.

Gand and Shadow finally came home a few minutes after four. I went down to the main house and headed directly to the bedroom

I'd once shared with Nix. It was Shadow's now. I knocked hard because Joan Jett's version of "Crimson and Clover" was blaring inside. I waited for her to say, "Come in," before I threw the door open and beelined right to where her iPhone was plugged into Gand's old amp. I yanked the cord out. *Shut it, Joan. I'm doing shock and awe.* Shadow had her bass and was playing along unplugged, learning, but she stood up, alarmed, and set the instrument aside.

"I'm getting in the shower," she yipped.

She looked like a refugee from a town that banned grooming, but—*oh, child. If you think that's the problem.* I fixed her with a steely eye and said, "Where is it?" in a brooks-no-bullshit tone.

Her eyes went wide in instant confirmation. She had the knife, all right. I should have known sooner. Shadow *had* seen me creeping up to the old tree house like a weirdo. I'd assumed she was too tied up in her drama to notice me, but no. She'd only been too tied up in her drama to ask about it right then. At some point, she'd Crime Girled around the yard and found the knothole. I'd been co-faux-momming this kid since Nix and I were children ourselves, but I was also her adopted sister and her cool aunt. That meant she told me truths she'd never tell Mom and Dad, and I trusted her in ways my canny parents didn't. Mom had probably clocked that Shadow was down deep into a mischief the second she took my side over Gand's, but I'd been fooled.

She tried to lie, anyway. Made big eyes. Said, "Whaaaaaaat?" stretching the vowel way past real surprise's expiration date.

"Stop. I need it. Now." I went full-frontal parent, holding a hand out like I expected her to insta-cross my palm with a bloody silver box cutter. Which I did. If my hand was shaking, it was only because she'd had it when the cops were searching the house. If they had prowled around outside the laundry room—God, it didn't bear thinking about.

I could see her teetering between doubling down and coming clean, could see the moment when her better angels won. She sounded both scared and sorry, with a little relief in the mix. "Jeff has it."

"Shadow!" I'd never spanked so much as her little hand when she was two and it was picking dangerously at the outlet covers, but now I wanted to go full evil nun on her. My resolve to be direct and inexorable instead of a shrieking harpy wavered. "Jeff? Really? Shadow, do you get how serious this is?"

She held up placating hands. "Yeah! I mean, we figured. We didn't tell anyone else. Not even Piotre or Darcy."

I spun away, pacing back and forth like something caged. "The only way two teenagers can keep a secret is if both of them are dead. You're lucky I'm only halfway mad enough to kill you. Call Jeff. I need it back. Now."

She gulped and scrabbled for her phone. While she did some rapid-fire texting, I looked for somewhere to sit, dizzy with all the awful everything that I was feeling. Shadow's room looked like a poorly organized garage sale. Her bed was where every old blanket and pillow in the house had come to die. Various ancient gaming systems and cartridges were piled on the desk and dresser. The sagging papasan chair in the corner was empty except for Nix's old giraffe doll, but I was not sitting down in that. Someone had set it out on the street for the garbageman a few weeks back, and Shadow had dragged it home. Mom had sprayed it down with Lysol until the upholstery crackled, but I still believed the cushion was stuffed entirely with lice.

She looked up from her phone. "He's on the way over. Like, right now."

"He's bringing it?" It came out so strangled. She nodded. I finally got a good breath in, and I immediately used it up to yell at her. "Shadow, why didn't you talk to me? That's what kills me. You spied on me, and then you snuck around behind me and took the—my—the—"

"Your bloody utility knife?" she interrupted, pressed hard enough to press back. Her nostrils flared as she finished my sentence like she was handing out a dare. "In an evidence bag."

"Yes," I said, and if this was a dare, I took it, stepping toward her, doing her one better. "Yes. My bloody knife. That I stole from the cops. That could send me to prison. And you gave it to Jeff."

She blinked, twice, and then she lurched at me and clutched me hard, bursting into tears. "Pen, I'm sorry. I tried to tell you, really. I asked if you were in trouble. Are you so mad?"

Of course I was. But I'd been mad for days now, maybe years, under my numbness and my awful sorrow. Maybe this was good, to have it finally coming out. I hadn't been honest, either, or asked for help from any of the people who loved me most. She blubbed and wailed and snotted onto my favorite sweater, and I patted her back and shushed and tutted, like I had when she was three and woke to find her betta fish had gone to Jesus in the night. "I should have noticed you were trying to talk to me. I'm sorry to come at you so hard, but why did you take this to some boy instead of—"

She reared back and interrupted, "Not some boy. It's Jeff!" as if that made it better. "Jeff is solid, Pen, he'll never say a word. He barely talks to people who aren't me, and then mostly about manga." Her eyes were big wet pansies, sad and urgent. Nothing left on Earth could move me like these dark eyes flecked with gold and green, so like my twin's.

I blew my breath out long, then said, "It's okay," even though it might not be okay, at all.

She was calm enough to let me go, so I pushed a stack of sweatpants onto the floor and sank down onto Gand's battered wooden desk chair. She plopped down at my feet between a pile of laundry and a scatter of school papers, reaching up to hold my hand. I waited, feeling as jumbled as the room, which was haphazard in three dimensions. The walls themselves looked fraught, crisscrossed in strings of fairy lights and papered with overlapping posters with cutout pictures of her friends glued into them. Jeff was packed in Barbie's dream car, while the taller girl from Wet Leg had Piotre's head. I could barely see the ancient carpet, what with all the books and dirty clothes and shoes and gutted dog toys and art supplies and Gand's old band detritus lying around.

Jeff finally poked his bug-eyed face into the room. He'd let himself into the house, which meant he knew exactly where to find the fake rock with our spare key in it. What, of my family's most secret businesses, did this boy not know? He was the quietest member of Shadow's posse, built solid and short with a thick chest, long arms, and stumpy legs. He was dressed exactly like her in ripped jeans and a huge stained hoodie. They looked like gender-bent refugees from Planet Grunge, him with his thin dark hair hanging in snarls, her scalp showing through her buzz cut. He pulled the evidence bag out of his back pocket.

"Sorry, Ms. Penny," he said softly, advancing with it held in front of him like an offering to an angry god.

I snatched it, and he scuttled backward until he plopped into the papasan chair, right on top of Nix's giraffe and any hepatitis that was lurking there. The weight of the knife in my hand was a relief.

Shadow peeped up at me, her voice hesitant as she asked, "Can I ask why you stole it from the cops?"

Gand had worried I was covering my own crimes. "I didn't hurt anyone, if that's what you're asking. That's not my fingerprint."

"We know!" Shadow hastened to assure me, and I felt more than saw Jeff shoot her a look. "Did you take it because she doesn't want, like, media attention?"

That made me sharpen and sit up. Thalia for sure did not want any kind of attention. Few murderers on revenge sprees do, not until the work is over, anyway, but how did these kids know the bloody knife belonged to a media-shy "she"? A cold hand closed around my heart and my anger took a little turn toward Midtown. Had Thalia approached Shadow as well as Gand? Thalia Gray, touching my stuff. She damn well better have stopped with my brother, who was an adult and hardly innocent. Surely she didn't—

When I didn't answer fast enough, Jeff chimed in. "If I was her, I wouldn't want publicity."

I boggled at them, and they exchanged a speaking glance, blatantly this time. Shadow pressed her hands anxiously against her cheeks. "Oh god, is that her blood? Is Clio dead?"

"No," I said. Clio? The name meant nothing to me.

"Told you, Shads," Jeffrey said. "You follow too much murder podcasts."

Shadow's gaze warmed. "You're protecting her. I knew it. I told Jeff you took the knife because the police would have run the print and outed her to the press. Then she'd always be *that* girl, like those missing kids whose dad was starving them to death the whole time in that hunting cabin. I'm right, aren't I?"

I became more alarmed with every hopeful word she threw at me. "Shadow. You didn't. Tell me you did not," I demanded, fumbling to open the plastic bag, a terrible, horrible idea blooming in my mind. I pulled out the box cutter, peering close at the thumbprint caught in the dried blood. Sure enough, a few tattletale grains of powder, finer than the finest sand, clung to the loops and whorls. It was a job of work to make my voice not shake. "You ran the print." They exchanged a guilty look. I rose to my feet. "How the hell did you do that?" This was the million-dollar question. They exchanged another glance, telegraphing information, having an argument in blinks and pressed lips. I stepped toward them, getting loud. "How?"

Four big eyes fixed on me. Shadow said, "Jeff got this Science Time Forensics Kit for Christm—"

I interrupted. "I know how to lift a print. How did you *run* it?" Neither answered. Shadow looked stricken. "You hacked it? You hacked the FBI's database? Oh, my god. Do you understand the consequences for hacking IAFIS? They will track you. You idiots. There's no way you—" I couldn't speak anymore. *How many felonies am I going to be complicit in this spring?* I wondered, near tears or hysterical, raw laughter.

"We did not hack IAFIS!" Shadow was vehement. "That would be insane."

Before I could feel any kind of real relief, Jeff said, "Wellllll . . ."

"Did you?" It was more of a shriek than I meant it to be.

"No!" Shadow gave Jeff a quelling look.

By then, I'd figured out enough to say, "Who *did* you hack?"

She held up placating hands. "A nonprofit. With a shitty website so full of holes that Bosch could get in there."

"A nonprofit? A nonprofit. Okay. Okay," I said, experimenting with the idea of not dying of stress right on the spot.

"One for the families of missing people," Shadow said, now a little pious.

"With access to the FBI's fingerprint database," Jeff added under his breath. Again, I thought my head was going to explode, and if they were both caught in the blast, I was furious enough to think they might deserve it. Jeff held up his hands, too, and added, "But it was cake, Ms. Penny, for real. In and out. Clean."

I started pacing back and forth again, my hands fisting in the hair I had carefully blown out into a confident shape before facing Thalia. This girl I loved like crazy cakes was suspended from school for hacking, and she had learned exactly nothing. The only thing that kept me from losing my entire shit was the understanding that in Shadow's place, with Shadow's skill set, Nix would do the same. If Nix were here, I knew what she would say: *Way to double down, kid.*

I turned toward them, trying for calm. "You can't possibly believe you can outfox the FBI's coders. You're hoping no one happened to be looking. Maybe you got away with it. This time. But every time you do illegal, wrongful shit like this, you up the odds that someone smarter, more experienced, better is going to notice. When that happens—and it will, if you keep pressing—there's your future, burned."

They gave me solemn nods, but their frontal lobes were basically made of Play-Doh. Yelling more might shut them down, and I needed these code monkeys to tell me what they'd so wrongfully learned. "Since the cat has left the bag for dead and crossed state lines, tell me everything. Let's start with a name, and then I want any aliases, known associates, known addresses. Does she have a record?"

Shadow looked perplexed. "A record? The only name we got was Clio Falkner."

Something bonged way down deep in my memory. I'd heard this name before. From Nix? I'd suspected Thalia Gray had known my twin; I'd even hoped that they had loved each other, but Thalia had denied it. She'd told me that she had her own sister story.

Jeff said, "It's baller that you found her. We didn't know who Clio Falkner was, but Google had a million hits. On real sites, too, like NPR and ABC, not only those picture things with all the ads. It was a big deal, back in olden days. Did you find Calliope, too?"

Calliope. That name bonged even deeper in my brain, and then I knew.

I hadn't put it together when he said "Clio," because I hadn't ever heard that name spoken alone. They were "Calliope and Clio," always said in tandem, always in that order, or sometimes "the Falkner sisters." Thalia Gray was one of them. Clio. The younger one.

I did know her, after all. So had Nix. Both of us had in fact known Thalia Gray since we were twelve years old.

21

We all have stories, not our own, that stick with us, the ones that alter or affirm the way we shape the world. Mom still talked about Baby Someone who got thrown down a well. She always got a little teary recounting how the whole country came together to dig her up. My soft-eyed father, the stray-dog gatherer, still mourned a little blond pageant girl who was murdered in her own home.

For me, for Nix, there was a time when the Missing Falkner Sisters was the loudest story in our life. All three of the kids had names from Greek mythology—Ajax, Calliope, Clio—and the story got national attention, which made them seem larger than life. At the same time, the parallels between our families made the girls feel very real, realer than anyone else we'd only seen on TV and the internet.

In the pictures, their mom and dad looked like our parents, regular people with normal jobs teaching English and Latin at a private prep school in Atlanta. The family was shaped like ours, too. Three kids, the only boy the oldest, except we had baby Shadow, crawling all over and babbling, and the Falkner girls weren't twins. They were both in middle school, though, like us. They lived in Grant Park, near the zoo. We'd been there. It was possible we'd driven right past their house, maybe seen the family walking down the street. Then, all of them but one were gone, baby, gone.

They'd left home for a vacation, but after hours of delay at the airport, their flight was canceled. They dragged home and went to bed. The next day, Ajax woke up late to find both his parents lying in the upstairs hall right outside his sisters' empty room. They were cold and open-eyed, each shot multiple times. The girls had simply vanished.

There were no signs of a break-in, and nothing, not even jewelry or electronics, had been taken. The internet (and presumably the cops) looked hard at the brother, who was sixteen and a little wild. He was quickly cleared; he'd sneaked out of the house to go to a party and was with a dozen kids at the time of death. He'd come home baked and gone to bed without noticing anything was wrong.

"Gand would do that," Nix whispered to me from her bed when this came out. Ajax was exactly the kind of boy my twin was prone to defending.

"For sure. You think Gand's in his room right now?" I whispered back and shivered. Our brother often slunk back into the house too late and too toasted to notice corpses or missing sisters.

After school, we took turns at the old clunky computer on the built-in desk in the kitchen, one of us playing with baby Shadow to give Mom a break, the other trolling for updates and photos, reading the endless internet hot takes out loud. The search for the sisters was exhaustive. How could girls so loved, so normal, one twelve and the other barely fourteen, vanish? Neither could drive, and Calliope's fat wad of babysitting money was still in her jewelry box, so they were not runaways. Clio still looked like a kid, all knobby knees and big teeth. If she was wandering around bus depots or hitchhiking, she'd be noticed.

"Oh. They are dead," Nix told me, peering at the monitor while I let baby Shadow carefully pinch Cheerios out of my palm, one by one. "Bank on it."

I wanted Nix to be wrong, but she was reading a web page full of statistics about missing kids who aren't found within the first seventy-two hours. We understood then why the mood of the search felt so changed; the cops and volunteers were hunting for bodies.

Calliope and Clio slowly dropped out of the news cycle, but then the cops finally allowed Ajax and his aunt back into the house to get his things. He realized that his mom's "glass flowers" were missing from the knickknacks clustered on the mantel.

These flowers were plainly visible in a photo of the mom that the

Atlanta Journal-Constitution published the year before, when she won a teaching award. Turned out, her garage-sale buttercups were a lost work in a series by Fabergé worth several hundred thousand dollars. This *Antiques Roadshow* Gone Bad twist renewed national attention. It peaked when a female body, singular, was found way up in the North Georgia mountains. Right size, right build, blond hair. It turned out to be a runaway from foster care, and Calliope and Clio gradually dropped out of the discourse once again. They joined other famous unsolved crimes on the internet, relegated to endless picture-heavy clickbait "articles." We forgot about them, too, until the *AJC* did a big story on the fifth anniversary of the crime. Their brother, Ajax, now in his twenties, had started a nonprofit called The Thousand, named for the number of bodies that go unidentified in the US every year. In its first six months, his organization had returned over a hundred sets of remains to their families.

We were in high school, and the story was a hot topic at the lunch table.

Nix said, "The Falkner sisters are at the bottom of Lake Lanier, and that place never gives the bodies back."

I still had my optimism. "You don't know that. They found that one girl alive, remember? The Mormon girl who got dragged out of her own house in the middle of the night by the crazy prophet guy."

Nix shook her head. "Pah, she was missing, what, not even a year? No way. Those sisters are bones."

The hot idiot that Nix was dating de-slouched and flapped his mouth-hole. "I hope you're right, Nicki. God, can you imagine if they did get found, alive? They'd be so messed up."

I felt the pause inside my sister, and then Nix turned toward this poor dumb boy. He was only saying things his parents had said, or that he'd picked up from the news or ingested with the water, because that's how deep this idea ran.

Oh, how slow she turned, how sweet her smile was. "So, if it was me, or your sister, you wouldn't want us back? No, I get it. I bet we'd be a handful. I bet we wouldn't be much fun. God, but that would be so hard. For you."

He got defensive, stammering out that he hadn't meant *that*. Within a week, Nix had a new boyfriend, and that was the last time we talked about Calliope and Clio. That may have been the last time I ever thought of them, except perhaps in passing. Until today. When my niece blithely announced that I had found one of them. Alive.

I was too blown away to fully process it; Thalia Gray was Clio Falkner. When I was a kid, I'd tried so hard to magic the Falkner sisters alive. I'd crossed fingers, said prayers, wished it on stars and eyelashes, while Nix had only wished for the cops to find their corpses and their killers. Now, almost a decade and a half later, I knew at least one had survived.

I couldn't imagine where she'd been, much less how she'd come back here with a fat pocket and a murderous agenda. I'd never bought the nutty internet theory that the girls themselves had recognized the flowers and done the heist, and I gave it even less credence now. Shadow at twelve, three short years ago, was ninety pounds of buckteeth and big eyes who secretly still liked to play with Barbies. Her sweat didn't stink, and her training bra's only job was preventing embarrassment in the middle-school locker room. I couldn't imagine a twelve-year-old cold enough to become a family-killing, high-end art thief.

I also couldn't fathom how Clio Falkner could blame the three men I hated most. Bowery, Castillo, and Banks were kids themselves when the sisters went missing. How could they have hurt Calliope? My brain jabbed these contradictions toward each other like wrong-end magnets, unable to make them connect. In an entirely separate operation, my brain was listening to Shadow pressing me for answers that I didn't have.

"Did Clio at least tell you what happened to her?"

"No," I said.

"I bet we could find out," Jeff said, and that recalled my full attention.

"Stop!" These kids were playing Crime Girl, and when they looked at the internet, they saw gaps in the code that let them slither into wrongful places. They had no impulse control and too much free time. I looked at their fierce, interested faces, the consternated eyebrows, the entitled questioning, and I realized exactly how right the word *playing* was. They had no idea how serious this was. "This is not remotely your business."

Jeff said, "It kind of is. The reward the brother raised is serious. Like, pay-for-college serious, and that's just for information that leads him to the bodies. You know where one is, alive."

Shadow snapped at him before I could answer. "Don't be a dick. Pen literally stole evidence from the cops to protect Clio's identity, and you want to out her?"

Jeff sat up straight. "Nah, brah. Pen could get the reward on the quiet."

"If she was an asshole," Shadow said, outraged.

Jeff shrugged and subsided. Subsiding wasn't good enough. Shadow stared him down until he pulled anxiously on his lank hair and added, "Sorry, Ms. Penny. I know you aren't an asshole." He was basically a good kid, but so far above the optimum IQ that he could be abrasive. I thinned my mouth like a person who thought the topic should be closed, but Jeff was also too far over optimum IQ to be good at reading faces. "Are you going to tell the brother, though?"

I said, "I'm going to tell exactly no one. Ever."

Instead of looking alarmed or even lightly quelled, Shadow's expression softened again. "Anybody else would go for the reward, and Clio's chance at a private life would pretty much be over." Shadow was bending the facts to fit a theory, that common rookie cop mistake Delilah had warned me against. Since Shadow loved me, her theory painted me as quite the hero. Her pure belief in my goodness felt much more damning than any amount of pious Karma-will-manage-it bullshit from Gand. Last I heard, Karma was busy dating Taylor Swift, and people with more money than morals decided how justice would work. Shadow's faith made me wish so hard that I was more honest. Less furious. Less ruined.

I was not about to disillusion her. Not when her theory motivated her to stop doing blithe felonies and poking my pet murderer.

Jeff was less misty about my altruism. "But, I mean, she killed that guy. The knife is from the outdoor mall? Right?"

I didn't want to give them a speck of information that might inflame their curiosity, but here, I saw an opportunity to make them back off. "It was used in self-defense."

Shadow looked smug. "Told you.

Jeff was thinking so hard his body was rocking with it, rhythmic and intense. "What we should do is—"

"Jeff! What you should do is nothing. You have violated her civil rights to hell and back already." That was direct enough to land with him. I was one of the very last Millennials, but Jeff and Shadow were Gen Z. Unfairness was a high crime with them. I pressed harder. "You solved it, okay? Now I need you to stop digging. You could go to actual, real prison." Worse, they could draw the attention of Thalia Gray, a murderer who didn't like it when anybody touched her stuff. "No more hacking."

They exchanged another series of speaking glances, all eyebrows and hard blinks, and came to some silent consensus. Jeff held up solemn Boy Scout fingers and said, "I promise."

Shadow never did the Scout thing, so she made the Vulcan peace sign and echoed him. "We promise. No hacking." Before I could say more, she added of her own volition, "We won't tell anyone about Clio. Not ever. She deserves her privacy."

"Thank you." Apparently, we all could agree to leave her alone, except for me. I tucked the bag with Thalia's weapon into my back pocket, and then I hugged Shadow, tight as I could.

She hugged me back, and whispered, "Love you, Pen."

"Love you, kid," I said into her ear, and then I let her go and added, "Can you two please find some nice, un-illegal way to spend your evening?"

Shadow laughed and said, "*Mario Kart?*" Jeff got up and went for the controllers.

I left them to it. I had to get on the road if I wanted to meet Thalia on time. I was relieved to have the kids off her scent, but under that, I felt a thread of strange jubilation. I wished that Shadow hadn't gone prowling—but since she had, well, I knew what I knew. For the first time since my nose had led me to Thalia, I had the upper hand.

Toy with my brother, will you? Come to my house, so scary in your mirrored glasses. Keep your secrets while you peel mine right out of my hide. Nope. Not anymore. I see you now, and I am coming to you. Clio.

22

The traffic gods were with me. I got to Midtown in a little over half an hour. I parked in a pay lot a couple of blocks down from the address, glad to still have daylight. This particular neighborhood looked like a great spot to be on the receiving end of a little light mugging. I locked everything but my keys and Thalia's knife in my car's trunk.

Just past the lot, I saw a sign with a red arrow pointing down an alley where a dozen people had gathered in ones and twos outside a chained-shut door, waiting. They were disparate ages, races, genders, but their layered clothes and ratty hair told me they mostly were unhoused. The door down there had another sign on it that said, simply, Clinic. *Methadone,* I thought, and that made my throat ache for these people and for my twin.

Thalia Gray's building was a block farther on, a concrete brutalist rectangle with banks of long, recessed windows. It looked squatty even though it was more than a dozen stories tall. The smoked-glass entry door was covered by a serious wrought iron security gate. There was no buzzer system with names or unit numbers, only a single black speaker with a button and a silver numbers keypad. I pushed the black intercom button and heard a hiss of air and static.

"Hello?" No answer. I tried again, getting antsier and antsier. "Thalia?" Nothing. I told myself to calm my tits. Nix's voice was a whisper in my head. *Calm as little swans upon the blessed waters.* I'd given up my cop gun, but I was armed with Thalia's knife, her thumbprint, and her real name. She had to talk with me. I hit the button again and got louder. "Hello? It's Penny. Albright."

"You came alone," Thalia said, right behind me. Close. So close she could have opened an artery in my throat or in my thigh before I got a scream out. I spun and leaped back at the same time, smacking into the iron gate, feeling like I'd left all my whole skin behind me. She smiled, but I had no idea if it got to her eyes. The aviators were firmly in place. Her hair was tied back in a thick, loose braid. She was monochrome again, but darker. Charcoal gray.

"Oh, hey," I said, like an idiot, my voice gone high. "Are we going in?"

Instead of answering, she said, "Phone," and put a hand out.

"I left it in the car," I said. "Are you going to search me again?"

She answered this question with a question. "Do I need to?" I shook my head in a fast no.

She twirled a finger at me anyway, wanting me to face away. *Right here on the sidewalk?* I thought, but I did it, turning toward the gate and pressing my palms to it, braced for her impersonal hands. This was a narrow one-way street, but it was still in Midtown. A car was passing us, and I could see another coming. The drivers would probably assume that she was a cop, undercover, and I was getting arrested.

Thalia didn't touch me, though. I heard her tapping numbers into the pad, and I realized she'd had me turn so that I wouldn't see her code. I dropped my arms, feeling like an idiot, and the heavy gate released with a grinding click. I glanced over my shoulder, and at her nod, I pulled it open. She braced it with a booted foot. I heard her inputting another sequence, then another click, and the heavy door behind the grate unlocked, too.

The smoked glass was so dark as to be almost impenetrable. When I swung the inner door wide, a wedge of sunlight spilled across a polished concrete floor, showing me only emptiness and dust. The room beyond was cavernous, taking up what looked like the entire first floor. The ceiling was high, and my footsteps echoed as I stepped over the threshold. I paused in the spill of warm light. This looked like an abandoned building. I glanced back, only to find that she had moved in silently behind me. I saw my own scared face, twice, reflected in her aviators before she turned to yank at the iron gate. It was age warped, and she had to bang it twice before I heard it catch. Then I was locked in with her.

"Go on," she said.

I felt my heartbeat pulsing in my throat. I went farther in, Thalia crowding behind me, never touching me, but close enough that I felt her as a haunting. I scuttled forward, out of knife reach. Behind us, the heavy inner door clanged shut on its own.

"You can't possibly live here," I said, my voice hollow and small in the emptiness.

She took off her glasses and tucked them in her jacket's inside pocket. "You think I'd give a fake address to a cop?" Her eyes shone in the faint light; she was making a joke. She moved to the side, boots echoing against the floor, and hit a bank of light switches. The ceiling was contoured into concrete rectangles, with an ugly, bare bulb hanging in each. Only about a third of them lit up, so that splotches of harsh light bounced off the floor. In the lit square directly above me, I saw cobwebs in the corners.

She came back toward me. "Did you bring it?"

I shifted, my hands going to my pocket. Not to get her knife out. To cover it. "You said you wanted to get out of this city. Remember?" I was still putting this together with the idea that she was Clio. She'd been born here, and this was where she'd spent the first dozen years of her life. Her brother still lived here. "So you don't live in Atlanta. But you own this place?"

"Yeah. I stay here, sometimes." I looked around at the expanse of dim filth, and something in my expression made Thalia chuckle. She pointed at the ceiling. "There's finished space upstairs." She turned her hand then, flattening it, palm up, silently asking for her box cutter.

I kept my own hand clamped over it. I'd let her leave a crime scene on the strength of a single word. I'd been up-front, telling her the three men we hated in common had hurt my twin. Now she wanted me to hand over her weapon. And then what? Quietly exit her building and her story? Hell, no. Not going to happen. "If I give you the knife, what do I get?"

Her head tilted as she assessed me. "Oh. Is this blackmail?" She sounded more amused than mad. I couldn't tell if she was serious as she added, "Do you take checks?"

"I'm not blackmailing you," I snapped, feeling mad at her, and at myself, and also a little bit bereft. "I want you to talk to me. I want to know why you hate the same men I hate. Why you killed—"

She flipped that extended palm up toward me in a sharp *stop* gesture. "Maybe I do need to search you."

"No," I said. "No, you do not." I leaned toward where she stood in her own pool of light, under her own bare bulb. I was looking for the woman I'd connected with at Danny Bowery's murder scene. The one who saw my dark, glad heart and opened, showing hers to me. "I'm not recording this. It's not a trap. I've covered for you, multiple times now. I've earned at least a drop of trust. But, okay. Let's do this." As I spoke, I yanked my lavender sweater off over my head and threw it on the dirty concrete floor. "If this is what it takes." I kicked my flats off, then struggled out of my jeans. Her gaze sharpened as I took the closed box cutter in its evidence bag out of the pocket, then held the bag between my teeth. I turned every other pocket of my jeans inside out to show her they held only my keys, then dropped these things to the dirty floor as well. I took the bag out of my mouth, already shivering, wishing I wasn't in silly pink-and-white-striped cotton underpants and my ratty old black bra. They didn't even go together. I spun for her in a slow circle, spotlighted in that harsh, bare bulb. "Good enough?" I asked, when I was facing her again. When she still said nothing, I cussed under my breath, and reached one-handed for the front clip of my bra.

Thalia held the same hand out, stopping me again. "I only want my box cutter back."

I snapped, "Not *only*. You also wanted to bang my brother. Apparently. Well, we all want stuff. I want you to talk to me."

For the second time since we met, I felt that she was having an actual expression. One she didn't curate or manufacture. It was soft, a little curious, a little wry. "Officer Albright," she said, solemnly, "I don't think you do."

I walked over to her, fast, mad, and freezing from my bare feet up. I held the bag out to her, the knife very flat on my palm. I looked at it, hard, until she did, too. Her eyebrows came together as she saw the thumbprint.

"I'm not the only person with a brother," I told her. She went so still then that she might have been a statue. Or a corpse. Her eyes flashed, and something cold and foreign rose up behind her human face. *Clio,* I thought, but by then it was gone. I'd pissed her off or scared her, one. She folded her hand over the box cutter and disappeared it into a pocket. She said nothing, so I pushed. "I know who you are."

Then she looked exasperated. Her voice went strangely gentle as she told me, "No, you don't. And if you did, how foolish would it be to talk about it. At all. Anywhere. But especially in what amounts to a soundproof concrete bunker with a dirt floor basement, all alone with a woman you damn well know has killed before. Christ, Albright, you just handed me a knife."

Well, when she put it that way . . . "You're saying I'm naive. Maybe that's fair. And I know I've been a pain in your ass, touching your stuff." I cocked one eyebrow and took a risk. "You were watching him, and maybe you were about to move on him, and there I was. Me showing up, it was a problem for you. You didn't expect me."

"I did not," she agreed.

I said, "I wrecked your plan."

Her eyes narrowed. "We're not going to talk about my plan."

I nodded. "No, that's good. The more I know, the more I'm—"

I stopped, and she said, "Culpable."

I nodded. "I still want—something. I'm not blackmailing you. I don't need money or to know what you'll do next. But we hate the same three—well, one now—men, because we both had sisters. I need to understand that. I have to know what happened to Calliope."

The name hit Thalia like Nix's could hit me. It was a blow and an invocation. After a stretched silence, she said, "You can come up."

She wheeled away and started walking across the huge, blank space. She didn't seem inclined to wait for me to struggle my pants back on, so I grabbed all my things and padded barefoot after her. There was a bank of three elevators to our left, but she went right past them, heading toward a thick fire door at the back.

I stopped. "Stairs? How far up is your place?"

"All the way," she said.

"The elevators don't work?"

She glanced at them, then back to me. "They work. That last one on the end goes to the top. You can take it. If you want to get into a box with only one real exit." She said this like I might say, *If you want to jump into a pile of spiders.*

"I do," I said. "I really, really do." I was in good shape thanks to the PT test, but I wasn't the kind of girl who walked up twelve flights barefoot in my skivvies unless I absolutely had to.

She backtracked to the last elevator, fishing out a loaded key ring as she walked, and she pressed the call button. The doors opened immediately, and I saw with some relief that it had at least a little dim light inside. She stepped in quickly, me in her wake. I could tell she didn't love it by the tension in her limbs. She twisted a small key in a notched slot under the buttons, then pressed the top one, marked *14*. The next highest button said *12*. I wasn't superstitious, but still. Even her floor had a secret identity.

"It shouldn't make any stops," she said, slipping out as the door closed between us.

Up I went, using the slow, shuddering ride to pull my clothes back on. She was letting me go up to her floor unsupervised, so I expected a hallway or a vestibule, but instead, the doors opened directly on an open loft so huge and glaring white that it was hard to take it in. I blinked, blinded, and put my hand up to shield my eyes. I stepped forward, but I could only go a couple feet. A white wrought iron gate was in front of me, attached to a thick twisting fence of the same material, blocking my way.

I looked left, then right. The bars ran from wall to wall and floor to ceiling. I pushed at the gate, gently first, then hard enough to rattle it, but it was locked. I felt more than heard the elevator closing behind me. I turned back to push the button, but there was no response. It didn't even light, and I saw another of those rounded keyholes under it. The elevator would only come, then, if she summoned it.

I'd stepped out right into a cage.

23

The industrial room was clinical enough to feel cold, but I was sweating, and my heart rate had jacked up. The living space I saw beyond the bars was nuts.

A single room took up the whole top floor, wide open with high ceilings, so brightly lit and so white on white on white that it felt eye-sharp. The floor was poured, pale concrete. To the left was a low, solid box of white wood with a thin futon mattress on it. White sheets and one flat, white pillow. Beyond that, near the center, was a strange, blanched art structure, part tree, part cube, made of intersecting branches. It was at least six feet across and seven or eight feet tall, decorated with hanging lengths of knotted rope, a chain of bells, and what looked like a macrame ladder.

I could hardly take in the rest, half blind still from the stark lighting and absence of color. I was trying to figure out what the hell the art structure was when I heard Thalia say, "Poor baby."

Her voice echoed, distorting as it bounced off the high, white walls. I startled, looking for her. There was no way she had gotten up before me, and there wasn't any place to hide. As soon as I thought it, I realized exactly how true this was. All the furniture was clear acrylic: a sofa, a chair, a desk, all see-through. She had quite a lot of sharply tailored clothes, all black or white or shades of gray, hung flat against the wall, which had white pegs for the hangers. Looking at the darker pants and jackets was a relief for my poor eyes. Her folding clothes were stacked in a bank of shallow, acrylic cubbies.

The bathroom was a cube of clear glass walls, and the shower was a smaller cube inside it. I could see the toilet from where I stood, no mercy wall or curtain. At the back was a kitchenette with a four-seater acrylic dining table. I could even see inside the shallow, built-in refrigerator-freezer with its sliding glass doors. There were no cabinets, but open shelves held white dishes, a host of cleaning supplies, and some white Le Creuset cookware. There were no curtains on the many windows. The glass was mirrored instead of smoked up here, giving me a gorgeous view of downtown.

"Hey, come on. Friends don't lock friends in giant cages," I called, trying for nonchalant and failing. I hated how my words came out so thin. I hated that I couldn't see her.

"Poor baby," Thalia said again, her voice echoing and coming from all over. "Awwwww."

She sounded odd, strangled, as if she was yelling at me through a pipe. Was she watching me like a creep on some kind of camera system? I didn't see any cameras, but I did find four flat, white speakers hung in the corners about ten feet up the walls.

"Thalia. Open this!" I kicked at the gate. The clang echoed itself and came back to me, muted and futile.

"Awwww. Poor baby," Thalia cooed. Then she shrieked it, so loud it bounced around the room. "Pooooor baby!"

My skin shivered. I thought, *I am not going to get out of here, not ever,* when a streak of pure and vibrant color dropped out from behind one angled speaker and soared across the room. To my whited-out, frightened eyes, it was the brightest and most perfect blue I'd ever seen. It came right at me, fast, zooming through this blank bad space, and I leapt back, releasing a startled shriek right before it resolved into a bird. A parrot.

A pretty damn big one, too, at least a foot and a half long. It was blue all over, but the wings and tail were variegated and more vibrant, and the head and belly verged on gray. It came to a rattling landing on my cage, grasping with gray-gold feet and hanging sideways, then biting at a bar with its wicked beak. It regarded me with one curious black eye that was ringed in gold. I put a hand over my pounding heart.

We looked at each other, and I felt halfway to hysteria; its wings were unclipped, and it was commiserating with a girl in a cage.

"Poor baby," it cooed in Thalia's voice. I tried the iron gate again, and the bird said, "Easy does it," and then made a *knock-knock-knock* sound in its throat.

It pushed off and winged to the massive structure, which I realized was a combination perch and parrot playground. It landed and began eating seeds out of a white dish that was attached to one of the posts.

I heard keys rattling and the clunking sounds of a huge dead bolt clearing in the thick metal door that was just past her hanging clothes. Thalia stepped inside. The heavy door was weighted to swing shut slowly on its own, and yet I heard another dead bolt turning while it was still in motion; it took me a moment to understand this locking sound came from the parrot. It was perfectly rendered.

"There you are." My voice sounded as shaky as I felt. Her eyebrows went up. "It— Your parrot scared me." I didn't want to say being in the cage scared me. I didn't want to beg to be let out. I wanted to pretend that this was normal, so very normal to be standing in a normal cage in a very normal room devoid of shadows or even color.

"He. Pierre." Thalia regarded me with her head tilted at an angle that matched his, and by then the door had closed. She turned the heavy bolt and started toward me past the outfits hanging flat on the wall, all monochrome, black jackets over black blouses hung over black pants, gray over gray, white over white. It was as if she was passing a host of headless Thalias as she searched on her crowded key ring. Good lord, but this woman liked a lock.

As she opened the gate she asked, "Something to drink?," like a normal hostess does when she is releasing her guests from the entryway trap. It was a weird question to find in her mouth, anyway. She wasn't used to having company, I thought.

I came out in a move that was more of a scurry than I would have liked. "No, thank you."

That was apparently enough chitchat for her. She turned on her heel and walked toward the kitchen area. I followed, honestly surprised she took her eyes off me. Then I caught movement above me, and I realized that she hadn't. The entirety of the high ceiling was covered in mirrors. I hadn't noticed because until we were moving through the room, everything that they reflected had either been monochrome or a huge blue squawking bullet that I thought might be attacking me. My gaze met hers in the reflection.

I said, bolder than I felt, "Mirrors. Is this, what, a sex thing?"

Her reflection grinned at mine. "I seldom have sex here, Officer. This is where I sleep." She said it like I'd suggested she sit on the toilet to eat salad. I blushed, but I was instantly more comfortable. She hadn't brought my brother here. Probably. I hoped. I decided to assume.

Thalia paused at the bird's tall, structured playground. The blue parrot sidled over, very coy, and tilted his head down for scratching. She obliged, releasing fine white powder and a teeny tiny feather, so pale the blue was almost white. It floated slowly downward.

"Love you, Clee," Pierre said. Standing by him, I heard less echo, and I could tell it wasn't quite her voice this time. Higher and softer. It was very similar, though.

"Love you back," she told him. She glanced at me, gold eyes gone bleak, and I understood. This voice belonged to Calliope. While I was gut punched by this understanding, she hit me with a question, hard and sharp. "How did you run my print, almost-ex Officer Albright? A private lab?"

"No. Don't worry. There's no paperwork, no computer records, no trail," I said, feeling again how very alone I was with her, thirteen stories up, behind all manner of insane security. A dirt floor basement, she'd said. If she killed me and buried me, who would know? Would my body be alone down there?

"The cop that was at your house when I returned your brother," she said, as if Gand was a library book, and I should be grateful that she hadn't torn the pages. Okay, well, fair. I was grateful. "Maybe you asked her to run it?"

I shook my head. "No cops. No official anything. I promise."

She raised a skeptical eyebrow. "Oh, do you promise? You sound four years old. And so sincere that I almost believe you. How, then?" The bird edge-walked away, eyeing me. His bright black-and-gold gaze was so like hers. He began locking and unlocking invisible doors, clicking out loud tumbler sounds so perfect it was hard not to check for someone coming in. She seemed inured to it. My gaze skated sideways to him, and she stepped between us. "How?"

I firmed my mouth and lied. "I hacked a database."

"*You* did." Thalia's disbelief was so instant and so blatant I felt almost insulted. Then her face cleared. "It was the kid. Shadow." My shock must have showed, because she added, "She's about the only thing your brother talks about. Can you keep her mouth shut?"

"Yes," I said, very firm. I didn't want her to dwell on Shadow. I didn't want her thinking about Shadow at all.

"It's two hundred fifty thousand dollars, last I checked," she said, and in case I didn't get it, she added, "The reward. For finding my corpse. Imagine what I'm worth alive." I inadvertently released all the air I'd taken in, and she smiled, mirthless. "You want to change your mind about that check?"

I swallowed, my hands fisting. "I'm not blackmailing you, Thalia. Shadow wouldn't, either. We'll keep your secrets."

"Mm. Do you *promise*," she said, so flat it wasn't a question. She made her hands into cool-guy finger guns and shot me. At the same time, she said, "Don't shoot!" to Pierre. He instantly made the sound effect to go with her skeptical gesture. *Boom! Boom!* He sounded so exactly like gunshots that I jumped. He even made his vocal bullets ricochet around the room. She turned and kept on walking to the kitchen area, fishing the box cutter out of her pocket and calling back, "Sit down, if you want," as she passed the acrylic four-top.

I came to the table and sat down, and even with my back to the bulk of the room, I could see every corner by simply looking up. She threw the plastic evidence bag away and turned the water on, rinsing the knife and then scrubbing at the thumbprint.

"This was sloppy," she said, irked with herself. "I was rattled. I was not expecting you to show up, almost-ex Officer Albright. You did, though. You do. You keep showing up where I don't expect you. It's becoming a theme. I don't love it." She dried the knife carefully on a dishtowel; I could see rust flecks coming off on the white; she hadn't bothered with bleach or hydrogen peroxide. She only wanted the fingerprint gone. She came over and set it down in front of me. "Souvenir?" I could still see his blood freckled in the hinge.

My stomach lurched. I didn't pick it up, but I felt less afraid with it close to hand. I thought that was why she'd done it. I said, "Knife to a fistfight."

She smiled again. "This isn't a fistfight, and if it was, you'd need a bigger knife." She sat down catty-corner to me and regarded me, unblinking. "What do you want?"

I told her, straight up. "I want you to tell me why you hate them, why you're killing them, how they connect to Calli—"

Thalia cut me off. "Let's talk in hypotheticals. Officer." Behind me I heard Pierre unlocking and locking another invisible dead bolt.

"I'm quitting, and you know it," I countered. "When Xav Castill—"

"Hypotheticals, future ex-officer." I started to ask another question, but she held up a hand. "If I ever met with such a person, then hypothetically, I wanted information. Hypothetically, it was damn inconvenient that someone killed him before I got what I needed."

"*Someone?*" I said. Unhypothetically, I'd long believed she killed him. "Not you?" She shook her head no. "Then who is someone?" She shrugged and I rolled my eyes. "Hypothetically."

Thalia leaned her forearms on the table, looming closer, though there was no one to hear us but Pierre. "Let's say there were three assholes who met in college and got into the habit of doing shady shit together. People who do shady shit get killed."

I negated that, immediately. "No. That's Gand's crappy theory, but Castillo died right before the anniversary of Nix's death. That's why I thought you must have known her."

She said with little irony, "Sorry to disappoint, but I didn't know her, and I didn't kill him." A thinking pause, and then she said, mostly to herself, "Maybe the answer's in the question."

I had no idea what that meant. "But you killed Bowery not two months later?" Her next shrug was a silent admission, more wry, with a half smile. "How can that be a coincidence?"

She pushed air out her nose, irked with my insistent directness. "Your three assholes were still smuggling, and that's a fact. Hypothetically, they sold something to a man I need to find. They have a way to contact him, maybe a name or even an address. When I hypothetically approached them, I was acting as a buyer. Infiltrating. I was close when—" Thalia mimed taking a good, solid swing with a baseball bat. "They got cagey, shut down entirely, until I offered too much money to ignore. I went to the restaurant in good faith. He changed the location so he could watch my arrival, make sure I was alone. A good tactic. I use it. So, fine. I went. But once he was sure, he revealed his bad intentions, as you well know, and I took him out of play. It's down to me and the money guy, so I hit him where he lives. There's a lot of cash in their business model. I found his. I took it. He'll have to deal with me now."

I mostly believed her, and I was so relieved. I almost believed her, and I was so disappointed. I wanted to stand up or cry or yell at her. I felt both absolved and angry. My feelings made no sense to me, and neither did her story, which I almost, almost believed.

"So. The other night, when we both staked him out—you weren't there to kill him."

I was speaking mostly to myself, but she had an answer. "He's the only one left breathing with the information that I need. My kid gloves are on, believe it. But hypothetically? I'm pretty good at self-defense."

That wasn't hypothetical. I'd seen Bowery's body. "You mean you'll only kill him if he makes you."

Her gold gaze bored into me then, so very cold. "I'll kill anyone who makes me."

I said it with her: "Hypothetically," and that made her smile.

"Awww. Poor baby!" the parrot said in Thalia's voice. Poor baby, indeed. Pierre wolf-whistled and then made a chuckling noise.

I said, "How is this connected to your sister? She disappeared years before they were dealing drugs at UGA. They weren't smugglers in middle school." The parrot jingled some bells, discordant and cheery, and I couldn't tell if it was a toy bell or a sound that he was making.

"You want to understand it," she said, like this pissed her off, but then she dropped her head and seemed to think it through. "I'd rather write you a check. But you want the story. You're telling me that's the price of your silence?"

I crossed my arms, protective more than angry. "When you say it that way, it sounds like I lack the courage of my convictions. I don't like it."

"I like it, though." Thalia looked up again and folded her hands on the table. "I'm comfortable with trades."

Her pale eyes met mine, and I felt our strange bond come alive again, a current moving between us. Not dark joy this time, but a parallel grief; I realized that she was not capable of simply telling me the story. She needed it to be a transaction, because to gift it to me was to admit we were connected, and the same, and that she maybe even cared about me. She couldn't bear that. She couldn't risk it.

I could, though. I'd lost Nix, but I had Shadow. I had Mom and Dad and Gand. And maybe—maybe—I had Michael. I already knew I cared about her, and that was not what scared me, so I gave her what she needed to push me away. "A trade, then. My silence for your story."

She got up and walked away immediately, almost before I saw that she was having some feeling that she couldn't keep off her face. She didn't go far. Only to the strange, shallow fridge to slide open one of the glass doors. The parrot gurgled like a stream as Thalia took out two bottles of water. When she came back, standing over me to hand me one, the emotion had been quelled.

She said, "It's a story to you. A thing you saw on television. Two girls sleeping safe in their room when strange men break in their back door. The men aren't particularly quiet, once they are inside. They don't expect the family to be home. One girl goes downstairs to see who's tromping around and she sees these strangers, sees their faces. She screams. Runs back to her sister. Their parents get between them and the men.

"There's no way to truly silence a gunshot. You likely know that, almost-ex Officer Albright. Suppressors work, but only to a degree. We both heard the gunshots, a sound like thin ice cracking, right outside our door."

She paused there to go back to her seat across from me. I wanted to take her hand, but I knew she wouldn't like it. I waited, barely breathing, pretending I wasn't there while the parrot clicked locks open and shut and whistled and told her that he loved her in her sister's voice.

"It's a story to you," she repeated. "If I say, 'The girls have pillowcases over their heads when they are taken from their room. They don't have to see what's in the hall,' that's easier on you. But this isn't a story." She closed her eyes. "This happened. It was me. This was us."

The difference between those two pronouns, *me* and *us*—it broke my heart. She was perhaps the loneliest person I had ever, ever seen, and she did want to tell me this. She wanted to say it out loud to a witness. Not just any witness. Not the bird or a therapist or a priest or a lawyer. She wanted to tell me. Because I was a me instead of an us, too. I held myself as still and quiet as I could, and I listened.

24

They came for the flowers. My mother's stupid estate sale glass flowers. They spoke French, but Callie had taken enough French to understand that much. We weren't part of the plan, but the man in charge knew how to traffic more than art. I guess that's lucky, or they'd have shot us dead, too.

They transported us in a van. Kept us in a shipping container. They said they wouldn't hurt us if we were good and quiet, so we were good and quiet. We were in there for days, I don't know how many. We had no way to tell time. Sometimes we felt motion, sometimes we were still. We had bottled water. A bucket. Jars of peanut butter, cans of fruit in syrup. We were scared, but together, and no one hurt us. They wanted us to be silent and still, like objects, so we were. We acted like one object, we were so twined together. Even when we were sleeping. We slept a lot because they drugged us, but I know they took us on at least one plane. Then they left us with the man who bought us.

We were lucky to go to one man, instead of to a place. Most girls like us go to a place where there are others like them, all lying drugged in little rooms. Heavy traffic. Those girls are dead within five years.

We thought the man was French, but I found out later he was Belgian. Small and wiry, but strong. In his forties. We called him Buddy, and we lived in a basement. No windows. No exit except a metal door at the top of steep stairs. It was a very nice basement, as these things go. It had electricity. A working bathroom. Books. So many books. Picture books, novels, textbooks. Books for learning English and French and math and science. Buddy wanted us to learn. We did homework, every day. There was a TV and a DVD player with language disks and old movies. *Goonies. Gremlins. The Princess Bride.* The one in the machine when we arrived had Russian subtitles turned on.

We each had a trunk of clothes that didn't quite fit. Weird things. Callie had prom dresses and miniskirts, pink fuzzy knee socks. A cheerleader uniform. I had pajamas with feet in them. Play dresses and leggings. The clothes had stains. Missing buttons. The name Hana had been carved into the baseboard. Someone had drawn tiny monsters, dragons and unicorns, into the margins of the math books.

Buddy wasn't always there. We'd be alone for days and days, even weeks sometimes. That was good. When he came, he wanted us to be nice and not cry. He wanted us to play Monopoly with him and to ask him to help us with our homework. He called us his wonderful secrets and wanted to pretend that he was Callie's age and she was his girlfriend. She had to hold his hand, be happy to see him.

I was the irritating little sister they had to babysit. We acted this way, or he'd leave. With the food. He might not come back for days, and then he'd say, *Aren't you so happy to see me?* If we acted happy, he made us eggs. Once we were reliably happy, it wasn't only food. French perfume for Callie. A teddy bear for me. We could ask for things. Specific books. A Nintendo. Calliope wanted a dog, but that pissed him off. How could we walk it? He didn't like us asking for things he couldn't give us. Like a pet. Or to go home. We learned to ask for things that he could get us easily and then to be grateful and happy.

He drugged her food, sometimes. Often. Not mine, though. When she got woozy, he put one of those old movies on for me, very loud, and then he took my sister upstairs. I watched those films a lot of times.

After a few months, he started taking Callie out. Overnight, or even for a few days. I hated it. Hated every hour I was alone. They went to parties in private houses, she said. Most were mansions. Estates. There were dinners and dances and poker nights. She saw other girls and boys there with men like him, but not a lot of them spoke English, and they were never left alone with one another. On one trip, after she'd been very good, he asked if she still wanted a pet. By then she'd learned to say, *Oh, is that a good idea? What do you think?*

He took her to a house that had a huge solarium with high ceilings, high humidity, green plants and birds everywhere. Rare birds. Calliope called the man she met there Parrot Man. Parrot Man didn't usually sell his birds, he said, but Pierre didn't like him, kept trying to bite. Pierre prefers women. Parrots are particular.

Buddy had cash, stacks of it in a sleek black case. He wanted Callie to see him paying so much for her pet and be impressed and clap and smile, so she did, but Parrot Man made her afraid. He had dead eyes and a wet mouth. He told Buddy he would straight-up trade Pierre for Callie. Right in front of her, he said it. Like a joke.

You know what Buddy told him? *Not today.* Like he was joking, too. Like them trading pets was so damn funny.

We were with Buddy for about two years. He was all about Calliope until he wasn't. We could both see it changing. She was starting to look grown. I was starting to look like she did when we first came.

My sister—

My sister did a lot. To hold his attention. Dressed me younger. Said she loved him. It worked. For a while. One day, though, he left with her on what seemed like one of their normal jaunts. I had only one frozen dinner, an apple tart, a bag of popcorn, so I thought he was taking her on an overnight. He didn't come back for four days.

When he did, he had a bag full of my favorites. Mushroom risotto. Steak. I could smell it. He was alone.

He told me about Callie before I even asked. All I cared about was where she was, but my eyes kept going to the food. He liked that. He said she was grown-up enough now to go to boarding school. In Switzerland. He told me she'd have a wonderful life, because she'd pleased him, and he was important, and he had a lot of money. When I was grown up, he would do the same for me, he said. I'd have a trust fund, like she did now, and I could go live with her. She was waiting for me. I think on some level, he believed what he said, even though he was expecting me to be a little bitch. *Don't be a leetle beetch, Clee,* he said in a half-jokey way. I knew if I was, he would take the food and leave until I wasn't.

I said I was happy for Callie. I smiled. I said I'd look after Pierre for her. He liked this.

He asked me if I wanted a little sister. I could tell he wanted me to want this, so I said I did. He had one coming for me, soon, he said, another blond one, from Ukraine. She knew some English, so I wouldn't be lonely. I thanked him. Until then, he said, I had Pierre for company when he was traveling. I thanked him, again, my eyes on that bag of food.

He heated up the risotto in the microwave and set the small, rare steaks on top. He left them at room temperature, so that they wouldn't toughen. He said this was our first date, and he lit a candle and made our plates while I set the table. He talked about how lucky it was my new little sister was still traveling and we could be alone.

I knew my food would be drugged, and that this would make it easier. Callie had told me. I knew if I was nice, it would be easier. My sister had told me that, too. I knew he had liquor upstairs, and liquor could help. When he brought our plates over, before I so much as took a bite, I giggled like she used to, and I asked if we could sneak some grown-up drinks. I said, *Maybe vodka? It's clear. We can add water to the bottle and your dad will never know.*

He liked that. He'd nicked a bottle of red wine, he said. It was already down here, in the take-out bag. He got up and opened the bottle. He poured us each some into juice glasses. I drank a little. It was sour and I hated it, but he drank his up and had some more. I smiled and said that I did bad on my math test, and he said he would help me after dinner. I told him he was smart and the best boyfriend. By then he was deep in the pretend, happy I was doing it right. He believed in it, but I did not. When Callie was there, I had believed in the pretend, too. So did she. It happens like that. He had the food, so he created the world. We loved him, because loving him meant we got to live. But when he didn't bring her back, he broke it for me.

I ate up all my food, which pleased him, and I flattered him and flirted like I'd seen Callie do, and all the while I wondered where he'd buried my sister. I asked if I could have a few new movies. *Do you know how many times I've watched* The Princess Bride*?* I asked it sweet, though, like I was teasing him. He laughed and promised he would bring me some new DVDs, next time.

He ate up all his food, too, and I really had watched *The Princess Bride* a lot. A lot of times.

When he turned his back to get the wine, I'd switched our plates. He ate whatever sedative he'd planned to feed me, and he'd drunk wine on top of it. He was the one whose limbs got heavy and slow. He was the one whose words started slurring. He wasn't a big guy, and he was getting close to fifty, but he was strong. All I had was steak knives. Still, I made it work.

Maybe the drugs and the wine made what I did to him with those knives easier.

I hope not.

25

Thalia's banks of mirrored windows had gone dark. To the south, even in her unforgiving light, I could make out the bright beauty of the Atlanta skyline. She had a million-dollar view, but I doubted she ever shut her lights off to see it well. We sat quietly together while the parrot clicked and hooted.

At last she spoke again. "I'm sure you have questions. Why didn't I call the police? Why didn't I go home? And then the big one. You're thinking it. It's the one I ask myself, all the time. I don't have an answer, and I'm not taking questions, anyway.

"I will say this; I knew my parents were dead. I thought my brother was, too. I didn't know what country I was in, and Buddy had convinced us he was so important that if we tried to leave him, no one would help us. We'd be disappeared.

"I got his keys out of his pocket and went up those stairs and out that heavy door for the first time in two years. It was morning. There was a clock, a thing we'd never had, and it said ten a.m.

"It was a green place. Beautiful. A simple stone cottage surrounded by pear trees and then woods, quaint and isolated. A black sedan was in the drive, but I'd never driven a car. There was a safe built into the floor of the bedroom. I dragged his body up the stairs. It took forever. He kept thunking back down. I had to use a clothesline and—well. Eventually, I got him up there. I used his eye, his thumb, to get the safe open. Inside I found different kinds of cash. Most of it looked pretend to me, but there were banded bundles of US dollars, and a stack of bearer bonds from Luxembourg. I didn't know what they were, but I took them, plus a small black notebook with a series of numbers that was useful, later.

"I found three brand-new passports for me. Different names, different countries, but they all said I was eighteen. I pushed his corpse back down the stairs and brought Pierre up. I never went back down there again, but I stayed in the house until the food was nearly gone. No one came. I spent the days teaching myself to drive and searching in the woods. I couldn't find a grave, and then it occurred to me, he'd traveled with Callie, many times, but there were no passports for her inside the safe.

"That was interesting.

"I thought, *He has bad friends. Someone else would want her. The Parrot Man did.* I had "Buddy's" passport, too, so I knew his name. I had a name, anyway. I thought, *What if I can find her?* I wrote down everything I could remember that my sister had told me about the parties, the people, and then I left and started looking. I'm still looking. I've sent some stolen children home. Or at least to safety. Shut some bad, bad places down. But I haven't found her."

My eyes ached looking at her. My throat ached, too. Thalia was so like Nix. She was diving deep to where the world got cold in layers, looking for any tiny piece of monster. She swam out too far on purpose, a knife between her teeth, then kicked down into the depths, reaching, with no one to pull her back. The people she was after were so insulated by money, privilege, power. Laws could not touch them. They knew no limits, faced no consequences. None, but her. Dangerous work. She could die doing it, and sink, and who would ever know or mourn her?

I began, quite hesitant, "Your bro—"

She cut me off before I could finish the second syllable. "No. I'm not the girl my brother remembers. That girl is gone, and he already mourned her. Anyway, how could I face him without Callie? Maybe if I find her. Or at least know what happened to her. If I made contact, he would ask the question, the one you're thinking. The one that haunts me."

She looked at me, so bleak, and I knew what the question was. I didn't say it, though. She did.

"She saved me in a thousand ways, hundreds of times. I didn't save her, though. Why? I ask myself that every fucking day. Why didn't I switch the plates at some earlier dinner? Before he took her off that last time.

"The only answer is, because I didn't."

She fell silent again. I wanted very badly then to hug her. I made myself stay still and let time tick past us, until I was suddenly so dry I was dizzy with it. I cracked open the water that sat sweating and ignored in front of me, and I slammed down half of it. Pierre made gulping noises. My eyes felt grainy and gritty, as if Thalia and I had come through some kind of bad desert together. She pushed the heels of her hands against her own eyes, then, as if she felt it, too. Maybe we'd both forgotten to blink enough while she was talking. Maybe we'd forgotten how.

I felt faint surprise to be in my body at all, breathing, my heart thumping along, thinking, *Here we sit, me and my personal murderer, like normal people at a completely normal clear acrylic table in a normal room that's white and wide open enough to work as an asylum, talking about all the invisible things that happen in this huge, bad world.*

Thalia wasn't checking boxes on anything as simple as a revenge-murder list that happened to match mine. Our hates and hurts were not the same. She wasn't going to kill Jordan Banks. Not unless he made her, and he wouldn't. Of the three of them, he was the weak link, the lackey, their delivery boy in college, now their money washer, left with the last spoils. She'd taken his cash, and without the other two, he didn't have the connections or the spine to keep it going and make more. He'd fold and give her what she asked for.

She reached for her own water and drank, too, watching me the whole time, the parrot providing more cartoon drinking sound effects, then she said, "So. Don't ask me."

It was easy not to ask. I knew the answer, anyway: *Because you were a kid, and scared, and starved into compliance. Because he was the only source of life for you and your sister, and he was clever and evil enough to use your love for each other against you.*

I didn't say any of it, though. Any reason I could produce, any absolution I could offer, she'd thought of it already. She'd said it to herself a thousand times, a hundred thousand, but she hadn't found a way to quite believe it. I knew because we were the same in this, too. My question was, *How could I let Nix slip through my fingers?* I knew, intellectually, that what happened to Nix was not my fault, but the road down from my head to my broken heart was twisted and snowed over. Her final phone call played forever in my head.

Thalia stared at me, almost angry, as if she expected me to ask. As if she wanted me to, so she could go cold, or rage, or be done with me. My real question wasn't why she hadn't switched the plates before, but rather, how the hell did she find the courage and the fortitude to do it in the end? I didn't ask that, either. I got up and walked away, over to the closest of the long, recessed windows. I was looking west, into stars and darkness. This way, somewhere, was my home, full of my family, holding my sweet, small, normal life. I stepped in even closer to the window to negate the white, the mirrors, the unabashed paranoia of it all, and I saw then that she had silently come up behind me. I could see the faint lights of the city and the stars shining through her pale reflection.

She said, "Don't tell Gand's kid. Let her be a kid. You can keep her mouth shut?"

I said, "I don't have to. Shadow knows enough to believe that keeping silent is the right thing to do."

Thalia cracked a skeptical smile. "You're saying she'll sit on all this. Because she thinks it's right."

I was. "Yes, actually. She cares about justice. She has a good, strong conscience."

Her smile widened into something almost genuine. "You think I need a conscience, Jiminy?"

I said, "Kind of?"

She stepped in closer. Her breath stirred my hair. "You volunteering?"

I held the gaze of her reflection. "I'm not sure I qualify for crickethood. Not anymore." She didn't want a moral compass, and she could not allow herself an absolution. All I could do was say a truth to her. "I think that you were really brave. You were a kid." Thalia's smile faded. I didn't look away. "You're still brave, now."

She backed away, her reflections disappearing off my shoulder. All I saw was the ghost of my own familiar face, so like my twin's, and through it, the city and the stars.

After a moment she said, "We aren't friends, Penny." She said it like she meant it, but she'd also called me Penny instead of by my last name or some snide cop reference.

I kept my back to her. "Well, I'm *your* friend. Whether you want me or not." I heard her blow impatient air out of her nostrils and I turned to face her. She'd gone back to the table, and I joined her there. "You didn't give me what I asked for, though. You never told me how these men are connected to Calliope."

"I did," she assured me. She looked right at Pierre then, and she asked in French, "Qui est un joli perroquet?"

He answered in a man's voice, deep tenor and oily: "C'est moi! C'est moi!"

My stomach lurched to hear it. I thought, *Buddy*. But that could not be. Pierre had lived with the Falkner sisters, who had girl voices and mostly spoke English. That voice could belong only to one person. "That's the Parrot Man talking. The one—he—who wanted to trade for Calliope. You're hunting him because you didn't find her grave. You think—you think—"

I faltered, but Thalia smiled and shot me with her finger guns again. This time, she bull's-eyed me silently, without cueing sound effects from Pierre. "Glaucous macaws were recorded as critically endangered, most likely extinct, in the 1990s, officially, but here's Pierre, and two years ago someone auctioned a hatchling for a cool two mil on the dark web. Your pod of assholes moved that bird. That, I know for sure. Bowery taped its mouth shut, stuffed it in his pocket, and walked it into the US personally. What I need to know is where they took it after that, because the buyer was either Parrot Man or someone who knows him. He's the competition when a bird like that comes up." The way she smiled made my blood go colder than this ice-white room. "I'll recognize his voice, Penny. I never met him, but I hear him talking." She turned her pale gold gaze onto Pierre. "I hear him every day."

She'd said that we weren't friends, but she was speaking so openly to me now. Calling me Penny, abandoning the word *hypothetically,* using their names, as if she finally believed that I was not recording her. It was her ease that let me know that we were finished. She'd made this into a transaction, so we were completely done. I would never see her anymore.

I felt it like a loss, right in my center. This person had seen all the way into the core of me when I was at my worst, and she liked it. More than liked. She shared it. I hadn't felt this since I lost my twin, and I didn't want it to be finished. I didn't want us to be finished. But she was. We were.

I said, "I'll keep your secrets. I'll stay out of your way."

She smiled at me, and it even reached her eyes. "Really? Because you've been bad at it, so far."

I smiled back. She was relaxed enough now to tease me. "Really."

She turned back toward the elevator, digging for her keys. "All right, then."

"Poor thing!" Pierre called after me as I followed her back across the room. "Aw, poor thing!"

Thalia unlocked the cage and held the door open for me like a footman, with a flourish, then unlocked the elevator call system. "The front door will close on its own, but the old iron gate will need a push. Shove until you hear it click."

This, for Thalia Gray, was a trust fall. It made leaving harder. Behind me, I felt her presence like a push, and I was already grieving the loss of our tenuous, fraught connection. Leaving her lit up my own loneliness, but nothing I ever felt about this woman was unpaired with its opposite; it was a relief to be done here. We were not twinned. We were a Venn diagram. In the space where we intersected, I had seen the worlds under the world, colder and colder, going down in layers.

A darkness I could hardly fathom existed beneath my nice house, my dad's gentle, slope-shouldered worry for me, my mother's sweet cherry pie kindness and her tart optimism. Even Shadow's vigilante tendencies were tiny and unworrisome. Comparatively, anyway.

Had Nix always known about the deeps Thalia inhabited? Had she always understood how much evil existed? I thought so. It was what made her fight so hard, fall so low, hold on so hard to joy when it came.

As for me, I would go home and finally try to learn how to be Penny with no Nix. I would help Shadow make up lost ground at school, cook my mom's favorite souffle and help my dad train rescue dogs, pester Gand to be home more often. These things mattered. These were the only things that mattered. In my world, we didn't extort people. We didn't kill people, even bad ones. I'd find some kind of regular job, and I'd make new friends, maybe find a nice man who wasn't sad much. Maybe I'd kiss Michael again, and see if I could love him. We might have babies, get our own rescue dogs, get fatter, get older, be happy.

I stepped into the cage, and she did, too, briefly, so she could unlock the elevator buttons with a twist of a weird, round key. Even though I knew it was coming, I still startled and whirled when she clanged the cage door shut between us. Framed in aching white, the wild, living blue that was the parrot squawked and whistled. Thalia's hand held one of the bars, and we looked at each other with this iron barrier between us. Her gaze was level, and I clenched my fists tight by my sides. I wasn't going to be weird or cry or ask her one more thing. She wouldn't like me to be moist-eyed and have feelings at her.

I pressed the button to make the elevator doors open, and as I stepped in, I tried to make a joke. "Gand said all along that the cases weren't truly connected. That bad people do bad things, and any number of people could have had their separate reasons. I'm tired of him being correct. Or correct-adjacent, anyway."

That made her chuckle. "Give him the win. He needs it. Your brother is the angriest man I've ever met."

That surprised me, and then I wished I did know if he had ever been here, trying to warm this whole, cold room. That wasn't my business, though. I held the elevator doors open and said, "You have Gand all wrong. He's the most peaceful person in the universe. All he does is eat fruit and say om and sniff at daisies like Ferdinand the Bull."

She fixed me with an eye as piercing and impersonal as Pierre's. "Penny. No one who has inner peace needs that much yoga."

She said it as if yoga was rage-medicine. If that was so, then he was on a heavy dose. I let the elevator doors slide closed between us then. I pushed the button for the lobby and wrapped my arms around myself as the elevator started moving. I was remembering the way Gand grabbed me when we fought. How hard he had to work after to re-create serenity.

I knew that I was going down, but the movement felt reversed, as if I had been deep underwater, and now I was full of air and rising. In Thalia's world, I was only foam or flotsam, but I had been allowed to come close and look down into it. She had let me because she needed someone to bear witness. Now that was done and she had let me go. I left Thalia deep under, down in the murky world that she inhabited. She wouldn't keep me with her there, and that was mercy. I didn't know how to breathe in the places where she lived.

I remembered Nix in her pink bathing suit framed against the dark expanse of the stingray's wings. It had been so near, but invisible, buried. I counted as core memory the way it rippled the sand off itself, how the force of its muscular body sloshed us upward. I thought that now I would break some surface and be back inside my life, but even as I was rising, her last words felt like anchors. Not on me. As I floated free of her world, I realized that Gand, my sweet-hearted brother, was still all the way down there, in the dark, alone. He had been hiding in those black depths all along.

26

I found Gand sitting on the built-in bench at the kitchen table, eating a huge plate of scrambled tofu. Maybe he was protein-loading before setting off on some night ramble, but he was here now, where he belonged.

I wasn't crying. I'd cried myself out on the drive home. He took one look at my swollen eyes and red nose and said, "Hey. What's up? Are you okay?"

I plopped right down on the bench and scooted over until I could tuck my face against his shoulder. "I'm going to be. Hard days. I'm so glad you came home. I'm so glad." He swapped his fork to his left hand so he could put an arm around me. "Where's everybody?"

He regarded me with bland kindness, as if I wasn't some storm that had driven him away multiple times, as if I wasn't a whole new hurricane bearing down on him even now. "Mom and Dad lost rock, paper, scissors, so they took Shads and Jeff to see that anime movie she's been so het up about. *Ninety Minutes of Pure Hell but You Get Popcorn,* I think it's called. The dogs are in the back."

I was glad. I had to talk to him, alone, and there was no place on the planet that felt safer than this wide-plank table. Here, we'd eaten pounds of mac and cheese and slipped our broccoli under for the inevitable dogs. We'd done best-worsts here, Garrett and Nicolette and Penelope, each of us sharing our nicest moment and our hardest one over tuna casserole or ham and creamed corn. Shadow had been introduced to solids on this pitted wooden surface, kicking her feet in a hand-me-down bounce chair.

I wasn't sure how to start, and I felt sorry already. I leaned my head against his shoulder. "I should have made the pancakes." He looked down at me, puzzled. "For you and that chick. Polly. Or whatever."

He chuckled. "Next time."

That pulled me off my inexorable course for a moment. "Are you saying there will be a next time? With her?" I wanted exactly no one I loved anywhere near Thalia's perilous orbit. If Gand had her number, he needed to lose it. A whisper-sly voice inside me, Nix's night voice, said, *Right after he gives it to you. Just in case.* I had no answer to my own immediate follow-up question: *In case of what?* "Do you have some way to contact her?"

He said, "I'm not going to." Which didn't mean he couldn't. He squinted up into some far horizon that apparently existed in the ceiling. "Polly and I had a moment. We were both fully present, but it was only a moment, after all. It meant something different to each of us, but if you think about it, that's true of every moment shared with another human."

I peered up at his eyes. "Gand. I need to talk to you. Are you high, because that was very Yoga Yoda."

"No. In a mood, I guess." He forked up another bite of his scramble, and I pinched a stolen bite off his plate. It needed garlic. "I'll see her again if I see her again. If it's fated." I made a tiny noise that might have been a snort. Thalia was a fate factory; she left as little as she could to chance. Gand bumped me off his shoulder, affectionately. "Penny, don't be a cynic. The pants that come with it don't fit you. All I mean is, Polly's a free spirit. Like me."

Like him. That was truer than he understood, and I wondered if I should let it all go. He hadn't, though. I couldn't because he couldn't. Thalia called him the angriest man she'd ever met, and through her lens, I saw my brother clearly.

I told him, "You were right. Bowery's and Castillo's deaths were not related. I couldn't believe that, especially since Castillo died right before the anniversary. The timing wasn't a coincidence, Gand, was it." It was phrased like a question, but I said it like a fact.

He set his fork down and said my name, "Penny," in a warning tone.

"You knew the person who killed Castillo had exactly nothing to do with Bowery's death. You knew it better than anyone."

His shook his head in a small, vibrating no, as if every word I said was hurting him. Delilah said cop gut took years, but she also said I had good instincts, and I knew what I knew. Castillo's death had been the sticking point for Gand, every damn time I'd said that the killings were related. He'd negated my theories, absolved Thalia, and he'd been absolute about it.

Now he wanted me to stop, but I couldn't. I put my hand over his, hoping he would feel acceptance in my grip. "When I called to tell you that Castillo had been killed, you seemed so surprised." He'd set the phone down and run away and vomited. I'd thought he was disgusted with me because I said I wished I'd done it. That wasn't it. That wasn't it at all.

"I was surprised. I didn't *know* that he was dead until you called me." His hand gripped mine back, so tight that I was losing circulation. His serenity was cracking, and Thalia had been right when she said the answer was in my questions. He saw my understanding, and his fingers flexed and spasmed. It was as if a chasm had opened under him, and he was holding on so hard it hurt me. I saw the face of a man who was afraid of falling, and who already had. "I didn't mean it."

I leaned in and pressed my forehead into his trembling shoulder. "Oh, Gand. What happened?"

He bent to me, hiding his face in my hair. I could feel his tears. I didn't think he would say anything, but maybe it was easier when he couldn't see my face. He started talking, quiet and fast, his words coming all in a tumble. This was a real confession, as if we were on separate sides of a black booth. He wasn't really talking to me, his sister. His words were more like prayer, mumbled and agonized, hard to hear. I lost words, whole sentences even. I tried to piece it together as the story erupted out of him like a poison he had swallowed.

We knew he was coming to be with us on the anniversary of Nix's death. We didn't know he slipped into Atlanta a couple of days early.

He wasn't being sneaky. He did this when he came off the road sometimes, he said, to reset himself to a domesticated animal. He had to find his way back to being a dad, a brother, a son. I hadn't known that. I wondered, *How wild is he, if the Gand I know is a tamped-down version?*

He'd been driving for almost twenty hours, and he'd microdosed peyote halfway through to liven up the drive and stay awake. It was stronger than he had thought. Ten hours later, he was still flying, so he decided to stay up. He took a larger dose, then parked his skoolie in a pay-lot and caught an Uber to a three-story Buckhead bar that had a DJ spinning endless dubstep in the basement. Gand wanted to see the music, move his body, let the bass-heavy, relentless rhythm get him out of his head. He wanted to be one with all the colors of the world before he had to sit with us in our shared loss.

That was when he saw Xav Castillo on the dance floor. The bar was close to Castillo's home. Perhaps Gand chose it for that reason. Subconsciously. I felt a faint ping of surprise to know my brother, who gave me such crap about my cyberstalking, knew exactly where Castillo lived. At first, Gand thought he was hallucinating. The anniversary was weighing on him, and Xav was spotlighted in a beam of crimson, frat-boy dancing like an asshole in three-dimensional sharp Technicolor, while the people around him were rendered as vague shapes and shadows. That made Xav seem unreal. So did the music, though. So did my brother's own feet.

Then he thought perhaps the universe had honored his fury by bringing Xav to him. Remembering this now, Gand's body trembled, and he burned hot. I could feel his rage roiling through him, battering at his bones from the inside. I said his name, but I don't think he heard me. When he could speak again, he told me, "Xav left. I followed him."

I thought Xav might have seemed "unreal" because he was never there. Gand probably followed a hallucination to the actual house. The Xav he saw, after all, had a black ribbon of light trailing behind him, making him very easy to track. Once home, Xav opened his front door and left it standing wide, like an invitation. Yellow light spilled across the green grass, and Gand heard Xav call into the night, "Bitch, I know you're out there. Come on in, let's get this done."

I thought then, *Thalia! She was already in contact with the group, infiltrating. Maybe threatening, by then. Castillo must have thought it was Thalia banging around outside his house.*

Gand went in, kicking the door shut behind him. Castillo had a baseball bat in his hands, and he was standing by a dog crate.

Xav asked, "Did she send you?" I knew Castillo meant Thalia, but Gand thought he meant Nix, and nodded. Castillo said, "Take another step, I'll let Betsy out. My dog'll rip your throat open. So you better talk. Where is she?"

He swung the bat a little. His dog began barking, looking like holy murder, but her protective woofs were hardly more than breathy puffs. Gand realized Xav had debarked her. It enraged my brother to see this upset dog in a crate with her voice taken away. It seemed to him then that the dog's soft fury became a bass beat that sounded out our sister's name, barking it over and over: *Nix. Nix. Nix.*

Gand wondered then if Nix *had* sent him, and set this rhythm, and summoned the swirling lights that he saw spinning through the room. When he went toward Castillo, it felt like a dance. Gand knew exactly where to step, how to dip, how to slip sideways while Castillo fumbled the cage latch. Gand plucked the bat right out of his hands, so easy, like picking a flower. As he lifted up the bat, it seemed to him that he held the thick stem of a huge poppy. Then he brought it down, and in the electric crack and shatter of first contact, Castillo's head became the bloom at the end, spilling wild red. Gand felt himself slowing, felt everything slowing. Castillo's body drifted down and settled, leaking color.

The dog went quiet, and Gand saw that she was scared. She was in the back of her crate, cowering, not even able to make her sad version of a bark. He felt so bad then.

"I stood over his crumpled body, crying because I'd terrorized this poor, mutilated dog. I thought, *What would Dad say?*" Gand stopped talking then. It was silent between us for what might have been one minute or ten. Finally he leaned back, so I could see his face. He'd stopped crying, but his eyes were agony. "That called me to myself. I looked down at him, and he was so still."

I wrapped my arms around him again, and I held him so tight. He was a big, solid man, my brother, but he felt so strangely frail then. He didn't want to know that I was glad, and so I didn't tell him. I wished I could tell Thalia.

"I didn't know for sure that he was dead. I wasn't sure if the red I saw was blood or light or— I was messed up. I should have called an ambulance. I didn't. I must have walked back to the skoolie. I don't remember. When I came to myself, I was at the Mouse Landing campsite. I didn't even know what day it was. I stayed there, not thinking, trying to simply *be*, moment to moment, until you called and told me he was dead. I didn't think that I'd ever come back after that. How could I be around Shadow when I—" He pulled back to look at me again, his voice still husky and so raw. "I only came because she was in so much trouble. She deserves a better father. She deserves—"

I had to be cruel now, but only to be kind. I turned my laser eyes onto my brother. "Well, too bad. You're the dad she got. She's half you, and she's all good, so you aren't allowed to hate yourself. As for what happened? Well. It happened. I'm not sorry."

He shook his head, his face crumpling in on itself, "I'm a killer. I'm scared to be around her. Around any of you."

I grabbed his shoulders and I shook him. It was like shaking a tree, he was so strong and solid, but he bent to me as if I was a wind.

"I'm not scared of you, you idiot. She's not either. No one who loves you has ever been scared of you for a second." Those words were a relief, I saw it, but I could not stop there. If what I had to say next was harsh, too bad, because this wasn't all about him, and he had to know. "You aren't that moment, Gand. You are more than that. I can forgive that moment, anyone with blood and heart and feelings could, but Gand, hear me. I won't forgive you, no one will, no god, no man, no institution, no philosopher or king will forgive you if you use this one night when you lost control as an excuse to abandon your kid."

It was harsh, but it landed. I saw it land even as he pulled back from me and straightened. I let him go, and he lifted his hands, palm up, then folded his middle fingers under his thumbs. He breathed in deep and long and slow, through his nose. His lips moved faintly, counting, on the exhale.

I remembered Thalia saying, *No one who has inner peace needs to do that much yoga.* She had him dead to rights, but what I saw now was a hurt man calling outer peace for his child's sake. He put his rage and guilt away like I might put socks into a drawer, then closed it up. In a dozen measured breaths, less than a minute, his forehead was as smooth and untroubled as a lake top on a windless day.

I sat with him, matching my breath to his. Not for me. For him. I don't know how long we did this, but it was enough that we both heard the automatic garage door start to scroll up. Shadow and my parents had come home.

His eyes opened. He looked at his hands and told me, "Shunya Mudra. It helps me empty out." He deliberately released the shape and stood up in one smooth, fluid movement. "I need to go."

"Gand—" I started, but he held a hand up.

"Just to my skoolie. I won't leave town. Shadow shouldn't see me this way." He had a point. For all his calm, his eyes were swollen and so haunted.

"Okay." We heard Shadow laughing as they came inside. "We'll talk later."

As he slipped out the back door, he told me, "No, we won't. Not ever."

He meant it. I looked through the window, but the kitchen light was on, and my brother had disappeared into the darkness. I scooted over into his place on the bench. It still felt warm, an illusion or a consequence of his jacked metabolism. I let Nix's voice unspool a sentence in my head: *Our gentle giant of a brother is a killer.*

I sat with that. He had done the thing I'd both wished to do and wanted to happen, but I mourned for him because it was wrong, and he hated it. It had rendered him so lonely. As lonely as I was. I made the hand shape he had shown me, the something-something mudra, and I closed my eyes and breathed the way he had. It didn't do a damn thing, as far as I could tell. I heard Shadow and Mom and Dad moving through the house, their bright voices overlapping. Shadow sounded so happy, and this was better than any hand shape I could make.

I dropped my hands, wishing for a way to contact Thalia. I wanted to say it to her as well: *I'm not scared of you.* My brother was done with the conversation, but hearing those words had helped him. Maybe Thalia needed to hear them, too. I'd never had to tell Nix, even though she was like them, full of storms. Nix knew. I wanted to tell Thalia, *Things like you need things like me.* I wanted to say it exactly like that. Things. Not people. Because we all had a little monster in us, me and Gand and Thalia, and we were all so lonely.

I sat in my brother's place on the bench, listening to my family heading up the stairs with no idea that I was in the kitchen. I let them go, and then I ate Gand's dead-cold tofu scramble, every bite.

27

It was the last of Thalia's three days, and we were down to the last of our three men. I got up late, my sleep cycle still reversed, pulling on sweatpants instead of bothering with clothes. I stayed holed up at home, reading a novel with zero comprehension, then messing up a fraisier cake so badly I had to dump it out. I stayed strictly off my phone. Even when I got on my laptop to draft my resignation letter for the Kennesaw PD, I disconnected from the wi-fi.

As the hours crawled past and the sun began to sink, my whole body became a held breath. I wondered if Banks felt the approach of darkness right along with me. He'd have to give Thalia the name and information that she wanted, or she would—what? Keep his money? Bury it? Bury him? If it went poorly, I might know when someone found a body. His or hers. If it went well, I'd never know. I had to accept that, and release it, and find a path back to being steadfast Penny Albright, a nice girl from Kennesaw who missed her twin. Then I could figure out if I was a chef or something else and whether Michael fit inside that life.

At that thought, I finally broke and went to get my phone out of the bedroom. He'd texted me every hour or so:

Penny, can we talk? Then, Maybe this went too fast. Did I press too hard? We can dial back. Then, Call me. Finally, I lost your whole family once. I don't want that again. Over a kiss. Reach out, okay?

I wasn't being fair to him. I flopped onto the orange love seat and texted back: I'm overwhelmed, not ghosting you. Let's get together next week. How's Tuesday? Instantly, he thumbs that up.

Phone in hand, I found it impossible to not do the thing I'd been avoiding. I opened Kaitlin's socials. Her internet silence had been due to an unplugged beach retreat with her bridesmaids in El Salvador. There was a freshly posted gallery of gorgeous black sand beaches, surfing wipeouts, and fancy cocktails. Nothing about her fiancé disappearing or being dead. I closed the app, then played the video I'd taken of Jordan Banks and his side chick while I was squatting in his bushes. The audio was plenty clear.

As part of letting go, I decided that if Banks survived this final night, I'd send this video to Kaitlin. Not to hurt Banks—that was Karma's job—but because I was a girl's girl, and Kaitlin deserved to know what she was getting. She might be another Beth Wyland, broken enough to pick this bad man anyway, but at least she wouldn't do it blind.

Another text landed from Michael:

Call me anyway? I had an idea. About how to find her.

I was tempted, in spite of all my resolutions. A Karma-fueled, enormous "it" was unfolding. I rightfully owned a share, yet here I sat, letting fate unspool. Could Michael's idea predict where Thalia would be tonight? I had the right training to be a useful backup for her.

I nipped that budding thought off at the root. I'd promised to stay out of her way. This was what she wanted.

It was an act of will to text back, Slammed. Tomorrow, okay?

Another text landed, but I turned off the vibration and stuffed the phone in my back pocket. I needed to be busy now, or at least not alone. I took a quick shower and got dressed for comfort in black leggings and Nix's old gray T-shirt with a tiger on it, and then I went outside in search of Shadow. As I came down the stairs, my brother emerged from his skoolie with a full recycling tub.

I'd planned to give him space, but he looked so relieved to see me. He called, "Want to help me with spring cleaning?"

"Sure," I said. He took the tub to the curb and set it down by two green biodegradable bags. Two was a lot for him. "That's all trash?"

"Yeah," he said, making his careful, barefoot way back toward me. "I'm moving out of the Shred Shed." He paused midlawn to take a bow, his serenity firmly in place. I tried not to do a big, fat cartoon double take at this, but I failed when he added, "I might sell it." I walked out to meet him on the grass. He tilted his head toward Mrs. Blanchard's house, and I saw she was sitting out on her porch under her bug zapper, tallying our trash with baleful eyes. "Except selling it might make her too happy. I should turn it into an Airbnb. That'll give her apoplexy, and me more income, and the whole family can still use it for camping. Win-win-win."

"Gand! Stop blathering and tell me where you're moving," I demanded, scared he would answer Budapest or Bali, anywhere a half a world away from a sister who knew all his secrets.

Instead, he told me, "Inside. Home. Back to my old bedroom." He lifted one shoulder, and I saw the barest flash of the brother I'd met earlier, eaten up by rage and guilt, seeking a path. "Come help me with these boxes." We went to the skoolie together. He braced the door open, revealing a chaos of open drawers and crates and Mom's wicker laundry baskets piled with his clothes. "Shadow goes to college in less than three years. That's a blink. With all that's happened recently . . ." He stopped there. Shrugged. "Life is fast. And finite. You made me face that I've been dealing with my shit all wrong. You know how I'm always telling you weights are better than cardio? Yeah. Time to stop running and lift."

He went in to grab another full recycling tub, tilting it so I could see it held books. I could make out the top title, white on a dark cover: *Radical Self-Acceptance: How to Forgive Yourself and Abdicate External Validation*. Yesterday, I would have snapped back that the last thing Gand needed was advice on how to hold himself *less* accountable, but that was yesterday.

"I also have to own my choices," he said. I dearly hoped he wasn't saying he was going to get confessional and stupid. I'd learned enough about our judicial system at school and on the force to know I didn't want him in it. He clarified, "If I'd chosen to be around, Shadow probably wouldn't have gotten suspen— Oof!"

His voice cut out because I'd launched myself at him, hugging him so tight from the side, while he struggled not to drop his box of books. "You're good," I told him. He'd given those words to me over and over, and now I gave them back. "Your heart is so good." That made him shift the tub and squeeze me so tight I couldn't say anything but "Oof" back.

As we broke apart, I saw a sleek, black Lexus had pulled up to the curb while we'd been preoccupied. I recognized it even before Michael got out, looking harried, and anxious, and apologetic, which was a lot of things to look like all at once. Especially for him, Lord Stoic of Poker Face. I muttered a guilty cuss under my breath.

He came right over to us, taking in the boxes. "Hey. You're, what, moving?"

"Not far," Gand said, jerking a thumb at the main house. "My kid needs me to stick closer."

Michael was distracted, but he took a moment to thump Gand on the arm. I felt instantly guiltier. Michael, too, must have this sense of huge beasts moving way down deep under us, pushing and surging, but unseen. At least I knew the whole story. He told my brother, "Look at you, ready to throw down a root."

"Just one," Gand said. "I only wish I didn't have a sister who gloats like the devil when she's right." He waggled his eyebrows at me, smiling. "You might want to look away from her, it's very unattractive."

"It's great," Michael said. "Not about the gloating sister, the coming home thing. Great."

I found myself measuring these two men. I'd thought of Gand as open, but no, the wrecked man I had seen in the kitchen had been hidden under serenity all along. Michael was a screwed-shut person, but he knew how to fit himself into my family, and he felt welcome here. He'd lost more than a partner when Nix broke up with him. Gand had lost us, too, deliberately. I wanted to fix all of it, fix all of us.

Michael turned to me. "Can we talk?"

He meant alone. Gand got that. "Good to see you, Michael. I better keep at it."

We left Gand to his boxes and went back upstairs. As Michael followed me inside, I tried to think of something I could tell him. Not that Thalia was Clio. Not what Gand had done. It was all connected. I didn't see how I could give him any piece of it.

As soon as the door shut behind us, I said, "You're going to have to trust me." A big ask, but Delilah had done it. Surely he had as much faith in me as she did. "All I can tell you is, it's almost over. We have to stay out of it."

He took three or four pacing steps past me and promptly ran out of apartment. "You found her. That's why you went quiet. You don't need my help."

"Don't take it like that," I said. "It's hard for me to let it go, too. I'm not avoiding you, I promise. If you want, we could order pizza. Watch a movie. We can let it go, together." I wasn't sure what "it" I meant, exactly. Thalia, or Nix? Michael believed we'd never love another person like the one we'd both lost. Maybe so, but loving each other just a little in the embers felt too bleak. Then I knew something I could tell Michael, and it might even help. "It was never about Nix."

He sat down heavily on my orange love seat and buried his face in his hands, then shoved them back across his close-cropped hair. "You talked to her?" he asked. When he looked up at me, I saw faint purple circles etched under his eyes. He took my silence as an answer. "Yeah. You talked to her. Where? How? Did you get a phone number or an address? We could—"

"Michael," I interrupted. "Let it go."

He stood up again abruptly. "Easy for you to say." It wasn't, and he saw this truth in my expression. "Easier," he amended. "You got some kind of closure. I can smell it on you, Penny. I smell *her* on you."

"Michael!" I said, more harshly. "Come on."

He wheeled, wanting again to pace, again finding no room, and so he came close and stared right down into my face. "How can you not trust me? I need this. Who is she? Where is she?" I swallowed and he leaned down. "You know where she is." His face was stone but his eyes burned. "I need to talk to her. Once. Just once. Tell me where she is. Take me to her."

"You're scaring me," I said. He was, a little.

He ran his hands over his hair again. "Sorry. Sorry." His pale face twisted with raw emotion. "I think about Nix dying, Pen. I think about it all the time. I dream it. It's like I'm there. I can see her in that bathroom stall, fading, lying on the tile. Scared and cold. Can you not understand that?" I could. The picture he painted already lived behind my eyes and haunted my dreams, too. "The music pounding, the darkness, everyone too high or drunk or busy to see a girl in trouble. I have to know." He was getting to me. I felt myself waver. I'd never give anyone Thalia's address, but Gand might have a number. I could call, ask her to tell Michael enough for him to find some peace. He saw me softening and leaned in. "I wonder if Nix said my name or thought of me at all. I was still in love with her, you know. She didn't love me back. Not the way I wanted. But I loved her. I love her, and it kills me to think that she might have known that she was dying, might have said my name. In my dreams, I see her brightness fading, see her feeling like a ghost already. Wishing for someone, anyone—for you, probably. Not me. She never loved me the way I—"

Michael was still talking, but it devolved into a babble of words and wind.

Nix said that . . . *feel like a ghost already*. I'd picked those words out of her final message, mostly lost under the relentless bass. How could Michael possibly say them to me now? So exactly? I'd never told him about that message, much less let him listen to it. That shame—I wasn't there, I failed her—that was mine alone.

Michael's voice sloshed and swirled like a distant tide. I talked over him, way too loud, "You can't know that." But he did. "How do you know that?"

He misunderstood the question. "She told me. The last time I saw her. She was rallying, talking about going back to school. I asked her to come back to me, too, but she said she didn't feel that way about me. She said—"

"No," I interrupted. Or maybe I was finishing his sentence, because Nix would never have put my plain brown boots back on. "How. Do. You. Know."

Nix's voice answered, ringing through my skull even louder than my baffled panic: *He heard me say them, Penny. I wasn't alone when I died. He was right there.* The very air around me felt compressed, gone thick and liquid. I remembered how her phone clicked off, midmessage. *Penny, he knows damn well I said his name.* She had said it. The missing parts of her message were filling in for me. . . . *cold and bad, Pen . . . I'm scared of my . . .* I'm scared of Michael.

I said, "You were there. You could have saved her." He didn't. He hadn't. Because she told him, *No.*

"Well, shit," he said, and with an almost audible click, all the emotion he was spilling onto me turned itself off. "What did I say wrong?"

Ideas and images were falling into place in my mind. No, not falling into place so much as raining down on me, coalescing and then rising in a river that could whirl me deep and drown me. Which way was up? Where was the air?

Three men. The one with the connections. Dead. The one with the infrastructure. Dead. Only the money guy left standing. Thalia and I had talked about them—*Let's say there were three assholes who met in college and got into the habit of doing shady shit together*—but had I ever said his name out loud? Had I ever said, *What are you going to do to Jordan Banks?*

She'd been so cautious, searching me, turning my phone all the way off, speaking in hypotheticals. I'd assumed Banks was her third because he was mine, because he was part of the trio who hurt Nix, but Thalia never knew my twin. Her mission had never been about Nix, and anyway, who moves a bird worth two million dollars and then buys a Mazda? Banks had always been the least of them. Castillo and Bowery graduated two years ahead of him and then moved to the swankiest parts of Atlanta, while Banks was a suburban guy with a middle-class job.

Her prey had never been Banks. Not ever. But I'd touched something—someone—Thalia Gray considered to be *her stuff*, and she'd absconded with my brother and touched the hell out of him. What—who—was *her stuff*?

I didn't want to ask these questions, but I could not stop the answers whirlpooling around me. In her glaring white loft, I'd said to her, *You were watching him, and maybe you were about to move on him, and there I was*. I'd meant Banks, but she'd also found me having a quiet wine-soaked dinner at Tasca. I'd said, *Me showing up, it was a problem for you. You didn't expect me*. I'd meant out at Banks's house, but Thalia meant she hadn't expected to see me with Michael.

Michael Sullivan, with his Lexus and his Beltline townhome. Michael, who lived large and urban, exactly like Bowery and Castillo, with the right car, the right address, the right scuffed boots, but needing more, always more, because no right he had was ever right enough for his family. This same Michael told me—oh. He must think himself so fucking clever!—that the men I hated didn't have the brains or the stealth or even the organizational skills to run a decent criminal enterprise. He did, though. He sure as hell did.

"God, Michael, was it always you? Even back in college?" My voice was a strangled whisper.

"Of course not." He was lying. One side of his mouth quirked up. Some horrifying part of him was glad I knew this, even proud. He wanted someone to see how smart he'd been.

I said, "It *was* you. Always. The drugs, now the birds, and God knows what else. How could you? How could you keep on working with them, after what they did to Nix?"

I didn't need him to answer, though. I wasn't stupid, I was only exactly that naive. Delilah and the academy had trained me to clock details, and even before that, I was a girl who paid attention. I listened so well, I heard the people who mattered talking even when I was alone. My twin's voice, most of all, then my mother's, but in recent days, I'd added a new one. It was Thalia's smoky voice that I heard now. Not a quote. Not a memory. She talked into my head as if she were with me, too:

Remember how the world is, ex–Officer Albright. Remember the cold deeps that Nix could always see. You know how bad people can be. The two dead men were his creatures. You think it's chance that they got Nix alone and hurt her? Right after she broke up with Michael?

He hadn't answered, but Thalia had done it for him. My chest felt so squeezed shut and airless, but I pushed words at him anyway. "You told them to. Because she dumped you. You say you loved her? You never loved her. You must have hated her. So hard."

Of all the things in play, this was the one that he could not let stand. "No. No. I love her. I never stopped. Not ever, Pen." My stomach clenched. "Yeah, she needed to get hurt, a little. I was hurt, after all. I wanted her knocked down enough to understand she needed me. I never thought she'd crawl off to Savannah."

The world telescoped, and all I saw now was his hateful face, shiny with sweat but still somehow cold as stone. He'd sicced them on her, his pack of awful dog-boys. "You wanted them to break her, so that you could pick up all the pieces like a hero. You thought that you could put her back together, and then keep her. But she didn't want your rescue. She wouldn't have you, even then."

Anger clung to his face and curdled. "She told me no. I came for her even though she was a fucked-up dropout, drunk and high all the damn time, looked like hell, and she still told me no."

I was tumbled and drowning in a sea of understanding. I hated it. I could taste salt and bile in the back of my throat. There was only one question left, and I didn't want to ask it. It would push me down so deep and cold, I might never see the sun again.

I couldn't ask, but I already knew. I couldn't stop myself from knowing. "Gand said that back in college, it was more than pot and mushrooms. You and your pack of assholes could get Molly, acid, pills. You gave it to her, didn't you? The fentanyl. You dosed her, you were with her on the night she died, and you gave her the laced drugs on purpose—" I could see it in his face, how right I was. His cold control had finally, truly slipped. "She told you she was never going to love you back. She was scared of you. She called me." His face twisted into deeper anger. He'd been right there, still ready to save her if she picked him, if she begged him, and still she'd turned to me. "You were in the stall with her. You took the phone out of her hands. You hung it up. That was you."

The revelation felt so loud, so sudden, but nothing was as sudden as his movement. He went past me, and I thought, *He's running. Yes. He has to run.* But I was still being naive. He didn't go. He had no intention of running. He only put himself between me and the door.

"Well, shit," he repeated. How could blue eyes go so grim-dark, be so cold. "I hoped it wouldn't come to this. I really did. You are so much more like her than I ever knew."

His big body stood between me and the door. I was utterly alone with him. I put my hands up, like a frail, small wall between us. I saw no way around him, no way out. I heard Thalia talking, far and faint, trickling to me under the roaring of my fear . . . *small and female . . . you can never, ever lose . . . go for a fast, definitive victory . . . bring a knife to a fistfight.* I wished then I'd taken Thalia's box cutter with its flecks of Bowery's blood still in the hinges. In the kitchen, I had chef's knives, sharp and deadly. My cleaver was out on the counter, even. I took one sidling step toward it, my hands still up as if I was surrendering. Three steps to go. I had to get to it.

That was when he put his hand into his jacket pocket, and he took out the gun.

28

We went down the stairs together, me first. I could feel the gun at my back. The suppressor he'd screwed over the barrel made it feel as wide as a fist pressing my kidney.

"Michael," I said. "This won't—"

"Shut up," he said, right into my ear. "Don't make me kill him."

He meant Gand. My brother was carrying another box into the house as we came down. He paused to watch us descend. "Hey. Shads went to Jeff's, and Mom and Dad are having date night. You guys want to go to Slutty Vegan? I'm craving fries."

I tried to make my face look normal. I tried to make my voice not tremble or squeak. "Oh, we already made plans." It wasn't great.

"What's wrong, Pen?" my brother said, eyebrows resetting into mild concern.

"Not a thing. Just, it's been a hard couple of days." That rang true. I bulled forward. "Michael and I need to talk."

Gand moved hesitantly out of the way, and I felt the pressure on my back ease as Michael dropped his hand to his side, using his body to shield the gun from Gand as we passed. If there was a moment to escape him, that was it. I'd been taught what to do. I'd practiced it with other trainees at the academy. Control the gun. Hit him hard and low. My whole body tensed, every muscle I owned screaming to make a move. At the same time, Delilah's voice sounded in my head, helping me think like a cop: *He didn't kill you upstairs because he still hopes to get away with it. He needs you to take him to Thalia; you have time, and if you move on him here, he could shoot your brother. He's that pressed.*

As we walked toward the car, Michael let me get ahead, shifting the gun to my back again, keeping his body between the weapon and my brother's view.

"See you later," Michael called over his shoulder, hearty and regular. Then to me, "Don't look back. You're going to drive." We stepped off the curb, moving around the trunk. "You're going to take me to her."

"Like hell," I said, barely louder than a whisper.

At the selfsame moment, my brother said, "What her? What's going on? Michael? Jesus. Is that a gun?"

Gand had followed us, stepping silently in our wake. Michael was a great liar, but I wasn't. I hadn't fooled my empathetic brother.

Michael shifted, turning the gun on Gand. I could tell by the way he handled it that he knew what he was doing. Gand eyeballed him, hackles up, having visible ideas. My brother had two inches and twenty pounds of muscle on Michael, and he was fast.

"You so much as blink at me, I'll shoot. First you, then your sister." Michael spoke with so little tone it froze my marrow. He had the gun trained on Gand's center mass, and all he had to do was squeeze. "Let me think." We all froze for two fraught seconds, and then Michael said, "Nope. There's no way out."

He shot my brother. He shot him twice, in his chest and in his gut. I knew it before I heard it. I heard it before I saw blood blooming red on Gand's bamboo T-shirt.

The world went slow. All I could think was, *Thalia's right. No way to truly silence a gunshot*. It was exactly as she had described it, a sound like thin ice cracking.

Gand was so surprised. His breath came out. He bent around the bullets, and then he spun and took one small step away from us. He fell so very slowly, first to one knee, and then he folded like he was moving into child's pose. His face pressed into the grass. Behind the tall fence, Brandy and Timbo started baying, their ruckus punctuated by the sharp, high barks of a Boston terrier going nuts.

I sucked in breath, and Michael said, "You scream, I put the next one in his head." I saw his foot move. He was alive. The air came out of me then, all of it, with zero voice behind it. Michael sounded calm, but his nostrils flared and his eye whites showed all the way around the deep blue irises "Penny. I need to think. I can't do it with you hissing at me like a cornered possum." He spoke with such soft reason. His face shone pale in the moonlight, gone shiny in a slick of instant sweat. I started toward my brother, and Michael's free hand closed in a blood-stopping grip around my arm. "Get in the car, or I'll keep shooting him."

He pulled me around the trunk, out onto the road. I let him, all my attention turned on Gand. I thought I heard him moan, which meant he was still breathing. I opened the driver's-side door, and as I got in, we both heard a frail old voice, querulous and insistent, calling over the dogs. "Are you doing fireworks? It's illegal to do fireworks." Mrs. Blanchard had heard the blunted shots and come down from her yard. She was right across the street.

"Move over," Michael told me tersely.

I scrambled over the gearshift into the passenger seat. I wanted to go. Now. No other neighbors had come to their doors to see if they'd heard fireworks or a car backfiring. They might not have even heard the retorts over their televisions. Once the car moved, Mrs. Blanchard would see my brother, folded in our too long grass with so much blood coming out of him. She'd call 911. My mother's neighborhood nemesis was now the best hope I had.

She hustled across the road. "Penny Albright! I know you hear me!"

Some real and very regular Penny part of me was irked, thinking, *How can she be so stupid? It isn't the Fourth of July. It isn't New Year's.* A colder, cop-trained bit of me thought, *If he shoots her, too, who will help Gand?* I was bisected neatly down the middle, both in the world where my family played at war with Mrs. Blanchard, and Thalia's world, where war was real and personal and deadly.

I tried to catch her eye, but Michael's body blocked me as he got in.

He slammed the door, and I said, "Stop before you do a thing that can't be taken back. You haven't killed anyone. Yet." He had, though. He'd killed Nix. We both knew it.

"I need my money. That bitch you're hiding has it." He pressed the button, and the Lexus's engine purred to quiet life.

Too late. Mrs. Blanchard moved in front of his car, blocking us, holding up her phone and peering in the windshield, scolding loudly enough for us to hear her through the glass. "Is that you, Michael Sullivan? I see that you have not matured a bit. You can't do fireworks here." She put a hand on her hip, her scrawny elbow jutting like a bird's wing. If Gand was moaning, she didn't hear him over the baying dogs. I wanted to call out to her, but there was nothing I could say. *Run?* She was a thousand years old. *Call the cops?* He'd shoot her.

Michael leaned forward, eyes narrowing. He yelled back, "Get out of my way."

Even now, no other neighbors emerged. Damn our older neighborhood, with its huge, wooded lots. Damn the dogs who barked like this every time the mailman came.

She waggled her phone at him like it was a trump card. "You are making me call the police!"

I said, "Michael. Please. No." Each word seemed to take every bit of my scant breath.

He had one hand on the wheel. The other held the gun down in his lap. I was so sure that he would shoot her.

He didn't, though. Instead, he put the car in drive and jammed the gas pedal hard down to the floor. I felt the double thunk as the wheels passed over her small, frail body. Front and back.

The Lexus was unfazed by this small barrier. So was Michael. He accelerated sleekly down my street, taking me away from her crushed form and Gand's crumpled one, taking me away into the dark.

29

Michael drove toward the front exit of my neighborhood, his face expressionless and tight. He'd tucked the gun under his thigh on the far side from me. A young couple who lived two blocks away were out walking their Sheltie, but they were going the wrong way to find my brother. It was full dark. We passed no one else on any sidewalk.

"You shot him," I said. My voice sounded so thick. "You ran her over."

"I didn't want to. They made me. You made me." He sounded flat, but the repetition told me he was panicking. Bad for me. Panicking people did dumb things, and I had to get help for Gand and Mrs. Blanchard.

"I'm sorry," I said. "Are you going to kill me?"

He honestly appeared to think it over. "I don't want to, Penny. Someone might have seen us, and we hit her." I hated that *us,* that *we,* but I didn't let the hate show on my face. He didn't see a way back from this. I didn't, either, and that made it hard to think, because it meant there was no way I'd survive. And Gand— Michael's cold voice froze my thinking. "She's all over my car." He swallowed, a loud, sick sound. "Forensics. Plus you know too much. And Gand—I'm fucked."

We were at a four-way intersection, and he came to a full stop, obeying the red sign like this was the law that mattered.

"If you let them die, if Gand dies, it gets worse," I said. "Let me call an ambulance. I'll send it right to my house. I won't say anything about you."

He flared his nostrils. "Give me your phone."

I did what he said, hoping he would make the call.

We were at the neighborhood's exit now, and he came to a full stop.

He hit the window button and threw my phone into the thick ivy that surrounded the Glenview Acres sign. I let out a short, sharp scream.

He said, "Shut up. I have burners in the glove box." He scrolled the window back up. "I'll call, if you take me to her. Now." I stared at him, uncomprehending. "The woman who killed Castillo and Bowery. The bitch with my cash. Your brother loses more blood, every minute, so, which way?"

I was talking before I understood I had decided. "Midtown. She lives in Midtown." It was too far. More than half an hour away. My brother was strong, but—

Michael interrupted my panicked thoughts. "I need an address."

I didn't believe that he would call, but if there was the slightest chance— "I don't remember it." He started to turn toward me, and I added, fast, "But I can find it. It's an ugly concrete building on the middle block of Bellway, near Tenth and North." What else could I do? I couldn't trust that the dogs would keep on making a ruckus until someone came, or that my brother had bothered to have his phone charged and on him for the first time in his life, or that he could somehow crawl all the way to the Phelpses. "Please call."

"He's fine," Michael said, snappish, like I was nagging him over some petty thing. "This is a .32, Pen. Small-caliber bullets, and Gand is strong. I'll call, once I'm sure you aren't lying."

He wouldn't. I was sitting by the man who had broken Nix to make her need him. He'd gone to Savannah, over and over, patient as a spider, hoping he'd ruined her just enough to make her cling to him. He'd stalked her at her lowest point, thinking she'd bend, but he'd underestimated her. She'd begun to forge her own way up, without him. I'd seen it. When she told him no, he dosed her, and he watched her die. A man who could do those things— He would let Gand die, and he'd kill me once I gave him Thalia. I knew it in my shuddering bones, and my body jacked into red panic.

I couldn't think or even move, now that I'd seen Michael plain. He was a reptile that had coiled its vile self around Nix's warmth. He'd come after mine because he felt her echo in it. It ruined me to remember that not two days ago, I'd found this sweet.

Remember Gand, Nix told me from inside my head. *And get your shit together.*

Her voice flickered my red fear into a rage. I understood my brother, then, because all I wanted was a baseball bat. Michael must have sensed it, because he plucked the gun from under his thigh and pointed it at me casually, across his lap. "I'm driving, so if you wreck us, who'll call 911?"

No one, Nix said, and Thalia echoed, *No one, whether you wreck this car or not.*

They were talking from the ceiling, and my heart stuttered and jerked so hard that I found myself hovering over the scene with them, dissociated. We all looked down at me, and from up here I could make such calm observations: *Oh, hrm, he won't help Gand. Oh, hey, I am being kidnapped.* I could also make my body speak. "Why do you want to go to her place?"

On my right, Nix whispered, *Good girl.* Thalia, to my left, said, *Yes. Get him talking.*

He still had the gun on me, pointed across his lap. "She has my money. She says she'll leave my cash where I can get it if I tell her what she wants to know, but that's bullshit. Why would she?"

I couldn't answer. I'd fallen back in my body, where there was a lot of urgency happening. My mind floundered and my stomach heaved. I tumbled in a whirl of fear and rage, and then I flickered back up to the ceiling of the car, watching my whole body shake and seize. I made it say, "So make a better deal. You must have a way to send her the information she wants. A number or an email. Use it to tell her she has to meet you, instead."

He shook his head. "Tried that. She texted back a video of her hand, feeding fifty thousand of my dollars into an ancient furnace. She'll start burning the rest at midnight, ten thousand every other minute. I need that money, Pen. I've lost both my partners to this bitch. It's going to take time and a lot of cash to get new connections in place." Did he think he could go back to his life? He must have heard how crazy he was sounding. When he spoke next, his tone was musing, like a man thinking out loud. "She's burned my whole life down, hasn't she? Shit. If she burns my cash, I can't escape this mess and make a good start elsewhere."

This mess was my brother, bleeding out in the yard, and Mrs. Blanchard, broken under his tires. This mess was me, a loose end who knew too much. I had to get down back into my body and find a way to fight him.

He angled his sleek car, exiting the highway. We slipped down this dark road, then that one, navigating one-way streets toward her place. He kept the speed limit. He stopped at red lights. His face was calm, but his hands gripped the wheel so hard the knuckles were white.

I asked Nix: *Is he going to kill me?* My twin snorted: *Of course, you dumbass.* Then Thalia, *Unless you get real smart, real quick.* Here, between them, I could calmly remember how Nix's loss had gutted Mom, how Dad had lost that sweet spark in his eye. What pulled them back was me and Gand and Shadow. It was too big a job for Shadow to do alone. That girl had already lost her bio-mom and Nix. *So I can't die here.* That was my own voice. Then I was back inside my heaving body, and I knew I had to stay, somehow, in the tumble of my red loathing and terror. I felt tears falling, unheeded. My heart was a rhythmless skitter, fast and high.

I shaped my fingers into Gand's dumb Mudra. I listened to my own, live breath. I did not disassociate again. I stuck. Maybe there was something to it.

Make him remember that he likes you, I told myself. He didn't, though. He liked remembering Nix. *Use that, then. Use anything. Make it about him.*

"You're smart, Michael." I sounded almost sweet. Nix, for all her fierceness, could be sweet, if she loved you. I said his name the way she used to, with her head tilt, her inflection. He glanced my way, and I made my face do one of her expressions. One eyebrow up, concerned but also daring him to rise above. "You could tell her what she wants to know. I think she'd give your cash back. She has enough money."

He almost smiled. "There's no such thing as enough money, Pen. She'll keep it. I have to take it back and handle her." Kill her, he meant. "She'll be my fourth." The fourth person he had killed, he meant, and I almost slipped out of myself again because I wondered if he was counting Gand. "They say it gets easier."

I didn't ask who they were, but god, I hoped that they were wrong. What he'd done at my house had come easily enough, and I was at his mercy. I pinched my fingers harder in the shape Gand said could empty me out and calm me.

"Michael," I said, so softly, as if it was a name I liked. "I know you care about my family." He didn't. He coveted them. "You care about me." He didn't. He only longed to own my sister's echo. "It's too much already to cover up, so letting Gand bleed out or killing me won't help you. You have to recalibrate. You need to get out of the country, right? You'll get your cash, and then what? Help me take care of you now."

He said, "Shut up, Penny, please," but his tone had gone weirdly friendly, and he tucked the gun back under his leg. We passed a gas station where two normal people were fueling up, blissfully ignorant of the evil that was passing by. "Good questions, though. Okay. The bitch wants one of my most important contacts. I bet he has no idea she's after him. What if I switch it? I can give her to him, you see?" I was trying to parse that. I started to ask a question, but he talked over me. "It's a good idea. Stay quiet or it's going to get bad for you. Understand?" I nodded, putting my hand over my own mouth. He reached across me to open the glove box and fished out a burner. He told it, "Okay, Google, call Monsieur—" And then he said a word that sounded like *ennui*. The French pronunciation. *Ahhh-nu-wee.*

He turned it on speaker, then set it on the dash in front of him. It rang four times, and with each ring, I felt Michael's body tense. His gaze kept sliding away from the road to me. I didn't like it. On the fifth ring, though, a man picked up. "Allô? Michel?"

My whole body went still. I knew the voice. It was as if Thalia's two-million-dollar bird had answered the phone.

Michael nodded to himself in a way that was almost rocking, and his voice came out all hearty, saying a word that sounded like, "Jher-vay."

I sat quiet and attentive as they talked, for all the good that did me. They spoke in French, of all damn things. Gand was the one who took French. Nix and I had taken Spanish. Michael kept saying that first word, *Jher-vay,* and I realized that it was a name. Gervais. He'd said the last name, too, a thing that sounded like Ennui. This was the man Thalia had been seeking. I repeated it to myself, over and over, so it couldn't slip away. *Jher-Vay Ah-nu-wee. Jher-Vay Ahh-nu-wee.*

A few minutes into the conversation, Michael straightened and began driving with more purpose. The set of his shoulders eased as they kept talking. Soon after that, they hung up, and he pocketed the burner.

We were past Tenth now, and he turned down Bellway. It was as I remembered, dark and narrow. We passed the lot where I'd parked, then the alley that led to the methadone clinic, deserted at this hour.

"Which building?" I pointed and his mouth compressed. "Bullshit. That's abandoned."

"No. I mean, yes. But not the top floor. It's a loft. She owns the whole building."

Michael cruised past, very slow, taking it in. "I can see this place having the kind of furnace I saw in her video. Maybe I believe you."

He kept going all the way to the corner, then turned. "We're going around the block. I didn't see cameras. No cameras? Is that front gate locked? Was there a buzzer?"

"Yes," I said. "Please, please call 911 now?" I couldn't let myself believe that Gand was dead, even though almost forty minutes had passed. Surely a neighbor had found him, or Shadow had come home. Gand could hold out. He was so strong. "Please."

He ignored that. "That man I called has a private plane. He wants to know who's after him. If I kill her for him, text a picture of her dead face, and get her phone or her computer, he'll have me out of the country before sunrise." Of course *Jher-Vay Ahh-nu-wee* could do this. The Parrot Man was world-breakingly rich. "If I get my cash back, I can start over. I won't need to hurt you then. Help make this happen. I'll call 911 for your brother, and simply leave. Okay? You have to get me inside that building."

He'd circled back to Tenth. The headlights from cars going the other way swept over us and away, light touching us in waves. I wanted to believe him, but his eyes were as cold and empty as ground glass. Nix always thought that he had some dark depth, some hidden vice. I wished now neither of us had ever had to see it.

I said, "She'll let me in," because what choice did I have? Even as I said it, I realized I believed it. I was banking, again, on that strange connection I'd felt between us from the start. Thalia would let me in, and I would get her killed because she didn't have a gun. She avoided fights like that, she said.

"Good," he said, then turned down Bellway for the second time. He pulled over in front of a decaying building that was two before hers and turned off the engine. "She started this. She contacted Xav, pretending to be a buyer. I'm almost glad she killed him; that idiot gave her my name."

I said nothing, because hope was both so mighty and so foolish. Hope made me let him keep believing Thalia had killed Castillo, in case he might still help Gand.

"Danny thought she was moving in on our business, or that she planned to blackmail us. I never believed that. He met with her against my advice, and look how that turned out. She means to kill me, too, I think, and I don't know why." I was uncertain why Michael felt the need to say all this to me, but I listened like a sweet, nice girl. He seemed to like that and peeped sideways at me, sly. "I think you know why, though, huh? I tell you the truth, here, Pen. I don't care. Knowing that she'll do it to me, that's enough. They say it gets easier and easier."

I understood why he was talking, then. He was psyching himself up. Not only to kill Thalia. He was going to stack his odds on getting out of the country clean. Not even my hope could survive this moment. He'd never call for help for Gand. Michael was a planner, a numbers guy, and he knew any loose end upped his risk. I was one of those loose ends. He was never going to let me leave her place alive.

30

Michael briefly trained his gun on me again, as if making a point. Then he got out and came around to open my door like a perfect gentleman. I wasn't sure I could stand on my shaking legs, but he grabbed my arm, hauling me up. No headlights were coming down this street. Most of the surrounding buildings were commercial use, closed and locked down for the night. There was only one person in view, walking down the other side of the street. A working girl. She glanced at us, and something about the vibe made her put her head down like a person very focused on her own business. She moved past us and away, going improbably fast in her heels.

The gun was a digging pressure left of my spine that pressed me forward down the jagged sidewalk. My feet landed on cracks with every step.

"Get me in, and I'll let you go. I promise." Michael was trying to sound soothing with a gun shoved up against my viscera. He didn't talk again as we got close.

The thick metal gate over the heavy-duty door made Michael frown. He jabbed at my back with the gun, and I pressed the single button under the intercom speaker. I had no idea what either of us would do if she didn't answer. We waited, the night stretching itself dark and taut around us. The street smelled like old rain and dog pee and motor oil. Michael muttered a word so quietly I couldn't make it out, but I thought it was a curse.

I put my finger to my lips, because it had occurred to me that she might not speak first. I could almost see her, standing in that cavernous, pale room, head cocked, listening. I leaned in close, and sure enough, I caught the faint hiss of live air coming from the speaker.

I spoke directly into it. "Thalia? It's me. Penny. Penny Albright." Silence. He started to speak again and I shook my head in an emphatic no. I pointed at the speaker, then my ear. "Thalia. I know you're there."

No answer, but Michael leaned in, and he heard the live air, too. He jerked his head at me, like, *Don't stop now.*

"I got the name you wanted. It was in Michael's phone."

He gave me a sharp glance, but stayed silent.

The speaker crackled. Her voice came out sharp with interest, maybe amused. "Damn, kid. That's the opposite of staying out of it."

"Oh, please. We're the same age," I snapped back and she chuckled. So heartening, that sound. Maybe I had a knife in my back pocket after all. If I could warn her, that was. I didn't see how, though. Michael and his pressing gun were right beside me.

"Are you going to tell me the name?" she asked, heavy on the irony.

I gave her her own tone back. "Are you going to buzz me up?" I was thinking about that huge white room, the mirrors. It had no hiding places. That was the point, but now this was going to work against her. She couldn't get the drop on him with no idea that he was coming.

"We're not friends, Penny," she said, like she was explaining college math to some cute, fat, gurgling toddler. "I told you."

I looked to Michael, and he nodded, encouraging, acting as if this was my chance to live. A lie, but he was selling it with such conviction. A lie, but if I could tip off Thalia—well. My stupid hope was back.

I said exactly what the gurgling toddler might, bratty as I could manage: "You're not the boss of me."

That made her laugh out loud, and then the buzzer sounded, and the lock clunked. Michael grabbed the heavy gate and yanked it open. A pause, and then a second buzzer came, letting me push open the smoked glass door.

Thalia spoke again. "Don't forget. The gate."

Michael looked to me, his eyebrows asking a question. I leaned back out toward the speaker and said, "I know, I know. It sticks. I'll leave it propped open until I go."

Last time, she'd told me to pull hard and make sure it latched. That was the only signal I could give her. Anything else, he'd be suspicious. Even with this, I was terrified that she would contradict me or correct me, and he would know.

"Good girl," she said, exactly like Nix said it, in my head. She didn't miss a beat.

Michael closed the gate slowly, leaving it propped, and we went inside. As soon as the heavy glass door swung closed behind us, he turned on the burner phone's flashlight and danced the light around the cavernous lobby, making sure that it was empty. He put his mouth down near my ear. His voice was hardly more than a breath. "Is this place wired for video? Sound?" I shook my head. I truly didn't think it was. Thalia wouldn't want any record of her own comings and goings, much less video or pictures of her face. She understood the world was full of Shadows that could find these things.

We crossed the poured concrete floor in tandem, and I thought this was deliberate. He was hiding the sound of his soft footsteps under mine. He looked to the elevators, but then walked me past them, to the stairs. He didn't want to be boxed in any more than she did. We paused at the heavy fire door, and he pointed his light at the handle. His hands were full, so I tried it, and it opened. He passed the phone to me to light our way, bowing as if to say, *After you.*

I started forward, but some small instinct or movement made me whirl in time to see his free hand coming up out of his jacket pocket with a hypodermic. I froze, staring at him with wide eyes, and he pulled the cap off with his teeth. The needle gleamed silver in the faint light that came from the red exit signs.

I went backward up two steps. "No. No. What is it?"

He smiled around the cap, and it was an absolutely chilling thing. He spit it to the side. "Calm down. It's an animal sedative. Ketamine. We didn't only move birds. It's safe. Pleasant, even. You'll go to sleep. And when you wake, I'll be long gone."

So would my brother, and I thought, *If he puts that in me, I die here.* I remembered the face of that boy who had ODed and then been dumped on Lester Street. His blue lips. I thought about Nix in that after-hours club, lying in a stall with Michael standing over her, pulling her phone from her lax fingers to hang it up. Waiting. To be sure.

I spoke quietly, but with such ferocity. "There's another fire door at the top, and she keeps it bolted. You can knock, but she's cagey. She might not open it if she doesn't hear me."

He thought about that, then said, "Pick up the cap."

I got it for him, and he held out the needle for me to cover. He pocketed it, then gestured for me to go up. I did it, half expecting to feel the needle anyway, entering my shoulder. It made me climb faster. Our feet shuffled and echoed against the endless concrete stairs.

Six floors up, Michael made me put the light out and drop the burner in his pocket. We stood catching our breath while our eyes adjusted. I could make out the shape of the stairs, barely, in the red light from the exit signs.

I wondered if my brother had been found, or if he was still alone, if he was hanging on or gone. I worried about Thalia, too. How could she possibly prepare? Michael, and a gun, and all that open space. The glass-walled bathroom. The mirrors on the ceiling. No matter where she was, he would see her, and he would shoot her. I didn't see another way it could play out if she was in that room.

I hoped she'd go down a floor, circle around, and try to flank us. As we began climbing again, I saw this had occurred to Michael, too. He sidled upward like a crab, looking up and down between each flight. At every turn, he sent me around the corner first.

When we reached floor eleven, I paused on the landing. "I know you're going to kill me." My quiet voice was thready from the climb and all my fear.

If I was hoping to distract him, it didn't work. He stayed ultracautious, but after half a flight he said with soft regret, "I don't want to, Pen." That was not the same as saying that he wouldn't. "I hope you know how much your family has meant to me. I mean that." I felt a red trickle of fresh anger. It was a line straight out of the thank-you note he sent my mother after the first time he spent Christmas with us. "I loved Nix. I will always love her." The trickle widened and flared. "She should have been mine. I should have been part of your family." He sounded genuinely sorry for himself, and the trickle became a flood of bracing rage that felt as much Nix's as it was mine. I was glad for it. I let it shore me up as we climbed. He had soaked in my family like we were a warm tub full of medicine for all the awful that was wrong with him.

At the last corner, Michael moved in close to slide an arm around my waist, and I hated it. He moved the gun up to nose against my temple, and I hated that more.

He eased us onto the final landing. There, a vertical line of soft light, thinner than a pencil lead, beckoned. The thick, metal fire door that led into her loft wasn't fully closed. The gold glow barely bothered my blown pupils, nothing like the hard white light I'd seen before. What had she done?

He checked behind us. Nothing. We both stared at the door. More nothing. He tapped the gun against my temple. I wasn't sure what he wanted, so I called her name.

"Thalia?" No answer, but this seemed to be what he wanted. I got louder. "Thalia."

Silence. He shifted uneasily and tucked me closer. We were now so pasted together that I had to swivel with him as he checked behind us once again. Nothing. No one. I waited while he turned us back and forth like a radar dish, trying to catch any sound or signal in the near darkness. Nothing. Maybe she was behind us. Maybe she was in the room ahead. Either way, she was as quiet as we were. She was also endlessly patient.

Michael was not. He breathed words into my ear. "What's on the other side of this door? Don't lie. I'll put one in your brain."

If I lied, he'd see immediately. I kept my voice as low as his, quieter than whispers. "It's one large open space. This door opens near a kitchen area. To our right is a long, blank wall where she hangs all her clothes."

I think he frowned. I felt it as a movement in my hair, right by my ear. "Where's the best cover?"

"There's not really a good place. No closet or couch. The bed is a solid platform. The bathroom is all glass."

"Big table? Desk?"

I shook my head in a faint no, hating how it made the gun grind against my temple. "There's not really any cover."

"Well. I have some." He meant me. I was a thing to put between his body and bullets. Imaginary ones, because Thalia didn't use guns. I was glad he needed me, even as a shield. Otherwise, with the door cracked, he might get the needle back out, and I was more afraid of that needle than the gun.

"We move together." His arm tightened on my waist. "The safety's off. Don't make your mother see you with half a head."

That hit me in the stomach like a blow, and yet I couldn't fold around it. The press of the gun kept me upright and compliant in his arms. Was I crying again? I wanted this all to stop with the kind of wishing left over from childhood. I wanted magic to swirl up and blink me away. More than that, I wanted Mom in one of her dog-hair-coated sweaters. I wanted to be in her arms.

Michael tapped my temple with the gun again, now hard enough to hurt. "When I go, you go. Be quick."

He stood, maybe counting himself down or getting up his nerve. I waited, and then I felt the surge of his body pressing me forward. My hands came up, palms slapping the cracked door. We moved fast, but the air felt like it was thickening around us, and time itself got slow, holding the tandem motion of our bodies in a terror-soaked eternity.

As the door slammed open underneath my hands, the faint gold light exploded into glaring brightness. It hit me in a blast, immediate and blinding. I closed my eyes, unable to help it, even as his momentum propelled us out into the room.

He yelled at Thalia, "I'll fucking shoot her."

She had to make a move, though. So he had to shoot me. I wondered if I would hear the gun before I died. This stretched half second felt like my last. I made my eyes open and was light-stung by glaring brightness. All I saw was white on white, and to my right, the dark shapes of her black and gray clothes hanging flat against the ice-white wall. The pale clothes were invisible, part of the dazzling glare.

In the next endless half second, he began to turn me away from the wall, and to my left, a splotch of blue that had to be the parrot appeared in my peripheral vision. Michael was now sucking in a shocked breath, trying to take in the room through light-blind panic.

No movement, save the parrot's, but there was no place to hide. *She evacuated*, I thought, bereft, because how could there be a living human person present? As we spun, his arm was an iron bar around my waist, the gun held steady at my temple. We were almost halfway through the revolution of our bodies, my feet leaving the ground as he dragged me in a whirl to face the kitchen; I looked back at the wall as we spun away from it, and then I saw her. She hadn't left me, after all.

We'd both been looking right at her, so light-blind we'd failed to see her. Now her form separated itself from the white wall. She wore all white, posed between a gray jacket and a black one. A white scarf, more sheer than a wedding veil, draped over her hair and head. She'd stood motionless, an absence of color on an absence of color, like a monochrome chameleon. I caught the faint gleam of silver in her white-gloved hand as she came toward us. I could see the predatory gold of her eyes gleaming through the gauzy fabric.

Just before his turning removed her from my line of sight, her gaze met mine for perhaps a hundredth of a second. In this slow endless spin, I had time enough to feel again that ripple of connection, and I knew that her best chance was already gone. The fight had not yet started, and it was over. She'd lost. She should have stepped up right behind him when we first came in, should have flicked the knife between his thighs to sever that artery she knew so well. It would have ended him. He would have had time enough to put a bullet in my brain, but he'd be down.

She hadn't. She wouldn't. Thalia might say that she was not my friend, but she was going to die here, in the wake of his next breath, because she had refused to risk me. Even in this awful moment, so scared I thought I might be peeing, so scared I had to clench my jaw to keep my teeth from chattering together, I knew she was with me. I was not alone.

Then we were facing the kitchen, and I whipped my head the other way, waiting for his revolution to bring her back into my line of sight again. Into his line of sight, as well. My dazzled eyes were recovering, so his must be, too. I could see the food in her glass door refrigerator as a smear of colors. In one beat of my wild heart, Michael would see her, and then this would be over. I felt his arm cinching me to him, and the gun's muzzle, as hot as a brand. He would turn it off me, onto her, and the booming sound would deafen me. I'd only hear the echo in my head, and then her white would bloom into bright red. She would fall. Once she was down, he'd wrestle me to the floor and put that needle in me.

Now, the bright pop of blue I had seen rising to my right was setting on my left: Pierre. His cool color was an instant calm that caught me in this timeless blink of time. Thalia had refused to risk me, and so I could not let Michael kill her. I could not allow it. That was all.

I found a little breath inside my body, and I used it to yell two words: "Don't shoot."

I wasn't talking to Michael. I was talking to Pierre. His answering gunfire was immediate, a perfect burst of violent sound that echoed in the huge space, exactly as it had before. It stopped Michael in mid-spin, keeping his back to Thalia. It was so real, I thought for a moment I'd heard Michael's gun, and I was dead. Pierre sent his sound bullet ricocheting around the room, and time began to surge a little faster. I screamed it again, "Don't shoot!" and again Pierre obliged me with a crack of sound. Michael thought I was talking to Thalia, unseen and shooting, not caring if she hit me, aiming for him.

He swung the gun away from my head, moving the black eye outward, sweeping it back and forth from the kitchen to the parrot's structure. His gun's eye sought her across the room, and he never knew that she was right behind us. I dug my nails into the bare wrist of the arm he'd locked around me, and I ripped at him. I felt his skin tear, and as his grip loosened, I yanked myself away, throwing my weight into it. I felt myself break free. As I stumbled forward, he lashed out, so fast, the gun still in his hand. The flat, hard side of it connected with my head, and I fell, seeing white stars bloom in the white floor. I barely caught myself, my hands slapping the concrete hard enough to sting.

I landed back in real time, rolling over as another gunshot rang out, and another, and another, and another, in loud layers of shot and ricochet. I had no way to know which were real and which were only sound. I smelled sulfur and burned air.

The parrot shrieked, "Poor baby!," and then someone shot again. I rolled onto my back. A real bullet bounced off a high white wall, echoing. Miachel stood over me, a darkness in the stark light, surrounded by white stars and dazzle. His shadow loomed, and now the gun swung down my way. The gun was all that I could see then. It was a gleaming black shape, and Michael was a shade behind it.

Then, she was there. She appeared behind him, so fast it seemed that she was made of light, white on white, a cold sun rising up behind his shadow. One hand held a length of white pipe that she brought down on his wrist with a crack that banged into my aching head as loud as yet another gunshot. The other hand was even faster. It had already snaked over his shoulder, flashing silver as it ripped back and away.

He grunted, or he gurgled. The gun arced to the floor and skidded off. His hands rose up toward his throat, one dangling at a helpless angle. He began to topple toward me, and I saw a thin, lipless mouth open up under his own real yawping mouth. Both openings gaped and flapped and made no sounds, and then my whole damn world went red.

I tried to scrabble myself backward, but I was dizzy, sick, and my hands could find no purchase. Michael leaned forward clutching at his throat, trying to hold in his blood as it ran down his front and jetted out between his fingers, splattering my legs. I closed my eyes, and the glare of white light burned me even through my lids. I felt his fall first as a rush of air, and then as a great wet weight that splashed and thudded painfully onto my prone body.

I called her name then. "Thalia!"

Michael heaved and gurgled. There was a moment of utter blackness. I must have lost consciousness. When I found myself again, I'd pushed him off me, or he'd rolled away. I crabbed sideways, streaking crimson across the white floor.

He was on his stomach, his face turned toward me, one hand still fruitlessly clutching at his throat. He looked so surprised. His blue eyes held such bold color in this space. Summer eyes, Nix had called them, and I'd been fooled into filling them with warmth; now they were going to glass. He tried to speak, but he couldn't. He tried to hold his life in, and he couldn't do that either. It came out red, in jagged, rapid pulses, the gush slowing as the rhythm of his heart slowed, too. His mouth worked, trying to speak or maybe scream. Thalia Gray stood over both of us, immaculate, still veiled and wholly white, except for the red-streaked silver knife in her gloved hand.

"Poor baby," Pierre said, mournful, and his voice was hers, echoing. She pulled the sheer scarf off to puddle at her feet, and I saw she did not share the bird's sentiment. Her eyes on Michael were measuring, devoid of pity, and yet the parrot sounded sympathy, using her voice. "Poor baby!"

I tried to sit up, but only made it as far as being propped up on one elbow, my head spinning. I was so sick and yet so glad, so fiercely glad, to feel that I was breathing.

"Gand," I said, my voice a rasp. I looked at her, pleading, my head ringing from the blow. I tried to sit up more and couldn't. I reached up and felt my head where he had hit me and it came away red, or perhaps my hand was red already. "He shot Gand. He left him bleeding in my yard."

"All right," she said. She was so calm. She turned her eyes to Michael. "Watch him. He needs another minute." Thalia backed up to her acrylic cubbies, setting the bloody knife down inside one that held five or six cell phones. She plucked one at random and called 911. I heard her murmuring with the operator.

I watched Michael bleed, the gush now sluggish, pulsing in slow surges. His hands had dropped away from the gash at his throat. The red pool spread across the white, coming close to me, and I crabbed away even farther. I couldn't stand for it to touch me. His pooling blood joined up with the streaky trail I left.

Thalia was back. "Someone already called. The operator said they were aware of the incident." She dropped into an easy crouch to examine Michael. "There we go. All done," she said, and the parrot echoed her, "All done!" exactly, the same voice, and the same inflection. Thalia was right. Michael had stopped living, but she said it like she'd finished watering the plants. She rose long enough to come to me, then crouched again, her face going fuzzy as it came in close to mine. "Your pupils are fucked. You definitely have a concussion."

I said my brother's name again. "Gand." My voice sounded so small in the big room.

"An ambulance is on the way, maybe it already has him. That's all we can do right now, from here," she said. Her head tilted in that birdlike way she had. "Next time, Penny, we need a code word that means *gun*."

I thought to myself, *Next time? Next time we what?* I finally managed to sit up. The whole world swayed around me, but I braced my palms against the floor and breathed.

"Good. Stay upright. You can't sleep." She moved to Michael's body on the unbloody side, bending to fish gingerly in his jacket pockets. "Where did he park?"

"Two buildings down, this side of the street, closer to the clinic," I said and started crying again. I felt like I'd been crying for a solid year now. Maybe two.

"That was good, what you did at the intercom. Quick thinking." She rose, holding his keys in one gloved hand. "You need a hospital, but we have to make some fast decisions. Me? I want to bury this fuck in the basement and put his car somewhere the cops can find it. It's better if he's a missing person than a murder investigation. Less heat on you, no heat on me. Can you live with that, Penny? The pressure. The questions. Knowing he'll be here, forever, and there will be no public justice."

A tear splashed on the white floor, tinged pink. I sounded pitiful, but I meant every word when I said, "I can live with it fine."

"Oh, no!" Pierre squawked. "All done!"

"Hush, buddy." She came back toward me, picking up the sheer white scarf and using it to clean his key fob, streaking the silk with red. "Okay. You have to tell the cops—"

I interrupted. "I know what to say. That he killed Nix. He did, Thalia. Because she wouldn't love him back." This was new information for her, thrown down with little context, but her gaze on me stayed steady. What the hell would it take to faze this woman? "I figured it out and confronted him, and he kidnapped me. He shot my brother. He ran my neighbor over." I cried harder. "All I have to do is tell the truth."

She thought it through. "Works." The fingertips of the one white glove she'd used to get his keys were also red, but once she peeled it off and dropped it and the scarf onto the heap of him, she was pristine.

I shook my head, and that was a mistake. The whole room swung around me, and I had to fight a gag. I said, "The GPS will show that he was here. He—"

She shook her own head then, and even her movement made me dizzy. "Oh, summer child, he ripped that shit right out of his car, likely the day he bought it. Sullivan was the brains of a very tight smuggling operation, and he did not play. How much does Gand know?" She came back over to me and knelt to check my eyes once more.

"About you? Nothing. I mean, I don't know what you said. I told him nothing."

She flashed teeth. "Good." My vision had cleared enough to see Thalia had a single drop of blood on her face, right under her eye. It looked like a red freckle, but I knew it was a piece of Michael, marring her. I reached for it, my eyes on hers. I felt more than saw her body tense. She didn't like it, my hand coming toward her. Any hand coming toward her. She would never like it, but she stilled herself and watched it come. She let me.

I pressed my thumb to her cheek, and I was shocked to feel how warm she was. She looked like she'd been carved of marble, but she felt so alive, like a woman burning up with fever. Or perhaps my hands were very cold. She leaned into the touch. A millimeter. I brushed my thumb across her cheek to wipe the freckle away and left a wide, red streak. I pulled my hand back and saw that he'd stained all my fingers, wet and red.

"You only blood for a first kill, Penny," she said. "But I appreciate the symbolism."

I realized all over again that I was soaked in it, in him. My stomach lurched, and I had to close my eyes and breathe as she got up. The parrot gurgled, making running water sounds. Even he knew how badly I needed a bath.

"Can you move? Don't try to walk. Strip down and crawl to my shower. Use the bar soap, even in your hair. It's better for blood and you have to get all of him off you. Leave your clothes by him, I'll burn them later. You can borrow some of mine. I'm going to ditch his car, then we'll figure out a good place with no cameras where I can drop you off. Something like an all-night gas station." Thalia went to her shelves and got fresh gloves with her bare hand, tucking them into her jacket pocket. "You go in and call for help, tell 911 that he whacked you in the head with his gun and threw you out of the car. When the cops get there, don't answer questions. Say your head hurts. Say you can't remember. Cry. Remember, you're the victim here."

"I can do that," I said. It sounded easy. I wanted to cry more. My head felt like it was made of pain.

"You should get a lawyer. Do you know one?"

I told her, "I have someone I can call." Not a lawyer, but I left it there. She wouldn't trust a cop, but I knew the person who could help me best was Delilah Williams.

Thalia started for the elevator. Getting in *a box with only one real exit* was proof that time was of the essence, but I had to say one more thing. In case she decided to take his cash, his car, and vanish.

"Jher-Vay Ahh-nu-wee," I said, and she stopped cold. The parrot had been twoodling softly to himself, but he stopped, too.

She processed fast. I saw her understanding break, and then she grinned. "Holy shit. Penny Albright. You really got the name. I assumed that was some bullshit to make me answer your buzz."

I'd learned better than to nod again, but I could repeat it. *"Jher-Vay Ahh-nu-wee.* I don't know if that's real or an alias, but that's what Michael called Parrot Man. I heard his voice, Thalia. It was him." I watched how the words quickened her blood. "Michael has his number saved in the burner phone in his pocket. If you can get it open, there might be more."

"I can get it open, kid. I have his face." Her smile lit up her gold eyes and made them warm in ways I'd never seen, even through the chill of her pragmatism. "Gervais Anouilh," she repeated, her accent so much better than mine. I really only spoke French menu. "I won't forget. Believe it." The way she looked at me, I knew she meant more than the name. She wouldn't forget what I had done tonight. The streak of blood I'd put onto her cheek gleamed wet and red.

I pointed at my own cheek and said, "You have a little, uh . . ."

She used her other white glove to wipe it away, then dropped that on the floor, too. Her keys rattled, and Pierre echoed the sound as she opened the gate into the cage. I pulled my shirt off over my head, so gingerly, then dropped it in a heap on the bloody concrete floor. She wasn't going to disappear. Someone had found Gand, and I had to believe that it had been in time. I would crawl into the shower, now, and make myself be clean, and she would come back. I believed she would come back and help me.

I began to struggle out of my soaked jeans, and she got in the elevator. As the gap between the doors narrowed, I realized we were smiling at each other. Smiling like we were the only two people left alive on Earth. And that was fine. Two was fine. Two, for me, had always been enough.

Epilogue

Every summer has to end.

Before school started back up, Gand and I drove Shadow toward the coast and then up the river to see Nix. He'd finished up physical therapy. He had two new scars, and no spleen, but his doctor had cleared him to refine his abs after not being allowed to do core work for weeks and weeks. It was the front end of August, brutally hot, the air so full of water that it felt like we were hiking in a spa, except with lots more bugs. Shadow brought Bosch, who dearly loved both a car trip and getting to go places that we didn't take the big dogs, the little monster. My niece set her fistful of daisies on Nix's spot under the willow, and then she took off with the dog to wade the river.

I'd never been away from Nix so long, but I hadn't quite felt comfortable leaving town before now. No one said, *Don't leave town.* Delilah told me to blithely give the finger to any cop who said that. I had called her from the gas station, not 911. A minute in, I heard her getting in her car, and she told me she'd meet me at Grady Hospital. On her way to me, she called an Atlanta cop she'd known since her academy days, and a paramedic that she used to date. At Grady, they took the concussion seriously given the state of my pupils, and the hairline fracture on my skull, and my memory gaps. Some of those gaps were even real.

I'm not sure how I got to Thalia's fishbowl shower, for example. I remember watching the water swirl to the drain, all crimson, and then in a blink, it was faint pink, and then Thalia's hands were on my face and she was saying, "Penny. Do not sleep." Dressing in her clothes (the pants were too long, a little tight, and still the nicest pair I owned), the drive to a dark street, and my weaving walk into the brightness of an all-night Shell—these things were a slideshow where all the stars and headlights had been painted by van Gogh.

I remember Delilah coming in like a storm, getting to the hospital before my mother, even, to stand over me and say, "This is a cop." I was so glad I hadn't yet mailed my resignation letter, so that technically, I was. "And a witness. And a victim. You handle her like she's your favorite frail dear granny, hear me?" I had no memory of who she said these things to. A doctor, a nurse, a cop? No clue.

Later, she told me what was happening behind the scenes, or as much as she could get, anyway. Michael Sullivan's disappearance was an Atlanta PD problem, and if there were holes in my story, well, I had a concussion, didn't I? Gand remembered less than I did. Or so he said. Maybe it was even true. He'd lost so much blood he'd flatlined for a full minute in the ambulance.

Poor Mrs. Blanchard died before she ever felt the second set of tires. I never thought that I would mourn that woman, but I did, sincerely. Mom, too. She made sure Mrs. Blanchard's grave was tended to a gloss-green, lawn-like excellence that would have pleased the tightest HOA. In typical busybody form, God bless her soul, our fussy neighbor had been recording. Her camera caught the gun her eyes had missed and documented her own cold-blooded murder at his hands.

It also helped that Michael had thirty thousand dollars in unexplained cash stashed in the trunk of his abandoned car, more than one set of books at a house that he could never have afforded, and cryptic files about transactions all across the globe in his computer. He had seven thousand pictures and videos of Nix, too, some taken in the bathroom stall of the club as she was dying. I didn't look at those. Delilah told me.

By the time I was out of the hospital, Thalia Gray was gone with no goodbye. I had a pretty good idea of where, though. Maybe the universe could find a scrap of pity to level at Gervais Anouilh, because I had exactly none.

At Nix's grave, I didn't have a lot to say. I didn't have to tell her any of it; she'd been with me. Gand sat down crisscross applesauce and caught her up on brighter topics: Next week Shadow would begin her junior year, and she'd worked out mathematically that she had an outside shot at salutatorian if she took enough AP classes. She and Jeff had done computer camp over the summer, building a game instead of tearing down firewalls. Gand cleared almost sixty thousand on the sale of the Shred Shed, and he'd put most of it right into her college fund.

He looked at me as he told Nix, "I'm living at home. For now. At least until Shads goes to college."

Shadow was so happy with him home. She seemed more balanced, her pendulum swings less wild. Our girl was blooming. If he really could sit still for two more years, she would leave him to embark on her own grand adventure, and that was right. That was good. What Gand did after that was up to Gand.

I told Nix, "He's doing great, for a born roamer." I echoed his, "For now." I didn't say, *I think this is his idea of penance, which is stupid, because, Nix, I know you're with me when I say, I'm glad they're dead.* There was no need. Nix always got my subtext. Only Jordan Banks was still breathing. As far as I knew. I'd sent Kaitlin the video, and then I hadn't looked again. I hoped I never would.

I did tell Nix I was almost finished with a (poorly) paid internship with a one-man private detective agency and readying to test for my license, and how Delilah called my new job "Private dick hunter" because according to her, all I did was track cheaters.

"Time well spent, though," she told me at our regular Tuesday coffee date. "The skills you're practicing will come in handy when you rejoin the force."

"You are incorrigible. Don't hold your breath," I told her.

She said, "Albright, I have good instincts. They tell me you're a woman who was born to fight the good fight."

"Maybe so," I'd agreed, but I knew that there was more than one way I could do that.

"She will not give up on me," I told Nix, smiling. "Any private dick worth her salt needs a good contact on the force, and cops need informants who aren't bound by all their rules. I think it's the beginning of a beautiful friendship. To be fair to her, I do spend a stupid amount of time tailing straying spouses.

"When people hire me, I tell them that they already know or they wouldn't be in my office. My boss says I better not cost him business, but they always need the pictures. Oh, Nixxy, people fight so hard, every day, to not see how the world is. You knew the whole time, didn't you?" I looked at Gand. My brother knew. "Me, I'm trying to look better. I'm trying to see the world exactly as it is, and then love it, anyway. It's hard. Delilah Williams does it, though. So it's possible."

That last bit made my eyes sting and my throat feel tight, and Gand put his arm around me. He tried to lighten the mood. "Pff, *love anyway*, she says, but Nixxy, she's not dating."

I said, "Pff, he's 'dating' enough for every single one of us."

"There she is. The Albright family umpire."

I grinned. "You need one, bubba."

My twin had been a force, but me? I was a fence. There was a time when I saw that as weakness. Now, I knew better. To shape a force as mighty as my twin—and my wild brother, and his bold child, and even Thalia Gray—this fence had learned to be a pretty damn big force herself.

Then all three of the Albright kids were quiet, two of us listening to the buzz and hum of bees and dragonflies and Shadow laughing in the distance. The heavy Georgia sun felt like a blessing. Far off, but not too far, we heard Bosch barking, too. A play bark. He and Shadow would come back soaked and muddy and destroy my back seat, and not one of us would care.

I asked Gand, "Do you remember that girl, Polly?"

It didn't take him even half a second. "'Course I do."

"Did you ever hear from her?"

He lay back, leaning on his elbows, squinting up at the bright sky peeping through the canopy. "Nah. I'll never forget her, though. She was something. At the same time, it was a moment, you know? It happened. It passed."

I could understand that. "You want to look forward. Not back."

He chuckled. "No, Pen. I want to be here, now. With you. And Nix, and my kid. If a now comes that has Polly in it, then I'll be present in that now. It's not today, though."

He didn't ask me why I cared, and I was glad. I didn't want to be coy, and I didn't want to lie, but some things were private. We'd never talked, never again, about what happened the night he followed his red-lit dream of Xav Castillo down into the darkness. That was between him and whatever he called God.

Bosch barked again, pure and joyful, and Gand stood up. "Okay. That's an invitation. There is some fetch happening, maybe some chase. That's what's now. I'm going to the river to play with my kid and a dog. You coming?"

I waved him off, smiling, and stayed with Nix. When he was out of sight, I set my bouquet down, too, between Shadow's daisies and Gand's bright spray of tulips. Mine was all gardenias, Nix's favorite. Bad flowers, the lady at the shop told me, because they "bruise too easy." Well, Nix had bruised pretty easy, when she was alive. I thought that was a strength, if the other choice was getting cynical. I remembered Nix telling me, *I should be more interesting and powerful now. Since I got raped. That's what I see in the movies.* I had a better answer now. It wasn't pain that turned us into superheroes. That whole story was a lie. What made women mighty were the partnerships we forged to get us through it.

I said, "Miss you, Nixxy" to the grass, and then I took my phone out of my pocket.

The text had come three days ago, and I was running out of time. I knew from experience that in less than a week, any answer I gave would bounce off a dead prepaid disposable, and I'd have to wait until she reached out again. That might be in a day, a month, or never.

Her text said simply, New lead. I could use a girl who doesn't know when to get out of my way. You ready?

Now, I put my hand flat on the grass, feeling the sun it had absorbed as a deep green heat.

"What would you do, Nix?" I asked my twin.

She didn't answer, but it didn't matter. I would always have her with me. In my history. In my blood. In my head, where her voice remained the best of all my better angels.

I got up and wandered toward the noise of people that I loved. They were so busy playing, they didn't notice me. I watched my brother wading out into the river with his lovely daughter, laughing, while Bosch made mad dashes through the shallows. Shadow and the dog were soaked to their young skins.

I finally caught Gand's eye. He lifted a hand and called, "You ready?"

What an excellent question. I smiled, and I called back, "No. No, not at all."

The three of them went back to romping in the river. Then I texted Thalia Gray, and I told her that I was.

Acknowledgments

First, thank *you*, person reading this book. I've been so excited for you to meet the Albrights. Glittery, especial thanks if you recommended it to your book club or to readers in your life or online. Novels live and die by word of mouth; you have given my books their heartbeats.

Thanks to the Kennesaw PD, especially Officer David Buchanan, Officer Erin Bright Ange, Officer David Hubbart, Lieutenant Chris "Muscles" Johnson, Sergeant Dean, and all the others who helped run the Citizens Police Academy. They took me to morgues and labs and squad rooms, answered my endless questions, and let me do actual cop training stuff (with non-actual guns). Everything I got right is thanks to them, anything I messed up is on me.

Gratitude and love to my longtime editor, Emily Krump (plus Paige Meintzer and the whole amazing team at Morrow); my even longer timer perfect agent, Caryn Karmatz Rudy; and my longest timest writing posse, especially Lydia Netzer and Abbott Kahler, the official darling assassinators for this book.

Onward Heroes is that time I looked back down the beach and instead of my lonely footprints, I saw I'd been carried by what looked like a drunk millipede and several cryptids.

Love and thanks to the Jackson and Winn clans, Mom especially, Dad always.

Scott, you have been both a necessity and the most luxurious delight in a time of tumult and change. Thanks for keeping the wheels on our bus *and* bringing the fun as we left the South and helped Sam and Maisy Jane launch their own singular, precious, unrepeated lives. I meant every word of my dedication, but secretly, you know they're all for you.

About the Author

JOSHILYN JACKSON is the *New York Times* and *USA Today* bestselling author of eleven other novels, including *gods in Alabama* and *Never Have I Ever*. Her books have been translated into more than a dozen languages. Jackson is also a former actor and an award-winning audiobook narrator. A recent expat from the American South, she has settled in a gently haunted Victorian rowhouse in upstate New York.